TREES *of* FATE

ANGELINA SCRIPTOR

Scriptor's Ink

This one? This one's for me
Angelina... You did it

PROLOGUE

EVERY NEW BIRTH WAS assigned to a Tree. And every new Tree meant a new era began.

For the first part of my life, there were three Trees—the last three Trees of our time. The Great Oak stayed far back, reserved for the outcasts and vagabonds. More than anything, it was used as a warning. The Lavender Crystalline was where I resided. From an onlooker's perspective, it was beautiful. To us, it served as a constant reminder that there was always better. Better, like the Great Cherry. That was where the Royals and their families stayed. Even when they could have taken domain over the other Trees, they were usually disregarded by people of such high standards. Besides, who would care about *us*?

Alaric did. He was described as tall and thin, yet toned, and oddly pale in comparison to the rest of his immediate family. His hair was dark and usually flipped over itself neatly, but, after being in the water, it was said that it was just a little too long for his parents' likings.

His parents, the next in line for the Great Cherry. They had two sons—the perfect amount to spread their rule over us all. All they were waiting for was their beloved father to die. The first time he fell ill, many of us Lavenderians thought it would finally be the end to his everlasting reign of power. Somehow, he kept recovering. Despite his age, despite his condition. After a few years, we were sure that one of the other Royals would take matters into their own hands. With all of the water around, it would have been easy.

Water. Everything we knew was surrounded by water. Some called it sacred, but most realized that we were under some horrible curse. Every day, the Lavenderians gathered to pray by our Tree. They felt like it connected them to the world we once had. To make space for such an activity, long docks were built in front of the thick bark, with steps that protruded straight from the water. I'd been told that every Royal wedding was on Cherry's own dock, and as Alaric was getting older, his parents were impatiently waiting for him to choose another Royal. At least, that was what we in the Crystalline were taught. They said that when he stayed silent, they grew angry. After that, he fled to the shadows, ducking in and out of homes, trying to fabricate a fate for himself. They rumored that the only reason we didn't see him at Lavender was because he was hiding in the twisted, decrepit homes of Oak.

The homes. To enter any of our homes, one's lungs had to be strong. Under the docks, in the Tree's great Roots, we constructed our living spaces by draining away the water. Sometimes, the only safety the Lavenderians had from drowning would be one room alone. Often, they would refuse to live like this. Always, they disappeared, shortly after their complaints were heard.

I lived with my parents and my sister once, but they, too, grew tired of this world. They remembered glimpses of the Old World,

2

and they longed for it. They were angered that none of the Royals were concerned enough to try to revert what they had done. Even when they promised change, many years before I was born.

I came about later in my mother's life. After The Collapse. They pulled me from the water, as they did most children now. I was unexpected, unplanned, and as some would argue, unwanted. But I don't believe that. I never did. To me, some just experience better timing than others.

As a child, I was educated by my parents. That alone is more than what most Lavenderians can say. I learned the basics, while the Royals were already finished with their schooling at the ripe age of twelve. After that, they shifted their focus fully to better things. Commanding, dancing, fencing, you name it, they probably did it.

I hated them. I hated them for all they were. I knew they killed my family, along with most of the people in this damned town. *They* were the ones who never cared. We never had a chance.

There was a point in my life when I stopped praying. I never believed in the "Tree gods," or whatever my town elders thought they knew. My mom used to tell me stories of a different God. A God that had control over *every* domain. A God that takes us home when we die on this earth. A God of not only the water, but also of the land and air.

At first, I did think they were just stories. If someone could hold *that* much power, why wouldn't they just save us now? But my mother told me to never be bitter, or she warned I wouldn't see the World Beyond after my own death.

I had forgotten all of this until my eighteenth birthday—the eighth birthday I'd celebrated alone. I was starting to grow in anger. In wrath. I felt stuck, and there was nothing I could do about it.

I knew that the more my intolerance grew, the sooner they would take my life, but I clung to the hope that maybe, just maybe, I could see my sister again when they did.

I went to Lavender Crystalline's dark, wooden dock, and I prayed. Gasping in the fresh air felt like sucking a new life straight into my lungs. I couldn't remember the last time I got to inhale it like this. Then again, that was exactly why people like me stayed intertwined with the Roots of Watertowne: Once we crave, we can never return.

Please, I prayed, to whoever would hear my words, *don't make me go back. I don't want to go back. Don't make me go back...*

And that was it. I know now that this was the exact moment my life ended. After this day, things would never be the same again.

ONE

"I'VE NEVER SEEN YOU here before." The unfamiliar voice was cut by rasp, yet smoothed in silk, and it made me second guess everything I was doing. As I continued to listen, his words sent a chill down my spine. Somehow, they were traced with the smallest bit of laughter. "I think I'd remember that hair."

Everyone in Lavender cuts their hair short. It's just easier with all of the swimming. My hands found the tangled mess that fell over my shoulder, and I knew he was watching me as they did. I tried to reply, but I couldn't process my own voice. It had been an absurd amount of time since I had last heard it, myself.

"Yeah..."

"Are you afraid?"

I didn't know what to say. I was stuck between a nod and a head shake: dropping my mouth slightly open and staring.

He didn't speak again. Instead, he looked around, sighed, and—to my shock—apologized. "Sorry. It'd probably be best if... I hope your prayer works."

And just like that, he dove behind the dock, and he was gone.

I stared over the edge, but any remnants of his existence were already lost to the reflections in the water. I turned around to see if anyone else had recognized him, but they were all still bowed over, stuck in their endless chants.

After staring at the rippling surface for just a moment more, I hurried back to my room, now with a plan to return at the same time tomorrow. My heart was racing. I couldn't think of anything other than him, couldn't hear anything other than his voice.

But he never came. Not the next day, nor the next. Before I knew it, my prayers were starting to shift, and I was begging for this stranger to return. I wanted to know who he was, where he came from, and how I could find him again. I started asking around town, but nobody here likes to talk. Who could blame them when their lives were made from nothing other than the sheer fear of their daily existences, or the complete devastation of remembering what once was?

That was when my mornings changed. I began keeping tally marks on my wall, carving them in beside the few couch cushions that made up my bed. It took two *months* for him to come back. Two, *grueling* months of swimming to the surface, breathing air, and fitting in with the very people I thought were insane. Finally, the waters were growing warm again.

I'm tired. I'm wary. I'm running out of food. There's no more jobs. The elders are dying. Nobody remembers the Old World anymore. There's no more children. The Royals went silent. Please... help us.

"You... really want to see me again, huh?"

"It's you! I-I can't believe it's *you!* Okay, okay... Hi." I suddenly felt my face growing hot. As soon as he finished pulling himself onto the dock, he stared at me, the smallest smile tugging at the corner of his mouth. I wrapped my arms around myself, and I sighed. "Where have you *been?*"

"...Really?"

"What?"

"You... you don't *know* me."

It took me a long time to realize that this was a question, rather than a statement. Regardless, it clicked. I *didn't* know him, and yet, I had been demanding his presence from an overworked, underpaid Deity. Who did I think I *was?* And what was I turning into?

"I'm... sorry." It was at that moment that I felt my curiosity die. I was set right back to seeing my impending doom. I knew I'd tempted my fate one too many times, and I decided once again that it was time to join my family.

Still, he smiled. It was far from menacing, but it teased. It led into this false sense of security, this false *hope.* I was sure I couldn't have been its first victim.

"You never did tell me why your hair was so long."

Now, I was fighting a smile. I reached for my crunchy, uneven, dead brown hair. Somehow, it felt beautiful.

To him, I only shrugged. He raised an eyebrow at me, and I felt my heart fall.

"Same time next month, I guess?"

"Wait!" I screamed before he could jump.

He froze and turned toward me. I never realized quite how tall he was until I was on my feet beside him. So close that I could feel his breath. To know he wasn't a dream.

"I'm waiting," he said as he crossed his arms.

"Where are you from?"

"You really don't—" His look of confusion began to morph. Before my very eyes, his smirk returned. "Around."

"Well... which family do you come from?"

"A broken one."

"You think you're smart, then. That's your thing."

"Are you bold, then? That's *your* thing?"

Time seemed to stop. I could feel my heartbeat in my ears.

"No, actually..."

For the past two months, I had been breathing the air above. I had been praying to a God unspoken of in the tomb of water we were all encased in. I had left my room, consistently, chasing after some mysterious shadow of my ever-fading memory. I was living more than I ever had before, in a time where that meant I should have been dead. Again, I found myself asking: who was I?

It wasn't until he dove off of the dock that I regained my new-found confidence. I followed after him, knowing it must have been a challenge. He swam, paddling above the water in a way I had never seen. Soon, we were leaving Lavender Crystalline, entering the deep void that surrounded the security of the Roots. I began to gasp for air, but every breath was far from enough. Then, without warning, I felt a searing pain in my right arm and leg. I tried to scream, but my eyes rolled back. My bubbles were rising upwards as I was being inexplicably dragged down. The sky above seemed to be getting farther away, yet still felt so close. As my vision faded to black, and my chest filled with water, I was certain I would see my sister soon.

When my eyes opened, I could barely remember my name. I coughed deep and repetitively, and the smallest bit of water sputtered from my lips. They tasted dry and shriveled. But my skin? My fingers? My *hair*? Now I was gasping for something other than air.

"Be careful! You'll hurt yourself."

My body forgot how to function as soon as I saw him. His thin black tank top was thrown over his shoulder, dripping in near-perfect time with his uneven hair. Both were damp, rather than soaked. I watched as his bare feet approached me, amazed by how swiftly he could control them.

"Drink this," he demanded.

"What—"

"Just drink it."

I found myself looking around. We were in a room of solid ground—no water was to be seen. I soon realized no people were to be seen, either. I took a sip of his drink.

"How're you feeling?"

I looked to the spot that was bringing me the most pain. My leg was bandaged, and I saw that my arm was, as well. I was only decent by my top and bottoms, the water-repellant undergarments that I always wore when going out.

"I do apologize for that," he interrupted. "I just had to make sure... I didn't want you bleeding out before we got here. Harpoons don't usually aim to keep survivors."

"Harpoons...?"

"Guards. Hired by the Royals to keep Treefolk from leaving their homes."

"And... why are you okay?"

"I have my methods."

"You're really cryptic, you know that?"

"So I've been told."

"There are others, then."

He smiled as he crouched beside me. "So I've been told... by you." He began to lean over me, placing his left hand on the ground near my shoulder. I backed up with my head and neck, but couldn't do much more. He appeared to be further investigating my arm, but it was without warning that he drew in a shaky breath. He quickly backed up, placed his fist against his forehead, and suddenly, he seemed much less menacing.

"I thought I *killed* you, you know that? I had no *clue* that the Harpoons were still vigilant there, I—"

"Where did you take me?" was all I could muster without my voice breaking. For the first time in years, I could actually feel the tears drying on my cheeks.

"I never meant for you to get hurt, Maliyah. I—"

I jumped to my feet. At least, I tried to. I stumbled back immediately, and he tried to reach out for me, but I pushed him away and fell back to the floor. I kicked fiercely from him as he came closer.

"How the *hell* do you know my name?" My voice was strong, but I was terrified. "What did you do to me? How long have I been here?"

"I know it's strange—"

"Is that the best you can come up with?!"

"No, I— Look, I'm sorry. I—"

"Who *are* you?!"

"*Alaric!*" As soon as he raised his voice, I fell silent. It seemed to echo throughout the room. He leaned against the wall, defeated, while his fist returned to his forehead. "I'm Alaric."

"Why... *why* are you *here?* I-I didn't—" I froze as a new thought took over. "Why didn't you let me die...?"

"Why would I?" he fought back. "You're one of the only people left that won't just *go along* with everything. Besides... I need your help."

"*Me?* What am *I* supposed to do? And, if that's the case, why didn't you take me sooner?!"

"It's more complicated than that, alright? Things don't always... Just stay here."

"Oh, now you're leaving me?"

"You used up all of my supplies. I'm going to get more."

"So take me with you!"

"So you can wander into trouble again? I don't think so."

"I don't—"

"Just stay here." Before he fully exited the room, he turned to flash me a forced smile. "Please."

Then, it was just me. I sighed, but it didn't take my focus long to shift. I began scanning the large, empty room. My hands traced the smoothed, thin lines in the floor.

Tree bark, I realized. Slowly, I shifted to my feet. My leg was throbbing, but I tried my hardest not to care. I wobbled, but slowly, I rose. I stood.

Of course, I've walked before. We all have. Most of us, like me, are just used to doing so in the gravity-defiant water, or for short periods at a time. I laughed a little as I slowly, monotonously lifted one leg and placed it on the floor again. My toes spread out strangely on the rough surface. I dragged my foot, sliding it back down, and my leg followed it. I fell to my knees, giddy with the new sensation. After lying on my stomach, I began to run my hands freely along the hard floor.

"*Ah!*" I quickly pulled my finger to my chest. A small black dot appeared where there hadn't been one before. I tried to pick at it, but every time I glossed over the spot, the sudden pain made me draw back again. Hasty footsteps grew closer and closer.

"Are you alright?"

"I thought you went to get supplies?"

"Tell me what happened," he insisted.

I turned my head away and held out my hand.

His smile brought my attention back. "Hold on, I'll be right back."

I continued to pick at it until he returned. He crouched beside me, set down a small bowl of steaming water, and held out his hand. I looked skeptically at him, but he simply sat there until I gave him my own.

"It's a little hot, but it'll help." He placed my hand in the water, and I looked back at him. "Just leave it in there for a few minutes."

"And it'll... just come out?"

"Not quite." He held up tweezers in his other hand. "That's what these are for."

"Is it... Will it... Y'know..."

"Hurt?"

I turned my head and nodded, slightly red in the face. How could I not *know* any of this?

"Only a little. But it'll be worth it once it's out." He reached for my hand again, but I pulled away. When he tilted his head and raised his eyebrows, I let him take it back.

He held my hand close to his face, moving the soft skin around in his fingers.

"There you are..." he seemed to challenge. He then brought the tweezers to my pointer. I sucked in air through my teeth as he pinched, but his firm grip never let me retract my hand. After only a few tries, he showed me the tiny piece of bark on the edge of the tweezer.

"See? All better." To seal my embarrassment, he brought my hand to his lips and looked directly at me as he smiled a kiss onto it. I ripped my hand back and turned away. He apologized, but he did so with a laugh.

"So," I tried after clearing my throat, "what do you... You said you needed my help?"

He sighed as he stood back up, then walked toward the arched exit of the room. "Why don't you follow me?"

I tried to stand again, but as soon as he noticed how wobbly I was, he rushed to my side. I tried to push him back, but the more I struggled, the less I focused on my gait.

"Do you... really not walk much? I would have thought that all of the times you went to the dock—"

"Doesn't matter," I demanded.

He silenced without hesitation.

As I stumbled to the doorway, he followed behind me, but as soon as I left the room, my jaw hit the floor. The wood stretched onwards, with seemingly endless hallways leading to more and more doorways. As I got closer to the end of the long hall, I couldn't help but gasp.

"Where... where *are* we?"

He walked ahead of me, over to a table, but my mouth was stuck hanging open. I held the wall as I looked into the wide, open space ahead. Outside, the water seemed to go on forever, but all of it was *below* my line of sight.

"Welcome to the Great Oak."

"How?"

Alaric stood up straight and bent one arm behind his back. His tone was that of mockery. "As the youngest prince of the Great Royals, Prince Aaron was first to pick—"

"No, not that! I mean... *how?* How is this *possible?* How are we *above* the *water?*"

"You don't know about—"

"No! *Nobody* does, Alaric! This is... this is *insane!*" I paused and dropped my voice to a whisper. "Alaric..." I tried the name out again. Tasted how it felt in my mouth. "You're... you're Prince Alaric."

"Yes, I did try to make that part clear."

"Then... *why?* Why did you... Why am *I* here...?"

Alaric shook his head and lowered his gaze. His black hair fell over his face, despite how he tried to push it back on his head. "Because I can't do this alone."

Now, I found myself staring. I wanted to tell him that we've all been alone. I wanted to tell him that his *family* was the problem. That at least he still *had* one.

Family. It had become a lost concept to me, but the word instantly brought me back. I started to think of my own, and I tried to remember what my sister might have done if I had said something similar. I was lost to the thought, and soon after, I wasn't even seeing him in front of me. Slowly, I approached. He silenced altogether and stared at me, more than likely befuddled by my sudden actions. Still, I hesitated, inhaled, and awkwardly wrapped my arms around his. He stayed unmoving, but I only tightened my hold.

At this point, I was fully aware of the strangeness in the situation, and I wanted to back out, but I was sure I would fall over if I did. I continued to squeeze my arms around his, and to my surprise, he actually moved one of his hands to my back. My eyes darted up to his when his other secured itself around my waist. I exhaled as soon as he used the grip to straighten me back to my feet.

"Um... thanks."

"Don't, uh... Don't mention it."

"No worries, I'd rather not." He smiled again, but this time, it was softer. I noticed the fragile state of his pale blue eyes, as if they'd been swallowed by a thousand tides, over and over again, until they lost their shine. But as swiftly as he was washed ashore, he was dragged back out to sea, for just a moment later, he cleared his throat, hardened his gaze to the table, and took a few steps back.

"Have you ever used a sword?" His question caught me completely off guard.

"*Excuse—*"

"A spear?"

"No! *Why* would I—"

"Alright. Dagger it is." He reached to the table, then grabbed a small blade. As he tossed it in my direction, I stepped back and let it clatter to the floor.

"*Alaric!*"

"Oh, you're no fun."

"Never in my *life*—"

"That's why you're starting today. Pick it up."

I wanted to refuse, but I could feel him staring through my skin. Into my soul. Judging his choice.

Slowly—carefully—I bent down and picked up the blade. The hilt was silver, but tightly wrapped with a light blue cord. When I looked back up, Alaric was holding a long, glistening sword.

"When you hold a weapon, make sure it always stays in a defensive position. Here, see?" He began to change his stance, hiding himself behind the blade. Maroon surrounded both of his hands. "But, obviously, you have to stay ready to attack. Just—"

"Are you really the most qualified person to be giving these instructions?"

"Do you see anyone else around?" This made me look back to the large opening in the bark. I was completely consumed by the idea, for I walked over to it, dropping my dagger altogether. I peered over the edge and stared into the blue abyss below. It felt so natural to want to jump in, as if Watertowne itself was screaming for me to come home. What was I even *doing* here? Why was I with this stranger?

What more would you be doing back home?

"Maliyah?"

I turned back around, blinking hard at the darker scene. It was so strange to hear my name again, let alone from him.

As I stared, he sighed, then nodded to himself. "Alright. Let's... let's take it slower. Are, uh... are you hungry?"

"Why would I need to use a weapon?"

"Dining area is this way." As he turned, my lips drew tight. The air seemed to change its pressure around my confused limbs. I forced myself to step out of the bubble that felt like it was forming around me, and I followed Alaric into the dining area.

I barely spoke as we trekked through the Tree, for when my attention wasn't stolen by walking, it was by the scenery. Most rooms were full of various furniture, wall hangings, and purposes, even if not everything matched. It felt to me as if we were going through a maze. We passed doorways, walked down ramps of roots, and eventually, we ended up at water level.

"I can't believe you just... *live* in here," I mused. "What about everyone below? You just... You let them suffer...?"

"Who said they were suffering?"

"All of us are!" I gestured to the water through another eye-level opening. *"Especially* the people of Oak."

"Have you... *met* the people of Oak?"

"I— But the... The people don't actually— Do they *talk* to each other...?"

"All I know," Alaric said as he walked to the opening, "is there's a reason I don't stay at Lavender for long." He gestured for me to look over, and as soon as I did, I wanted to know everything. Multicolored lights from below seemed to illuminate the water's surface. It felt as if loud noises should have been surrounding me just to accommodate the boisterous scene.

"But I thought—"

"Which rumor? The prison? The slaves?" Alaric turned back to me with a confident laugh. "As soon as I took charge of this place, I *liberated* it. I took out the guards, broke through the Roots. As soon as I told the people my plan, they *helped* me to fix everything."

"Why doesn't anyone know about this...?"

"Because we made a deal. If they helped me break free of the Royal's rule, I would supply them with everything they needed. I just can't allow them to leave. Not to the other Trees, at least. Not yet."

"You talk like there's... like there's *more* than the Trees. And how would the Royals not find out about this?"

"You think they *care?* They don't care about *anyone,* so long as they don't interfere with their petty lives. Hell, they don't even care about *us!* Do you *know* the last time I spoke to them?"

My mouth felt glued shut. Alaric tightened his fist, slid it down the thick bark that surrounded the opening, then dropped it altogether. "Come on. I'm sure you're hungry. Besides... I got you something."

"Something like...?"

"Just come on."

We walked through our final doorway, and finally, I saw the dining room. It was a wide space with a square, marble table in the center and a few unmatching chairs around it. I must have made a face, because it didn't take Alaric long to answer my silent question.

"The people gave me most of what I have. It's not like I could go ask Cherry for help with my interior decorating."

"What's it like?" I found myself asking. "The Great Cherry."

"Corrupt." Alaric's expression instantly tightened. "But... I guess it was beautiful. Once. Before the king lost his mind."

"Your grand—"

"The *king*. He— Look, I don't want to talk about *them*. Do you want your gift or not?"

I nodded, so he reached for the table and tossed me a bag that had been sitting on it. As I peered inside, he sighed.

"It's a hair brush. You just— Oh, what the hell? You know how to use one. I'm going to make you some food."

As soon as I was alone, I stared at the brush. I'd used one before, but never without my hair being from dripping to drenched. I raised it to the top of my head, but it didn't go through as smoothly as I was used to. I tightened my expression and grunted as I pulled, but I eventually had to rip it back out from the top, my hair even more tangled than before.

I heard a small laugh coming from the joined room. "Do I have to teach you *everything*?"

I was frustrated by his mockery, but he came in holding two plates, and suddenly, I couldn't care less. My stomach may as well have grown hands of its own to reach for the shockingly colorful platter.

"What *is* all—?"

"After you eat, I'll give you some stuff to... to make yourself more at home, I guess."

Up until this point, I hadn't even considered that I might be staying here for a while.

"How long—"

"Until it's safe for you to go back." Alaric swallowed a bite of his food. "Until we've defeated the Royals."

"*Excuse* me?" I found myself shouting. "You never said *anything* about—"

"I need people like you. People who aren't afraid to lose something, because they have nothing *to* lose. Fighters."

"I am *not* a fighter! I can barely speak up when I—"

"You're fighting me right now, aren't you?"

My heart beat loud in my ears. For as much disbelief as I was in, he continued to make his point.

"You *are*, Maliyah. You don't like to lose. After I left, you kept coming back. You didn't let me win. You—"

"This is so stupid. I'm going home." When I stayed in my seat, Alaric raised his eyebrows at me. I sighed and put my head in my hands.

"I'm not asking you to learn right now," he continued. "I shouldn't have rushed into it like that. I am, however, asking you to see what I see. You and I, we're stuck. We're stuck living the same damned day over and over again until we die. And until people like you start helping people like me, we'll never be free."

"People like you," I scoffed. "Who even *are* you?"

"And who are you?"

"I didn't ask for this!"

"You did, though. Every day for the past two months. You *begged* for this."

I stood up and looked out of the nearest opening in the wall.

He challenged my gaze. "Go, then. I'll find someone else."

Without a word, I went back down the hall. I traveled until I found the largest opening in the bark, leading out to what must have been Oak's dock. I almost looked back to see the Tree from the outside. When I caught myself, I forced my eyes to lock on the water.

It'll be better this way, I told myself. From there, I drew in a deep breath, and I jumped.

TWO

THE WATER FELT COLDER than I remembered, despite the beaming sun. I held my breath tight, but my body was instantly begging to gasp for fresh air.

Where are you going, I chided myself. The truth was, I had no idea. On the inside, I already wanted to go back. Not to my home, but to Alaric. I wanted to tell him he was right. I wanted to look his grandfather in the eyes while I stabbed him through the middle. But now, I had a different point to prove. I looked to the closest light, and I continued to follow it. Down, down, down, until my head was throbbing. I grabbed a Root from the Tree and ducked inside, taking a long, suffocated breath.

"Oh, hello," someone greeted. "Forgive me if I'm wrong, but I haven't seen you here before, have I?"

"No," I carefully replied. "I-I don't... I don't get out much."

"Ah, I see. Well, you're welcome to a warm meal or bed, if you need it."

"That's alright. Just needed to catch my breath for a minute."

"Why the rush, sweetheart?"

"I—" I paused. "My sister's waiting for me."

She sent me a sweet smile. "Mustn't keep her waiting, then. Have a nice night, love."

I nodded at the woman and took another deep breath. To my surprise, I wouldn't need to hold it for long. Just ahead of me sat a long, transparent structure, where people were walking to and fro. *Walking.*

Water flowed over every entrance, but it never seeped farther than that. The citizens of Oak swam in and out as they pleased, but inside, they chatted and sat—they carried on *living.* I swam into the tunnel of glass, where I saw a flashing, neon sign. In bold lettering, it read,

Welcome to The Tube!

Beneath it were arrows pointing in various directions. Some referenced clothing shops, others restaurants, and just in my eyesight, some people even *gardened.* I'd only ever *heard* of such a task before. As I looked closer, colors I couldn't even identify were popping out of flaky, brown earth.

I felt my teeth begin to grit. How could I have lived in such a depressive world for so many years, while the so-called "vagabonds" were thriving in their own, secret society?

"Incoming!" a child yelled as he ran by me. As I stepped aside, a few others dashed by, and I traced their footsteps to find their parents laughing in the distance. I began to walk in their direction, gawking at every new, colorful sight. While the Roots of Oak were incorporated into the buildings, it didn't limit them. The people used their own materials to build off of the Great Tree, rather than barricading themselves inside of it. For layers and

layers, they laughed, worked, and breathed, and it appeared there was no intention to stop there. Over most buildings, construction continued upwards, stretching toward the surface. Automatic stairs helped people standing in place to climb, bright lights invited the lost in to dine, and everywhere, people smiled. A single thought crossed my mind:

Of course nobody ever left. Why would they want *to?*

I continued walking through The Tube until something unexpected caught my eye. My speed nearly doubled as I chased after the figure, but as soon as I reached the storefront, I stopped. I watched as Alaric spoke to the cashier, who then pointed toward what appeared to be a wall full of woman's clothes. My brows knitted, but I entered.

"Good evening!" a teenage-looking girl eagerly greeted. "Is there anything specific I can help you with today?"

"No, I... I'm just looking."

"Alright! Let me know if there's anything I might—"

"Thanks." I followed where he went, peering around the corner as he shifted through the clothes hanging on the rack. He held a few next to each other, occasionally draping them over his arm as he continued to look.

"Excuse me"—I turned around to face the new voice—"but is there something I could help you with?"

"N-no, I was just—"

"Maliyah." His voice made me whip around yet again. "I'm sorry if I— Look, I'm sorry. I wanted to do something nice to try to make it up to you. Do you think— I'll be blunt, I have no clue what I'm doing here. Can you just pick something so I can get it for you?"

"What...?"

"I took you away from everything without a warning. Including your money. I... admittedly took too long to realize that. But I also know that you're not swimming all the way back to Lavender, so could you please just pick some stuff to fill your room with?"

"My... my room."

"The empty one we were in earlier. If it's to your liking."

I tried to look around, but of course, there was no one else to look to. Reluctantly, I let myself cave in to his instructions.

"Do they have anything in orange...?"

Alaric's smile returned. He gestured with his head, and there began our first night as housemates. For the rest of the night, he showed me around the town, lent me some money, and helped me fill my room.

By the end of the day, we had assembled my bed, a small couch, a desk, and a dresser, and we had filled a closet with clothes. I didn't want to admit to him that it was more than I ever had to begin with.

As the sky fell much darker, what I learned was called Oakview lit up in a new way. The neon flashing slowly grew dark, and softer house lights took their places in windows throughout the Roots. The Tree itself was mostly dark, but with a few lamplights placed in the corners of each room, the deep brown color of the walls and floor stayed warm.

As Alaric and I finished rolling out a fluffy white carpet, I leaned against the bottom of my new couch. "I... I'm sorry."

"I am, as well. My room is just down the hall if you need anything. You should try to get some rest soon."

"No, I—"

"I know. Just... get some sleep." As Alaric stood and began to leave the room, I noticed him fiddling with a chain around his neck. The more he did, the more I could see a pink shape escaping the neckline of his shirt.

"What's that?"

"Hmm?"

"Around your neck?"

"Oh... Another time. Get some rest." With this, he was gone, but I could hear his faint laugh echo through the hall. "We need to get some doors in here."

I sat on my new bed and tried to take in everything that had happened. I had nearly forgotten about my wounds, which hadn't pained me since Alaric finished treating them. I didn't even realize when the bandages fell off, leaving only small amounts of discolored skin in their places.

Prince Alaric... I thought as I lay down. *Maliyah Adley... What the hell do you think you're doing?*

As my eyes began to open, I struggled to remember where I was. The feel of the new bed confused me as much as the feel of the wood against my feet as I stood up. Beside them was a pair of pink slippers. I couldn't help but chuckle.

Alaric really did get me everything. I paused once I felt them against my toes. *Alaric.*

No longer could I call myself a citizen of Watertowne's Lavender Branch. Now, I would be one of the hundreds who disappeared.

"She prayed for one too many things," they'll say. I stood and moved to the wall. Felt the wood under my hands. *They'd say, if there was anyone left to recognize that I went missing.*

I cleared my throat and made my way to the kitchen. I looked through various doorways as I passed, but Alaric was nowhere in sight. When I entered the dining area, I saw that a plate of food was already made and set by the chair that I had used the day before. I passed it to enter the kitchen, where I grabbed a glass and poured myself some water.

"Alaric?" I called as I sat down. My voice traveled through the many empty rooms, but nothing called back. I stared at the food for a moment. Never before had I seen some in such bright colors and loose textures. My heart filled just knowing there was still something left to *produce* such a thing. Still, I put my curiosity aside, and I ate my breakfast in silence.

Once I was done, I peered out of the front entrance. The sky was dark and clouded, and a light rain rippled against the surface of the water. I took a step onto the long, wooden planks that connected to the dock, and I held my face to the sky. I smiled with every tiny raindrop that touched my skin. The sensation was bringing something out in me that I hadn't felt in a long time. Soon, I began to laugh.

"Good morning."

The sudden voice made me jump, but I was still smiling as I turned to face Alaric. "It's raining!"

I nearly grabbed his hand and pulled him toward me. My chest was moving up and down, breath hastily escaping through my lips. I could see confusion cloud his expression, but he never mentioned it out loud. Instead, he stepped forward, blinking a little extra as the steadily increasing rain splashed on his face. I breathed in, and when I looked over, I found Alaric already looking. My smile dropped that same instant.

"I... am being stupid."

"Not at all. It's a good reminder."

"What is?"

"You. The rain. To breathe."

I paused and changed my expression a few times, but before I could speak again, Alaric was holding out another bag.

"Here, I got you something. Feel free to use any of the bathrooms for as long as you'd like. I'll be in my room." As he walked back inside, I opened the bag to see not only a bottle of shampoo, but also conditioner, something my mother used to buy me and my sister on special occasions.

I smiled, but he was already gone. I walked to one of the bathrooms closest to the entrance, and as I set them down, I noticed what the labels read: *"Orange-scented."*

During my shower, I thought about many things. While the topics came and went, I began to wonder what my parents would think of me. Staying with a stranger, but hoping to make things right. Leaving home without as much as a coin, but keeping in mind the way things used to be. The way things were before I was even brought into this world of blue. *I'm fighting for a life that I was never meant to be in.*

While I rinsed off, a strange scent caught my attention. I blinked a few times, and it took me a minute to realize that the smell was coming from my hair. I pulled it to my nose, and I began to laugh.

"Orange," I whispered. "Huh." I turned off the water, wrapped a towel around myself, and walked back toward my room.

"Oh. Maliyah, you're here." As Alaric's voice grew closer, I held the towel tighter to my chest. "I want to show you something when you have a moment. I realize you haven't been made familiar with it yet."

"Yeah, sure. Just... let me get dressed first?"

"Forgive me," but I saw him crack a smile before he was fully turned.

As he continued walking past me, I made my way into my bedroom and sifted through my new clothes. After I threw on a loose top over my underthings, I knocked on the frame of Alaric's door. He was unwrapping some material from around his reddened knuckles.

"Training," he answered. "But I figured, since you're going to be here for a bit, I'd show you how to use the dryers."

"Dryers?"

"In The Tube, and a lot of household doorways. Come, I have one at the front."

I followed him back to the front entrance, where he pointed out a pushable area on the side of the door. Then, he gestured to the middle of the arch.

"Stand here."

I did as he said, and he hit the side of his fist against the button. Hot air instantly started blowing on my head and sides from tiny, missable holes.

"How did you even—"

"A lot of time and renovations. But it helps from getting water everywhere. How's your leg doing, by the way?"

"Better."

"The tea helped, then?"

"The... the tea?"

"What I had you drink when you woke up. It's made from the petals of the Great Cherry. That's... why the Royals were so eager to claim it." His expression turned to something much darker. "And why the king refuses to die."

I wanted to ask him why he had such a passionate hatred for his grandfather. It *couldn't* have been the same reason as the rest of us.

After all, they were family. Again, it crossed my mind: at least he *had* a family.

My thoughts were interrupted when Alaric sighed. "I'm glad it worked. It doesn't, always. The more severe the wound, the more it takes for it to heal."

I stayed quiet, and the air turned off.

"Warm yet?" he asked. "Or would you like another round?"

"I'm fine, thanks."

"Good. *Now* try your other gift." Alaric tossed me my hairbrush, and I couldn't help but laugh. I looked angrily at it, but I tried to brush it through my hair. Before I could fully make contact, Alaric jutted out his hand. "Start from the bottom."

"What?"

"The— Here, look." Alaric stole the brush back from me, then took my shoulders to guide me to the nearest chair. He crouched beside me, gathered my hair over one shoulder, and bunched it together at the bottom. I physically flinched when I saw it.

"Is everything alright?" he asked.

"It's— I thought—"

"Maliyah?"

"Look!" I gestured to the bottom of my fluffy, tangled hair. "It's— I haven't even *seen* this color before!"

"A darker auburn, I'd say. Have you really not—"

"Never! It— it looks so—"

"Just wait." A twinge of excitement entered his voice. He began running the brush through the bottom of my hair, slowly working his way up, moving his hand with it to prevent it from pulling. Once he reached the top, he spun me around so he could brush it over my back. Then, he guided me to a mirror.

"No... *way.*" I nearly cried. I could barely even recognize my-self. My hands kept going to my hair, over and over again. Words couldn't describe how I felt.

"It looks... nice."

"How did you know how to *do* that?!" I yelled.

He only smiled weakly, but I noticed him fiddling with the chain around his neck. As soon as he caught my gaze, he dropped his hands.

I tried again with a nod in its direction. "A girlfriend, maybe?"

"Another time" was his only reply.

I wondered if that time would ever come.

THREE

THE DAY PASSED MUCH slower than the one before. I ventured through the town while Alaric disappeared into one of the unexplored rooms of Oak. In just a short time, I found myself acquainted with many of Oakview's inhabitants.

My first stop was after I stumbled upon a Greenhouse, as it was labeled. Inside, artificial lights blared from the cemented ceiling. There was less glass in this building than many of the others, but once I entered, I was surrounded by colors.

I spoke to someone who called herself a "Life Keeper." She tended to all types of crops, livestock, and even small trees and bushes. I found myself smelling various new scents, approaching every individual plant to out try the sensation. Tiny, buzzing creatures seemed to float around me, landing happily on all of the colors.

I followed one of them to another tree, this one dotted with orange. As soon as I got closer, I gasped at the scent that matched the one in my hair.

Orange-scented, I remembered. I inhaled deep through my nose, practically rubbing their rough surfaces across my face.

Soon after, the Life Keeper approached me, holding a mysterious shape in her hand. "If you want to smell something, try this."

"What is it?" I asked, staring at the long, green base she held it by.

"It's... just a flower."

"A flower?"

"They look nice. People like to give them to each other as gifts. You can take one, if you'd like. I have plenty."

I nodded enthusiastically and took the one she offered me. I kept it close to my chest as I walked home.

The middle of it had small black and yellow bits, but the largest area was purple. Its scent wasn't as strong as the orange in the tree, but it still held a gentle, pleasant aroma.

When I returned to Oak—after shielding my new finding in a waterproof bag—I called out for Alaric. It took him some time, but eventually, I met him in one of the sitting rooms.

"Enjoy your trip?"

"I found something. The Life Keeper said they're gifts, so... I wanted to thank you for everything you've given me." As I held out the flower, Alaric's serious expression melted. He took it between his fingers and admired it for just a moment. Right after, he brushed my soft hair from my face and planted it behind my ear.

"Purple looks good on you."

Before he could fully lower it, I held his hand to my cheek. My smile faded as I felt it linger. My chin seemed to twitch forward and back, not knowing which direction to lead my head. I let out a shaky breath.

Then, Alaric stepped back. "I'll take it you did enjoy your trip, then."

My lips folded into each other, and I nodded.

"I... I'll be back to my work, then. Holler if I can—"

"Alaric—" I didn't know why I was so quick to stop him. He raised an eyebrow as I breathlessly asked, "Why me?"

"I already told you why."

I crumbled inside with his blunt reply, but he smiled before he turned away. "Besides... you can't miss that hair."

Once he was gone, I found myself exploring the Tree more. Most of the rooms were as expected: a few places to sit, dining areas, and extra spaces that I'd assume were once bedrooms.

Eventually, I stumbled into a very tall part of the bark. The room was completely hollowed out, save for a circular column in the middle that seemed to be carved into repetitive shelves. The sides of the room were turned into long ramps, curling up around the entire space. Light beamed from the green at the top in rays, shifting with every small gust of wind. As I began to climb, I leaned over the side railing, caressing my fingers over the leathery surfaces that fit in each hole. As I took one in my hands, I saw black lines of letters fill the contrasting white pages as soon as I opened it.

Books.

My mom used to read me books. I tried to read along, but I was a very slow reader. I much preferred to close my eyes and listen. I'd imagine what she was saying, taking it in as her every word painted a new picture in my mind. She told me about creatures that once existed, plants that once thrived, and tales of what I could only imagine to be a complete fantasy.

I wonder how many I can find in this town. I questioned how she'd managed to leave out flowers. I closed the book and put it back on the shelf.

Tomorrow, I decided. I continued climbing up.

My walk sped to a jog, and eventually, I was sprinting to the top. My legs seemed to be moving themselves as my breath escaped through my lips in short puffs. The ending seemed painfully far away, but before long, I found myself pushing into the green. The gentle rustle alone was enough to change my breath altogether. A long, wooden platform was built across the entirety of the Treetop, and a short bar was put in place to prevent anyone from falling over the edge. I crept to the one closest to me, and I peered over. The blue seemed so far below, but closer above than I'd ever thought it could be. I reached into it, feeling the soft leaves brush my fingertips. My arm stayed there as I sank to my knees, then settled on the platform. I pulled my hair from under my back and let it sprawl lifelessly around me. Lifelessly, in a world of blue and green. I stared deep above me, and soon, I closed my eyes, letting myself fall into a dream.

I was lying on my back, floating on the surface of the water. There were no Trees in sight—only clouds that shifted in color as the warm sun rose. My sister floated beside me, giggling as her long brown hair curled around her. Small creatures swam in the water with us. I kicked my feet. Gently. I pushed my arms, and I flew. Gracefully.

When I turned back around, Alaric was there. We stood in my old bedroom, but it was oddly full of water.

"Maliyah."

My name echoed around the space. I turned to him, and ripples formed around my waist. He came closer, but I found myself backing toward the wall.

"Don't be afraid," he said.

"I'm not."

"Why?" It was my sister's voice now, hovering all around me until it could sink into my skin. "Why don't you fear?"

His hand closed around my hip, and I stiffened, but his grip only tightened. He brushed my hair aside, and I leaned into him.

Slowly, his hands began to wander. They explored, like I did to his home. I welcomed, as he did to me. His lips crept forward, reaching for my neck. I lifted my head, using my hands to guide his own.

I have nothing left to lose.

I sat straight up, and my hand grabbed at my chest. I tugged at my damp shirt and repetitively smoothed back my hair.

"Bad dream?"

I let out a breathy yelp as I turned toward his voice.

"Or, perhaps, a really good one."

"Holy—" I cradled the back of my head with my arms, then pressed it hard against my knees. As I did, I let out something of a whine. "What am I *doing* here...?"

I felt a hand on my back, but I quickly ripped myself away.

"Hey, easy," he warned. "I'm not the villain here."

"How am *I* supposed to know that? I-I don't even *know* you! Geez, I— We *just* met, and now you're—"

And now you're invading my dreams.

"Why don't I give you some space, then?" He stood up and took a few steps back. His expression was stern, but clouded with something else.

"No!"

It shifted. His forehead relaxed.

"No, I—" I stopped and made myself take a deep breath. "How long was I asleep for?"

"Maybe an hour or so. I'm not sure, I wasn't here for very long."

"How'd you find me?" I prayed it wasn't because I was talking in my sleep. It took him a minute to answer.

"Just... figured I'd find you here eventually."

I winced. Waited. But he didn't continue.

"Are you hungry?"

I shook my head.

"I... Should I leave you to your day, then?"

Stay. I flinched. *You're crazy.* I breathed. "Well... what do *you* normally fill your day with?"

"Do you... Would you like me to show you?"

I nodded, and he offered me his hand. I took it, and I almost didn't let go. It was a moment too long before I forced myself to.

We walked in silence. If he spoke, I didn't hear him. My mind was screaming too loud. My thoughts conflicted. My heart pounded.

Alaric guided me down. Down the ramps, down the stairs, under the water. Through thick glass windows, Oakview glowed.

I wonder if Lavender could ever be like this... We crossed a final doorway, and the floor turned cold on my bare feet. The thickest of Oak's Roots twisted around us.

"Welcome," Alaric gestured, "to my training room."

The room was long, empty, and bitter. A single, rectangular table defined its purpose. There, I saw the wraps that Alaric's hands had been tied in before, along with the reasons for wearing them. Beside the table, a hole was being messily formed in a thick root. There were also swords of various lengths, to which I matched slashes in the walls. The patterns repeated throughout the entirety of the room. A ridiculous part of me questioned if he'd chiseled out the whole space that way.

"This is..." Alaric rubbed the back of his neck. "This is where I train, obviously."

"What, exactly, are you training for?" but I already knew the answer. I tensed as he sighed.

"Something has to be done. And it won't be done peacefully."

"Are there others?" I was suddenly asking.

"Others?"

"Other... fighters. People who can help?"

Alaric's lips tightened. "I've tried to recruit people before, but... everyone is *happy* here. They don't *want* change, and why would they?"

"But everyone else—"

"They haven't *seen* everyone else. And they never will. They're making so much progress here, and—"

"One person," I decided. "There has to be *one* person who wants to—"

"Maliyah... That one person is you."

"No. No, I— I can't—"

"Maliyah—"

"Stop saying it like that!"

Alaric's head jolted back. "Am I pronouncing—"

"No! No, you just... forget it."

Stop making my heart stop at the sound of my name. Stop speaking, so I can remember how to breathe.

"You know what?" I froze before I continued. *There's no going back from here. You can choose something else. You can choose your nice room. You can choose—*

I scrunched my brow at my own thoughts. *You can choose to be better than everyone else.*

"Give me the knife."

Alaric smiled and picked up the blue-stringed blade. "First of all, it's a dagger. Secondly, be careful not to cut yourself. It's sharp."

"I'm *not* gonna—"

"You'd be surprised." Alaric pulled off his shirt, exposing tiny scars all around his sides, arms, and stomach. Only a few were really noticeable without looking.

"Alright." He picked up a sword, twirling it in the air, only to catch it as he jumped into a ready position. "Swing."

"What?"

"Swing at me. Let's see what you can do."

I hesitated, opening and closing my mouth, but there was nothing I could think to say. I stepped forward and swung the blade.

Alaric stepped around it and laughed. "Alright, I didn't mug you, I damned a generation. Try again."

This time, I slashed.

His expression tightened. "That's more for a sword. With a dagger, try staying low. Sharp. *Jab.*"

I made a swift cutting motion near his ribs, and he had to jump out of the way.

"That was better! Now try to follow through with it—you have to stay close."

"What are *they* going to be using?" I couldn't believe I was asking.

Alaric only shook his head. "That's for later. If you can get at least a *little* comfortable with this, I'll be happy. I want you with some level of self-defense before we worry about anything else."

"The dagger's my self-defense, then," I reasoned as I handed it out to him.

"Keep it. I'll give you something so you can sheath it on your leg."

I paused and stared at my reflection in its shimmering surface. "This is *insane.*"

"This is *real.* Come over here."

I walked toward him slowly, but he grabbed my hand and spun me into him. I let out a small breath as he looked over my shoulder and readjusted my grip and stance.

"Hold your elbow more like this, but make sure your wrists are always guarded. I'll get you some gear that will fit you tomorrow."

"Can I come?" I turned when I spoke. My breath was low, right near his neck.

He cleared his throat and stepped back. "If that's what you'd like. But first, come this way." He led me to a thick, hanging root. Slashes had been dug heavily into it. There was seldom a surface unchipped. "You can practice on this for now."

"Just... keep going?"

"That's what my training is. I'll correct you. But... we should start going on runs or something. Help build up your stamina."

"Can you show me how to swim like you did?" It came out much more excitedly than I had originally intended it to.

His laugh ended in a steady smile. "If that's something you're interested in, then of course."

I smiled back at him. He swung his shirt over his shoulder and ran his fingers through his hair. He looked at me as if he wanted to say something, but he never did.

My gaze returned to the room. "How *long* do you spend down here?"

"Few hours every day."

"But... for how long? I mean... how long have you been *doing* this for...?"

Alaric shook his head. "Come on, let's go swim. I need to cool off, anyways."

"Alaric." I grabbed his wrist, and he turned to me. His expression was tight, but I just looked at him. I wanted to find something—*anything*—but there was nothing there to read.

"How long have you been alone...?" I softly added.

"I'm not alone. I have the people."

"But you said it yourself, that you can't—"

"Ignore what I said. It was just... I wasn't feeling like myself, alright? I'm fine now. Shall we swim?"

"If I can beat you there," I tried with a smile, "then you have to answer a question."

"A quest—"

Before he could finish, I began to sprint. I was laughing as I ran, but I didn't turn back until I was there. I knew I was far ahead after I stopped hearing his footsteps behind me. When I stepped onto the front dock, dropping my hands to my knees, my mouth fell open.

"How," I demanded with a breathy laugh. *"How* did you do that."

"I've lived here for *much* longer than you have. Now... does that mean that *I* get a question?"

I could feel my heart thump in my ears as soon as he finished asking. I nodded slowly.

"So tell me..." He paused and thought for a moment. I watched as the slowly fading rain dropped against his light skin. His hair was easily displaced by the wind. He nodded in small, private amounts. The silence was killing me.

"Do you trust me?"

"I do."

"Why?"

I felt frozen. *Why, Maliyah? Why* do *you trust the stranger?*

"You said *one* question." I spoke over my breaking voice.

"Actually, *you* said it," he countered. "Besides, it's a part of the same question."

"Fine." I let out a breath. "I guess... I thought you were coming to kill me. After my parents, I thought that's what the Royals *did.* So... the expectations bar was pretty low on that front."

"Your parents were killed?"

I winced. This was never something I'd said out loud before, yet here I was, without even realizing it had come from my lips.

"They were... Eight years ago, they went up to the docks to pray with my sister. I never saw them again."

A look of darkness crossed Alaric's face. "Your... *older* sister?"

"Yeah? But—" I stopped when he clenched his fists. The tightness made me take a step back.

"Did you *see* them die?"

"How could you *ask* that?"

"Because there's a good chance that they *didn't* just *die.*"

Bitterness filled my mouth. A million thoughts ran through my mind, but not one of them could surface past my lips.

"No... No, if they were still alive, they would've come back for me. They would've—"

"No, I— Look." He pressed his fist against his forehead. "I don't mean to get you thinking like that. Chances are, they would have been killed by now. They never keep anyone past a few years."

"What are you *talking* about?"

"The Royals take *slaves,* Maliyah." Alaric refused to meet my wide, desperate eyes. "Lavender is their harvesting point."

My entire body began to shake. "What... what did they do to them...?"

His gaze was focused only on the ground.

"Alaric...?"

"Anything."

I had to throw my hands over my mouth, but my pained scream still escaped. I remembered my sister. She was beautiful. I always wished I could look more like her. I cut my hair only when she did. Dressed in the same colors as she did. I don't know how soon after I started sobbing.

Alaric held me. I left nail marks in his skin, snot and tears on his chest and shoulder. It was ugly. I *felt* ugly. I squeezed, with both of my arms, behind his neck, and he tightened his hold around my ribs.

"I can't say for sure what happened to them," he explained. "Maybe they *were* killed sooner. But..." He didn't have to finish. "I'm sorry."

We stayed like that until my exhaustion took over. When I woke back up, I was lying numb in my bed. I had absolutely no urge or desire to move.

"Maliyah?" he tried.

I didn't answer. Instead, I curled up and stared at the blank wall.

Alaric sat still at the foot of my bed. "I... I don't know what to say."

He rested his hand on the thin blanket that was draped over my leg. I wanted to kick him away, but I didn't have the energy.

"Are you hungry...?"

He sighed when I failed again to respond. I didn't know how to feel as he leaned back and rubbed my leg.

"You're doing well, Maliyah. You're going to make things change. You... you have a good heart."

Everything felt loud. The lamps. Heartbeats. Breath. His voice was muffled, but so, so loud.

"I wasn't... I wasn't always alone." His words finally cut through the noise. "I had a sister once, too."

I lifted my head a little, so he helped me to sit up straighter against my headboard. He stayed sitting up, across from me, but his gaze was now fixed on the bed.

"Can you—" My voice was raw, and my breath was staggered. "What happened...?"

Alaric's eyebrows knitted together. He fiddled with his chain. Now that he was shirtless, I could clearly see the pink shell that hung from the end of it.

"She... used to live here. With me. When I took domain over Oak, I... I took her in, but she mostly—" Alaric breathed hard and shook his head. "She did the decorating around here. That's why I couldn't—" He gave a frustrated groan, but I didn't ask him to stop.

"Her name was Alana, and she was born after Aaron. Obviously, they didn't want a girl, because they went back to the egregious royal customs that the king liked, so now I'm here. For the third Tree. They didn't— I don't know *why* they didn't just— Forget it. She started talking about rebellion, about how stupid it all was, and she went to... to talk to them about it. She never came back."

"You never talk about Aaron. Is he—"

"I don't *want* to talk about Aaron."

"But isn't he your brother? You've *gotta*—"

"I don't *have* to do *anything*. He's the same as the rest: a disgusting, pompous idiot. And, as far as I'm concerned, he's *not* my brother."

When I fell silent, Alaric sighed. "I didn't mean to—"

"Is the shell from your sister?"

Alaric looked down, but shortly after, he nodded. "It was her necklace. She got it from our mom when she was little. She... It came back instead of her."

"Your mother," I tried, "she's still alive, right? Why don't you talk to her?"

"Because they'd kill her if she knew where I was."

"*What?* Why?"

"Because they hate me! All of them! I—" He winced. His entire demeanor changed. "My mom's the only one of them who's worth it. Her and Alana. They're the only reason I'm doing this anymore."

"What about your dad?"

He shook his head hard. "Just them." When he finally looked up at me, he tried to change his tone to urge the conversation in a lighter direction. "You're lucky you got me to talk about my mom."

"She's next in line, right?" I hopefully suggested. "When the king dies, she'll be the queen with your dad?"

"It's... not that simple."

"Then why—"

"I'm glad to see you're doing better." He patted my leg a few times, then stood up and offered his hands. I took them, and he pulled me to my tired feet. "Now, come on. Why don't we get you something to eat?"

FOUR

THE REST OF THE day went by quietly. Alaric made us food, we ate, and every attempt I made to pick his brain was shut down almost immediately. Eventually, I went to my bed, and I tossed and turned for what felt like hours. Even after I could fall asleep, nightmares woke me every chance they got. By the time I was awake, I couldn't remember them, but they were enough to leave me shaken up. That was when I gave up on sleeping and decided to explore a little early.

I walked toward Alaric's room first, guessing he was the type to rise before the break of dawn. I'd never actually been to his room, and I was curious to see how he lived. I peeked past the doorframe, and I saw him stir in his bed. I jumped back to the side instantly.

"Oh... Hey, Maliyah." He tried to make his voice higher than usual, but the morning had already taken its toll. "Can I help you with something?"

"I-I didn't mean to wake you, I was just—"

"Don't worry about it. I've been, uh... I've been up for a while."

I laughed while he stretched and rubbed his eyes, then watched as he reached for his bedside table. His waking motion was to slide on the necklace that was lying there. It made me wonder how many times he'd done it before.

Right after, he stood up, stretched out his legs, and pulled a thick string on his wall. I gasped as it pulled a piece of fabric aside, unblocking yet another large window, allowing the blinding sunlight to flow through.

"Neat, huh?" he laughed. "Well, don't just stand there and stare at me. Come in."

I shook my head and walked into his room. It was a large bedroom, but then again, so was mine. He had furniture, including a bookshelf and somewhere comfortable to sit near it, a dresser, a closet... I don't know what more I was expecting.

"It's... a room," he mused. "Feel free to... I don't know, pick through my personal things? What is it that you wanted from me in here?"

I laughed, but my inner thoughts were teasing me with a simple answer: *you.*

"Just... feeding curiosity, I guess."

"Is it all you've ever dreamed and more?"

Now, my laugh was sincere. "Did you sleep well or something? Perhaps a... really good dream?"

"I don't know. Just trying to... I don't know."

I rolled my eyes at his response, but I continued to smile. He saw me looking at his bookshelf, and he asked, "Do you like to read?"

"I haven't, actually," I began. His eyes went wide as I finished. "Read... anything."

"You are *missing out*. Here, take this." He ran over and held up a book, but I hesitated. I was struggling to ignore the fact that he was only wearing his tight, shorts-like undergarments.

"Please, I *know* you're going to like it."

"I-I'm not that good at reading, actually. I used to just listen when... while my mom read to me."

Alaric slowly lowered the book. He smiled and gestured with his head for me to come sit.

"No, no, I... I don't want to—"

"Come on, you're not hurting anyone. Let me read you this first chapter, then we can go do whatever you'd like. You wanted to come with me to get your gear, right?"

I pursed my lips, but I sat on the small, round chair close to the floor. It squished as I sat, and I fell into it more than I expected. When I gave a small yelp, Alaric laughed. He sat on the floor, leaning into the cushioned chair and over me. Each of us held a side of the book. He began to read, but as soon as I closed my eyes, he took it back. He shifted to lean his back against me, and occasionally, I looked over his head to see the page.

It was like I could see the girl in the story—how she sat, cloaked in black, at her brother's funeral. She was somber, but I knew she hadn't always been. When the second girl appeared from the bushes, insisting she come with her, I was begging Alaric to keep reading. I leaned into him, brushing my head against his. He turned so I could rest on his shoulder, instead. In one arm, he held me. In the other, he turned the pages.

"'...and they ran back into the cave. The one that she had once run from, the one that killed her brother. But there he stood, a ghost of her memory, as if he had never died at all.'" Alaric closed the book, and my lips were stuck apart. I held his arm, looking longingly at the front cover as he held it. "We can read more later, if you'd like, but I think it might be a good time to go get that gear now."

"Thank you," I forced, suddenly feeling embarrassed. "That was... Thanks."

Alaric smiled as he helped me off of the chair. "It seemed your style."

"Was it really her brother, though?" I found myself asking. "Did he... How were they at the funeral, then?"

"I guess you'll have to wait and see," he said with a playful shrug. He started to walk away, but as his hand slipped past mine, I gently took hold of it. He whipped back around as soon as he felt the small tug. I looked there, where we both connected, and I wanted to say something. I could tell that he did, too.

"I'm sorry about yesterday," he blurted out. "I didn't mean to make everything so—"

"It's okay." I let go. "I just... don't want to think about it."

He nodded and continued walking forward. I followed him quietly.

The energy shifted as soon as we got to the dock.

"Alright," Alaric said as he backed toward the water. "First, we should check Julie's. There's a lot there that you might want to use as... You might want it underneath your gear. Then, I'll take you to Smithy's. He hand-crafted all of my gear, and I think he might have something already made that he'll be able to alter to fit you. I need you as safe as you possibly can be, so we can make sure to—"

"Aw... That's cute." As soon as I spoke, he paused and rubbed the back of his neck.

"I... did not mean to get so chatty there. Sorry."

"No, it's good. I mean... I'm glad you care."

"I just don't want more blood on my hands."

"More?" I took a step back, but he began to smile.

"I'm *kidding.* Shall we?"

I exhaled, but I could feel the tension in my chest. *You don't know him at* all, I realized. *He could be waiting to do* anything *to you. He just needs to gain your trust. And you already told him he has it.*

"Maliyah?"

I shook my head. "Yeah. Let's."

"Are you alright?"

"I am. I-I just—"

"I didn't mean to spook you, if I—"

"No, I'm fine. Really."

"If—"

I cut him off by jumping into the water. I felt a splash behind me, and there was Alaric, reaching out his hand. I took it, and he began to swiftly move his legs. I copied his motion, and our speed instantly picked up. He pushed the water behind him with his arms, dragging mine to do the same. In no time, we reached The Tube. I began to walk in, but still holding my wrist, Alaric stopped me. He pulled me back and pressed the button on the side of the entrance. I couldn't help but laugh as we dried off. My loose, netted orange top flapped freely around me, and my deep blue undergarments were visible even as the light over-layers dried.

"Alright, this way." Alaric pulled my arm as he guided me through The Tube. Nearly everyone smiled and waved as he passed. Some older people even bowed.

"Must feel nice, huh?" I asked as we walked. "To have so many people who adore you?"

"It all means nothing without someone who loves you." His expression wavered for only a moment. Quickly, he added, "Come on, we're almost there."

I wanted to tell him that people did love him. He had his parents, grandparents, and even a brother. But the look in his eyes whenever they were mentioned made me feel cold.

"Julie," Alaric greeted as we entered the small store.

"Princey. Been a while, no?" The girl at the counter flicked her ponytail as she spoke, but a sour expression crossed his face.

"Yeah, well, I haven't exactly had a *reason* to come here."

"*I'm* not a good enough reason?"

"That's—"

"Can you go? I have actual customers to see."

"I was—"

"*Alaric,*" she demanded through her teeth.

Alaric sighed and rolled his eyes. "I'll tell Clarissa you said hello, then."

"You know what? Nobody *likes* you, Alaric. You're just like the rest of them. You're a snobbish, *arrogant—*"

Before she could finish, Alaric slammed the door shut behind us, despite the eyes that were staring.

"Who the hell does she think she is?" It took me a minute to realize that I was much angrier than he was. "Aren't you the *prince?*"

"To some, maybe," he calmly responded. "To others, I'm a hero. Then, there's... Well..." He gestured to the door.

"Who is she, anyways? You'd think you had a history, the way she acted."

"She was..." he sighed. "She was my sister's friend, a *long* time ago. And, yeah, she had a thing for me, but that was an even longer time."

"Was it... mutual?" I wondered if he could hear the fear creeping into my voice. Regardless, he shook his head. I decided, against my better judgment, to continue the question. "Because... there was someone else in mind?"

Now, he laughed. "I'm not concerned with... with *that*. I mean, I wasn't. I— I had different things to worry about."

"And now...?"

I could tell he was biting the inside of his lip. He was quick to look to the next store down. "Come on. Clarissa's a lot nicer."

I shook it off and nudged his shoulder. "Why didn't we see her first, then?"

Alaric's smile slowly spread to one side. "Like she said, it's been a while, and... I knew she'd get *pissed* if she saw you."

I couldn't help but laugh as we walked toward the next store. "You little *bastard!*"

"You have no idea."

Just a few seconds later, we were inside the store, and the dark, curvy girl near the counter began to squeal. She wore a top with a light gradient of colors that ended just above the chub of her stomach. I had to step aside while she tackled Alaric in a hug. The one he returned was weak, but I could tell there was still some sentiment behind it.

"Hey, Claire."

"I *missed* you, Alaric! Why don't you ever come to visit?!"

"I've been—"

"It doesn't matter. Is this your girlfriend? *Tell* me you—"

"No. No, she's... I'm looking for something for her to wear under her gear."

Claire stepped back and hugged herself. "You're doing this, then. For real."

Alaric nodded solemnly.

"What's... what's wrong?" I asked.

"Hon, I don't mean to call you incapable—I don't even *know* you—but... The last time someone tried something like this—"

"Someone has to try again," I quickly insisted.

She gave a small smile. "Well... here's to hoping you're the right girl for the job. I know Alaric would *die* before he let anything happen to you, so... Let's just hope nothing happens to you." She turned back to Alaric. "When do you plan on leaving?"

"Not yet," Alaric replied, "but I'm not swimming through cold waters."

Clarissa nodded slowly. "I'm on your side. If there's anything I can do..." As she sighed, I could tell she was fighting to keep her smile. "Why don't you come with me, love?"

"Oh, I'm Maliyah."

"Very cute!"

I couldn't help but chuckle. "Thanks."

She tilted her head to guide me toward the racks at the back of the shop. We sorted through various styles and sizes of clothes, and I tried on many different articles, but after nearly an hour, I found something that would work.

"I know it can get hot, but it's supposed to help the armor stick on. If you need to run, or something like that, you can shed a few layers and still be okay. Plus, the top is the same material as your under stuff, so it'll help in the water, too. Not to mention you're looking *fine* in those pants."

"I really appreciate the help."

"Please, come by any time. I love making clothes like this. It's... kinda my whole thing. Just drag the Royal *Pain* down with you, please."

Alaric laughed as he walked over. I did a small spin to show him my outfit. We chose a black, long-sleeved shirt that ended just below my ribs, and dark brown pants on the slightly bulkier side. They had a large pocket on one side, but they fit me nicely and weren't very heavy overall.

"Not bad," Alaric said.

"Not *bad?*" Clarissa crossed her arms. "Why don't you just tell the poor girl she looks hot?"

Alaric rolled his eyes. "While you do look nice, that isn't what this is about."

"Why don't you go change back?" she suggested. "I'll get another set all packed and ready for you by the time you're out."

I nodded and entered the dressing room.

This all feels so normal, I thought. *More normal than I've felt in years. And yet, this is the least 'normal' situation I've ever been in.*

As I stripped off the tight shirt, I sighed. *What even is normal? Was life ever normal?*

But I knew it was. Before me. Before everything was covered in water.

When I walked back out of the dressing room, still pulling on my orange cover-up, I found Clarissa and Alaric arguing.

"...could have it so good. Why would you go and throw your life away *now?* You could finally just *live.* Be *happy!*"

"I'll never be happy." Alaric lowered his voice. "Not until they're gone."

"We... doing okay out here?" I tried.

He nodded, but Clarissa's expression stayed solid. He glared at her, then held up a see-through bag. "I have your clothes, so... whenever you're ready."

"Thank you. I wish there was some way I could pay you back for all of this, but—"

"Trust me, you do enough already." When Clarissa raised one of her thin, shaped eyebrows, he was quick to clarify. "It's nice to finally have some company, is all."

"Don't bother visiting me, though," she retorted.

Alaric moved his hand to the back of his neck. "Want to go look at gear now?"

I nodded, then turned toward Clarissa. "It was nice meeting you. I'll come visit soon."

"Yes, of course. And remember to bring *him* with you!"

We shared a laugh, and Alaric tipped his head. After Clarissa waved, we walked out of the door.

"Smithy's is this way, but... I'm glad you and Claire get along. She could use a familiar face every now and then."

"Why don't *you* visit her more?"

"I— I'd like to, but... It's hard sometimes."

"Because of training? I mean, what else do you—"

"It's not that." He stopped and looked into my eyes. A sad smile sat on his face. "They make me think of her."

"Oh..." This made me think of my own sister. I wondered when I had stopped longing for her to return. When, instead, I began questioning when I'd join her. If it was better where she was. If, maybe, there *was* a home after death. If she was happy there.

"You're right, though," he finally said. "It's not their fault."

We walked in silence until a middle-aged man called out to us. His hair was brown, but slightly peppered with grays. He was surprisingly built for his general appearance, especially in his arms.

"Alaric, my boy! How have you been?"

"I'm doing well, Smithy. I was hoping you had some gear for my recruit?"

"How strong we talking? Leather, metal, mail?"

"I was thinking... Well, you judge it. She's inexperienced and needs lightweight, but I want her to be as safe as possible."

He began to circle me, and I found myself laughing.

"I'm John, by the way, but my friends call me Smithy."

"It's nice to meet you, Smithy."

"Did I say we were friends?" He stopped and stared at me.

I blinked a few times, and soon found myself standing up straighter.

"Ah, I'm just kidding. I think I can have something by... Give me two days and come get it at noon?"

"That would be perfect. You're a legend."

"Where'd you pick this one up?"

"Lavender, actually."

"*Lavender?* What the hell were ya doin' at *Lavender?*"

"Has this happened before?" I asked. "Have you... Have you recruited people?"

"No," Alaric turned to me, "no, it's not like that at all. Smithy is just—"

"Oh!" Smithy yelled out, causing us to turn back to him. "Oh, I see how it is! Defend *her* case—throw your lifelong pal in the dust—just for some pretty lady. Make it three days."

I coughed up a laugh, but I could feel my face flush.

"You know it's not like that," Alaric fought. "Why don't you come by for dinner tonight? I'll treat you."

"That's funny. You're real funny, kid. I'll see you in two days."

Just like that, they both turned and walked off in opposite directions.

I shook my head and increased my speed to catch up. "He seems fun."

"Fun," Alaric laughed, "that's one word for it."

"So... where to next?"

Alaric squinted his eyes as he thought, but soon, he began to smile. "You know what? I have an idea. Follow me."

FIVE

I NEVER DID GET fully used to walking through The Tube. During every trip, my eyes were drawn to some new color or sight. I constantly pointed and asked questions, and almost always, Alaric smiled. In one particular moment, he had to quickly lower my finger as he waved at an elderly lady. We laughed, but he didn't let go after that.

We picked up the pace shortly after, and appearing in the distance, a great mass of green caught my eyes.

"What *is* that?" I asked.

He only smiled back at me as he gripped my hand tighter. "Come on, we're almost there."

As we approached, I read the green words that were painted onto the worn-down, wooden sign:

Welcome!
Oakview's Greenland Preserve
Always contribute, never take

"Alaric... what *is* this place?"

"We call it Greenland. It's our park. Any leftover saplings and seeds get planted here, and we help them to continue spreading. It's basically— Here, come look."

He pulled me through the arched entrance, which was laced with many different types of vines. Some were thick and thorny, others had small buds of flowers, and some were incredibly leafy. As we walked, I saw countless amounts of the small trees I'd previously seen scattered around in Greenhouses. Among the green, the entire place was bursting with vibrancy. Even the stone path was lined with colorful grasses and flowers.

I started to let go of Alaric's hand, but he hooked the very end of my finger with his own. He let me pull him around as I veered from tree to tree, flower to flower, feeling like the small, buzzing creatures I'd seen before. I smelled everything, and I often made him bend down, as well. Eventually, I sat under the shadow of a lush tree, in an area where a few people were doing the same. Tears filled my eyes as I spread my hands and legs in the soft grass. As Alaric sat beside me, I lurched over and held him in a tight hug. Before I knew it, I was sobbing into his thin shirt.

"This is *beautiful*. I— It's so beautiful!" Before I could think of a way to continue, Alaric reclined, gently taking me with him. He guided my head to rest on his chest, and as I did, I began to twirl my fingers in the grass. My soul felt like a new part of it had just been uncovered. How could all of this just *exist?*

"The whole world looked like this, once," he softly mused.

"Did you ever get to see it...?"

"No. I'm not much older than you are, I'm sure. So I was born into this, too."

"How do you know, then?" I propped my head up to look at him. "What it was like?"

"Before they burned all the pictures, my mother snuck a few into her room. They whipped her for it, but... they couldn't stop her from painting her memories."

"Is she... How does she still *live* there...?"

Alaric's eyebrows knitted. He tried to turn away from me, but I leaned over him and looked right back into his eyes.

"People do funny things when they have power. It doesn't matter who they hurt. It doesn't matter who they know, or once knew. It's... It just needs to stop." His voice dropped to a whisper. "I will *die* trying. At least then I won't have to watch it anymore..."

"What do you think happens," I found myself asking, "after you die?"

"I don't know, but... it has to be better than this."

"My mom... She used to tell me stories, but... I don't think they were stories to her. She said... She said we'd come *home.* That there'd be no more pain. No more suffering. That we'd go somewhere where everything is beautiful. We can see the ones we loved and lost, and... and just be happy. Forever."

"It sounds a little too good to be true, don't you think?"

"I know, but... sometimes it feels nice to believe."

"Yeah... Maybe it does." He exhaled and rolled onto his back, so I rested the back of my head against him. We stared upwards, through the trees and beyond the glass. Past the endless waters, into the sky. The ongoing sky. The one that decided if our world was blue or gray. The one that watched us, but never spoke. I wondered if there was anything past it.

"Maliyah..." His hand curled to find my arm. I held his fingers in mine. "I'm glad I found you."

I laughed softly in response. "It took you long enough." I closed my eyes, but I could imagine his smile. The smile that teased, but eventually melted. The smile that made mine grow brighter.

I love this. The words seemed foreign to my mind, but I let them drift around. *This is happiness. And, if this is living, then I never want to die.*

I remembered what Alaric had said to Clarissa, about never being happy. It made me question if he felt the same as I did in this moment. If his worries slipped his mind while the waters above us danced with the wind, as the grass brushed against our skin. Or if he was stuck, forever thinking about his next moments. When he would fight. If he would win. When he would die.

I never felt brave enough to ask him.

I can't recall how much time passed before we moved. It seemed like the sun should have been setting at any minute, but the commotion around us was the same as when we first laid down. Alaric sighed as he sat up. His arms rested over his knees.

Lie back on him, my brain screamed. *Let him hold you. Just a minute more.*

"I..." I had to swallow before I could speak. "That was... That was nice. Really, really nice." I turned to him, only to catch him staring into the distance, absently nodding. His mind seemed to be somewhere else entirely. "I wish... Thank you."

He tried to smile, but it appeared to me as nothing more than a twitch. As he sighed, he ran his hand over his face. When he rested it back on his lap, I placed mine over it, but he drew it back almost instantly. His mouth kept opening, but no words ever came out.

"Alaric...?"

"I... I'll be back. Just— Wander or something, I-I don't know." He stood up and quickly started walking in the direction we came from.

I stood, speechless. *What did you say? What did you* do? I began to take small steps back and forth, but I was interrupted almost immediately.

"Excuse me?"

I turned around. The girl approaching had to have been close to my age.

"Yeah?" but I was still breathless, torn between absolute bliss and ruin.

"Were you... You were with Prince Alaric, right?"

I nodded at her.

"How?"

"I don't think I—"

"He *never* comes here. We *always* ask him to—every time we *see* him—but he *never. Comes.* So, *how?* How'd you do it?"

I froze. "I... didn't."

"Who even are you, by the way? I don't think we've met."

"No, I... I'm new here."

"New? There are no new people."

"There are when Alaric brings them."

The girl raised an eyebrow at me. "Whatever. Just tell him to come back soon, alright? Remind him why we made it."

"Why... *did* you make it?" I asked.

The girl stopped and laughed, but when she saw that I was being serious, her demeanor changed entirely. "It's... it's a memorial, of sorts. His sister always wanted to see the Old World, but she never could. I, uh... hope you like it. See you around, I guess."

I flinched as she walked away. I began to walk around again, but now, the trees had even more color to them. I swear I could pick out more yellow in every flower.

After a small while, I felt a hand tighten on my wrist. I whipped around, but there stood Alaric, glossy-eyed, lip-bitten, and face-to-face with me.

"Maliyah, I... I didn't mean to leave you, I just—"

"You did, though." I reminded him. I almost took a step back, but his grip tightened.

We've all lost someone, you know. Especially in Lavender. It doesn't mean you can run away from the things you have now, just because you don't want to remember the past. I pondered on my words before I said them. *But isn't that exactly what* you're *doing?*

His words stopped my brain altogether. "Dammit, Maliyah, you... you make me *feel* something, and I... I don't even know what to do with it. I-I want—"

I could tell how hard he was biting the inside of his lip. He fought to shake the tears from his eyes before he went on. "I haven't felt like this in a really, *really* long time, and I don't know if it's a good thing. I was so focused—I was so *ready,* and... I didn't mean for this to happen, I really didn't, but—"

Kiss him, kiss him, kiss him. My brain was *pounding* in my ears. But I thought about his words, too.

You don't *know him. He was ready for change. And now you're making him feel like... everyone else.* I watched as he sucked in a shaky breath. *Is that such a bad thing...?*

"Should I... Should I go...?"

"No." His tone was firm. "No, I can't— You—"

Shock took over my body as he dropped his head onto my shoulder and laughed. My heart picked up as I reached over to place my hands in his hair.

"I don't want to bring you into this anymore." His voice was nothing more than a breaking whisper. "I don't know what I was *thinking*. I—"

"I want to go."

"Maliyah—"

"I do. I *want* this. I want your *drive*. I... I want to win or die trying. Then... I want to go home."

"I can't—"

"I *want* to do it. With *you.*"

"I would kill myself if I lost you." Alaric took a step back and looked straight into my eyes. His were beaten with red.

"Don't say that. You... you don't even know me."

"I know," he said, lowering his gaze, "but that's the scary part. I've never wanted to die for a stranger before."

"Alaric—"

"I think I—" He stopped himself, but still bit down on his lip. He inhaled deep as he looked up at me, sideways. "I think I'm going to do something crazy if we stay here."

"Do it, then," I challenged. I lowered my hands, and he took a hold on my wrists. I felt like there was a hole deep in my chest. My ribs were yanking my insides to fill what was missing, dragging my lungs behind them. His hands tightened. I inhaled. Prepared myself.

Then, he let go, and he took a step back.

"You, my dear," he said with a gritty smile, "are going to ruin me."

SIX

ALARIC BOUGHT ME SOME food on our way home. Already, through my short time here, I'd tried countless unfamiliar and completely new things. Nearly everything tasted better than the small fish I was used to. We stopped at a park bench while I ate, but as soon as some people began to approach Alaric, we got up and left.

Our conversation was little, as I was mostly in my head. My heart was still trying to recover from what had happened earlier. I was stuck wondering what I had done to trigger Alaric like that, and I wondered if I could do it again. I kept glancing at him while we walked, but he seldom looked back. A few times, I nearly reached for his hand. Nearly.

As we approached our end of The Tube, however, Alaric did offer me his hand. I took it, and we jumped back into the cold water. I watched as he gracefully moved his legs, swiftly back and forth, and just like before, I tried my best to replicate it.

Alaric pulled himself easily from the water, then reached down to help me up. When I landed, I sat on the dock, dripping from nearly every surface. I laughed as I tried to steady my breathing. I noticed as his eyes flicked over me, then stared firmly into the sky. I nudged him with my arm, but he shook his head, stood, and offered me his hand again. After he pulled me off of the dock, we stood in the doorway together, and I waited for us to dry off.

"Is it true that the Royals get married on these docks?" I asked.

"Please," Alaric scoffed, "there hasn't even *been* a marriage since..." When he trailed, I looked up at him. He began to nod, and I knew his mind was set on one thought only.

"Do you think..." I sighed as I stepped back. "Do you think it's actually possible?"

"I don't know. Before, it was just me and Smithy, and I know Clarissa can help with some things, but... she won't actually go *into* Cherry."

I'd never thought about that before. That I'd be *seeing* the Great Cherry. *Entering* it. Only then to destroy its legacy.

"We're going to need a lot of surprise on our side," he decided, "but... I was hoping you could help with that. How's walking been feeling, by the way?"

"Not bad, actually. My legs get sore at night, but... could be worse."

"Good. I'm glad."

I noticed his eyes flick over me again. I raised my eyebrows at him.

"Sorry. I— Sorry."

I laughed and rolled my eyes. "You know what's *really* been sore, though?"

"What's that?"

"My throat." As his expression clouded with confusion, I laughed and swatted at his chest. "From all of this damn *talking*.

I haven't actually held a conversation in... I don't even *know* how long."

He laughed quietly, but his eyes were stuck on me. Softly. I could feel my face getting hotter, so I looked down.

"What do you think of me, Alaric?"

"What do I—"

"What were your first impressions? Did I meet them, or am I... something else?"

"You're *definitely* something else," he laughed. "But that's not a bad thing. I was expecting persistent, I guess. Resilient. From the way you kept coming back. And... that's why I waited. I needed to know if you would *really* fight for something you believed in. And you do, it seems. You're just... *more.* "

"More," I repeated. "How so?"

"You're funny sometimes," he answered with a smile. "And you're good company. I enjoy talking to you. But..."

"But...?"

"I realized you're not something I can throw away. You know, I'm not... I'm not fully confident that we come out of this. I-I don't—"

"I told you my thoughts already. I'm sticking with it."

"Headstrong," he added. "That's the word."

I rolled my eyes as he crossed his arms.

We went inside, and I followed him back to his training room. After enough questioning, he showed me more basic positions and maneuvers to use while holding my dagger. A few times, he'd throw it from my hand and watch my attempts at recovering it. He offered pointers and guided my movements with his own. We practiced until I was sweating and panting.

Then, Alaric grabbed my wrist. He twisted it behind me until I yelled. I could feel the tip of his blade against me. His breath was on the back of my neck until he loomed over my shoulder.

"What would you do now?" he demanded.

"I don't know!"

"*Think,* Maliyah! What would you do?"

"You're hurting me!" I cried.

He let go and took a step back. He put his fingers to his forehead as he sighed. "I'm sorry, I... They're ruthless, okay?"

I picked up my dagger from off of the floor. I only needed a second to breathe. "Let's go again, then?"

His eyes widened at my request. "Are you sure?"

I charged at him, and he barely had time to step to the side. He stuttered through pointless sounds before he shook his head. He threw a punch at me, and I dodged. I swung at his neck, and he bent back.

"That was good!"

"You're going easy!" I shouted. "Come on!"

He hesitated, so I swiped at him again. He tried to get around me, but I kept him in my sight. Then, he reached around me altogether. I didn't know which part of him to swing at. He held my arms to my waist, trapping me in a hug. I kicked my legs, but I couldn't lose his grasp. He grabbed onto the hilt of my dagger, and I fought him for it. I tried to kick at his shins, but he kept moving away. Finally, he took it. He spun me around, pressing me into the wall. He held its blade under my chin. I could feel my heartbeat quicken.

"What do you do now?" he questioned under his breath.

My reply was simple: "I die."

Alaric rolled his eyes and took a step back. I tried to grab my dagger, but he pressed his forearm across my chest, pushing me back into the wall. I exhaled hard as my body slammed into it.

"You never stop, you hear me? I don't care how bad it hurts, or how much you want to. You keep *fighting.*"

I lowered his arm with my hands and slowly slid away. "I'm going to need some more training first."

It was reluctant, but he nodded. "Why don't we stop for now? If you'd like, we can go again tomorrow."

"Can I try the sword?"

"*Absolutely* not. You haven't even won with the dagger yet."

"You think I'm *ever* going to beat you?" I forced a laugh when he hesitated. "Alaric... I don't know if—"

"You'll get better with time. You haven't even *held* a weapon before yesterday, and you're *already* pretty good at defending yourself with it. In a few months—"

"Alaric." I kept my tone serious as he met my eyes. "I'm never going to be better than you. Hell, I'll never even be as *good* as you. You've been training your entire life, and—"

"And I'm still not good enough," he admitted.

"What?"

"Do you *know* how much training the Harpoons have? *Especially* the ones in Cherry. They're *bred* for this. That's why I asked Smithy to come with me. *That's* why I was looking for more backup."

I didn't know what to say. I felt helpless.

Alaric sighed and took a few steps back. "You should... get some rest. I'm going to shower."

You should join him, teased my brain. I shook my head as fast as the thought arose, but I couldn't help but stare as he fought his shirt, forcing its wet form off of his skin. It clung, but he tore, and finally, it splat on the floor by the table.

"You should—" I don't know what he was about to say, but whatever it was got my heart beating fast. He was quick to clear his throat. "Sorry. Thinking out loud."

My voice felt trapped with all of the thoughts running through my mind. Then, just like that, I was alone. I let out a frustrated noise, tossed my dagger onto the table, and made my way back to my room.

The next day, I went straight into the training room. Alaric was already there, punching and kicking a large root, yelling out as he did. I watched as his knuckles hit, over and over again, chipping at the dense wood. He didn't stop until a piece flew off.

"Damn." Finally, it was I who made Alaric whip around. I crossed my arms as soon as he saw me. "What'd that root ever do to you?" His expression lost some of its tightness, and I smiled.

"It's... early," he commented.

"Well, good morning to you too."

"That's not— Aren't you sore?"

"Yeah, but that ain't stopping me! We push through the pain here, right?" I started laughing as I punched meaninglessly into the air, but I was already heating up.

You sound like a total idiot, my head decided.

Even Alaric scoffed. "I don't want you to injure yourself."

"I'll be fine. We can stop early. I wanna go again, though. It's... kinda fun."

"We'll see if you're still saying that a month from now," he warned.

"Wonder if I'll have abs by then." I poked at my stomach, and he shook his head, smiling.

"What is *with* you this morning? Surely you can't be having *that* many good dreams."

I only shrugged. "Come on, toss me Celia."

"Celia?"

"My dagger. Don't people, like... name their swords and stuff?"

Alaric shook his head. "Not... really. But when they do, it's usually after a battle. Like... like Bonesplit, or Bloodbringer, or—"

"Celia," I repeated with a smile.

His laugh filled me with genuine joy. *"Wow.* I am training a *dimwit."*

He tossed me the dagger, and I caught it by the hilt. "Silence! Else, you'll face the wrath of my Celia!"

I swung at him, and he instantly sidestepped to grab his own short blade from off of the table. As they clashed, my chest tightened. "I... thought we weren't doing this yet?"

"Why? Are you afraid?"

"Of course not," I teased, "but I think Celia might be. Just a bit."

Alaric pushed forward, and I pushed back. I slipped to the side, but I tripped in the process.

"Definitely don't do that." Alaric offered me his hand.

I poked at it with Celia. "No kidding." I jumped back to my feet, but before I could swing again, Alaric tossed me a longer sword.

"But—"

"It's... just for fun." His smile twitched, and it made me look away. I slid Celia back to her table, admiring the long silver blade in my hand. It was heavier than I'd imagined.

"Celia, Jr.," I whispered in astonishment.

"*No.*" but Alaric had a big smile on his face. "Besides, that one's mine."

"What's her name, then?"

"Desiderium."

"That's lame."

"That's *Latin.* And it's a lot better than Celia, Jr."

"What's it mean?"

"Tap me once and you'll find out."

I tried to hold the sword over my shoulder, but it was already awkward in my hands.

Alaric laughed at my struggle. "Alright, come here." He helped me to lift it, then to position my hands more accordingly on the hilt. He kicked the insides of my feet to have me spread my legs, then reached around me to help me keep my stance.

"I miss Celia," I pouted.

Alaric laughed with his response. "Oh, you like the *easy* ones, huh?"

"Well, I never said *that.*"

"What... What *do* you like, by the way?"

"You mean... in a *person?*" I was astonished by his sudden question. He shrugged a little, so I furrowed my brow. "Why don't you tap me once and find out?"

Alaric stammered, but I dropped the sword and ran back to the table. He followed me, so I grabbed Celia and slid under it. Once I popped around the other side, he stood defensively, watching my movement closely. I started to smile, and Alaric leapt over the table altogether. I screamed as I tried to move over, but he grabbed my waist and pulled me to the ground.

"So," he started, pinning my wrists to the sides of me, "what's your type?"

My eyes flicked him up and down. I saw his lips part, just a little, but he acted as if he hadn't seen it. I smiled to one side. He let go and sat beside me, so I joined him in a sitting position.

"Honestly," I began, "people in Lavender don't... *talk* anymore. And, recently? I don't even know if I've *seen* other people my age."

"That bad...?"

"Not to mention, everyone stopped having kids. Once people started vanishing... they gave up. It was a miracle to meet someone who hadn't lost someone."

Alaric paused. I could tell he was starting to travel somewhere in his mind.

"But," I smiled, "I guess I like tall boys."

"Oh, really?"

"Yeah. Dark hair. Blue eyes. And I guess it's cool if he works out."

As soon as he caught on, Alaric hit my shoulder. "You're a witch."

I shrugged with one shoulder and flicked back my hair. I couldn't stop my giggling.

"What about you?" I asked a moment later.

"Me?"

"Yes, *you*. Have you had girlfriends before?"

A sadder look crossed his face. "I already told you—"

"Yeah, yeah. Doesn't mean you can't look, though. There's a lot of girls that seem to like you. Are any of them—"

"I can't. Not... not them."

"What if you met someone new," I tried. "Someone you'd never seen before. No associations. What would you do then?"

Alaric stood up and acted as if he was pondering my words. With a sly smile, he replied, "I guess... maybe I'd trick her into moving in with me?

My mouth fell open but still curled in a bewildered smile. "Oh, sure, but *I'm* the witch!"

"Come on," Alaric laughed. "Let me make you some breakfast."

We ate our breakfast rather fast, then, to Alaric's continuous surprise, returned to training right after. The day sped by, and by the end, I was exhausted. I showered, rung out my hair, and without thinking, my feet carried me to Alaric's room. I peered in as I knocked on the frame of his door.

"Refreshed?" he asked without looking up from his book.

"Yeah. I, um... What're you reading?"

He pat the bed next to him, but I sat near his feet. He tilted his head at me and raised an eyebrow. Again, he gestured to me with his head. I smiled and moved closer. He pulled me into him until I was leaning against his chest. I closed my eyes almost instantly. He reached to his bedside table and opened the book we had been reading before.

As he read, my breathing slowed. I felt Alaric's heartbeat against my back, and I used it to time his words. I watched as the characters in my mind ran, fought, yelled, cried, and hugged. *Lived.*

Alaric stopped to take a breath. I looked up at him, and his eyes met mine.

"You never did tell me the name of your sword."

"*You* never tapped me."

Fighting my exhaustion, I lifted my hand and flicked back my wrist. My pointed finger landed against his bicep. "Tap."

He didn't fight his smile. "Longing."

"What?"

"Desiderium," he reminded me. "It means longing."

"And that's less cool than Celia? I don't think so."

He chuckled quietly at my remark. "It was my sister's sword. She trained with it, then gave it to me when Smithy made her a new one. So…"

Silence settled on us for just a moment.

"You know," he suddenly added, "Celia is kind of a cool name."

I turned back to him with a dumbfounded expression stuck to my face. "No, it is *not*. Please, enlighten me with your reasoning."

His laughter continued before he did. "It's like *caecus.*"

"Which means…?"

"Blind."

It took me a minute to think about it. "So… it sounds like the dagger got its name… because I blinded someone. Which is a complete lie, but the Harpoons don't need to know that."

"That, or because you're a blind swinger," he teased.

I hit him in the arm, but I was fighting to keep my eyes open. "Do you care if… Can I just stay here a minute?"

I felt as he nodded against my head. It only took me a little longer to fall asleep.

SEVEN

WHEN MY EYES BEGAN to open, I turned to my side. I felt Alaric still lying there, and I wrapped my arm around his chest. My head rested comfortably between there and his arm.

"Good morning," he grumbled.

"Not yet..." I hugged him a little tighter, but when I felt his hand on the skin of my back, I sucked in air and straightened.

He curled his hand around my waist. "You're..." He didn't finish his thought.

"I thought you were gonna move me to my room...?"

"I did, too."

My lips curled into a smile. "You have to stop me before I make a habit of this."

"Stop you?" His finger began to trace small shapes against me. I wondered if he knew he was doing it. "Why would I do that?"

I turned to my other side, but Alaric was still holding me. He turned and pressed his form against mine. I felt his knee with my heel.

"You *are* tall," I laughed.

"Your legs are *not* straight."

"You're still tall."

"Maybe you're just short."

"Maybe you're just wrong."

His arm curled around me, and I turned into him. His lips were dangerously close to my neck. I could feel my breath threatening to shake on every exhale.

"Your gear should be ready today."

"Noon," I countered. "Not yet."

Then, without warning, he pressed a small kiss to my shoulder. "I'll see you soon, then."

My eyes shot open. I blinked a few times as I watched him slip on another thin shirt. My lips were slightly parted, and I was left questioning if I had truly woken up or not. As Alaric left the room, my fingers lingered over the exposed skin where he had breathed.

When I finally stood, I felt like white noise was running from ear to ear. Every step seemed to thud against the wooden floor.

You're going to break yourself. You can't get involved with someone who wants to throw his life away. I looked over my shoulder at his bed. There were two distinct shapes left behind, merging in the middle.

Is one good month worth a lifetime of pain? I shook my head. Why was I even *thinking* these things?

I soon found myself in the training room, leaning against the frame of the door. Alaric punched at the same spot in the wall, and the hole only deepened. I watched as his punching grew continually harder and faster until he finally stepped in and launched his fist with his shoulder. Another chip was formed in the wood, and he was left cradling and shaking his hand in the other. He whispered something under his breath.

"Hey," I finally said.

He turned around and sighed. His knuckles were bleeding. "So she finally joins us."

"Are you... okay?" I gestured toward his hands. "Is that normal?"

He laughed coldly. "Maybe. Probably. Yeah, I'm fine. Just... Intense session, I guess."

"How does that work?" I ran my fingers over the wounds, despite how he flinched.

"How does what work?"

"The intensity. Isn't that just... you?"

"More or less. Sometimes I... I need to get the anger out."

"Anger from...?"

"Life. Memories. Dreams." He met my eyes. "Anything."

"Do you... do you dream of angering things... often?"

"Yeah." He looked to the floor again. "It's, uh... Yeah."

My voice lowered to a whisper. "What'd you dream about last night?"

Slowly, his slick smile returned. "That's for me to know."

My stomach fluttered. *Damn.*

"Do you, um..." I nearly laughed. "What time is it?"

"Around ten, maybe? Why, you rushing to get somewhere?"

We were so close. All I needed to do was rise to my toes for our lips to connect.

I bet he would kiss me back. I wonder how hard he could. I felt insane.

He took his hand back from mine and continued to shake it out. I watched him ignore his wince as he wrung his wrist in the other.

"So, what's the plan?" he finally asked.

"Are you sure you're al—"

"I'm fine. Do you want to—"

"Alaric." I looked straight into his eyes. "Are you okay?"

He nodded slower this time. "I think it... I just need to get my focus back."

"And it's gone because...?"

"You're doing well so far." His lack of an answer was all I needed. "I think... If we keep practicing the dagger, you'll have a good amount of safety. Do you want to try defense next? Or, we could... Without a weapon. Just... overall?"

I let him sit alone with his mind for just another moment. He shook his head soon after. "I'll be—"

"Let's do it."

"What?"

"Show me. How do you... I don't know, punch good. Or something."

As I smiled, his followed.

"First of all, that's *offence.* But sure. Come here." He wrapped his arms around me, positioning my arms and legs like a doll. "Make sure your stance stays strong. You have to—"

He stopped as soon as I looked over my shoulder. He squeezed his eyes shut before shaking his head. "Wow, I am *not* with it today. I... Do you want to do something else?"

"Not really." I forced my grin. "I'm good right here."

He gave a single, breath-filled laugh. "You are the *worst.* "

I tipped my chin up as I smiled. "So you stand like this. Then what?"

Alaric let out a long puff of air, then slowly mocked the motion of punching me.

"When you go to block, make sure to hold your arms tight— Yeah, like that. Nice. Always protect your head and face. Try to keep your muscles tight, especially if you think there's going to be an impact."

We continued like that for a while. Soon, I was alternating between punching and blocking, letting him correct my every move.

Eventually, I tried to sneak in a kick. He grabbed my leg, and seconds later, I was on the floor.

"Do you *always* have to get ahead of yourself?" Before I could answer, he offered me his hand. "Come on, let's clean up. Smithy'll be ready for us soon."

We walked the same route as before, but this time, people didn't wave at just Alaric. As we got closer to Smithy's, Clarissa ran out of her store.

"Hey, guys! How are you?" She was quick to pull us both into a hug.

"Do you have a minute?" I asked. "We're going to pick up my gear, and it would be fun if you could—"

"I *always* have time for my two favorite people. Shall we?" She interlocked our arms, and we continued our walk. Alaric smiled weakly as we did, but he stayed quiet.

"Smithy!" she shouted before I could even spot him.

"Is that my girl Claire over there?" he returned from the distance. "Why, it's been a while! How are you, stranger?"

She rushed ahead to give him a hug. I sped up just enough to stay within earshot of their hushed conversation.

"Not many people come to the shop anymore," Clarissa was saying, "but business is alright. Julie still gets more customers, though."

"Have you ever thought about relocating?"

"I have, but—"

"Alaric!" Smithy interrupted.

Although her eyebrows turned in, Clarissa held her smile.

"Afternoon," Alaric returned.

"How goes it, my boy?"

"It... goes. Is the gear ready?"

"That depends. How much of a rush are you in?" As Smithy clapped him on the back, he raised his hand in my direction. "Right this way. Gear is in the back."

I followed him into the back of his shop, where a few sets of gear were set up on wooden stands.

"There's usually something you'll want to wear underneath your—"

"Wearing it," I stopped him.

He gave me a quick look up and down. "That... That'll do nicely, actually."

"I got it from Clarissa's."

"How nice. Why don't you try on the chestplate? That's usually what needs the most adjustments, for obvious reasons."

I grabbed the leather top from off of the stand. There were two belt-like straps that wrapped around the back, and Smithy helped me to tighten them.

"The more you wear it, the quicker you'll get at putting it on. But, that goes without saying." On the front, a more metallic plating was built into the leather. "How does it feel?"

"Not bad." I tried a few different movements, and at first, it was difficult to adjust. Smithy tampered with the belts on the back until my arms had their full range of motion again.

"It's not too heavy, actually."

"Hold your horses, little miss. Try this first." He handed me two leather pads to strap to my shoulders. Each of them had a line of that same metal surrounding their perimeters.

I tried moving my arms in circles and stretching in them. "How often should I *wear* all this?"

"I think you know."

I looked up at him. *Breathe.*

"It's best to practice anything you might want to use while fully armored. I'd assume that Alaric is teaching you how to handle a dagger?"

I nodded. He handed me a band with another belt-like strap on the back. A piece of leather dangled from it, and at the bottom, a thinner strap mirrored the first.

"You can slide it right in there. Just make sure you get the bladed part in the leather. Want to try the shoes?"

I managed a laugh before I asked, "There's shoes, too?"

After I tried on all of the gear, Smithy put everything other than the chestplate in a bag. We exited the room to see Alaric and Clarissa talking. I noticed a slight shine on each of her cheeks.

"It's nice to see you two together again," Smithy shouted, turning their attention back to us.

"How did it go?" Alaric called back.

"Not bad. I have the little details in the bag, but I want to make the chestplate a little more... fitted. I think it would be easiest for her to move that way."

"How much do I owe you?"

Smithy raised an eyebrow at his question.

"No. You're not—"

"Your services are enough. If you come back home to us—*both* of you—you can pay me then."

"Are you going to be coming with us?" I asked.

"I am, but... there's only so much I can do. I'll get you both through the door, but after that, it really comes down to Alaric sneaking you in."

"Would they attack you?" I turned to Alaric as I asked. Clarissa was hugging herself.

"The moment I enter the Cherry, they're going to drop *every-thing* until I'm dead."

"But your family—"

"*Killed* Alana."

Something in my ears pounded. How had I not considered that before?

"They won't hesitate to do the same to me."

"They would." Smithy corrected with a half-hearted laugh. "They'd torture you first."

"Can we... can we *not* think about this right now?" Clarissa was practically begging. "It's... I really don't want to think about it, alright?"

I turned to her, my look as melancholy as hers. "Do you want to come over tonight? I... I'd love to chat with you a little more."

She tried to muster a warm smile, but it never fully formed. "I'd love to, if that's alright with Alaric?"

We both turned to look at him.

He sighed, then smiled. "Yeah. I think that would be nice."

After thanking Smithy, we walked with Clarissa as she closed her store for the day. We returned to Oak in relative silence, but as soon as we broke the surface, a bittersweet smile crossed her face.

"I forgot how beautiful it was up close."

After we dried off, I gestured with my head. "Come on, I'll show you where my room is."

She followed me, and Alaric disappeared somewhere behind us. As I showed her around, she settled comfortably on my small sofa.

"So you really came from Lavender?" she eventually asked.

I nodded as I sat on the side of the bed.

"What's it like there? I hear it's a beautiful Tree."

"It is *not.*" As soon as I started, something was unleashed from deep inside of me. "It's dark and gray and everything is falling apart. Nobody talks to each other, but you're supposed to believe that you have it better than everybody else. Some part of you is always wet, and it's claustrophobic, and it's *lonely,* and... And nobody *does* anything about it!" I don't know how, but tears started forming in my eyes. As soon as they did, Clarissa came over to the bed to give me a soft hug.

"You really like hugs, huh?" I wiped my eyes with the part of my shirt that went over my hands, wrapping around the bottoms of my fingers like gloves.

"I just know that I won't always get them." Now, she wiped her own eyes.

"Do you have any siblings?" I found myself asking.

"I'm the second of four. My brother's the oldest. He has his own house and stuff now."

"So you still live with your parents?"

"They're helping me while I try to get my Boutique off the ground. It's been a few years, but... What about you?"

"Me?"

"Your family. I'm sure they miss you lots."

"I... haven't seen them since I was ten."

Before I could even finish, her hands flew to her mouth. "No... Maliyah, I am so, *so* sorry. Were they—"

"Do you guys really not know what it's like there...?" I began to tear up again. I wished I could live in such beautiful ignorance. "It... People just go *missing,* and you never see them again. Alaric said—"

"You don't have to finish. I... I'm sorry."

"I... had a sister."

"What was her name?"

"Leilani." I flinched as soon as it came from my mouth. "She..." My hands began to tremble. Almost instantly, Clarissa pulled me closer with her arm. I felt totally comfortable leaning against her. It was as if I'd known her for the entirety of my life.

We stayed like that, shakily breathing, until Alaric knocked on the frame of my door. "Is everything okay...?"

Before answering him, Clarissa turned to me to respond. I nodded.

"Well... I made some late lunch if anyone's hungry." He turned around again, and I smiled at Clarissa.

"Thank you. I... Thanks."

"Any time, alright? You always know where to find me." She smiled at me, and after giving her one last hug, I gestured with my head to the door.

"You hungry?"

"Are *you?*"

We giggled together, then stood back up. Alaric was waiting for us just outside of the room, and the three of us walked together to find the dining area. There, Alaric had already made our plates.

For a while, our conversation was kept to mainly small talk, where Alaric and Clarissa caught up. They smiled at each other often, even when she began reminiscing over the past.

"So... how long ago did you two meet?" I finally asked.

Clarissa was quick to reply. "Maybe four, five years ago? When Alaric first came here, he was all business. It was mainly Alana that introduced herself to us in the town. But they did a *lot* to help us reclaim our properties, rebuild our homes... stuff we never even thought needed to happen."

"If we *were* able to take back Lavender," I suggested, "do you think you'd do the same there?"

"No." Alaric's voice was steady and stern. "We would go straight for Cherry, and from there, we'd fix it *all.*"

"How, though? The three Trees have never even *communicated.* There's no way to—"

"Because I would be the only one left to rule it."

We sat on his words. I, especially, was thrown deep into trailing thoughts.

You could be his queen.

I tried to distract myself as Clarissa filled her mouth with more food.

"This is *really* good," she complimented. "When did you learn to cook like this?"

"Excuse me for a moment." Alaric stood, but he didn't walk toward the direction of his bedroom.

Clarissa sighed as she watched him leave. "I wish he could just... let it go. Breathe."

"He does, sometimes."

"Only with you then, hon, 'cuz I *never* see him out of go-go-go mode."

Only with you. The words spread like a plague through my brain.

"He's really... *always* like this?"

"He *was.* Honestly, I could hardly tell you about now. He stopped visiting after—"

"Right." *Only with you.*

"What do *you* think about him?"

"Huh?" Her question snapped back to my senses.

"You've been staying with him for a few days now, right? What's he like when he's alone?"

My mind began to sing. *He's passionate, but afraid. He's soft, but cold. He's caring, but lost... He's broken.*

"I think he's... confused."

"He won't rest until they're gone," she added. "He *can't.* But... they're his family, too."

"Do you mind if I go check on him...?"

Clarissa shook her head, so I stood. I looked into each doorway as I passed, and I stopped in front of the nearest bathroom. I knocked.

"Just a moment."

"Are you alright?"

"Of course," he returned. "Why wouldn't I be?"

I heard him turn off the water to the sink, so I walked in. He was leaned over the white porcelain, his face and hair dripping with water. He stared at me blankly.

"You know... Clarissa and I were talking about something I didn't even *think* I needed to bring up. If you ever just want to—"

"*Why* would I need to talk? I'm *fine*, Maliyah. Alright? Let's go back to the—" He tried to pass me, but I threw my arm in front of him. He looked at me, then forcefully made his way past.

Confused.

"This was wonderful. Thank you so much for having me." Clarissa gave me a tight hug as we stood by the front entrance. She turned to

Alaric with an urging expression. "I really hope we can do it again sometime soon."

He nodded, and I waved. Then, she was gone, lost like a puddle to the great sea. Without a word, Alaric turned and began to walk off.

"Hey," I tried, "where are you going so fast?"

"I... need to train."

"I do, too. We can try out some of my gear."

"No, I... I *need* to do this. *Alone.*" As he spoke, he twisted one of his wrists in hand.

I shot him a glare. "How's your hand feeling?"

He paused and dropped them both. *"Fine."*

"Alaric, take a *break!* Let yourself heal a little!"

"Whatever happened to pushing through the pain?"

"Alaric..."

"Why don't you go take a walk or something? You like that."

"I like it better with you."

He stopped. Before he was fully able to turn around. I stood up a little straighter with the anticipation.

It was only a moment before he looked back down, turned around, and left.

EIGHT

I SAT AT THE dock with my bare feet in the water. I moved them slowly once my eyes were closed. I thought about what it felt like to wake up next to Alaric. To lean over and wrap my arm around his bare body. How he'd placed such a gentle kiss on my shoulder before he left.

Was that really only this morning?

I tried to think of something else, but every time, my thoughts shifted back to him. Lying in the grass, learning to swim, fixing my hair, even taking a piece of wood out of my careless finger. With everything he did, he did it with tough determination. But it was always full of tenderness.

I scoffed, stood up, and began to walk to the training room. I could hear him yelling from all the way down the hall. As soon as I did, I sped up, tunnel visioned, until I arrived at the room.

I stared as he beat up the root. He punched it from all angles, using his knee, his elbows, *anything*.

"Alaric...?"

He picked up my dagger and implanted it deep in the crumbling root. *"What?"*

I jumped back—even closed my eyes—at the force behind his volume. When he turned to me, I could see how red his eyes were. Both of his knuckles were unwrapped and bleeding, along with his right knee. Even his forearm and wrists were heavily scratched from the wood.

For every step I took forward, he took one back. He aggressively wiped his face with his arm, but all it did was smear the blood around. His chest moved up and down rapidly. Unsteadily.

"Why don't you come here?" I tried. "Let me help you."

"Help me? I've been on my own for— I don't *need* your help." He met my eyes, and I held his gaze. I could feel my worried expression taint his. The truth was, I was *terrified*—but not for myself.

After what felt like forever, his eyebrows curled in, and he fell to his knees, shaking. I ran over to him and dropped to his level without any hesitation. He tried to push me away multiple times, but I kept grabbing for his hands. He looked away, and I placed my hand on his cheek until he turned toward me. I moved his wet hair out of his face. Every breath to his lungs was a challenge, and he was fighting it in his throat.

"You're not... supposed to be here..."

"But I am, so you're going to have to get over that part."

"No. You-you're not supposed to be here at *all.* I'm supposed to be alone. *Focused.* I-I didn't think—" He stopped as I wrapped my arms around him. He dropped his head onto my shoulder, and I finally felt his body give in. "I'm so tired..."

I stayed quiet. I wasn't sure *what* to say.

Only a minute later, my expression was tainted with panic as his choppy breaths turned into weak laughter. I took his face in my hands and forced him to look at me. His eyes were wet, but he was stuck in a distressed smile. I tightened my grip and widened my eyes, but I froze as soon as he spoke.

"Maliyah... I told you you'd ruin me."

After a short while, I helped Alaric to his feet, but he sucked in a sharp breath every time he moved his hands.

"Geez..." It was hard for me to look at them. "What were you *thinking?*"

He didn't answer. We both knew the real answer wasn't meant to be spoken.

As we started toward the stairs, I noticed him fighting a limp.

"What the hell?!" I was more surprised than anything else.

He, on the other hand, actually laughed.

"No, this isn't *funny! How* did you even—"

"I already told you. Training gets intense." He laughed again, but I couldn't unhear the weakness in his voice. He was dying inside, and I needed him to let it escape.

I looped my arm around him. Although he still tried to fight me, I was adamant on staying.

You're lucky I'm just as stubborn as you are, I thought.

Going up the stairs, his knee buckled, and he fell completely against me. I hit my back against the wall to keep us from falling all the way down. He lifted his head but was quick to rest it back on my shoulder. After letting out a few breaths, I could feel him stiffen.

"Oh, what the hell?" He pushed against the wall, stretched, and finished going up the stairs on his own. I shook my head as he left my view. By the time I got up the stairs, I heard the echoes of a shower running. I sat outside the door and waited.

Every now and then, I could hear him wince and suck in air. It was always followed by some sort of motivational insult. This went on for a painful amount of time.

Eventually, the water stopped running, but he didn't come out of the bathroom. I barely waited before I stood and peaked in.

Alaric was focused, but struggled to look through the cabinet above the sink. The white towel around his waist was already dotted with red smears.

"Please let me help you."

He jumped at my voice. I could tell a question lingered on his tongue, but he didn't ask it. I walked in, and he stepped aside. As I asked him what he needed, he pointed his shaky hand, and I retrieved it for him.

He sat down on the lid of the toilet, and I took his hands in mine. I poured some clear liquid onto a cloth, and I recoiled at the sudden smell. He squeezed his eyes shut as I dabbed it across his knuckles, then on his arm.

When we were done, he let out a slow breath. "Alright. Can I have the—"

"Let me do it for you."

"Maliyah—"

"*Alaric.*" I tilted my head and raised my eyebrows, and he sighed. I began to wrap his hands.

Once I was done, he tried to stand up. I quickly sat him back down and poured more of the liquid onto another cloth. I then kneeled, dabbing at his knee. I looked up at him, past his towel, as I did. It was hard to read his expression.

I wrapped his knee, and he stood up.

"Thank you," and then he was gone.

I continued to follow behind him. He entered his bedroom and threw his towel to the side. I looked away, but I listened to him rummage through dresser drawers, still sputtering frustrated sounds. Finally, he was silent. I entered.

"What are you, my shadow?" He was lying on his bed, hands folded over his forehead, staring at the ceiling. I walked up to him. He wore only his black shorts and necklace.

"I'm worried about you."

"Well don't be," he scoffed. "You said it yourself, you barely even know me."

"Let me, then." I leaned into him, and he moved his hands. I rested myself across his stomach and chest, still staring into his eyes. To my surprise, he put his hands behind my back. "All you have to do is tell me."

"I... don't know what to say."

"Then it's settled." I propped my chin up with my hands. "I know all there is to know about you. Like we were never even strangers."

He rolled his eyes, so I let out a breath and let my head relax.

"Alaric... Why did you *do* that? You scared me..."

"I..." He swallowed, as if he was dealing with a new sensation. "I didn't think..." Finally, he shook his head and exhaled. "It was just a training session. I've done it plenty before."

"You have me now, alright? No more stupid stuff."

"It's not—"

I interrupted him with a soft laugh. "Don't scare away the lady of the house. We're delicate little creatures, you know."

"I don't think I could scare you away if I tried."

"Oh, really? You think I'm that tough?"

"No." He lowered his volume. "I think you'd keep coming back to me."

I opened my eyes. He was smiling.

"Says you, who couldn't go an hour without me the first time I left."

"*You're* the one who came to *me* in the store. You could have just let me shop."

"For women's clothes?"

"You don't know my hobbies!"

As he smiled, I found myself laughing. "Tell me, then. What *are* your hobbies?"

"I... can't even remember. It's been so long since..." He shook his head.

"Since...?"

"What about you? What did you like to do before I changed your daily agenda?"

"Nothing, really. When you live in Lavender, you either work, you sleep, or you pray. So... I worked until I was out of a job, I slept, and then I prayed."

"What did you work as?"

"Anything I could. It's really just different forms of giving people what they'll pay for."

"Well... What did you pray for...?"

I paused and looked up at him again. *I prayed for you.*

"I prayed to leave." I met his eyes. "I prayed for change."

"Do you think... Do you think someone was listening...?"

"I mean... I met you, didn't I...?"

We stayed quiet after that. I wondered if my mother really was right. I could assume he was wondering the same.

"Why do you—" He shifted to sit up. I slid off of his chest and sat next to him. "Why do you care?"

"Care?"

"About... *me.*"

"Why would you say it like that?"

"No, I just... You really *don't* know me. And yet..."

"Well," I tried as I looked back into his eyes, "at what point does a stranger become a friend?"

He mustered a laugh. "Probably before the point where they move in together."

I smiled at his comment, but I couldn't help but notice how he was avoiding my eyes.

"You... You *are* a good friend. You know that, right?"

"You don't know that."

"Alaric, you're trying to change *everything*. And you were trying to do it *alone*. You're only, what? Like, twenty-something?"

"Close enough."

"My point exactly. You can't... You can't *hate* yourself when things go wrong."

"I never said—"

"You didn't have to." I looked at his hands again. He tried to hide them from my view.

"Why do I care," I repeated to myself. "Well... maybe it's because you're the only one worth caring about."

"How could you—"

"I don't really have anyone else to change my mind, right?" I smiled sadly at him, but he turned his head. "It's nice to... to not be alone."

"Yeah." His voice was low. "It is."

We sat there for a while, neither of us feeling the urge to speak. I leaned against him and listened to his shaky, quick breaths. He tensed at them. I think he hated them.

Time was quickly lost. I closed my eyes, and I think he may have too.

"Maliyah?" He sounded tired and worn.

"Yes?"

"Thank you."

"For?"

"Staying." He finally turned to look at me. "Trusting."

I could feel my body growing hot again. I wanted to move closer, but we were already touching.

"Thank you for ruining me."

NINE

I STAYED WITH ALARIC for hours after that. Even when the sun began to change the color of the water, I lay on his chest, running my fingers over his skin. He barely spoke. After some time, his breathing returned to normal, and he shifted to his pillow. I went with him without a word.

My head rose and fell with his breaths. Eventually, the pace slowed. He let out a soft exhale, and I turned. His eyes were closed.

"Alaric...?"

When he didn't reply, I smiled. I readjusted myself and closed my eyes with him.

You barely even know me, and yet you'd show me your most vulnerable parts. In a world ready for war, you'd lie asleep at my side. With your unsettled mind, you'd show me your heart. Maybe that's the reason I'd consider us a little more than strangers.

When I opened my eyes again, it was still dark out. I groaned and turned over, but I squinted around the room as soon as I realized Alaric was gone.

"Alaric?" I grumbled. When there was no response, a bitter taste rose to my mouth. "Alaric!"

He's probably just in the bathroom. Don't be paranoid. Still, I stood up, fixed my top, and started out of the room. I peeked into various doorways as I passed, but somehow, my legs knew where to take me.

As I approached the first room, I saw his silhouette on the dock. His feet were in the water as he stared into the black ahead. I didn't speak as I sat down next to him. He didn't turn to me when I placed my hand gently over his. I tried to follow his gaze, but there was nothing to latch it to. Instead, I decided to stare at the stars. They could never look this beautiful from under the clouded water.

"You really believe that," he finally said. "That when you die, you go somewhere... better."

I nodded, but I was only deciding for myself in that very moment. *He needs this.*

He sighed and looked toward his feet. "Do you think... do you think I'll see her there...?"

"Life got easier after I started living with the hope," I told him. "If I'm wrong, then... we'd be too dead to care, right?" I laughed shallowly before I continued. "Besides, why punish the living with thoughts of the dead?"

He hesitated a few times, but finally, he dropped his head against my shoulder.

"How're your hands?" I asked.

He only shook his head.

"Can't you, like... Drink that tea or something?"

"I keep most of the blossoms at Smithy's. That way, I'm not tempted to use them outside of emergencies."

"This isn't an emergency to you?"

"This will heal. And... maybe it is time I take a little break. Then, as soon as I'm better, and after you get your chestplate, we can start training for real."

"If you weren't already training 'for real,' I don't want to live in your world."

He let out a soft laugh. The sky was slowly shifting into a deep blue color, and not long after, the clouds began to turn into pink and orange.

"Wow..." I whispered. We watched, silently, as the horizon erupted in pink. "It's so... *wow.*"

"It makes me think of you." He was still staring into the distance as he spoke.

"Your sister?"

"No." He turned to face me. *"You."*

"Why...?"

His gaze was stolen back by the growing colors. An orange began to drip onto the canvas, and I smiled. We sat there for just a few more minutes, our skin getting hit with sudden warmth, before Alaric let out a long breath. He stood, and I could see the blood seeping through his bandages. He looked at his hands no longer with anger, but with immense disappointment.

"Do you... want to help me with these?"

"Yeah, of course. What were you thinking to—"

"I just want to clean them again."

"Oh, yeah. Yeah, definitely."

He began to laugh as I got to my feet. "Why so surprised?"

"Because you're actually *asking* me to *help* you, that's why, you stubborn—"

"Just come on," he said as he walked by.

I reached for his hand, but a frown tainted my expression. I followed a few steps behind him until we reached the bathroom.

Again he sat on the lid of the toilet, but this time, he didn't hesitate to place his hands in his lap. I retrieved everything we needed, and a few times, I could feel his gaze on me. With slow movements, I began to unwrap his hands. Instantly, dry blood took over my view.

"Dammit, Alaric, *how* did you—"

"Not now." His request was soft enough for me to feel it in my chest, but his eyes were burning into my head. I let out a breath and continued to unwrap.

I could barely recognize what I was seeing by the time I got to his hands. I began to dab the wet cloth onto him, but he instantly threw his head back and held his breath.

"Maybe we *should* go get the—"

"No! I-I *can't* run out of them. The next time I'm in Cherry, I'm there to *destroy* it. We can get all of the blossoms we want then."

"Alaric..."

"I *won't* waste them on my ignorant decision. Alright?"

A smile poked through my worry. "So you *do* admit that it was stupid."

He rolled his eyes, and I continued to clean his hands. He flinched hard enough to make me steady him. I had to switch the cloth I was using multiple times.

After a while, I re-wrapped his hands. He tried to bend his fingers, and while I was grateful to see that he could, it was a slow and painful process even to watch.

"They're not broken," he decided. "I'll be fine."

"Oh, wow. I'm glad *that's* your standard. If the bar wasn't already on the floor—"

"Calm down, drama queen. I'm a big boy, I can take care of myself."

"Clearly. Because taking care of yourself is—" I fell silent as soon as he stood up. He took a step forward, and I took one back. When I hit the wall, my palms seemed to cling to its surface. He leaned his arm near my head and smiled. Slowly. I felt my insides heat up and crumble.

"Huh," he said in a breath. He backed up.

What do you mean, 'huh?' I wanted to counter. But I was suddenly afraid of what he might answer. He squinted at me and nodded a little. Gave me a quick look up and down. My throat was dry.

"Well... thank you," he simply stated. I felt a pressure lift off of my body. I wasn't sure if I loved or hated that he had so much control over it.

"Don't mention it." My voice was breathier than I'd expected. Another smile flicked over his lips. I pushed away from the wall, and he took a step back.

"So what's the plan for today?"

"Maybe we could..." but my mind was somewhere else.

After a brief moment of silence, Alaric shook his head. "I don't know, either. Do you want to read more? I wouldn't mind going back to bed for a—"

As if on cue, my stomach made a sound.

Alaric stiffed a laugh, then met my eyes. "Or we can eat. That works, too."

I smiled as we made our way to the kitchen.

The next few days continued like this. We stayed in the Tree, and I helped Alaric clean his hands after we woke up. Often before we slept, he would read, and I would help him turn the pages. It was a gamble as to whether I fell asleep by his side or went back to my room.

Soon enough, we were falling into a routine, and I was comfortable in it. I nearly forgot the real reason I was there. We hadn't spoken about it since.

That Friday marked our first full week together. Alaric had more motion in his hands now, but I'd already gotten used to helping him out. When he cooked, I knew where to find and put away what he needed. We were eating breakfast when someone knocked on the frame of the door. Together, we got up and approached the sound.

"*Smithy!* I haven't seen you *here* since—"

"Yeah, well, the last time *you* didn't come to pick up your armor was after Alana left." His tone was more serious than I'd ever heard it. He cleared his throat and continued slightly lower. "I was getting worried."

Alaric stayed quiet.

"He was hurt," I admitted.

Smithy's eyebrows turned inwards.

"No, I'm—"

"See?" I grabbed his bandaged hand, even when he fought me on lifting it up.

"Oh, Alaric..."

"I'm *fine*, okay? It was just... I was *training.*"

Smithy shook his head, but he held up the bag that was in his hand. "I brought the rest of her gear. If she wants to try it on—"

"I'll go change." I hastily left to change into the clothes from Clarissa, but this time it wasn't from excitement. In my mind, I was rewatching how hard Alaric had punched the root, over and over again until his body was a tattered mess. All over a single thought of what had happened. Of what might happen. What *does* happen.

A darker part of me questioned what he would do if he lost me. I wondered if I meant that much to him. He *said* I did, but what were words in comparison to a real moment?

I took out my clothes, and I began to change.

When I met up with them again, one of Alaric's hands was unwrapped in Smithy's. He was examining it, a nervous expression plastered onto his face. I could tell it took everything in Alaric not to flinch at his touch.

"Hey," I said, as calmly as I could.

Smithy sighed and held onto Alaric's hand for just another second. When he let it go, he turned back to me with a smile. "Ready to try this on?"

I nodded. He came over to me, and I held out my arms. Instantly, I could feel the top fit over my shirt. It was much tighter, lighter, and easier for me to move my arms in. He started to strap on the back, but quickly stopped.

"Alaric, come do this."

"But—"

"I need to see if you can. Until she figures it out, you're going to be the one helping her with it."

Alaric sighed and walked behind me.

"You don't have to," I tried to whisper.

"Yes, he does."

"It's alright," he whispered back. A chill traveled up my spine as soon as I felt his fingers there. I tried my hardest not to make it visible.

He fumbled with the straps, but eventually, the plating was tightened to my chest and ribs.

"How does it feel?" Smithy asked.

I stretched my arms and moved around. "How does it *look?*"

"Why don't you go get the rest of your gear and find out?"

I nodded and went back to my room. I clipped on the shoulder and leg pieces, rolled up my pants, and jumped into the shoes. It was heavy, and I felt like stones were tied to my ankles, but I knew that it was necessary. I looked into my mirror, and I turned.

I look ready for battle. It seemed like an obvious thought, but it sat strangely with me. I wasn't a warrior. I wasn't even a fighter. Yet here I was, training and preparing for the fight that would change the world. *That, or kill me.*

They were standing in silence when I returned, but I saw a small smile creep onto Alaric's face after he saw me.

"We should do a training session while you're all geared up," he suggested. "It'll be good practice for your movement."

"I suppose I'll be off, then? Everything fits well?"

"Wait." Alaric turned to him. "Why don't you help?"

"Help?"

"Help her train. She's getting better with the dagger, but—"

"Alaric, I haven't trained anyone in *years.* You know I'm not cut out for—"

"You are. You're the best we *have.* Come on, please? It'll be fun. And... you can ensure her safety when we do go out."

"No. I want *no* responsibility over her death. Not this time."

"That's not— Smithy..." As Alaric trailed, I was hit with a sudden understanding. I watched as their eyes found the floor.

"Hey," I tried, grabbing their attention back, "you already made the gear, so chances are, you'll be blaming yourself anyways. What's the harm in trying to prevent that?"

Smithy sighed, and a sad smile grew on his face. "You're cunning, you know that?"

Nobody spoke. I could feel the anticipation in the air.

"Fine. Let's go."

As soon as we entered the training room, Smithy's hands balled into fists. He rushed over to examine exactly where Alaric had been punching at the root. He traced along the intricate design of its exposed innards. Chips flaked away and fell off with every touch.

"Alaric!"

"Don't—"

"Did you even wrap your hands?!" He turned around, but I could see the panic in his eyes. *"Anger* is not *fuel.* It is *destruction.* Do you understand me?"

Alaric nodded slowly, and Smithy let out a long breath. "Which one is hers?"

"Light blue string."

"Ah." He picked up the dagger and admired it. "I remember when I made this... Do you know why I wrapped it with blue?"

Alaric looked down, but I shook my head.

"It was the first blade I made after my wife... The blue string is what she once used to tie her hair."

"I-I didn't— Do you want it back?"

"No. No, I... I parted with it for a reason. Figured it would be better in Alana's hands, anyways. And now, my dear, I hope it brings you safety." He handed me the blade, and it felt heavier in my hands. I stared at it, following the string with my thumb. It ended in a tight bow near the hilt.

"Now why don't you show me what you can do?"

TEN

SMITHY'S TRAINING WAS MUCH more strict than Alaric's. He showed me how to better move my feet, hold my arms, and even position my wrists. Alaric watched from the table. His expression was tight.

After what had to have been an hour, Smithy turned his gaze to Alaric. "Grab your sword."

"Smith—"

"Grab it! You're not going to heal if you don't try to fight it. It's been four days, you said? That's plenty. Come on!"

Alaric picked up his sword and ran at Smithy, who took his own and blocked it. As soon as they made contact, Alaric grabbed his wrist and yelled out in pain. The noise the sword created as it clattered to the floor made me turn away. I didn't want to watch as Alaric fell to his knees, doubled over and cradling his right hand.

"Dammit!"

"Get up, Alaric," Smithy instructed. He prodded him with his foot. "Get *up!*"

Alaric jumped back to his feet, fighting to hold the sword in his left hand. Smithy didn't struggle to swipe it from his grip and kick him back over.

Again, Alaric retrieved his sword. He finally took it in both hands, his gored right knuckle curling around its hilt. He charged at Smithy, and when they connected, he screamed through gritted teeth. This time, I could see his grip tighten. He swung a few more times, and with a hard bang, Smithy was knocked off his feet.

"Good!" he called as he stood back up. "Very good!"

My mouth was hanging slightly open as Alaric turned to look at me. He was panting.

Smithy clapped his shoulder. "You two will make a good team. *Always* look out for each other."

"Thank you."

"I'll come back soon, I think. I... I'd like to see how you progress together."

Alaric nodded once in his direction.

"I'll see you soon, Maliyah. Come visit me at some point, alright?"

I waved as he left the room. As soon as his footsteps faded, Alaric walked toward me. He dropped his sword on the table and let out a pained yell. I could *see* his hands throb and twitch.

"Why is he so hard on you...?"

"He has... He has a history. It's—"

"Does it involve how he lost his wife?" There was no shame in my words.

Alaric stifled a laugh, but soon after, he let out a long breath. "John Feeney was a Harpoon."

My eyes shot open, but Alaric continued. "He was assigned to look over the Oak Branch. With... me. Alana... She always talked about fixing everything. She went after the Cherry, and I... I started the revolt here. Riled up the people. He killed the ones who went after us. She told me she had inside help, but I didn't even know they..." He sighed. "I didn't know she meant it for *me*. Alana never came back, and I met up with the only Harpoon left."

"And his wife...?"

"Cherry executed their families as an example. He warned her not to go, but she thought it would be suspicious if she didn't."

"What...?"

"When Alana showed up, there were already rumors that she was staying with me, but it never surpassed that—a *rumor*. They had no *clue* what went on here, but... Just in case she *was* from Oak, they invited the families of our Harpoons to a banquet. Then... they slaughtered them all. To *warn* them that they were failing, and that Cherry knew about it. Smithy... Smithy was the only one left to feel it." He balled his fist, so I dropped my hand over it. Even after he relaxed, I kept it there. His skin felt tattered and raw against mine.

"Then...?"

"Then he came to see me. Here. He trained me like he did with her, but this time, he was tougher. We fought *hard*, nearly every day. He didn't stop until..."

I urged him to continue with my expression.

He laughed softly. "Until I broke my wrist."

I stared down at his hand again, but still, he continued. "He wasn't sure if he should baby me or make me work it off. We waited a few days, and he cooked for me, and... then I didn't want to start again. I started thinking about my sister. I realized... I realized why he really came. I knew she wasn't coming back. It wasn't long after that my mom sent me the necklace." He closed his eyes and drew in a long breath. "That's when he made me start fighting again. That's when I knew that... I was *going* to be the end of this. Even if it killed me." His gaze shifted back to me. He looked directly into my eyes. "Even if it kills me."

We sat in silence, but I was already pondering his words. He stared at the table where I sat.

"I thought Smithy said he gave the blade to Alana...?"

"He *made* the blade for Alana," he sharply corrected. "Smithy... was in denial for a lot longer than I was."

"And... and I thought you fought the battle *alone?*"

"I did, to my knowledge. It wasn't until after that I learned about—"

"This is insane." I sighed and jumped off of the table, but Alaric caught my arm with his hand. He opened his mouth to speak. I thought he might threaten me, but he never did. Instead, he let go. I still didn't move. I couldn't.

"I never thought I'd..." He interrupted himself with a sigh. "I always *said* I was going to, but I never... I never actually *thought*—"

"It's okay," I whispered, but I couldn't think of a follow-up. We stayed quiet, and I listened to our breathing sync. Slowly, I slipped my arms under his. We finally let time move forward, holding each other softly as we did.

The days continued to pass, and we continued to train. Smithy came by every now and then, and he instructed us on not only how to defend against each other, but also how to work together. It didn't take long for me to match Alaric's movements. Where I practiced jabbing with my dagger, he prepared a swing with his sword. I became a distraction, opening a new chance for him to deliver a blow to our opponents.

"You have to remember," Smithy constantly warned me, "that they will spare no mercy. You have to be ready to look them in the eyes as you sink your dagger through their very soul. Leave *nothing*, or they *will* kill you."

As morbid as it was, I knew it was true. At night, when I was alone in my bed, I thought about what it would be like to take someone's life. I doubted that I actually would.

After another week, Alaric woke me up. I was dressed only in a loose top and the undergarments to my lower half, which was covered by a thin sheet.

"Everything okay?" I asked as I rubbed my eyes.

"I was going to head into town to restock on some stuff. I was wondering if you wanted to come...?"

I smiled and slid out of bed. I saw him turn his head, and I went to my dresser to more properly clothe myself.

"What're we going to get?"

"Just, um..." He cleared his throat. I started to laugh as I turned around, but his eyes darted away from me. "Groceries and stuff."

"Can we stop to see Clarissa?"

"I mean, I wasn't going to go that way..."

I forced my lips into a pout as I slipped on my cover-up.

He rolled his eyes as he finished, "but I guess we can find the time."

As we shopped, I was back to gawking at everything I saw. There were so many foods that I had still barely even heard of. An entire section of the store was kept cold, just to house different animal products. I couldn't believe all of these creatures had managed to survive The Collapse.

After going back to the Tree to put away what we needed to, we swam back to The Tube, where I led Alaric the way I was most familiar. As I ran my fingers over his hand, feeling the healing skin, I was sure some of it would scar. When he tried to pull away, I wrapped my arms around myself. Only a moment later, he took a few steps forward, trying to steal my hand back. I glanced at him and smiled shyly.

"Maliyah!" I heard soon after.

"Hey, Riss!"

"Where have you *been?* No one's seen you around in a bit!"

"Alaric went and hurt himself, so we've been stuck inside, but—"

"Wait, what happened? Are you okay?"

"I'm *fine.* Just a... a training incident."

"Alaric..." She stopped to sigh. "So you've just been, what? Lying in bed this whole time?"

"Have you not talked to Smithy at all?" I asked.

"No? I didn't think—"

"He's been coming back to Oak to help us train. We've been... It's been a lot of work." My excitement died as soon as I realized what I was saying.

"How long do you think it'll be before you leave...?"

I turned to Alaric.

He shook his head. "Not yet."

Before I could even turn back, Clarissa was hugging me again. I noticed the tears starting to form in her eyes.

"We're coming back," I tried. "All of us."

"No," Alaric countered. "If we can win, I need to stay at Cherry. Then, there's a lot of work to be done." He must have noticed our expressions, because he quickly added, "but anyone will be free to move from Branch to Branch, if they so wish."

"Do you think you'd move to Cherry?" I chimed.

Clarissa forced a sad laugh. "Maybe a relocation will help my shop. I'll... have to see what my family thinks."

"I want to build roads," Alaric explained, "but not underwater, like The Tube. I want to go back to the surface, where people can breathe *real* air. I want to connect all of the Trees that way."

"You've... really thought about this, huh?" Now, Clarissa hugged herself.

"Every waking moment." Alaric's eyes flashed toward me, and he lowered his voice. "Every waking moment... until I met you."

I couldn't believe he actually said it out loud. I had to turn my head away.

"I don't understand why you can't just stay." Clarissa fought with a sigh. "I-I mean, I *do*, but... We're *happy.*"

"And the people in Lavender are suffering, yet believing they have it better than us. I can't live comfortably in a world where that's happening."

"People give up every day there," I added, sadly. "They lose their mothers, sisters, fathers... And most times it's *completely* against their will. I've been happy here. Really, *really* happy. But if Alaric didn't show up, I would still be one of them. If he doesn't do for others what he *knows* he did for me, then... I wouldn't be able to sleep, either." I turned to face him. "Although... that's not to say I *want* to live in your world."

"I can help," he insisted. "I've done it before, and I can do it again. If I die trying..." He paused.

You have nothing left to lose, my mind chanted. *Just say it, you have nothing left to lose.* I waited. Saw him glance again in my direction. He never finished the thought.

"Have you been doing well, though?" He asked after he cleared his throat.

Clarissa shrugged. "Business is even *slower* than usual. I swear Julie's been stealing *more* of my customers."

"Maybe a relocation *would* be good for you," I suggested.

"Yeah, if I could *afford* it."

"Honestly..." I sighed, then shared a glance with them both. "It sounds like we could all use the fresh start."

The more time passed, the harder our training became. Before I knew it, an entire month had gone by, and Alaric had stopped holding back. Smithy would even come over to fight against the both of us, testing what we were capable of doing together.

It was in that month that I became completely comfortable with my dagger. I could move it around myself with ease, have full control over where it went, and pour my strength into every jab. A few times, I tried my hand at the sword or spear, but I could never adjust to it as easily as I did with Celia.

The waters were warm and refreshing. Sometimes, people didn't even dry off after they entered The Tube. Kids ran around, I saw more families than ever, and Alaric was growing angrier by the day.

One day, while we were training, Clarissa was watching. She flinched many times as we moved, but not once did we cause each other harm with our blades—we knew how to dodge in perfect motion with the other's swings.

Alaric's expression was more stern than normal. Even when I giggled, he stayed a stone. It was without warning that he threw his sword. Clarissa and I stared as it implanted itself deep into a root. We cowered as he screamed, dropped to his knees, and slammed his fists into the floor.

"He *killed* her!" He was angry, but with every new breath, sorrow was taking over. He doubled over on himself as he continued to scream. *"Why* does he get to live another year?"

"Alaric...?"

"It's Aaron's birthday." Clarissa's voice was chilled. "Isn't it?"

Alaric looked up at me through his matted hair. "I... I'll *kill* him."

"You're still brothers." My voice was weak. "I'm *sure* you'd be able to—"

"He's *not* my brother!" We both flinched at his tone. He stood up and brushed himself off with a force that hadn't made itself known to me outside of training. "He is *not* my brother..."

ELEVEN

IT WAS ONLY A few weeks later when we began to make our plans. After we got our boat, we would pack it with the smallest amount of necessary resources: weapons, gear, food, water, and any and all leftover blossoms.

Clarissa would be our driver. She'd get us there, drop us off, and take a wide circle around the perimeter until one of us broke the surface again. No matter who came back with her, she'd spread the news of our outcome.

Smithy was our guard. He brought Harpoon-grade weapons to fight off as many of them as he could. While he was out of practice, he was our best shot at getting us in.

I was our diversion. Wherever Alaric went, I would go first. I needed to take the attention—from Harpoons or otherwise—off of him. As soon as he was recognized, this would no longer be seen as a simpleton's wistful venture to return a long-forgotten peace to Watertowne. This was an assassination attempt.

Alaric was the firepower. He would guide me straight to the main bedroom. The king. He made it clear that there was no room for reasoning. If we tried, we would die. I would barricade the door while he announced what he had done. Everyone would surrender to him, or they would follow the same fate as their king.

Finally, after endless weeks of training and preparing, it was time. As soon as we started to pack, Clarissa was in tears. Her entire family came to Oak to wish us safety. Crowds gathered on the dock to watch us set off, and when they ran out of room, they tread the water, anticipation laced in their every breath. We opened the Tree to anyone who may have needed it until our return. Clarissa and her family were set as the temporary rulers, if anything was to go wrong. Alaric trusted them, and so did I.

I was in my room, looking over my things one last time, when Alaric entered. He didn't speak. He only walked over, backing me straight into a wall. My breath was heavy as I stared at him, and his hands found both sides of my face. I looked directly into his eyes—they were so sure, yet still so afraid. He lowered his hands. I rose to my toes and cupped the sides of his neck. He squeezed my waist tight. Our words escaped through desperate puffs of air.

"Don't go. Stay here and take over if something goes wrong. You're trained—more capable than *anyone* else—a-and the people *love* you! I think it would be the perfect way to—"

"I *can't* leave you now, Alaric. You *know* that. If you died… I-I don't know what I'd—"

"*No,* Maliyah—"

"Thank you." My voice stayed a broken whisper. Hot tears fell from my eyes, but I hoped I was pressing myself hard enough into him to stop him from noticing. "Thank you for ruining my life."

As we got into our boat, my head began to spin. Not once did I fully process what we would be trying to do. The journey would be easy, but painful on the mind. To avoid any early sightings, we decided to take a path far away from any Trees. Then, we'd come up behind the Cherry and sneak in through an underwater entrance. I prayed that Harpoons wouldn't find us before we got there.

As we departed, the crowd's cheers were deafening. All of Oakview wept, screamed, and chanted. I could feel the adrenaline building inside of me.

Clarissa kept waving at her family, tears streaming from her eyes. "I love you! I love you more! I love *you* more!"

"I love you..."

I whipped my head around. It was so raspy—so *quiet*—as if he was trying it out for the first time. He never looked up. I settled with the thought that I had imagined it.

Without much time having passed, everyone fell silent. The sun had just fully risen, and the people we knew so well were fading into specks in the distance. The farther away they got, the quicker my chest rose and fell. I tried to keep it under control, but it must have been noticeable, because Alaric dropped his hand on top of mine and gave it a tight squeeze. I turned to him, but he wasn't looking at me. He was staring at the water ahead, his own breath slipping through slightly parted lips.

"Oh, damn," Clarissa exclaimed from behind the wheel.

"What'd you forget?" Smithy asked with a laugh.

"No, I— I just realized... Did anyone say bye to Julie?"

We shared a laugh, and in a single motion, Alaric dropped his arm around my shoulder. The action surprised me, but it wasn't enough for him to look my way. Still, as he held me close to his side, I gratefully leaned in.

The wind was sometimes hard on our faces, and the water occasionally splashed into the boat. While it moved on its own, Clarissa was happy to steer, and the noise of our movement faded from my ears after some time. I watched the water, feeling its surface with my hand. I wished there was some sort of creature in it to travel with us.

"If we get back—" I started.

"When," Smithy corrected.

A silence settled on us. I closed my eyes at my own words. "When... *When* we get back... What are you going to do with all of the creatures your people have been raising?"

"I want to keep some of them with us," Alaric replied without an extra thought, "to make sure that they're properly adjusting, but I do want to slowly release them. The aquatic ones will be easy, of course, but the ones that were once on the land... I want to make more parks, like Greenland, but not just underwater. I know we won't be able to drain Watertowne completely, but... I want to see what Cherry has hidden from us, too."

"How *did* everything flood in the first place?"

Everyone turned toward me.

"You... don't know?" Clarissa asked.

"You *do?*"

"The Collapse wasn't named just by what it did to us," Alaric began, "but by the events that *caused* the flood. Before, when everything was *normal,* there was a group of scientists stationed here. They *began* work as officials in trying to help our climate—or so the people were told—but because of that, nobody batted an eye when they started to manufacture a giant, indestructible Tree." He shifted his gaze directly at me. "That Tree was what became the Lavender Crystalline."

"Many of the Lavenderians look to it as sacred," Smithy chimed in, "and that's because they're still following the original ways. It was the first Tree—the first era of 'new'—and they were mesmerized by it."

"After they knew Lavender would work," Alaric continued, "they started growing the other Trees. They wanted to make them look more organic, but also have them serve as their bases of operation."

"Wait," I interrupted. "Why would they need a base? What was—"

"War, Maliyah," Smithy replied. "It's always a war. And it was getting *bad*. So bad... that we'd rather *drown* than fight."

Alaric shifted his view from him to me. "After the Trees were successfully growing, and societies were thriving around them, they started their next project—finding a way to produce *water*. After *decades* of secret studies, they found a way to create it on their own, working with molecules and machinery. Then... The Collapse."

Smithy picked up again from there. "As soon as the flooding started, the scientists ran to broadcast it. It was reported as 'breaking news,' but instead of *actually* stopping it, these people only promised that they would, all while tucked away in the safety of the Great Cherry... And they were glorified. Everyone trusted them, and because of it, they forgot who actually *caused* it."

"But how could you know—"

Smithy didn't let me finish. "Because our *king* was the one who ran the entire operation, and every machine was safely secured in the base of a Tree."

I didn't know what to say. All I could do was stare.

"The town was under a foot of water in no time," Alaric went on. "It destroyed *everything*. Homes, schools, *people*... It took *weeks* just for someone to *attempt* to fix the plug. Instead, they used the walls built at the start of the war to contain it. That was the area that became Watertowne."

"And when we turned to the Trees," Smithy declared. "Because of the 'state of emergency' we were already in, no one was allowed to leave, and we had to adapt. We quickly realized that the Trees were the only things strong enough to survive The Collapse, but we weren't allowed inside. So, against authority, we started building. We dug down, fighting the water, to make *sure* the Roots were left safe. Really, we should have just evacuated."

My voice was soft. "You talk about it like... like you were there."

"I was." Smithy's blunt words brought a dire realization to my understanding. "I was a lot younger then—barely even an intern—but I *was* there. I *watched* as the people lost their lives and the lives of those closest to them. *Everything* was gone..."

"But after finding sanctuary in the Trees, the people turned their praises to the very authorities that brought their demise. Their eyes never opened again. Us Harpoons, though... We knew. We were brought in right from those scientists, whether we were their kids, or apprentices, or 'rescues.' What we *really* were was the first tests at making the perfect little guards. And while some of us were losing our minds, a few of us were opening ours. All our town *was* in the Old World... was some giant experiment for people who thought they were better."

"Wait..." I froze. "Is there land that... Does the Old World still exist...?"

My eyes only continued to widen as Smithy began to nod. "We've been taught that we're the only ones on this planet. In reality, we just didn't want to face what was happening on the rest of it. We took ourselves out of the equation so we couldn't be bothered."

"Wh-why didn't I know any of this? Why was this—"

"Why *would* they tell you?" Alaric challenged, his voice tainted with bitterness. "They're the 'saviors,' remember?"

"So... if we *can* take back Cherry..."

"Then we can tell the people the truth. Give them a *real* safe haven from the war. I don't know how long it would take to find the ends of the walls, but I *do* know that they end. And if people want to find them, I'll give them their boats. We need to build above the water again. *Especially* over Lavender. But... if we can take back Cherry... we can give the people their choice back."

"Why don't we leave now? If all of Oakview knows, then—"

Clarissa chimed in with her own reply. "It's the same reason there's only four of us on this boat."

"People are happy here, Maliyah." Smithy put his hand on my shoulder. "They don't think they *need* change. Truth is, they don't know what change *is*. So here they sit, carrying on with their lives, until we tell them we're leaving. *Then* they all gather, they all cheer, in the name of 'change.' They still don't know how many people are gonna be coming back with us. They don't know how much land they'll be gaining, how much their lives *will* be changing. And when they get a taste of it? That's when I suspect they'll really sing our praises."

"This doesn't stop when we win Cherry," Alaric finished. "Winning Cherry is when it *starts.*"

When the sun began to set, we stopped the motor on the boat and brought out a few blankets. We laid them out on the seats while Smithy marked his compass with the direction we were facing as a precaution against getting turned around during the night.

Clarissa was the first to pass out. As soon as she hit the pillow, before it was even dark, I could hear her breathing change. In a way, I envied her.

"I guess we can get an early start tomorrow, then," Smithy reasoned with a laugh. He was quick to lie down, but even with a mask over his eyes, I could tell he wasn't as fast to his rest.

I stared into the water, watching as the sunset changed its color. It seemed like there was nothing below or around us. I turned when I felt a hand on my back. It slid across me until I was wrapped in a tight embrace.

"Alaric...?" I whispered.

"I'm... afraid."

"What? We're so prepared, a-and—"

"No." I looked up at him, but he was staring into the blackness ahead. "I'm afraid of losing you."

I leaned my head against his chest and let him hold me. Inside, my body and mind were clawing at me, begging to escape at once.

"I know there's a chance Smithy and I can make it out," he was suddenly saying, "and I *know* Clarissa's going to be fine, because she's not even going in. Worst case scenario, she takes the boat, and she leaves us. But... I really, *really* don't want to lose you."

"If it comes to it," I realized with a shaky breath, "you need the priority over me. You're the only one who—"

"No." His laughter made me hold him tighter. "No, I *can't*. I-I don't... I *really* don't think—"

"You need to sleep. Why don't you go lie down?"

"Stay with me. Just another minute."

I nodded against him. More than a minute passed.

Our breathing was slow, and I could feel our occasional shivers. It was colder over the open water than by Oak. Still, I didn't want to move. I was happy there, holding onto him, but thoughts were creeping into me like another foreign weed that had never crossed my view.

What if you don't *make it back? Are you still happy to die for this? What if there* isn't *peace after death?*

"I'm okay with dying." Our matching thoughts almost scared me more than his words. "I hope I go where you say I will, but even if I don't... You're leaving here *alive*. The only way you don't... is if I don't, either. That way you won't have to be alone in death."

"Alaric, you can't. You need to help—"

"Smithy can—"

"No." We froze at Smithy's tired voice. He laughed as he sat up and slid off his mask. "Yeah, I've been listening to your poetic little love song. Alaric... We *need* you. I'm sorry to say it like this, but—"

"You can't control whether I live or die."

Hearing him say it like that sent a chill down my spine. I finally sat down.

"I'm doing everything in my power to keep *everyone* alive, but Maliyah is right. You're first."

"But—"

"No 'but's. You're the only one with enough power, influence, and authority to help us after this."

"*Maliyah* has authority!"

"*Maliyah* doesn't have the *experience,* Your *Highness.*"

We fell silent. Clarissa stirred in her sleep, but she only readjusted her position before she continued her soft breathing. I closed my eyes—I really did envy her.

"Now"—Smithy lay back down—"why don't we all try to get some rest? We're going to need it."

Alaric sighed and put his head in his hands. I don't know if I'd ever seen him that stressed.

"It's going to be alright," I tried. "Regardless of how it ends up... it'll be okay."

"I should have never roped you into this."

"Well *I'm* glad you did." My voice was firm, yet positive. He turned to look at me, so I continued with a forced laugh. "Who knows? Maybe I'll be the one who turns the tide."

"In whose favor?" Finally, he smiled.

I hit him in the shoulder, but he let his body relax. When his eyes closed, I turned to lean against the tall end of the seat, and I moved his head to my lap. I ran my fingers through his soft hair. It was a nice change from how slick it usually was. A final thought crossed my mind as I listened to Alaric's breathing:

Now I know how Clarissa does it.

I woke up to the sound of Clarissa revving the motor of our boat. After recoiling from the light, I saw Smithy pointing into the distance. Clarissa turned the wheel to match him.

"Morning, love bugs!" she shouted.

I laughed as I shoved Alaric off of me. At some point in the night, I must have slid down from my forced sitting position. "How much sleep did we get?"

"*I* got plenty. Don't know about you noisy folks, though."

"Do we have the time?"

"I mean... it's past sunrise. That's all I can really do for you."

"How much driving do we have left?"

"Girl, slow down! Good morning to you too!"

We shared a laugh, and I turned to Alaric. Already, he resumed his staring at the seemingly endless water. I slipped my hand in his to grab his attention.

"How did everyone sleep?" he mindlessly asked.

"Better question," Smithy interrupted, "what's for *breakfast?*"

We shared another laugh, and Clarissa pointed at her bag. We sorted through the food in it, picking mostly solid items, like granola bars. Smithy split his third with Alaric.

"Hey, make sure we have enough for the rest of the trip!" Clarissa warned.

"It's only, what? Another day?"

"Only if you don't plan on coming back!" Her tone was playful, but it left a foreboding silence. We finished eating under the sounds of the water and motor.

An hour after eating, I began to feel ill. I leaned back on the chair, and I must have fallen asleep a few times, because when I opened my eyes, Alaric was holding me. He was chatting with the others, and he seemed calm enough, so I closed my eyes again, reasoning that it would be best to get my rest while I could.

For the remainder of the day, I ducked in and out of dreams. In some, I saw my sister, and I might have even recognized my parents. But in most, I was with Alaric. Floating on the surface of the water, reading in his bed, but most memorably, sitting in long grass. It looked like the Greenland Preserve, but it expanded as far as I could see. It was soft as I lay down in it. Alaric held me gently in his arms.

When I finally opened my eyes, it was dark. Alaric was still holding me, watching the still water behind us.

"Sleep well?" he softly asked, brushing my hair from my face.

My heart was already beating fast. I nodded.

He smiled before returning his gaze to the water. Clarissa was asleep across from me, and Smithy was at the other end of the seat that I was on, his knees bent to make more room for me.

"Why aren't you asleep?" Somehow, I was still groggy. I curled up more against him.

"I'll sleep soon. Just... thinking."

"About what?"

"Get some more rest. I can tell you need it."

"What about you?"

Slowly, he bent down and kissed my forehead. It left a warm smile on my face and sent me into an even deeper sleep than before.

TWELVE

"Up!" I SUDDENLY HEARD. It felt as if I had just fallen asleep, but the sun was shining bright in my eyes. "Up, up, up! *Now!*"

"Harpoons!" Smithy announced. As soon as I turned, I realized he was strapping on his gear.

"What's going on? Where are we?"

"Change of plans: we're swimming the rest." Smithy tossed me my gear as he spoke. I noticed that Alaric was also putting on his.

I whipped my head from side to side. *"What?"*

"Harpoons are guarding the waters!" Clarissa shouted, guiding the boat to take drastic turns. "I have to turn around! I'll circle the area, but I can't get too close, or *none* of us are getting home!"

"I'll fight through 'em." Smithy was ready to dive into the water, but Alaric was still searching for his sword. "Clear the way so you can follow."

I finished sliding on my gear, and Alaric was right behind me to yank the straps that went across my back. It took my breath away at first, but I was quick to slide my dagger into its tight hilt.

My heart was pounding against my chest. We took a sharp turn at what must have been full speed, and I nearly fell over. Alaric had to grab my arms to hold me up.

"I'm going to the other side of the Tree," Clarissa warned us. "You'll have to swim more, but it'll be safer when I pick you up. You're *all* coming back to me, you hear?"

"Thank you," I breathlessly said. "Thank you for everything. I—"

"No goodbyes!" Smithy shouted. "You can thank us when it's over!"

Clarissa stopped the motor. The silence was deafening.

"Well... this is it."

"I'll see you all when this is over." Smithy saluted, and there he jumped.

As he swam down, I stood at the edge, prepared to follow. "I guess I'll see you on the—"

"Wait."

I turned back, and Alaric grabbed my wrist. He looked deep into my eyes, his chest moving rapidly. Up and down, up and down. He rose up on the chair. Met me on the edge of the boat. He hesitated for only a moment. Then, his lips were tight against mine, only leaving for a shallow breath of air, just to return, even more desperate.

"You're coming back to me," he said as I gasped in a sharp breath. "Do you understand?"

I nodded fast, but tears came to my eyes. He grabbed the collar of my black shirt, pulling me in yet again. My hands fumbled for his top, feeling the ridges of his gear. It was less than mine, but enough to stop my hands from wandering. His, on the other hand, crept to my sides. They crawled to the edges of my top, sliding under it, taunting my skin. I rose closer and closer toward him, kissing him more and more, again and again.

"Only if *you* come back to—" I was unable to finish. He was against me again, and I was breathless. I felt like I could fall over the boat at any moment, crashing into the water, just to be swallowed by it. A part of me welcomed the complete consumption, but only if Alaric was to follow me down.

He took a step back. On the edge of the boat, I was above him, looking down. Breathing. *Breathing.*

His hands were tight around my hips. He looked directly up at me, and he laughed. One, breathy laugh. But it was gone only moments after. "Smithy—"

"I'm ready," I said with a final exhale. I only wished the situation was different. I wanted dearly to be back in my room in Oak. I wanted to stay with him. I wanted to feel his skin against mine. I wanted to feel what more he could do.

"This isn't over," he insisted with a smile. He looked at Clarissa. Her eyes were laced with tears. Then, with a sound nod, Alaric jumped into the water.

As I followed him, I tried to copy his motions, but all of my training seemed insignificant compared to this moment. I held my arms straight and let my gear sink me as far as it could. I panicked that I hadn't taken a good enough breath, that my journey was over already. But Alaric took my hand, and I felt ease fill my body. We kicked in unison, fighting against my heavy boots, to follow Smithy's path. According to Alaric, there was an air pocket ahead, and if he was successful, Smithy should have cleared it of any unsuspecting Harpoons.

I was kicking anxiously as we approached the jagged piece of land under the water. There sat Smithy, wiping his blade clean. Around him were the bodies of three fully armored men.

"Are they...?"

"Love," Smithy laughed, "get used to it now, because you're about to see a *hell* of a lot worse."

A frown tugged at my lips, but Smithy solidified his prior statement. "Always aim for the stomach, if you find one of these. Just above the belly button. There's a gap in the gear there."

"Smithy..."

"Are we ready to go? We need as much daylight as we can get before we reach Cherry's interior."

We nodded, and I felt Alaric's hand brush my fingers. I wanted to reach for him, but I knew we had to move. Again, I sucked in a deep breath, and we swam.

Seeing the Great Cherry through the surface of the water was like knowing you're in a dream, but still being unable to wake up. The colors were vibrant, and petals floated carelessly all around us. They acted as if they were being pulled to the bottom of the endless abyss below, but still fell with a grace unknown to me.

Smithy began pocketing as many as he could. Slowly, we swam closer and closer to the Roots of the Tree. They were a pale brown—nearly even a white or yellow—as if they had been stripped. I was tempted to caress their surface. I wanted to feel it. Breathe it all in. Alaric's words and stories suddenly held more meaning to me. *This* was dangled right in front of his face for *years*, by the people who had damned us all. It was no wonder he snapped when he did.

Finally, we broke through the surface. It felt as if our every breath was one of betrayal. We were painfully silent, relying on the knowledge that we had approached unseen. Hopefully, they watched Clarissa leave and passed the entire situation off as a mistake. I prayed that no one went after her.

Now, it was Alaric's turn to guide where we went. We ducked back under the water with the most silent breaths we could take. My eyes were stinging from the amount I'd used them while forcing my way through the blue. Still, I followed Alaric wherever he swam. The Roots grew larger with every new kick, and finally, I saw our entrance.

As soon as the Harpoons pointed at us, Smithy kicked off of a Root to meet them. Alaric grabbed my arm and pulled me behind him. I was running excruciatingly low on breath by the time we swam into the opening.

Because of Smithy's struggle against the Harpoons, we were given an opportunity to run ahead. Alaric clutched my wrist as he pulled me in the direction we needed to go. I was coughing, gasping for air, and I nearly tripped multiple times over my own weight. My thick, wet shoes felt awkward around my ankles, and I was tempted to jump out of them altogether.

My thoughts ended as soon as we ran into more Harpoons. I grabbed my dagger, but Alaric yanked me into another room.

"Did they see me?" Even his whisper was panicked. Through the chaos, I had managed to forget how crucial that part of the plan was. I turned to him, then looked back to the opening. I shook my head. He nodded, and again, we ran.

He continued to lead me through a maze of rooms. At one point, I questioned if he knew where we were going at all. Then, we entered an area completely full of men, women, and Harpoons.

I froze as Alaric tore me back into the room. "There's another way we can go. I just need to—"

"We had a plan." Inside, I was screaming. To him, my voice was certain. "Now it's my turn to follow it."

"There's too many of them here. We can—"

"Alaric." I grabbed his face. Looked him straight in the eyes. "Get to the king. I'll handle the guards."

"I—"

"I'll see you soon, okay?" I turned, but he still clung to my wrist, forcing me to turn back to him.

"Come back to me."

I let my impulses take control, and I found my grip around his chain. As I rose to my toes, I used it to pull him in for a tight kiss. I had to force myself to draw away from his sweet taste. His longing breath. I sighed, but I stayed close. Then, I let go, turned, and ran.

As soon as I was in the hall, the Harpoons turned to me and drew their swords.

"How did you get in here?"

"What's your authority?"

Their questions were answered almost immediately.

"Word from the Roots! Treefolk have stormed the Cherry!"

They wasted no time in running toward me. I sprinted into another hallway, running without direction. As I ducked behind a wall, I slipped off my shoes, and I chucked them behind me. I felt my toes against the wood, and I ran even faster than before. Against my better judgment, I also dropped my shoulder gear. I pumped my arms harder now, hoping that anything would help me to lose them.

"Find her!" I heard someone call. I looked around, and I noticed stairs. I ran to that hallway, climbing them as quickly as I could, panting heavier than ever. I looked around for something to block the stairwell, but I decided instead to keep running. I climbed every staircase I could find, up and up and up, to get as far away from the Harpoons as possible. The thought that there might have been more on the upper floors never even crossed my mind.

Lucky for me, the farther up the stairs I got, the more people I saw calmly conversing. It seemed that entire families were in the upper floors, dressed in lavish gowns and suits.

They don't know we're here.

I tried my hardest to control my breathing. I looked around and took another turn. A few people glanced my way, but I was able to enter a new hallway without gaining any more attention than that. People in more casual attire hastily walked by, carrying trays of food and drinks, and I couldn't help but wonder if any of them were from Lavender. I shook off the thought, but it was replaced by a much more bitter one.

I saw another staircase, but this one was guarded by Harpoons. They stood with not only spears, but with the guns Smithy had warned us about. I held my breath as I turned back around.

I continued to creep around like this, never letting my dagger out of my hand. I tried to keep it behind my back, my only hope that doing so wouldn't make me look more suspicious than before.

It took a while, but I finally found a room that was empty. There were a few chairs, a table, and a red carpet running down the middle. I looked around, and I let out a long, deep breath. Then, my heart stopped.

"Leilani...?"

I whipped around, staring, with wide eyes. A tall boy with short black hair, parted neatly in the middle, was staring back at me.

"I... You look... Who the hell *are* you?"

"I was just passing through." My heart was slamming against my chest. I could feel my face burning just from looking at him.

"No." His hand went to his side, where I swore a sword was hanging. I was too afraid to realize that it was only an empty sheath. "No, I asked you a *question. Why* did you come in here?"

"I-I got lost! I didn't mean to—"

He began walking toward me, but I stood my ground. He didn't stop. I was regretting my decision just as fast as he was approaching. The closer he got, the slower he moved. He blinked a few times, then smiled. I noticed his eyes flick me up and down, the motion quick and subtle. If I wasn't as afraid, I might have missed it. It sent a chill down my spine.

"Could I... maybe help you find your way?"

"I was just heading to the... to the, um..." I flinched as he stood over me. I hated myself for running out of words. He smiled. His finger found my chin, then tauntingly traced my face. I sucked in a breath as his other hand found the bare skin around my hip.

"What's wrong? Surely I don't *scare* you... Do I?"

In one swoop, I pulled my dagger from behind my back. I aimed right for his neck, eyes glued to the spot I wanted to strike. I audibly gasped when he caught my wrist. Slowly, he started to bend it backwards, a smile stuck on his face.

"A fighter... I can handle that."

"Let *go!*" I screamed, but I was quickly hit with a painful real-ization—nobody here was going to help me.

Suddenly, he was kicking out my feet, wrestling me to the floor, and all of my training meant nothing. I was kicking, punching, swinging my dagger, but I couldn't get my hands free of his grasp. He hit me in the stomach with his knee, and I doubled over. Again, I screamed, and I winced at myself. I didn't know if screaming would attract anyone, and even if it did, would they help *him?* Would they kill me?

Then, he was above me, holding me down with his body. I continued to struggle, but I knew it meant nothing against his muscular form.

Thin, but muscular. Tall. Dark hair. I wanted to bite off my tongue.

"What did you say your name was? We should... get to know each other."

I spat at him, and it only made him hold me down tighter. He looked at my dagger, and he smiled again. He inched his hand slowly from my wrist until it was over the top of the hilt. I tried so hard to hold onto it, but it only took a flick for him to knock it away from my fingertips.

Now, he moved his head closer to my neck. I tried to move away, but he kept my wrists pinned with his right hand. I kept trying to pull them back, but there was nothing I could do against the full strength of his body. I felt weaker than I ever had. He took Celia in his left, thrusting her close to my side.

"I asked you a *question.*"

"Maliyah." I hated myself more for telling him the truth. His next words chilled me beyond my core.

"Maliyah... Adley?" He set the dagger down and moved his hand back to my hip. From there, he traced it along my body, making his way to my front side. He pulled on my top from under my gear, feeling if it was sturdy. He followed it to find my tight straps. He didn't bother to look at my face as he threw out his next query.

"Did you know that your sister was my lover?"

My insides hurt. I wanted to puke and scream and punch and *die.*

"Leilani Adley... She was the most beautiful creature I'd ever laid my eyes on. I'll never forget the way she could *move.*" He smiled again and took a hold on the strap near my ribs. He tried to lift me to find the buckles, and *finally,* I was able to shove him away. I immediately rolled aside and jumped to my feet. After grabbing Celia, I bolted toward the back of the room.

Don't stop fighting. Never *stop fighting.* Alaric's words rang in my ears. I couldn't escape the vision of when we had first started training, after he had me pinned down for the first time. *They're ruthless, okay?*

"Hey!" Just the sound of his voice made me want to close my eyes. I held my dagger straight in front of me, but my entire form was shaking.

He is not *my brother.*

"Hey... I'm not going to hurt you, alright? Let me tell you a story."

I didn't move. I kept my eyes on him as if my life depended on it. A part of me knew it did.

I'll kill him.

"The very first time I saw Leilani, I *knew* that she was perfect. It felt like *forever* until they went to pick her up. When she finally got here, well... We wasted *no* time in getting to know each other. And whenever she got homesick... she talked about *you.* I made her tell me every little detail."

"When?" I didn't know my voice could sound so broken, yet so strong, at the same time.

"When? Oh, it was a few years ago. I can't *fully* remember. Girls come and go, you know? But *Leilani?* I'll *never* forget her. *Especially* with someone of her... She was so *pure,* you know that? So innocent, so naive... I was *shocked* by how *good* she was with..." He paused, only to fill the air with his bitter laughter. "With *every-thing.*"

I wanted so badly to close my eyes and curl up. I wanted to go back home. I wanted to be with my sister. I wanted to be ten years old again.

"*What* did you *do* to her?" It took everything in me not to start crying.

"Anything I wanted to, my love. We had some good times together, the two of us. *Best* years of my life."

"Years? How many years? Was... Is she here...?"

"Oh, I wish... She wanted to find you, you know that? More than anything else, it seemed. So, of course, she tried to leave. I warned her not to—*begged* her, even—but... they all do, eventually. And that was the end of the beautiful Leilani."

"Find me? How did... How would she—"

"You're so sweet. So young, like I was. And innocent, *just* like her. I can't tell if she'd be proud, or so, very disappointed. I tried to tell her you'd be dead, left alone without a family, but... I guess she was right. You *are* a fighter." He took another step forward, but I continued to hold out my dagger.

"Come on, baby, don't fight *me!* At *least* let us talk a little more first! I don't want to *hurt* you, I swear! I just—" He was close enough now that I could jab with my dagger. The way he stepped aside with such ease was nearly enough to break my stance. He tried to grab my arm, but I jumped back. I tried as hard as I could to think of Alaric and his training, but everything was cloudy. I swiped as if to clear the fog in front of me. I could hear my sister's voice, her screams, and her pain. I wanted to kill this man, even if it killed me. He couldn't win. He *couldn't.*

I kept swinging, but he moved as if the wind itself was on his side. It wasn't long before the carpet bunched up under my bare feet. I tripped, and he caught my arm. I yanked it back with all of my might, but he bent it forcefully behind my back. My yell turned into a full scream as he slammed me against the wall with his body. My mind flashed back to Alaric.

You're hurting me!

I could feel him fiddling with the straps on my gear, and nothing mattered to me anymore. I screamed and screamed until my throat felt raw. My face was hot with tears. My chestplate loosened. I felt his lips on my neck, his hot breath against my ear. I was trying so hard to tune out his whispers. I tried to hit him with the back of my head, but he was pressing himself too tightly against me. I begged for a Harpoon to come. I begged that it would shoot me dead.

He grabbed a cluster of my hair, and I wanted to cut it all off. He yanked until I was leaning against his shoulder, and the harder I fought, the harder he pressed Celia into my side. I was so tempted to ram myself into it, but I had no control over my movements. My chestplate clattered to the floor, and I was quickly thrown after it.

He held me down with his body again, but this time, it was only my tight black top in the way of his filthy hands. I thrashed against him, trying *anything* to get away, but nothing worked. He cupped his hand over my mouth and shushed me.

My sobs were muted, but I continued to wail and thrash. Cautiously, he removed his hand from my mouth, only to drag it down my face. It reached my chin, and again his mouth found my neck, slowly working its way to my cheek. I tried to move away, but he followed my every flinch, whispering into me as if I was already his. He smiled as his hand continued to lower, lower, lower.

It found the single gold button on my dark brown pants. He fiddled with it. *Played* with it.

Then, just before he could slip his finger under my belt, he gasped. *Loud*, as if he was choking. The rapid beating of my heart seemed to come to a complete stop. He started coughing, and as I looked up, he sputtered blood onto my face. As he fell forward, I kicked away from him and scattered to the side. Through fast, shaky breaths, I looked up.

There stood Alaric, Desiderium bloody in his hands.

"Aaron!" His voice pierced my skull. I squeezed my eyes shut, begging myself to wake up. "You're *dead!* You're *dead!"*

"Alaric...?" Aaron clutched at his wound. As he struggled into a sitting position, I could already see the blood soaking into the back of his loose, white shirt.

I rubbed hard at my face, my body, *everywhere.* I wanted to change out of my own skin.

"Look at you... Look at you, a-all grown up..." But Alaric kept walking forward, only tightening the grip on his blade. Panic rose in Aaron's eyes. "Alaric, *no.* N-no, I— *Please—!"*

"You're *sick!"* Alaric was screaming, slicing his sword through the air. "You *killed* Alana, and now you— You— You're *sick!* You're a sick, twisted *bastard!"*

"No! No, *you're* the bastard, Alaric! You know *exactly* what you are! I *never* hurt Alana! I *loved* Alana! More than you *ever* could!"

Alaric dropped down, pressing his knee directly into Aaron's chest. He was wheezing as Alaric grabbed him by his collar. He looked him directly in the eyes as he spoke, but not before fishing his necklace into view. He dangled it right in front of his brother's face, as if in a challenge.

"You meant *nothing* to her, and you mean *nothing* to me. *Look* at me, Aaron, 'cuz it's the *last* thing you're gonna see!"

He grabbed his sword again, but I screamed. I screamed so loud that I couldn't even hear myself screaming. My entire body trembled, and my only working sense was my tunnel-visioned sight. I stared as I saw the figure sprinting over to Alaric, and I stared as he jabbed a spear directly into his back—I knew it would fit right between the straps in his leather top. Tears were streaming down my face, spit was flying from my mouth, but I couldn't feel a single thing.

Alaric's eyes widened, and he dropped his sword. The man behind him unsheathed a dagger from his hip, and he fought to stab it into Alaric's shoulder. He was screaming, too, but my ears were filled with high pitched sounds. Alaric whipped around, reaching for his blade. He was met with a slash across his chestplate, and I frantically moved over to him as he was kicked to the floor.

Sound came back to me all at once. It slammed into me with a force great enough to make me collapse. There I lay, directly on top of Alaric's bleeding form. Aaron was behind me, and the man reached for him as he wept. Alaric fought to sit up, and I didn't know what to do. I held him, hugged him, and cried. I was losing him, and it was all because I was too weak to fight my own battle.

Then, Alaric got to his knees. He leaned on me, using me fully to support his weight, but he fought his violently shaking hand to take a fistful of cherry blossom petals from his pocket. He swallowed them in one go. Instantly after, he jumped back to his feet and lurched himself forward. He swatted a cup away from the man, who was trying to make Aaron drink. I watched in horror as he pushed Alaric back, but this time, I caught him, forcing him back to his feet. I felt *disgusting*, but I refused to let it end like this. *Not* for Alaric. I grabbed Celia from the ground.

Aaron was completely limp. His eyes were open, but not even his chest moved. The man hastily returned to his side. Alaric took a step forward, but he nearly collapsed. I turned to the spear on the floor. Even part of the shaft was coated in his blood.

"No..." The man began to shake Aaron. It became more and more violent until he was pounding on his chest. "No! *No!* You *bastard,* you killed him! You killed my *son!*"

"His—" My breath escaped in one foul choke. "Alaric...?"

He was struggling just to stand. I could see the life leaving his eyes with every breath. He was using Desiderium as a crutch, stumbling even then.

"You made a *monster,*" Alaric spat.

The man balled his fist. "I made a *prince.* Your *whore* made a monster!"

He took a few steps closer, and I wanted to run to Alaric's side. I wanted to grab him and pull him to safety. I wanted to do so many things, but my legs were frozen in place. I only stared as he approached, as Alaric fought his arms to lift his sister's sword.

"Maliyah!" I turned my head to see Smithy—cut up, burned, and bleeding—running straight toward us. My throat betrayed me and gave no words. He tried to grab me, but I immediately pulled away. I was *still* shaking. It seemed to be all I *could* do. Alaric finally collapsed beside us.

"Take it!" Smithy shoved his bag into my arms. He then launched at the man, moving his sword more rapidly than I'd ever seen. *"Go!"*

I looked at Alaric, then I watched Smithy. The man put up a fight, but Smithy was quick to hit him in the head with the hilt of his sword. Again. Again. Again.

The floor shook as he fell. Smithy wrapped Alaric's arms around his shoulders, practically dragging him out the door.

"Maliyah!" he shouted again.

I wanted to run as much as I wanted to tear off my skin. Instead, I stood there, as motionless as Aaron's corpse. Again, Smithy tried to grab me, and again, I shook him off. I repetitively shook my head until he reached down and slapped me across the face.

That was when I saw Alaric. *Really* saw him. The back of his shirt was soaked in blood, and it even began to drip from his shorts. My vision was still blurry when I tried to look between him and Smithy.

Before I could fully process a thought, we were going back the way I had first run. I could only see directly ahead of me, barely able to make out Alaric's drooped form. When we made it to the exit, Smithy threw him at me. He was barely conscious, only groaning meaningless sounds of pain.

"The *tea*, Maliyah! Give him as many petals as we have."

"But—"

"Go, *now!* I'll hold them off!"

"I—"

"I'll meet you when I can."

I nodded, and I held Alaric tight to my unbloodied side. Smithy launched himself at more of the Harpoons, and now, beams of light seemed to be flying through the water. I crept around the side we had originally entered, and I took a deep, deep breath. I jumped in, and the mass of red spread all around us. I kicked my feet as hard as I could, but I felt weak. I felt *worthless.*

I continued to kick until I reached the surface. Clarissa helped me pull Alaric onto the boat, but I retreated to the back of it. I was finally able to just hug myself and curl into a small shape.

"What *happened?*" I could barely hear Clarissa screaming. Tears were still falling from my eyes. *"Maliyah,* what *happened?"*

I did it, I did it, I did it.

I closed my eyes, and I didn't have any intention of opening them again.

THIRTEEN

I GASPED AS I sat up, my body encased in chills and my hair dripping with water. Clarissa sat over Alaric, murmuring words of desperation. She held a cup to his mouth, but most of the liquid spilled out to the side. His thin shirt was on the floor next to him, soaked in blood. The inside of his gear looked no better.

Somehow, I ended up on the floor of the boat with them. I held a cloth to his back, but it was fully saturated within seconds. I threw it to the side and grabbed another from our bag.

"Maliyah, what *happened?*" She kept asking, but I kept shaking my head. I questioned if she even wanted the answer, or if her mouth was just trying to fill the murderous silence.

I started to sob again, and I leaned over Alaric's chest. The blood didn't bother me anymore—there was already so much smeared on me that I couldn't tell who any of it belonged to. We stayed in this hopeless state until Smithy finally jumped back onto the boat.

"*Drive!*" He practically threw Clarissa back onto her seat. Right after, he crouched by Alaric, crushing petals with his hands and pressing them tight against his wound. At the same time, he fished a canister from his bag and poured more into the empty cup.

"*What* did Aaron do to you?" His tone was firm and accusatory, but I flinched just at his name. He looked me up and down, and his eyebrows tightened.

"*Aaron?!*" Clarissa whipped her head back. Tears made endless paths on her cheeks, but she continued to drive. "Maliyah... I..."

I only shook my head. I continued to shake it until everyone was quiet. Again, I sobbed, and I pulled my knees to my chin. All I wanted was Alaric's arms around me, and I knew it was that one thing I couldn't have.

Smithy propped up Alaric's limp form, and he began to wrap the area around his ribs. I could see his chest occasionally move up and down, but without that, there was no proof that he wasn't already dead. The way he barely opened his eyes made me want to squeeze mine shut.

Help us, my mind begged. *Help us,* please.

The morbid silence settled on us once more. Smithy continued working on Alaric's wounds, major and minor, until they were all covered and sealed. I sat on the floor next to them, still hugging my knees. I couldn't say a word.

I thought about what it would feel like to lose Alaric. I wasn't sure I could ever speak again. I thought about how empty Oak would feel, and I questioned if I could ever go back to it.

Would I try to find what was beyond Watertowne? *Was* there anything beyond it? I *knew* I couldn't return to Lavender.

I closed my eyes, and I imagined the Great Oak. I visualized its every room, and I thought about how it felt when I first got there. Everything was so new, and I remembered Alaric's face as he looked at me. How my expression alone made him smile. Even something as simple as removing a splinter from my finger seemed to stand out in this moment as delicate and precious. Tears continued to bubble in my eyes as I thought back on how he helped me with my hair in our first few days together. I wanted so badly to go back to that day, to lie in the park with him, to feel how it felt just to brush my hand against his.

Soon, my thoughts shifted into dreams. I was remembering everything while my mind mixed in its own content. In every image, Alaric was smiling, and I was with him. It was all I wanted to see.

When I woke up, Clarissa and Smithy were talking loudly. They were both standing, jabbing their hands into the distance.

"What is it?" My voice was hoarse and raspy, but I couldn't escape the panic that had already set in. "What happened?"

"Look!" Clarissa shouted. She threw her finger in front of her, and I froze where I stood.

"Wh... *what?*"

"There's no *way* it's always been this close. I-I was only driving for a few hours, I— This can't be *possible!* I-it *can't* be!"

"We have to take back Cherry," Smithy decided. "One way or another. People... The people need to know about this."

"This whole time?! It *can't—* "

I could only stare as my friends spoke. Behind us, blue stretched on for ages. The endless blue, only broken up by the giant, pink mass, now not even a speck against the massive horizon.

But ahead of us, past the blue, before the sky met the sea? There, in the distance, was brown. And we were speeding toward it at an immeasurable pace.

The clamor was soon to die down, and as Clarissa drove, I found myself staring at Alaric. I watched until his chest rose again. Only then would I exhale, drawing my eyes back to the steadily growing land in the distance.

It was a color unlike any other I'd seen. It was far from the rich soil in the Preserve, but more muted and dull. I thought its vibrancy would grow as we approached, but the only change was the amount of it in our view.

As we finally came close, I didn't know what to think. A thick, white barrier stood at the edge of the water, stretching in both directions as far as I could see. Clarissa stopped the boat, and I climbed over my seat. As soon as I touched my toes to the barrier, I felt that it was sturdy. In fact, sturdy would have been a *severe* understatement. I put my full weight on it, even bounced up and down a few times, and it held, as strong as a Tree's interior under my feet. It took me a few steps to fully get across. I stared into the distance, and behind me, Smithy began to laugh. Clarissa's hands were cupped tight to her mouth. In front of us remained that endless *brown*. The ground was crumbling, full of deep craters, and felt indescribable underneath me.

"This... this is *all* wrong."

"What?" Clarissa questioned Smithy's remark.

"It didn't look like this. Before. It was *beautiful*. Green grass, full trees... This? This is *dead.*"

"Dead?" I could feel my heart slam against my chest. "What do you mean *dead?*"

"Dead," Smithy repeated. "We killed it. Finally... someone must have won the wars."

"But... what about all of the people?" Panic crept into Clarissa's voice. "I thought—"

"My dear... The world was a *lot* bigger than just us. Imagine hundreds, millions, *billions* of people, all in different lifestyles and places. The Old World was *full* of 'em. Couldn't go a day without seeing one, it was so packed. And now... I couldn't tell you who was left."

"We-we have to find them, then! We have to—"

"Darling... We can barely save our *own* people."

"But we have to! We can't just... They can't just be *gone!*"

I only continued to stare. I took a few steps forward, then lay down in the dirt. In the solid *ground*. I felt how it crumbled through my fingers, and I rubbed it against my face, regardless of how it stuck to where my tears had been. I heard Clarissa begin to sniffle behind me. I could imagine Smithy taking her in his embrace. I only stared into the sky. I'd never felt so *steady* before.

Even then, my head wouldn't stop spinning. Smithy asked me something, but I couldn't hear him. I barely noticed as he and Clarissa worked to carry Alaric from the boat. They placed him carefully on the barrier next to me.

Soon, there was quiet. I listened to the wind. It felt fresh against my skin. Occasionally, I shuddered, but out here—*alone*—I welcomed the feeling.

I wasn't sure how much time was passing, but I was still watching the clouds move above me. They changed more in color the longer I stayed still, and slowly, the sun disappeared into the distance. The sky looked so vast with nothing to obstruct its view. I felt petty in my little world of problems. Tears kept rolling down my cheeks, but now, they were silent.

"Are you going to be out here for a while?" I didn't answer Smithy's question. "Clarissa is finally asleep. She needs it. I... I need some too, but if you wanted to rest, I could keep an eye on Alaric. I just want to give him one more drink before I... before I sleep."

I didn't look toward him. I heard him crouch next to me, but after a moment, his footsteps began to retreat.

"Maliyah... I'm sorry. I hope..." He let out a troubled breath. "I'm here to talk, if you ever so pleased."

Another tear rolled down my cheek. Everything was so silent that I started imagining my own noise. I continued to stare at the colors changing in the sky. I tried to focus only on them. With everything else, I just wanted to forget.

I imagined myself flying with the clouds, but this time, I was far from drifting into sleep. I pictured images in every shape, using the colors to help form what my mind's eye came up with.

The sky was finally turning dark when I heard horrible coughing erupt from the side of me. Without any hesitation, I bolted upright and whipped my head around.

"Alaric?"

He was gasping for air, clutching at his chest. He sucked in sharp breaths and bent his knees. His entire body seemed to be pulling toward his torso. I frantically dropped to his side, and my hands immediately began to search. I grabbed at his face, pushed his hair away, and squeezed his hands tight all in mere seconds.

"Alaric, please breathe. Stay-stay still. Come on, look at me, can you see me? I'm here, I'm right here, I—"

"I failed you."

"What?" My jaw hung open. "No, no look at me! I'm right here, I'm okay! I—"

"I'll *kill* him!" Alaric coughed again, but he clutched at his chest every time he did. *"Aaron,* that—"

"You *did!"* My voice rose higher as tears fell from my eyes. "Alaric, he's gone. He's *dead.* He— He won't—" I couldn't bring myself to finish the thought. I turned my head away.

He'll never touch me again. He'll never touch anyone *again.*

"I... He—"

"He's gone. He is. He's— He's gone."

Silence was upon us for only a moment. My sobs growing in volume was what broke it. I threw myself onto him, despite how he flinched and exclaimed. Slowly, his shaking hand moved to hold my arm. I cried into him, loudly, without any hesitation in mind.

"I thought— I saw you—" I felt his hand tighten around me, but I bent over and covered my face. I couldn't control my panicked breathing. "I can't lose you. I *can't* lose you. I can't—"

"Maliyah..."

Hearing his voice made me sit up again. It almost sounded normal, as if he had just woken up beside me. I squeezed my eyes shut and pretended we were in his bed again. It was only his skin and mine.

"I'm here."

"Alaric?!" Clarissa's voice was nearly as raspy as mine. It sounded much more haunting coming from her. "Is— Was that...?"

"He's—" I couldn't finish. Clarissa came sprinting toward us, then slid the rest of the way on her knees. Her hands hovered above him, not knowing what to touch. I could already see the blood crawling onto the bandages that were wrapped around his sides.

"How do you feel? I-I know you must— But— Alaric, I—"

"I'm okay." He forced a smile onto his face.

I wanted to hit it off of him. *No, you are* not.

"I'm okay," he repeated. This time, he looked at me.

"You can move your legs? You can feel everything? Smithy thought he hit your spine. We didn't know if—"

"Is Aaron really dead...?" Alaric's voice was both insistent and desperate.

Clarissa turned to me, her eyes wide.

I nodded.

He let out a long exhale and closed his eyes. "I... I should *never* have put you in that position. I—"

"You couldn't have known," Clarissa tried. "There was no *way*—"

"I should have." When Alaric's expression tightened, I pulled my knees to my chest. "I *should* have."

"But you didn't," she tried again. "It's done now. You—"

"Failed."

"What? No! Alaric—"

"It's not over until the king is dead. I kept fighting, but... he wasn't even *in* his room. You all did your part—risked your *lives*—and I... I failed you."

"I—" My voice broke, but I forced myself to continue. "I should have fought harder. It wasn't your—"

"No. " His sureness sent a chill down my spine. "Maliyah... Don't you *dare* blame *anything* to do with *him* on *you*. He—" He was interrupted by another coughing spell, so Clarissa helped him to sit up. I wondered if Smithy could see his shaking from the boat. Every motion left him wincing and sucking in tight breaths. Then, his eyes widened, and his mouth fell open.

"Where *are* we?"

"Welcome to the Old World," Clarissa answered. "Or... what's left of it, at least."

"How...?"

"It was only a few hours from Cherry. This whole time, it—"

"But—"

"Before we continue," Smithy's voice echoed through the nothingness ahead of us, "I need to first make sure that *everyone* here understands that the outcome of today's events was *nobody's* fault but the Royals. Is that understood?"

Clarissa nodded, but Alaric looked toward me. When I turned my head, Smithy continued. "Now... I know we're all excited, but I think it's crucial that we get some rest. Especially you, Alaric. Please, lie back down before you hurt yourself again."

"Smithy," Alaric was breathless. "I... I'm glad you're with us."

"You're delirious, son. Lie back down."

"No, I *mean* that, Smithy. You changed my life, and I never thanked you for that. You—"

"Do you want to stay out here or on the boat?" Smithy's voice was certain, but I saw Alaric turn to look at me.

"I need to talk to Maliyah."

Smithy nodded, then gestured with his head for Clarissa to follow him.

"I'm going to try to rest," she said. "I... I'm glad I'm with you, Alaric. Until the end, alright?"

He forced a nod, but almost instantly, he turned back to me. "Please look at me."

I didn't want to. It hurt just to see his eyes.

"Maliyah... I'm *sorry.*"

"You didn't do anything." A sad smile crept onto my face. "I wish you did *less.*"

"Maliyah—"

"I didn't— I thought I *killed* you."

"No. Maliyah—"

"You should have just let me die..."

"Never. Maliyah, *never. I* should have cut off Aaron's hands before they finished growing."

I hesitated, but I leaned toward him. A long sigh escaped my lips. "Aaron... said something. When we were... When he was—"

"I should have cut off his tongue, too."

I couldn't help but smile. It was weak, but it was there. Just hearing him speak again made it easier to breathe.

Alaric stared into the sky. His hands were folded on his stomach, but I could tell his every breath was pained. His chest moved unevenly and staggered.

"He... took my sister," I finally said. "He thought I was her."

"Maliyah... I—"

"He... killed her. Years later. When she tried to escape."

"I-I didn't—"

"But... that's not... *all* he said." I turned slowly to face him, but it wasn't hard to notice his hesitation. "Alaric... who *is* he to you...?"

"A rotting *corpse.*"

"No, Alaric. I mean—"

"I *can't*—"

"I *need* to know. I really, *really* do." Tears fell around the rim of my eyes. I was slowly getting used to the feeling. "Alaric... Who *are* you...?"

Alaric sighed, long and deep. The pain behind it almost made me wish I hadn't asked in the first place.

"My... When I talk about the Royals, I... I don't even know what to *call* them. But I guess..." He sighed again, loudly groaning as he readjusted his position. I couldn't *imagine* the pain he must have been feeling.

Still, he propped his arm under his head, let out one more breath, and started again.

"When the king—Favian—first moved into Cherry, he had a son with him. That son was Avon, who would marry a woman named

Natasha. That part... that part is true, but... it's about the only part that is. The rest..." He shook his head and swallowed.

"Aaron was eventually born to them, but... *Dammit, Maliyah...*" All of his pain seemed to filter into his expression. I only bit my tongue.

"Aaron was born to them, but he was the *only* one born to them. Avon went sterile, maybe from Favian's lab, maybe from *Favian,* but... he wanted more kids. He blamed Natasha, and he took his anger out on her. Favian saw this, and... and he told her she deserved better. She was happy with Avon, once, but now their entire *world* was different. Favian promised her a better life if she went with him. He told her she would raise the future, produce an heir to the final Tree. She fought him, insisting that her *husband* was the one she needed to be with, *despite* what happened to them in their marriage. That was their *promise,* said on the dock in front of that very Tree.

"Favian took her anyway. She... she went screaming until he threatened to kill Aaron. Then... Alana was born. Despite the circumstances, Natasha loved her daughter. But Favian wanted a *son.* So he kept *taking* her, even after she lost the babies. She became so disgusted and torn that... that she nearly took her own life. The only thing holding her together was her unending desire to protect her kids. She wanted to be there for them, to watch them grow, and more than anything, to make sure Favian would never lay a finger on them. And finally, almost two years later... I was born."

Alaric paused only to let out a shaky breath. All I could do was stare.

"Favian wanted to kill Alana, but my mother promised she would go with her. He told her... he told her he would find another woman, but she reminded him that there was no other female already in the direct line of the original Royals, and he only had one son to marry off. It was... Alana was the only one I considered family for a long time. I thought— I *used* to think Avon was my dad. I mean, it would make sense, right? Aaron and I... we *were* brothers. Once. But Avon raised him to *hate* me, told him I took what was rightfully his. I went to Oak, *despised* by them, and I took Alana with me. I didn't... I didn't want any part of what they were doing anymore. And..." His voice broke. He pressed his palms hard into his face. I was absolutely speechless.

"Alaric—"

"Don't. Just... don't. It's not even worth it."

We sat quietly, but after only a moment, he began to laugh. It was bitter beyond words, and it slashed through the silence like a tired blade.

"How does it feel to have kissed the bastard son of a tyrant?"

"It didn't." I spoke in the first breath that left my mouth. "But it felt *great* kissing *you.*"

"Maliyah, that *is* me. I—"

"No. Really, no. If you're trying to tell me that your *lineage* is the only thing that defines you, then—"

"*You're* trying to tell *me* that it doesn't *bother* you?"

"Yes, it bothers me! That is *the* most *messed up* thing I have *ever* heard! But that doesn't make it *your* fault! You never *asked* for that! *Oh* my—" I drew in a long breath as I pressed my palms to my forehead. As I exhaled, I reset my volume. "Of *course* it bothers me, Alaric. But that is *exactly* why we need to take control of Cherry."

Alaric was silent, back to staring into the stars.

"How... how are you feeling?" I tried.

"Nobody but Smithy knows about that. And he only knows because he was there. I... I haven't even told Clarissa."

"I meant... more on your..." I gestured to his chest.

"Oh, yeah. That."

"Well...?"

He forced a half-hearted laugh. "If I don't move, and I barely breathe, then I want to die a lot less."

I sighed, but he reached for my hand.

"The blossoms are working, though. They won't... they won't *fix* it, but it's a lot more numb than it was. I should be able to walk again soon, and... and if I keep taking them, I'll be fine until we can get help. So long as I don't bleed out, we can get back to Cherry tomorrow."

"*What?* Alaric, no. You need to—"

"I am *not* leaving. Not without success or death."

"What about me?" Alaric turned to me as I spat the words through my teeth. "I thought you wanted to protect me?"

"Of course I do. I-I don't understand—"

"*How* can you *protect* me if you're *dead?*"

He froze. "Maliyah..."

"No! You can't just... you can't just overlook death like that! What if I never see you again?!"

"Don't lose your faith, Maliyah. Not over *me*. I... I really liked that about you."

"I *need* you..." At this point, I was squeaking out words. My entire face felt tingly and hot. I leaned into the battered hand he was offering.

"Come here," he whispered.

My voice broke instantly. I was back to my loud weeping, dragging myself onto the barrier. He pulled me in, and I laid my head on his arm. It was all I wanted to feel.

"Think about where we *are*. We *did* this! *Together.*"

"Not really." Somehow, I still brought myself to smile. As soon as he saw it, his look of concern melted. "You were... pretty out of commission for that journey."

"Come on, I got *stabbed!*" he joked. "Cut me some slack here!"

I sniffled, and he put his other arm around me. He winced and continued to suck in air, but he pushed through it just to lean into me.

"If I wasn't here, you wouldn't be like this..."

"You're right." His words stung me to my core, but his next ones brought me to shock. "If you weren't here... I'd be dead."

"That's not—"

"Do you know how *badly* I wanted to wake up, just to see if you were okay? I... If you weren't here, why the hell would I *bother?*"

"If I wasn't here, you wouldn't have gotten hurt in the first place."

"If you weren't here, I wouldn't have *tried.*"

I squeezed my eyes shut. "Don't... don't *say* that!"

"When we were in the park, lying in the grass, I... I *felt* something, Maliyah. And I knew it was over for me then, because I wanted to go home with you. I wanted to see tomorrow with you. I... I wanted to *live* with you."

"Alaric—"

"You gave me a *reason* again. A reason not to just run in there and finally be *done* with all of this. You... *You* saved *me*... and I almost told you the *one* thing going through my head that day."

"What... What was...?"

"Maliyah... I think I'm falling in love with you."

Tears escaped through my closed eyes. All I could do was shake my head. "Y-you couldn't... You *couldn't* have—"

"At what point does a stranger stop being a stranger?" Alaric shot back. "Maybe... maybe it's when one of those strangers starts to feel it in his chest."

In one motion, I leaned into him, and I pressed a deep kiss against his lips. It was disgusting, wet, and full of tears, but I went back for another, and another, and another. I held his face, and he grabbed at my hips. I leaned fully over him until he let out a yell.

His entire body tightened and flinched. I threw myself back, staring at him from a distance. It took him far too long to get his breathing back to normal again.

"S-sorry..." he mumbled.

"Don't *apologize. Damn...*"

Alaric's laugh, no matter how strained, brought the smile back to my face. "Damn at me, or damn at what just happened? Because, either way, I guess I'll take it."

I only shook my head at his remark. "Why don't we get you back to the boat? I think... I think it would be for the best if you got some rest."

"Only if you come with me."

I looked out into the horizon, where the endless lifelessness stretched. I never thought something could look *more* dead than water.

"Maliyah?"

I turned back to him. He was struggling into a sitting position.

"We're going to make this work."

I wrapped my arm under his and tried my best to pull him to his feet. He was grunting and breathing through his teeth, but he eventually stumbled into an upright stance. He leaned on me heavily, and it was hard not to touch his back, but we managed to hobble our way back to the boat, step by step.

After I helped him settle onto the deep red of one of the leather seats, he held my wrist. I turned to him, and I could see him fighting tears.

"It's okay," I said. "Just... keep breathing, alright?"

"Stay with me. Maliyah... Stay with me."

"Alaric..."

"You're all I want." His eyes were squeezed tight. I wondered if Smithy was right—if it *was* the pain making him spew out his words.

"I... *Please.*"

I went to sit by his legs, but he gripped my wrist tighter.

"Alaric, I don't want to—"

"You won't hurt me. You could *never* hurt me. Just... *please.* Stay."

I sighed, but I moved toward him. He pulled on me, weakly, until I was squeezing in beside him. Most of my body overlapped his, and I felt his fingers crawl to my hip. The motion made me tense, but it was far from being my focal point. Lying on his chest, I could feel how quick and uneven his breaths still were.

I wrapped my arm around him, and I closed my eyes. A final tear fell from them before I could finally fall asleep.

FOURTEEN

I NEARLY JUMPED FROM my seat when I heard Alaric scream. We were all sitting up and staring at him by the time he grabbed at his chest, coughing and yelling indecipherable words.

"Clarissa, grab my bag!" Smithy shouted.

She tossed it to him without hesitation. He reached into one of the pockets, grabbed a handful of petals, and crushed them in his fist. He then rushed over to Alaric and tore off his saturated bandages. I helped prop him up as Smithy jammed the remainder of the petals into his wound. Alaric screamed even louder, and it rang my very soul. I reached over and squeezed my arms tightly around his shoulders. Finally, his breathing began to steady.

"We have to go back. We have to go back *now.*"

"Hold on, son. You're hurt, remember? What're you—"

"I-I can't believe I was so *stupid!* I didn't *think*—"

"Alaric!" Smithy shouted. "Use your words!"

"They'll go for Oak!"

All of us froze. I could hear the breath leave Clarissa's throat, and I feared it wouldn't return.

"Avon *saw* me, Smithy! I *killed* Aaron! They *know* I was there, and they *know* I'm from Oak! Avon *lived,* Smithy!"

Clarissa's hands moved to her mouth. They were trembling. "They... they can't defend themselves. There's no way. I... *No...!*"

"I can't *believe* I didn't think of it. I— *Why* did you let me *leave,* Smithy?! We were supposed to do *one* trip! *One* trip, to *kill* the king, whether we were *dead* or *alive!*"

"Because you're my *boy,* Alaric!" We all fell silent. Smithy's eyes were glossed over, and his breath left him in shaky puffs. *"How* could I have let you die, when I *knew* that you didn't have to...? Alaric... You're my boy..."

Alaric let out a hard breath. He threw his head into my chest, and I tightened my grip around him. His entire form was threatening to collapse.

Smithy fell to his seat, his fist crammed against his forehead. "You're right. They *will* go for Oak. And chances are, they already left. We don't have the speed to catch their cruisers. Our only shot is... is if we try to stop them from the inside."

"How many blossoms do we have left?" Alaric questioned. "I'll take some straight, I can—"

"Alaric, *no!* That'll *kill* you, it could—"

"I already did!" He tried to sit up again, but his entire body tensed and caved. I steadied my hand against his chest, but underneath, I could feel the rapid thuds of his heart. My own were beginning to catch up.

"What do you mean it could kill you, how could it—"

"The petals have immense healing properties," Smithy explained, *"especially* when ingested. But taken *straight?* That could completely overwhelm the body. That's why we dilute it in a drink or rub it on the skin. Alaric, *when* did you—"

"Against Avon." His voice was cold. It felt like a part of him was missing. "To stop him from... from bringing Aaron back."

My mind did a double take. *He did it for you.*

"Alaric, *no...*" Smithy sat down as he spoke. "No, you... You *can't—*"

"I told you, I already *did.* I'm not dead, so it must have taken. I built my tolerance. I can—"

"Is *that* why he was out for so long?" Clarissa realized. "Alaric, I thought you were *paralyzed!* There's no *way* you can—"

"Start driving. We're *going* back."

Clarissa sighed, but she made her way to the motor. After revving it up again, she sat back in her seat, and we were off. This time, it was Smithy who stared blankly into the distance.

As we approached the back of the Great Cherry, I could feel Alaric tense. I knew he was planning something, even though he never spoke a word. With my worry, I rested my head on his shoulder, and I continued to hold him.

"When we get there," Smithy was explaining, "I'll go in first. Clarissa, keep an eye on Alaric, but make sure you get away. Maliyah..."

"I know," I assured him. "It's alright."

"I'm going to try my best to keep you safe, but... I need you to help me get to the king. Clarissa... drive the boat a good distance away. We'll—"

"But you two—"

"Will be fine. So long as I can help it, I won't let anything happen to Maliyah. We just need to reach Avon and make him call off the Harpoons. Then... we'll do what we can."

Clarissa looked like she wanted to say more, but she clenched her jaw and nodded.

Smithy turned to face me. "Stick by my side. We'll be alright."

I nodded at him, and I felt Alaric exhale. His silence left an unsettled feeling in my gut. Smithy stood and began to prepare his gear again, and I froze as soon as I remembered where I had lost mine.

"Take mine," Alaric finally said. "Whatever fits."

I turned to him hesitantly, then to Smithy. He was already holding the gear in my direction. I sighed and strapped on his thigh and shoulder gear. I left his bloodied, scratched chestplate near Clarissa.

We stood, preparing to jump in as she drove by. She would slow down just enough for us to control where we landed, then immediately speed back up to gain as much distance as possible. She planned to return to us every fifteen minutes, but if Harpoons spotted her, Smithy told her to get even farther away.

"Friends..." Smithy said as he approached the edge of the boat. "I'll see you all again soon."

I smiled sadly at Alaric. His hands were stuffed into his pockets, and his body was propped against the arm of the seat. I frowned when he didn't look toward me. Internally, I was wishing he would say something. *Anything.* Just in case.

Instead, he continued to stare. I could tell he was deep in thought. It scared me.

Smithy dove in, and just before my feet left the ledge, Clarissa's panicked shrieks filled my ears. I squeezed my eyes shut as I passed the water's surface. The screaming was muffled now, and I tried to focus on speeding toward Smithy.

Just before the boat's motor faded into the distance, I heard another splash above me. I didn't want to imagine what it was. But as a hand grabbed my wrist, I, too, wanted to scream. Alaric didn't hesitate to swim ahead of me, and I found myself being pulled faster toward the bottom.

As soon as we reached the first air pocket, Smithy crossed his arms. He tried to appear stern, but I could see right through it: He was terrified.

"You didn't."

"You need me."

"I need you *alive,* Alaric. You're— What happens when the effects wear off? What if you—"

"Then I take more."

"Alaric, you *can't—*"

Already, Alaric was pulling me ahead again, swimming fast toward the next Root pocket. Harpoons were guarding the area, so we turned and went another way.

Slowly, the density of the Roots increased, and eventually, we began to walk. Smithy stayed quiet, even after he passed us. He was holding one of the guns from earlier, but I knew we didn't arrive with it. I could only imagine he took it from a fallen Harpoon.

The entrance was swarming with guards. Smithy gestured for us to stay back, and Alaric took the opportunity to reach into his pocket. He revealed a few blossom petals, but I snatched his wrist, concern laced in my expression. It didn't stop him. He inhaled deeply, raised them to his lips, and swallowed. A shudder ran across his body, and his grip on me tightened. As he stood up straighter, I could only stare.

Then, everything echoed with a noise I'd only heard from inside of Cherry. My eyes widened as Smithy ducked behind the root with us. The weapon in his hand was smoking. He held up his palm, and I held my breath. I heard footsteps growing closer, and Alaric slowly unsheathed his sword. My own hand moved to Celia.

A Harpoon turned the corner, and Smithy's weapon jolted. That same noise filled the room, and my hands flew to my ears. The Harpoon dropped to the ground, and Smithy let his weapon fall. He switched to his sword, and he and Alaric started swinging. I stood, watching, with my dagger in hand. As they ran forward, I followed. Alaric wore his chestplate, but from behind, all I could focus on were his bandages. In my head, I was waiting for him to collapse again.

We fought together as we broke into Cherry. There were more guards than ever before, and my movements went into autopilot. I dodged, ran, and ducked, as if I was still in training against Alaric. I knew that I had no protection this time, so it mattered now more than ever. Many times, I could feel the wind of a blade barely miss my skin. As I rolled over Alaric's hunched form, swept my leg across the floor, and swiped Celia through the air, I could hear my heart beating slow in my ears.

Alaric continually pushed Harpoons away from me. Whenever more than one began to fight me at a time, he jumped away from whatever he was doing to intervene. As many times as we could, we bashed the hilts of our weapons into their thick helmets. I still turned away every time Smithy ran his weapon directly into someone's middle.

We approached the ground level soon after. Working as a team, we kept the Harpoons at bay. The most we fought at a time was seven or eight.

When we made it back to the upper floors, we sheathed our weapons. There were less people than before, but still, Royals in extravagant outfits were gathered around the room. Aaron's name was a hissed whisper, in what I could only assume was a rumor. A dangerous thought crossed my mind: *Maybe they didn't find out yet. Maybe Oak is still safe.*

I saw Alaric look around and duck into a quiet room, so I peered around the corner at him. He was breathing heavily, leaning against the wall. He reached into his pocket and tilted his head back.

"Alaric...?" I kept my voice low.

He didn't turn to me. His entire body was back to trembling. As soon as I approached, I could see that he was clutching his left bicep.

"I'm okay. I-it's just a—"

"You're *bleeding!*"

"I'm *fine!* Just... don't tell Smithy."

"Don't tell me what?" Smithy asked as he approached.

Alaric shook his head, but it was impossible for him to cover the blood spilling from between his fingers.

"When did this happen?"

"I'm fine. Let's keep—"

"Invaders have stormed the Great Cherry!"

The announcement made Smithy throw his hand over Alaric's mouth. The room we had come from was filled with gasps and screams.

"Please, return to your rooms! The situation is under control, but as you may have heard... our dearest Prince Aaron has been lost."

Whispers turned to wails, and screams turned into shrieks. As they were being ushered away, we peered around the corner. Harpoons were flooding into every room, swords, spears, and guns at the ready.

"We will be holding a funeral for the Great Prince in the Lavender Crystalline tomorrow. His domain will weep for their loss."

"Do you think... Maybe they don't know it was Alaric...?" The smallest hope tinted my voice.

"I think," Smithy challenged, "they don't want everyone *else* to know it was Alaric."

"Who *are* all of these people?"

"The products of *years* of incest and slavery."

"All of them?"

"There were only so many scientists. Most of them were too consumed by their work to raise a family before any of this. Then... priorities changed."

I shuddered, but my attention shifted as soon as Alaric began to cough. He was holding his stomach, and his shaking had worsened.

"How many blossoms did you—"

"I'm *fine!*" He grabbed my arm, and I helped him back up. "I... If they were sent away, they'll all be in their rooms. Surely... Surely the king is left in his."

"Alaric," I tried, "maybe you should—"

"No! I-I'm coming with you."

He reached into his pocket again, but Smithy pulled his hand away. "When was the last time you—"

"Fine." Alaric yanked his arm back, but he winced as he did. "Let's go."

"You don't think the king was moved to... I don't know, a special security room or something?"

"Only one way to find out." Alaric walked ahead again, but he nearly twisted his ankle just by taking his first step. I tried to reach for him, but he held his hand out to gesture that he was fine. Seconds later, he started running, and he drew his sword at the Harpoons guarding the stairs. Smithy sprinted beside him, and I watched behind us.

"Incoming!" I shouted as another Harpoon approached. This time, he held the same gun that Smithy had before. I dropped to the floor, yanking Alaric down with me as he shot it. Smithy jumped to the side, letting the pulse hit the other Harpoons. They fell to the ground, and I jumped back to my feet. I noticed Alaric's hesitance in getting back up, but I was too preoccupied by the approaching Harpoon to help him.

After they had been cleared, I dropped to Alaric's side. "Come on, before more of them come." I was tugging on his arm, but again, his chest was moving unevenly.

"I just... Just a second..." He squeezed his eyes shut and reached into his pocket. Smithy jutted his hand out, but Alaric pointed his sword at him. *"Let* me do this."

Smithy shook his head, but he took a step back. Alaric swallowed another few petals, and he squeezed his eyes tighter. He leaned his head against the floor, groaning loudly, and I felt myself tense.

"Alaric...?"

He sucked in a deep breath through his nose, then jumped back to his feet. "Let's go."

He waved us ahead, and we ran up the stairs. I could hear Smithy grumble something under his breath.

Alaric began to lose his speed before we were even onto the next floor. I saw him reach into his pocket again, but he hesitated and brought it back out with nothing.

We kept moving. I crossed the doorway first, but as soon as I got through, something slammed into my face. I lurched back, black and white splashing across my vision. I grabbed my nose as I stumbled. Alaric was the only reason I didn't clatter down the entire staircase.

Smithy launched forward, slashing his weapon at the Harpoon who got the jump on me. A few more were quick to leap out, but Smithy fought vehemently against them. I winced, and when I looked at my hand, it was covered in deep red blood. Alaric had a look of panic on his face, but I pushed him ahead.

"I'm okay, go help Smithy!" I wiped my hand on my pants, and we continued on.

Soon, I found myself staring into the room that had halted our progress before. Desiderium was still lying in a puddle on the ground. Alaric rushed over to it, sheathing his own weapon as he grabbed it. He looked it over, and he flicked his half-brother's blood off of it.

"They know," he said. "They have to know."

"Why?" The new voice made us all turn. Smithy and I held our weapons tight. "Why do *you* get to live, when *he* has to die...?"

Alaric took a step forward, and I threw out my arm. Anger radiated off of him like a freshly detonated explosive.

"No one *has* to die," Smithy countered, "but some do damn well deserve it."

Avon was puffy-eyed. I turned to Alaric, and I could see the words biting at his tongue. They were begging to be let free.

"Let me speak to my son."

"I am *not* your son. If *that's* what you wanted, you had nineteen *years* to mention it."

"How? How could you *do* such a thing to your brother...?"

"The same way he would do that exact thing to me! Hell, *you* would do the same to me! Don't act like a *saint* now that he's gone!"

"Who *are* these people? Who did you find, with the ability to kill a Harpoon? What dark magic do you hold over their souls?"

He drew his sword, but Smithy held his own out stronger. "Take one step toward him, and I will *gladly* remove your head from your shoulders."

Avon stepped back again, but he kept his sword firm in his hand. "This is your sister's doing, isn't it?"

Alaric tried again to run forward, but I used both of my hands to hold him back.

"What do *you* know of Alana?" he spat.

"I know that she attempted this very thing. She came here, a sword just like yours, waving it around as she demanded we stop what we were doing. She spoke of pain and suffering, and we all *laughed.* My father told her to look around—we're all doing *fine.*"

"And, what? You *killed* her?"

"Oh, no. Not at first. *Aaron* had a few words for her before then."

I felt a thud in my ears. Alaric ran past me with a scream, and their swords clashed. Avon yelled over their movement, every bitter strike backing him closer and closer to the wall.

"She was a beautiful *slave,* you know. She brought us *exactly* what we needed, whenever we needed it, and when she didn't comply—"

"*Shut up!*" Alaric swung harder, but I could see him losing his balance. Smithy ran over to them, and for a moment, Avon fought them both. I began to run forward too, but he was already sprinting out the door. Alaric tried to chase after him, but Smithy grabbed his shoulders and yanked him back.

"*Don't!* He'll bait you into the Harpoons. We need to get to the king before—"

Alaric interrupted with a pained scream. He threw his blade to the ground, but before he could do anything else, he was doubled over on the floor. He fought to get his hand into his pocket, but Smithy wrestled its twitching form away from him.

"*Alaric!* You *can't* keep—"

"Get *away* from me! I can do—"

"*Hey!*" They both turned to me, and I sheathed my dagger. "*Why* are you *fighting* right now? Is this *really* the time?"

Alaric grunted and picked up his sword. He seemed almost dazed as he stumbled forward again. Smithy held him up by his forearms.

"I'm doing *fine* with them, Smithy," he spat. "My body can handle it."

"How do you know when you'll have one too many? Grow to rely on it, and—"

"I. Am *fine*. We need to— *Forget* it. Just follow me."

We climbed the staircase in silence. Alaric led us down multiple corridors, but the halls were eerily empty. As we passed the many locked doors, I smiled sadly at Alaric.

"We... never did get those doors, huh?" When he didn't answer, I hugged myself. "We should do that. When we get back home."

He glanced in my direction but gave me nothing more. I frowned as we approached the final staircase.

"This is where he'd be. I..." Alaric sighed. Again he looked at me, then returned his gaze to the floor. He turned out his pocket, grabbing the final blossom from inside. "Are we ready...?"

I turned to Smithy as Alaric swallowed the petal. He shuddered minimally this time, and I saw him tighten his grip on his sword.

"They're in there!" Avon's voice echoed through the halls. We turned, but already, Harpoons were sprinting toward us. We ran up the stairs, but from the top, more Harpoons were running down. We were stuck in the tight corridor, dozens of them waiting for us to strike.

Smithy clutched his sword, knuckles white, but their weapons were set on us as their only targets.

"Take them to the king," Avon directed. "I'd like him to see what his *son* has become."

I saw Alaric flinch. With weapons jabbed at our backs, we sheathed our own and walked up the stairs. I felt Alaric's fingers slip around mine as we went.

At the top of the staircase, the Harpoons parted, but the ones behind us never moved their weapons from our sides and backs.

At the end of the massive room, a crackling fire was encased in stone. Furniture was spread around it, and a red carpet led down the center of the floor. Over all else, my eyes were drawn to a bed larger than any I'd seen before. From it rose who I could only assume was King Favian.

"Not you," he cried as a red robe, lined with white fur, was draped around his shoulders. A bejeweled, golden crown was quick to be placed atop his balding head. "Not my precious boy."

"I am *not* your boy!" Alaric's threats were laced with agony. The spearhead against me was pushed deeper into my skin.

"You are, by what's inside. You are, by your mother's will. Still... I always feared that your sister's *curse* would get to your head."

"Alana was *right!* She was the *only* one who was right! She—"

"Fetch his mother." I could hear the cold breath leave his lips. Avon stuttered behind us, but Favian shouted again. *"Fetch his mother!"*

"My... She's...?"

"Not another *word* from you! Don't you see what you've *done* to me? All I wanted was a proper son. A son that could *see* what I left him. A son that could—"

"And *Avon* wasn't good enough? For what reason?! He's more inclined to your world than *anyone!*"

Favian rushed forward, and I bit my teeth together as his hand connected with Alaric's cheek. I could see Smithy fighting to break free from the Harpoons who held his arms, but the more he fought, the more they prodded all of our backs. As they kicked in his knees to fight him to the floor, another came to hold him down.

"Avon was a *fool, blinded* by love! He needed to know *why* I did what I did, but he never could! Instead, he chose that *woman.* Beautiful, yes. Tantalizing, of course. And yet... A *woman!*"

"So the solution is to take her for yourself? How would that *ever—*"

"Silence!" Beside us, Smithy choked out an agonizing sound. We whipped around, but the Harpoons only tightened their grips around my arms.

Alaric began to scream. *"What* did you do? *What* did you *do?"*

"John. Feeney. I know *you.* I remember your *wife.* She was the only woman without tears on the day of all your deaths. Tell me, John... What happened that day at Oak?"

He was pushed forward, and I could see the blood that spread from where his armor parted. They pressed him to his knees in front of the king, but he only spat at his feet. "Go to Hell, you son of a—"

"*What* did you do to my Harpoons? *Why* is it always from *Oak* that I have to *execute* my own *people?*"

"*Don't touch him!*" Alaric was thrashing, exerting all of his force, in a vain attempt to break free of the Harpoons' grasps, but too many of them held him back. "It's *me* your quarrel is with!"

"You *care* for him, do you? You care for him like what? Like a *brother?* To replace the brother you *murdered?*"

"*Stop it!*"

"Like a *father*, perhaps? To replace the *loving* father that you *abandoned?*"

"*Don't! Touch him!*"

"Would that *hurt* you, son? Would that cause you *pain?* You're just like Avon: *plagued* by the inability to *focus!*"

I froze at his words. Suddenly, I was right back in Alaric's training room. His voice rang in overtaking surges throughout my mind.

Focus, I need to get my focus back! I was so focused, *so ready!*

My mouth fell open as he grabbed Smithy by his short hair. I stared into his eyes, but his gaze was directly on Alaric. Even as a single tear rolled down his cheek, he smiled.

"You've always fought well, son." He was met with another yank for his words. His sword was on the floor in front of him. No other weapon sat in sight.

"*Stop!* Let him *go!*"

"This? *This* is the man you care for?"

Alaric lurched forward, and one of the Harpoons nearly lost his footing. They took him by the hair, yanking his head in the direction of the king. Harpoons prodded Smithy's every breath with their spears.

"It's been an honor to fight by your side. Thank you, Alaric. Thank you for giving me hope."

"Stop it!"

"Thank you for being my boy. Alaric... I'm proud of—"

Then, I screamed. It clashed with Alaric's, whose was even more tormented than mine. The noise was deafening, but it was more than enough to drown out the horrendous gargling that overtook the room. A Harpoon grabbed my head, but I still tore my wide gaze down to the floor. After only a glance, the image was branded into my brain:

Smithy's body crashed to the floor, but hanging from the king's grip, dangling by his hair, was his head.

"No, no, no, *no*—" I didn't even know I was whispering. I felt vomit rise to my mouth, but it never went farther than that. My breath was leaving me in tight puffs. I forced my eyes to close, and I couldn't open them again. I *refused* to look at what was in front of me.

"Look at him, Alaric!" Favian was screeching. *"You* caused this! Your lack of *focus,* your lack of free will, *bending* to the behaviors and dreams of those around you? *You* did this!"

I turned my head toward Alaric. I needed to see him, but I still couldn't open my eyes. Smithy's headless body was piercing through the black. I wanted—*desperately*—to turn back time.

Why, why, why, why, why, I repeated in my head. It was the only thing I could do to keep my thoughts away from the present.

Alaric was still screaming. His voice was cracking, and I'd never heard it so pained.

Look at him, Maliyah. Look *at him!* But I still couldn't open my eyes. All the sounds were blurring together. Everyone was talking—everyone was *screaming*—and I just wanted to go home.

Then, everything went silent.

"Alaric...?"

"Mom."

"Favian, what... What's going on? Why is— Who's body is that?"

I heard a thud, and something wet rolled into my foot. Despite lifting my closed eyes to the ceiling, the awful taste returned. My hair was being pulled, but I didn't care. I *needed* to disappear.

"Natasha, is this not the child we created? The beautiful baby boy of my seed and your womb?"

"Alaric... Why are you—?"

"Avon! Is this not the boy who *killed* your son? *Slaughtered* him under his own *roof?*"

"No..." The woman's cold voice finally convinced me to open my eyes. She was beautiful, with porcelain skin and long, flowing black hair. She wore an elaborate black gown and gloves that stretched to her elbows. I knew she had been crying. Her eyes were a dead giveaway, even with the lacey veil draped over her face.

"Alaric... It's not true. *Tell* me it's not *true!*"

"Aaron was a *monster!"* Alaric was still screaming. Tears were pouring from his eyes.

"Aaron was my *son!"* Her voice broke fast, but it was her sobs that made me turn away.

The sobs of a mother. I refused to look at the ground. *But which son is she weeping for...?*

"And *what* was Alana? Was she not your *daughter?* Was she not *tortured* and *murdered* when she came back here? Mom, you *know* this is—"

"Don't. Do not speak her name to me. And *do not* call me *Mom."*

Alaric's expression weakened. He began to blink faster, and he would have fallen to his knees if it wasn't for the Harpoons holding him up. "I— *What?* How could you *say* that to me...?"

"Get him away from me. Get— Get him *away!*" She threw her hands over her face, and she was quickly escorted from the room.

Alaric was breathless. He coughed out only choked sounds.

"Alaric—" My voice was weak, but it was the only sound I could make. Before it could fully develop, a pain erupted in my already bleeding side. I let out a sound laced with pain.

"And who is *she,* Alaric?" Favian resumed. "Who is *she* who you brought into my home, brought to aid you in your evil transgressions?"

Alaric didn't say a word.

"Hey!" I was thrown forward without any thought or care. They brought me to the king, who quickly held his bloody sword to my neck. I nearly tripped over Smithy's corpse as I was dragged to Favian's feet.

My breath quickened as soon as I realized who was holding me. His grip on me was tight. I held my neck as straight as I could to try to keep it away from the blade. I couldn't swallow without feeling its edge.

"Who is she?!" he demanded again from Alaric.

"She's..." but his voice was weak. I could see him begin to stumble, and his eyes were even fluttering shut. He started to cough, and I felt the king's grip on me loosen.

"I asked you a *question!*"

"Don't do it... Just... Just kill *me...* Just kill me..."

Favian's hands slipped away. The Harpoons were all turned toward Alaric, yanking him back to his feet.

I saw what he was doing. In the split second that I had, I did something that I never thought I would actually do—I reached for my dagger, slid the blade between my fingers, and I jammed it right into the king's stomach, as hard as I possibly could.

Everything after happened in a whirlwind. The king sputtered and coughed, and the Harpoons rushed to his side. I was thrown next to Smithy's body, and I curled up in his blood. I braced my head as more ran past me, all trapped by their panic. My dagger was still sticking out of him.

Alaric ran over to me and yanked me to my feet. He grabbed Desiderium from the floor and shoved it into my hands. The next thing I knew, we were fighting back to back, swinging our swords at numbers of guards. Avon was screaming nonsense while trying to shove petals into his father's mouth.

Alaric and I continued to fight, but it seemed like the Harpoons never ended. I was messy with the sword, and a few times it was nearly knocked out of my hands, but I let my adrenaline control me. It was working until I finally heard the noise.

At some point during the battle, a pulse was fired. It sent the same, shocking sensation down my arm as that first day that I swam with Alaric. Internally, I was praising his gear—it absorbed the impact just enough for me to only drop my blade. Alaric tried to turn to me, but he was quickly overwhelmed. Harpoons slashed at him, his chestplate useless as they made countless gashes in his back. The straps of his gear were cut, and it fell to the floor. I barely knew what I was doing as I jumped into them.

It was just enough to let Alaric turn around, but there were still Harpoons surrounding us. They grabbed us again, securing us tighter than before, as they called out to Avon.

"Status on the king, sir?"

"Dead." A silence filled the room. "He's... he's *dead.*"

I killed him. My thoughts rushed forward before I could even understand what they meant. *I killed the king of the Great Cherry.*

"Summon my wife," Avon was saying. He slowly reached for his father's crown. As he turned to face us, placing it on his head, he finished, "Tell her... Tell her to come meet her *king.*"

Fifteen

Every second that passed felt like an eternity. Alaric was coughing and sputtering, and every wheezing breath made me flinch.

Hang in there, I wanted to tell him. *Don't leave me now.*

When Natasha entered the room, she was wailing. The Harpoons were dragging her by her arms, her vail had fallen off, and her hair was an unruly mess.

"*No!* I don't want to see *any* of you! Let a mother grieve in *peace!*"

"Natasha," Avon began. She was brought to her knees before him. "There was a time when you were my world. I married you on the dock, and I thought it was the most wonderful day of my life."

Natasha didn't stop crying. If it wasn't for the Harpoons pulling her hair, I doubt she would have made eye contact.

"Then... we had a son. We had a son, and he was *perfect.* We would watch him grow, and... and do you remember what I told you? I wanted another son, didn't I?"

I watched Alaric drop his head. The gashes in his back were beginning to drip with his blood.

"What did you do when I couldn't have that son?"

"Avon..."

"What. Did you. Do?" As Avon screamed, spitting every word into her face, even the Harpoons around me tensed. When she didn't answer, he launched his foot forward, kicking his wife directly in the chin. She would have flown back if it weren't for the Harpoons. As she cried out, I saw blood drip around her.

"My *son* is *dead!*" Avon continued to scream, and Natasha was hoisted to her feet. Then, his voice returned to the unnerving calm that it was before. "My son is dead, and yet... you still have yours."

"Avon, *please!* Has there not already been enough death to-day?"

"Kill him." He snatched a sword from a Harpoon, just to throw it at her feet.

Alaric's head whipped back up at the sound. I tried to turn to him, struggling again against the Harpoons, but they still held me firmly in place.

"Kill him!"

"Avon, don't be ridiculous!"

"Kill! Him! Feel what I feel! *Feel* what it's like to lose your only son!"

"I already *lost* my son! *And* I lost my daughter! Can you not *understand* that—"

"Kill the bastard! Right your wrongs! *I am your king!"*

The Harpoons pushed her forward, forcing the blade into her hands. After turning her around, they pushed her in front of Alaric, holding him steady. They blocked her from looking back at Avon.

Alaric didn't say a word. His eyes were wide and glossed, but they only stared through his matted hair at his mother.

"Alaric..."

"Please!" Their grip on me tightened, but I found myself begging. Natasha turned to me at the first sign of my presence. Tears were falling with the blood from her lip, nose, and chin. I felt like I was living through a hazy nightmare.

"Please, I-I'll do anything! *Anything,* miss! Just don't... don't take him from me... *Please."*

She took a step toward me, and Alaric's breaths turned choppy and staggered. I could visibly see him fighting his pain. As he choked on his words, he spat blood onto the floor beside him. *"No.* D-*don't* do this."

"Listen to me," I said as soon as she turned back to him. "I... I *know* that Alaric loved his sister. He loved her more than *anything. He* felt your pain. A-and I don't *want* to know what that pain feels like. *Please...* Alaric *is* your son. And he loved *you.* Don't... don't let it end like this. Don't—"

"Silence, wench!" Avon shouted.

I squeezed my eyes shut, but I raised my volume. "There's an entire *world* left out there! I've seen it with my own eyes! Why do you settle for one, *single* Tree, when there is *so* much more? *Why* do you confine yourselves to the same, monotonous, *pain*-filled life, when you could be out there, *living?"*

"Kill her!"

"Kill me, and you'll never know what else there is! What else you could *have!"* I didn't know what I was saying, but Natasha took another step toward me. I prayed that at least if she killed me, she would spare Alaric.

"Who *are* you, that you come here with my Alaric? *Why* have you done this— these *horrible* things to my family...?"

"I said *kill* her! *I* am your king!"

"My name is Maliyah Celestia Adley. My sister was a slave to your son. She was *tortured* by him until her dying day. Then he tried to... to take *me*. Alaric was only acting to protect me, as he vowed he would always do. A *vow*, like you once had with your husband. I mean you *no* harm. I-I just... People are *hurting* out there. *My* people. And... I can't live like that. Not anymore."

Natasha stayed silent. She gazed deep into my eyes. Then, she finally turned back to Alaric and dropped her husband's sword. "No more."

Before my smile could fully form, Alaric was screaming again. Natasha began to sputter, and she reached for her stomach. Blood was instantly forming near the sword that stuck through her. It twisted, then ripped itself back out. She fell to her knees and collapsed between us, a messy red puddle beneath her in seconds. In its reflection, there stood the king, staring at what he'd done. As his blade clattered to the floor, he dropped by his wife's side, cradling her lifeless form.

"You did this," he whispered. *"You* did this!"

He jumped back to his feet, and in the same motion, he charged at Alaric, who struggled against the Harpoons still restraining him. The ones holding me back immediately let go to assist the havoc to my left.

With the time I had, I scrambled for a blade. Desiderium was still on the floor. I swung it as hard as I could, landing it on anyone in front of me. I kicked them down, forcing my way through to reach Alaric.

As soon as I saw them, I froze. It seemed that everyone had. All we could do was stare as the king thrust his blade deep into Alaric's stomach. It cut through his hands as he fought to keep it from going in any farther. Nobody held him back anymore. In fact, every Harpoon seemed to take a step away.

Everything was silent to me. I rushed forward, and I swung. Avon screamed as he ripped my sword from his shoulder, but still, the Harpoons didn't move.

Our blades clashed. My limbs felt like jelly as I continued to swing. In every blink, I saw Smithy's face, but it slowly shifted into Alaric's. I began to scream, and my sword moved with more intention than it ever had.

As we backed our way toward the bed, I saw Celia lying on the floor, removed from the king and soaked in his blood. In one motion, I pushed Avon's blade with my own, swooped to the ground, and implanted her deep into his shoulder wound. He instantly began to choke.

I twisted the blade, and I looked deep into his eyes. "Alaric is a better king than you could *ever* be."

He dropped to his knees, and I kicked him over as I ripped my blade back, but not before twisting and digging just that little bit more. I returned Celia to her sheath, barely bothering to flick away the blood. Desiderium felt good in my hands.

When I turned, the Harpoons were staring. But my heart fell as soon as I saw Alaric.

I rushed to his side, screaming for everyone to move away. They did. Alaric was choking, blood was spilling from through his hands, and all at once, I forgot how to breathe.

"I need blossoms! Someone get me a—"

"My lady." A Harpoon kneeled, holding a cup in one hand, and a handful of petals in the other. I didn't have time to think about what was happening. Alaric continued to choke, his body pale and shaking. I grabbed his shoulder and pulled him toward me. Every movement made him squeeze his eyes shut.

"Drink!" I commanded. "Alaric, *drink!*"

Blood weakly spilled out of his mouth in his pathetic attempt to spit it to the side. "I can't— I *can't—*"

"Don't *do* this to me, Alaric! You *can,* and you *will!*" I forced the cup to his lips, and while shaking, he gulped. Again. Again. The liquid spilled out around him, but I didn't care. While he drank, I pressed my handful of petals to his wound. I held it there, tight, despite the blood rushing out of it, despite how he screamed in pain. My own vision was blurring, and I knew that my side was bleeding, but nothing mattered to me. Nothing, except for Alaric.

"Alaric, *look* at me!" I shouted. His breathing was slowing down, and his eyes were beginning to drift past me. I slapped his face a few times, but his head was already drooping to the side. "Alaric! *Alaric!*"

"My lady."

I whipped my head around, and I felt my own hyperventilations beginning to take over.

The Harpoon there took a step back. "Please, allow us to help."

"I'll kill all of you!" I was screeching without intending to. My heart seemed to have grown a mouth of its own.

"I swear it," another Harpoon added, "that we will ensure the safety of our king above all else."

I froze. *Our king.* I turned back to his limp body. His chest was still moving. *Alaric... we did it.* Tears were still running down my cheeks.

"I... I need to get to the surface. Can someone—"

"Your escort, m'lady." They gestured to a Harpoon with a gun.

My head was spinning as we walked, and my entire body was throbbing to the beat of my heart. The Royals gasped as Harpoons approached their doors. Some screamed and slapped their guards. But I didn't care what was happening. I needed to get to Clarissa.

While I was swimming, I began to feel numb. My vision was darkening, and I saw blood floating around me. I had no clue how much of it was actually mine.

As soon as I spotted the boat, I flailed my arms and yelled out to the nothing. All it took was one shot from the Harpoon's gun for her to begin bolting toward us with immense speed.

"Here!" I was more pleading than shouting, beyond ready to give up on treading the water. "Clarissa, here!"

"Why... Who is *he*? Where's Alaric? Where's—?"

"You need to come with me. *Now.*"

We swam back down, and Royals stared as we ran. We were going up a staircase when my legs finally gave out.

"Maliyah!" Clarissa shouted. She reached down for me, and the Harpoon readied his gun.

"You're *dead* if you touch her!" I screamed. He lowered his weapon, and she turned to me with a shocked expression. I was struggling to rise higher than what one knee could get me.

Clarissa reached around me, but I gasped at the touch and dropped back to the floor. Her hand was coated in what must have been my blood.

"*Oh* my—"

"We won," I finally said, "but Alaric... Alaric is hurt."

"We... we won?" Clarissa let the words sink in. "You... you did it? Where's Smithy?"

I tensed. My eyes found the floor. I was ready to crawl into it. Her eyes widened. "No..."

The rest of my strength left me all at once. Clarissa's scream was the last thing I heard before I fell back and slammed into the floor.

SIXTEEN

THROUGH ALL OF THE confusing haze—somehow—a dream made its way to my mind. Even then, it was nothing like I'd seen before.

I saw flashes of faces, all moments that I'd lived, in mere seconds. I saw my parents smiling, Leilani's back as I followed her, Alaric holding me to him, Clarissa's bittersweet embrace, and Smithy's body lying limp on the floor.

I saw my sister run to me, a stranger kiss me, a friend scream, and an enemy die. I saw a demonic king, a manic husband, and a lost woman all get struck down. Smithy's severed neck interrupted my view.

Then, I saw myself, holding the bloodied blades that had ended it all.

I gasped as I sat up, and Clarissa burst into tears as soon as I did. She tried to hug me, but I pushed her away. I was hyperventilating, grabbing aimlessly at my black top. My side was still throbbing, yet was overtaken by a strange numbness. I turned to look at it, only to notice that it was covered in a dark pink and red substance.

"Nectar, my lady," a Harpoon quickly clarified. "Made from the blossoms themselves. It helps to quicken the healing—"

"Where's Alaric?"

"He... has yet to awaken, my lady."

"Let me see him. I need to see him, *now.*"

"Right away."

Clarissa followed behind me, and I could see the panic in her eyes. Only the smallest part of me still cared. I *needed* to see Alaric. I needed to know if he was still alive.

When we entered the king's room, he was laid out on a table. Clarissa screamed as soon as she saw him. His hand was limp, hanging to the side of him, and his entire body was covered in cuts, bruises, gashes, and blood.

I rushed over to him, despite the pain that shot up my side every time I took a step. *"Alaric!"*

"He cannot hear you, miss. He is in a very deep—"

"How many petals did he take...?" Clarissa asked from behind me.

I turned to her, and finally, I *saw* her. She was crying, shaking, and holding herself tight. That was when I realized: We had left her, afraid, confused, and *alone.*

"I-I tried to stop him—I really did—but—"

"It's not your fault," was the first thing I said. Then, I ran to her, arms wide. She held me tight, sobbing, as I collapsed into her completely.

"What... what *happened?*"

I took a step back. Turned to Alaric again. *Still breathing.* I sighed.

"Avon found us. He told everyone that Alaric killed Aaron. We got cornered. *Right* before we got to the king. He..." I let out a breath. "Alaric kept taking the petals, even when Smithy tried to fight him. He wouldn't *stop,* Riss. He took them *all.* By the time they had us, he *needed* them. He was shaking so bad, and coughing, and— and... And they *killed* Smithy! They killed him right there, right in *front* of us! He— He cut off his freaking *head!*"

Clarissa's hands flew to her mouth. She closed her eyes as tears fell from them. Now, I couldn't stop.

"They tried to bring in Natasha, but Aaron was dead, and they almost killed me. Alaric distracted him, and... I killed him, Clarissa! I *killed* him!"

"Y-*you...?*"

"I *killed* the *king!*"

Clarissa stared at me in complete and utter shock. My hands began to shake. My body was soon to follow. Everything was silent again, even when Clarissa's sobs filled the room.

"Avon wanted Natasha to kill Alaric. She— she wouldn't. So he killed *her.* They just— I—"

"Maliyah—"

"I killed *him,* too!" I felt something tight in my chest. It felt *wrong.* "I looked him in the eyes, and I— I *killed* him. But... but not before he... He..." I turned back to Alaric. I froze. Stared. *Still breathing.* Exhaled.

"I-I didn't..." Clarissa couldn't find the words. "Is Oak okay...?"

As soon as she asked, I straightened and turned to the nearest Harpoon. "Send word to Oak... Alaric is the new king."

"Oak...? With all due respect, m'lady... Isn't the Great Oak barron?"

"*Send* word to Oak!"

"Right away." He hurried off, and Clarissa stared at me.

"They just... listen."

"They don't know any different."

"Maliyah... how are we *here?*"

Because I'm a murderer. Because I killed them. Because Smithy is dead. I didn't answer.

Alaric's choking had never sounded so beautiful. Clarissa gasped, but I ran to him first. I forced her to watch as my hands flew to his wound.

"Alaric. Alaric! Can you hear me?!"

"He's... gone."

"We *did* it, Alaric! You—"

"No... No, Smithy... Smithy's *gone.*"

I froze. A sudden sadness washed upon my soul. I felt his absence like a ghost breathing down my neck. It sent a shiver through my entire body. "Alaric..."

"Why am I still here...?"

"What?"

"Th-the petals... I—"

"Alaric... y-you didn't... you didn't think..." I couldn't finish my thought. *"Alaric..."*

He closed his eyes, allowing a single tear to run down his cheek. With his trembling breath, I wrapped my arms around him.

"We did it, Alaric." I spoke into his neck, and my lips caressed his skin. "Cherry is free. *Lavender* is free. We *saved* them."

"The Harpoons—"

"They healed you. I-I told them, and they did it. They *listen* to us, Alaric. You're... you're the *king!*"

Alaric let out another shaky breath. He tried to sit up, despite still groaning at his motions. I held the jelly-like patch to his stomach as he rose. He turned to Clarissa, who smiled sadly and waved, then continued to look around. After his scan, his eyes settled on me. I took a step toward him, but he only continued to stare. His face was... blank.

"Alaric...?"

Without warning, he pulled me toward him. I stumbled forward, barely catching myself against the table he was on. I stood between his knees as he yanked my face to his, trapping me in a tight kiss. It was strong—*hard*—unlike anything I'd ever felt. He bit down on my lip until I let out a noise of pain.

But his hands against my jaw were trembling violently. His entire body was. I knew there was something he still wasn't telling me.

"Alaric—" but he took my breath once more. He stole it for himself, sucking it in as if his life depended on it. Then, he began to fall forward.

"Alaric!" I grabbed his shoulders, but his eyes were flickering, barely fighting to stay open. A few Harpoons ran in our direction. Even Clarissa took a few steps forward.

"Maliyah, I..." His voice was a whisper. "I'm weak..."

"We did it, Alaric. We *did* it."

"You did it." Somehow, his words stung me.

"Alaric, no. No, *we* did. I-I wouldn't *be* here without you. I would have never—"

"You... you..." His voice was already trailing. I tried to shake him, but his blinking was getting slower and slower.

"*Hey!* Hey, hey, hey! *No,* Alaric. Y-you can't *leave* me now, alright? Do you hear me?"

Through it all, he smiled. He smiled, and I felt it stab me in the chest. "It's okay. I-I just—"

An idea shot to mind. I looked down, to where Alaric's stomach was patched. I tightened my expression, and without waiting, I jammed my hand against the spot. The second I made contact, he threw his head back and screamed. The Harpoons all drew their weapons.

"You *witch!*" He clutched his hands over the wound, spitting his words through his teeth. Finally, I smiled. I rose to my toes to lean another kiss against his lips, but when I drew back, his eyes begged me for more. I leaned my whole body into him, and I began to laugh.

"We did it," I repeated in a breath. "Alaric, we—"

"Just shut up and kiss me." He pulled me toward him, and I ran my hands across his chest, sliding them onto his shoulders. He leaned farther into me, and I felt my chest press against his. Slowly, I led my hands around his arms, crawling toward his back, but he flinched away. He was left sucking in a tight breath of air. He tried to lean back into me, but I took a step away from the table.

"Let me see."

"Maliyah—"

"Let me *see.*"

He sighed, but he carefully swung his legs over the table. I leaned over, and my hands shot to my mouth. Slashes spread across his entire back, all coated with a thin layer of nectar. I didn't know what to say.

"It's... Maliyah, I'm—"

"Can I, um..." Clarissa's voice made me turn completely around. I'd nearly forgotten she was there. "Don't mind, but I think I have the right to an interruption."

"Claire..." Alaric smiled deeply as he focused on her.

She only shook her head and rolled her eyes. Inside, I knew she was fighting her panic.

"How long have you been— Are you two...?" She didn't finish. A slow smile spread across my face. After wiping her own with her sleeve, she managed a small laugh. "I just— This is *Alaric* still, right?"

I turned back toward him, and he moved forward on the table. He stumbled as soon as he touched the floor, but I held him tight to my side.

"I wouldn't—" With just one look from Alaric, the Harpoon silenced.

With just one look from his king.

"Prepare my old bedroom, and one for my friend. Gather everyone in the dining hall, and tell them their *king* has an announcement to make. And... have this room cleared out immediately. I have plans for it."

"Yes, sire."

"Right away, sire."

The Harpoons scrambled, each of them heading a different direction. I turned to Alaric with a sudden bewilderment. He spoke with such authority—such *sureness*—and somehow, it felt strange coming from him. I thought about each of his words for longer than I should have.

My old bedroom. This was his life, once. He *did* control the Harpoons. He *did* live in this Tree. He watched the servants come and go, and he had every ability to pick the next victim, if he chose to. But that was exactly it. He never *did* take that choice.

One for my friend. A smile crept onto my face. I knew that he didn't mean me.

Then, we were moving. Alaric insisted on walking, despite how he grunted with every weak limp. It wasn't long before Clarissa and I both wrapped our arms around him, practically dragging him down the stairs.

"*Wow,*" Clarissa whispered. "We *did* it." Her expression changed at a morbid speed. As her eyes met his, I couldn't help but flinch. "Alaric... you *family*—"

"Was dead long before they were killed." He jutted his chin forward, and I prompted our walking again. We traveled the rest of the way in silence.

SEVENTEEN

CLARISSA STARED AT ANYTHING and everything as we passed through the Great Cherry. Her eyes weren't once settled directly ahead of us. Every piece of furniture, every wall hanging, every carpet caught her view, and she whispered something to herself each time they did.

"Turn left," Alaric directed. We entered a hall of three doors, with immense space between each one. Alaric sighed.

At the end of the hall was a single door. There was an inscription—worn, but still visible—above it.

Avon's Wing
Home to Prince Avon and Natasha
Left: Prince Aaron
Right: Alana and Prince Alaric

I held Alaric tighter. A Harpoon walked from the first door on the left. He bowed when he saw us.

"Which room would you like for your—"

"Prepare Alana's room."

"Alaric, no," Clarissa was quick to fight. "You can't—"

"I want to." A sad smile sat on his face. "Prepare Alana's room. Just don't... don't change too much."

The Harpoon nodded, and he quickly entered the next room over. We made our way to the first door, and Alaric sucked in a breath. As he steadied himself against his doorframe, he forced his eyes away from the name that was engraved over the door. Instead, he turned his gaze inside.

A large bed was made in the center of the huge room, and a dark red carpet covered nearly the entire floor. Furniture filled the extra space, including a seating area off to the slightly lowered left side. On the right wall, above his desk and drawers, was a large painting. It was of three children, all with dark hair. My heart sank seeing her face for the first time.

"Is this... This is where you lived...?" Clarissa asked.

Alaric nodded slowly. "I haven't been here... I haven't been here since..." He let out a long breath.

I turned to Clarissa, but I jumped as the Harpoon standing behind us spoke.

"Miss, your room is ready for whenever you please to enter it, and a wardrobe has been filled for you."

She nodded, and the Harpoon set off to fulfill another task. A second appeared to take his place.

"Sire, the stage will be prepared in fifteen minutes."

Alaric didn't answer. Instead, he continued to stare into his room.

Clarissa put her hand on my shoulder. "I'm going to... I'm going to take a minute and... and get changed and stuff. Alana..." She let out a puff of air as she nodded. "Alana was a... a good friend of mine, so this is..."

"Take your time," I said with ease.

She smiled, and the door closed behind her. I entered the doorway with Alaric. He was shaking as he clutched it.

"Alaric—"

"They're gone." His eyebrows were twitching as he stuttered through his words. "They're... they're *all* gone..."

I didn't know what to say. A sudden guilt filled my insides. Alaric stumbled into the room, and he sat on the carpet. I entered and shut the door.

"We... we used to be a family. We did. I... I had a brother and a sister. A mom and a dad. We... we were *happy...* "

"Alaric..."

"Avon... Fucking *Avon*—" His voice broke, and he covered his face. I cloaked him in a hug as soon as I could reach him. He leaned limply against me. His very breath was shaking.

"I... I *miss* them, but... I *know* that wasn't *them.* " He stared downwards as he repeated what he had decided earlier. "They... they left a long time ago."

"I'm sorry, Alaric, I'm so *sorry...* " My voice was nothing more than a whisper.

Alaric let out another long breath. "It's... it's done now. We should... we should get changed."

"Changed...?" I questioned.

Alaric forced himself into a smile. I stood, and I pulled him up after me. He gestured to one of the large wardrobes on the left side of the room.

I stared at it, then laughed. "But... we *just* got here."

"Welcome to the life of luxury, I guess. Just..." He interrupted himself with a soft laugh. "Don't get too attached."

I smiled, and slowly, Alaric began to walk again. A few times, he stumbled and reached for his wound, but already, his gait was growing stronger. He was fast to open his wardrobe and start sorting through everything, so I shook my head and approached the one that had been filled for me. It held long, flowing dresses, large hats, and articles I couldn't even name. I closed my eyes and imagined my sister. I pictured how we used to play dress-up with our parents' clothes when we were kids. Looking back, I think she only played along for me. I shook the idea away, turned my back to Alaric, and stripped off my tight, wet top.

I screamed only seconds later as I felt arms wrap around my stomach. I was quick to cross my arms over my chest, but Alaric was laughing, and the sound brought me joy. My face burned as he pressed a soft kiss onto my bare, upper back. His head rested against the now tingling spot.

"You're beautiful."

My skin felt hot. My hands clutched my shoulders. Slowly, his moved away from me, but he didn't just remove them. He slid them across my body, dragging them back to his side. Then, he resumed the shuffling in his wardrobe, as if nothing had ever happened.

From my own selection, I found a long, purple dress. I held it against myself, took out Celia, and began hacking at the fabric until it ended around my knees.

"You know they have tailors for that, right?" Alaric teased.

I rolled my eyes. I slid on a tight top piece that nearly fit me, then threw the purple over it. There was a small part of me, long ago buried deep inside, that felt like a princess.

Like a queen.

I slid off my thick pants and left them in a pile with my top. The sudden change left me feeling exposed. I almost wanted to put my tight articles back on, welcoming the feeling of the damp fabric's cling.

When I turned back to Alaric, I almost laughed. He was wearing black pants and a loose, white top that cuffed at his wrists. Gold buttons and chains accented the entire piece.

"Want to see the best part?"

I nodded, and he pulled out a long, red cape, with white and black fur along the trim, similar to the one Favian had been wearing. Now, I did laugh.

"It's only for the speech. They... I need them to take me seriously."

"Oh, right. I'm *sure* what'll help is looking like a—"

"Don't even—"

I rose to my toes and pulled him into another kiss. This time, his smile twisted and warped into something else. It was more devious, yet still somehow happier. He grabbed my waist and pulled me in tight, but I winced. I drew back entirely, even to the point where I had to close my eyes.

"Maliyah?" A look of concern washed away all else.

"It's nothing. It's—" but he was already hoisting up my dress. I slapped his hands away, but he was fast to slam me against the wall. I let out a quick exhale as he did. He held my hands back as he lifted my dress, bunching one side near my ribs, and turned me so he could more closely inspect the area. His lips parted. It wasn't hard to miss the large, thick patch of nectar there.

"Maliyah!"

"The nectar works really well, right? It's kinda cool how it—"

"Why didn't you tell me about this?! When did you—"

"Alaric, it's *fine*. Did you *see* yourself out there? You were barely even—"

"*When* did this happen?"

I moved my hand over his, holding it gently to my wound. Doing so let my dress fall, but the various layers of fabric were still propped up by his arm. My nose brushed the side of his.

"I'm alright. I promise. But... I won't let it stop you from checking on me later tonight." I closed the space between us one last time. His hand tightened on my side, making me flinch even closer to him. He stumbled backwards, and eventually, we tripped over one of his couches. I laughed as we flew over his armrest, but he yelled out in pain as we connected with the soft seat.

"*Holy*— We are *not* in good shape."

"Thank God for nectar, I guess," I joked.

Alaric laughed, and I ran my hands through his hair. I smoothed it upwards, despite the pieces that fell, and we shared another laugh.

"Little Prince Alaric."

He smiled, and I dropped my head on his chest. As soon as I did, there was a knock on the door.

Alaric threw his head back and scoffed. *"What?"*

"The people are ready for you, sire."

Instantly, his face snapped back to business. He turned to me, then looked back at the door. "Could you get Clarissa? I... She's in—"

"I know." I patted his chest as I stood up. "I'll be right back."

I bit my lip as I left the room. I knew why he was sending me, but there was a part of me that didn't want time to move on yet. The part of me was larger than I was ready to admit.

Clarissa was wearing a two-piece dress when I found her. The top showed just a slice of her stomach and back with ruffled sleeves around her shoulders. It continued with a skirt in the same, muted pink color. Her distinct curls were quickly reappearing as her hair dried. She was sitting on the bed, staring at a painting of Alana and her brother, as I opened the door.

"Hey, Riss." I kept my voice soft.

Her eyes were glossy when she turned to me. "She was really... She was my best friend, you know that? For as long as I knew her. She helped me start my business—she helped me follow my *dreams.* I never thought... It's hard to think someone could actually just *leave,* you know?" Her voice rose higher and more troubled with every word.

I nodded slowly as I took a seat next to her on the bed.

She sniffled before she continued. "I really wanted Alaric to visit more. Some days I just sat and waited. I never *told* him I was, but it... it would have helped."

I put my hand on the arm farthest from me, and she didn't hesitate to lean in.

"He... He does *crazy* things sometimes. I-I get scared for him. I just... I never know when it's gonna be his last big stunt. He..." She sighed, and I let her fall forward onto me. I rubbed her back as she quietly cried, her hands clamped over her face.

"When I saw him take the petals, I thought... I was ready for him to drop. Right there, right in front of me. I-I told him so many times, you have Maliyah now, just *settle down.* Just be *happy.* But he just... he *wouldn't.* He *couldn't.* I—"

"I'm sorry." The voice made us both turn. There stood Alaric, looking right at us from the doorway. "I... I know I should have

come. And I know I didn't care as much as I should have. And...
I'm sorry."

"I know you were hurting, Alaric. Of *course* you were... But I
was, too. I had to sit there for so many hours—so many *days*—just
wondering if you were alright, and—"

"I know. I know, but—"

Clarissa stood and ran. She practically jumped into his
arms—despite how his expression strained—and wept into his
shoulder. He sighed as his hand found her back, and I saw him
glance around the room. I could tell he was trying not to think
about it.

"I'm about to give a speech to the remaining Royals. I... I plan
on introducing you two. You won't have to say much, just... Are
you ready...?"

Clarissa nodded and wiped her eyes. "Thank you, Alaric.
Thank you for... Thank you."

"You shouldn't have to thank me. I... I know I could have been
better, I know—"

She hugged him again, and I saw a smile tug at his lips. When
his eyes found mine, I stood up and made my way toward them.
Alaric's arm slipped around me, and Clarissa sent me a smile
through her tears. I exhaled. My throbbing heart was finally starting to relax. Somehow, in this crazy moment, I felt like I was
home.

None of us felt the desire to move until the Harpoons began
getting closer to the door. Alaric was the first to break off the hug,
and Clarissa wiped her tears as he did. She sent me a soft smile, but
an unsettled feeling sat in my chest while I watched them speak
to Alaric. Clarissa tried to tell me something, but I held up my
finger and continued to stare through the crack in Alana's door.

It didn't take me long to rush back to Alaric's room. When I knew no one was looking, I slid my holster up my bare thigh, and I cut a small slit in the side of my dress to reach it more easily. By the time Alaric found me, I had already let my dress fall, and I felt more ready for whatever was to come.

Alaric returned to guiding us through the Tree, and Harpoons surrounded us until we reached our destination. After a short while, one held out his hand, and Alaric slipped through a large door. He left it cracked in order for us to hear from the wide hallway we were in. The chatter and murmur ahead of us silenced as soon as the king cleared his throat.

"Good evening, Royals. I'll spare your precious time by getting straight to the point. As you may know, today was a day of great loss, beginning with the death of your late Prince Aaron. That being said... his was not the only loss of the day."

Many people gasped, and I turned to Alaric. My knuckles were turning white over the hilt of my dagger, but Clarissa discreetly dropped her hand over mine. I stared her down with wild eyes.

They're going to turn on us. This is a trap.

Hers looked back with complete patience and trust.

"Please, stay calm, but as you know, when one member of the Great Royals passes, their title is immediately given to the next member by birthright. While that has never been officially *done* in our history since The Collapse... Today, I come to you with an announcement, beginning in that your new *king* would like to share a few words."

Everybody gasped. Some even screamed. Questions buzzed in the air like an invasive swarm.

"Silence!"

The mere speed at which the room died covered me in chills.

Alaric began to pace with his hands folded behind his back and his chest out proud. "As much as some of you may not want to admit it, your lives are about to change. For *years,* you have been living under the unchecked tyranny of King Favian. Today... that king has fallen."

The crowd again erupted into mixed noises, but as soon as Alaric held up his hand, they were forced back into silence.

"Not *only* has your king fallen, but so has his firstborn, Avon, along with his wife, Natasha. Hence... *I,* solely, am left to rule as your king."

"Murderer!"

"Arrest him!"

"I am your king! And my first *demand* as such is for all servants and slaves to step forward *now. "*

Many Royals threw their servants ahead. Some scrambled forward on their own. Only a few reluctantly followed.

"By a show of hands, how many of you originated from the Lavender Branch?"

One hand went up instantly. Two more followed. The numbers grew exponentially until nearly everyone who had stepped forward was holding their hand in the air.

"To any of you with your hands raised... I call upon you to implore for your help. Maliyah?"

I took a step forward, but he continued to hold out his arm. I walked until I was standing beside him, but I couldn't make myself let go of Celia's hilt. All eyes were on me.

"This is Lady Maliyah, and you will *only* refer to her as such. She is my representative from Lavender. With your help and hers, I believe we can restore the desolate Roots to a beautiful utopia. Clarissa?"

Now, Clarissa ran forward.

"This is my representative from the Great Oak. Years ago, unbeknownst to the Royals, my... my associate and I worked to liberate it. Today, it is a flourishing city. Markets and stores run, families grow, and livestock from the Old World is shared. Not only is there suitable housing, but also transportation, occupations, and an overall way of life."

"I've lived there throughout its entire growth," Clarissa added, "and there's nowhere I'd rather be."

"Help us to save Lavender. Help us to connect our societies. Together, we *will* thrive once more."

Everyone in the front began to cheer. A few even rang out in song.

"All hail the king! All hail the king!"

"I don't want to be your king," Alaric finished, "but I do know what has to be done. I want to rule in your best interest—not as your overseer, but as your ally. In turn... my second demand is to set you all free. May you return to your families, spread the word of what has happened here, and return to help only when *you* see it fit."

The cheering continued, and I turned to Alaric with a smile. He held his stern expression, but I could tell he was fighting the corners of his mouth.

I whipped back around as soon as the crowd's hails turned to screams. In the audience, a girl in the front row fell to her knees, then flat on the floor. Behind her, a Royal was drawing a sword from her back. Harpoons sprinted into the crowd as the servants parted ways, holding each other in fear.

"*You* do not control us! We have lived this way since the flood itself! Some of us were *there* with your grandfather, our *true* king! *This* is our birthright, and you *cannot* take it away!"

Two Harpoons dragged him away while two others retrieved the fallen body. I turned back to Alaric, but his stance was unwavering.

"Tonight, we rest. Tomorrow, you must pack your things, for the cruisers will be prepared, and we will set a course for Lavender. Any who feel my cause shall come with me, and I swear the Harpoon's protection upon you. All else will remain here, but I cannot promise you everlasting safety, nor food and health. The choice is yours. I hope you will find me... just."

The Royals continued their protests, but the servants resumed their chanting, undefeated by their fear. Alaric turned and walked back to the door without another word. Clarissa and I followed after him, and the noise was silenced as soon as the Harpoons shut them behind us.

"That was *amazing,* Alaric! You're a *natural!*" Clarissa cheered.

Alaric leaned the back of his head against the wall. "I... forgot what that felt like."

"You've *done* that before?"

"No. Well, not exactly. I mean... I used to listen to Avon give speeches. And Favian. But... I practiced with Alana. She'd humor me for a while, and I..." He sighed and shook his head. "Do you mind if I settle down for the night...?"

"No, of course not. I'm one door down if you need anything, alright?"

Alaric nodded, and the Harpoons continued to escort us through the halls. As we reached the bedrooms, Clarissa softly called out, "Alaric... I'm proud of you."

After that, our doors were tightly shut. I quickly made my way to the bathroom, and as I showered, Alaric went to a nearby room to do the same.

Once I was satisfied, I wrapped a towel around myself and went back into the bedroom. Alaric was lying in the bed, staring at the ceiling. He didn't speak as I walked over to the wardrobe.

I sorted through the undergarments until I found something more my size. I slid the bottoms on under my towel, then dropped it to the side of me. My back still to the bed, I found a white button-up shirt that was far too big to be my size. I slid it over my arms, buttoned the top, and closed the wardrobe behind me. When I turned back, Alaric was still staring.

"Are you... are you doing alright?" I nervously asked.

He only fiddled with the shell around his neck. Other than his hands, he was completely still.

"Alaric...?"

"There's a Harpoon outside the door. Could you ask for more nectar...?"

I made a dash for the door and poked out my head.

The Harpoon turned to me without hesitation. "Lady Maliyah, how may I be—"

"Is there more nectar?"

"Of course. Shall I fetch the medic?"

"No. Just a few patches is fine." I barely had time to turn back to Alaric before another Harpoon was running over. He handed me a surplus of what I needed, and I lent him a smile before I shut the door again.

As the thought crossed my mind, I pulled up my shirt, and I admired my side. Already, the wound was closing. I wondered if it would even leave a scar.

Regardless, I tore off a small piece for myself, and I stuck it to the spot. Right after, I slid into the bed. Alaric didn't meet my eyes.

"I can—"

"Let me see."

He sighed, and I pulled away the blanket. His stomach wasn't bleeding, but the gash was grossly flesh-like. I wanted to turn my head at the sight.

"I can just—"

"Alaric."

He returned his gaze to the ceiling. Slowly, I lowered the patch to his wound, and he flinched. I held it there for a moment before I reached for another patch.

"Turn around, please."

"I'm—"

"Alaric," I said again.

He sighed, but he turned over, mostly using his arms to do so. This time, I did turn away. Every gash on his back was still raw and red. I had to suck in a breath before I could continue putting the patches over them.

He shivered as my hands slid down his back. Even after the patches were on, I continued to keep them there. I ran them around his side, past his ribs, until I found his chest.

"Look, I know it's bad, but I also know there's nothing *there.* "

I smiled as he faced me again. I leaned on him, and he draped his arm around my back. Slowly, he used his thumb to brush my hair from my face. It traced my cheek, and I leaned even more. I closed my eyes and let my body relax.

"Maliyah..." He couldn't finish. My lips hovered above his. I felt his breath, and I lingered there for a moment. His thumb reached my lip before I moved forward again.

He spun me around him as he kissed me, the motion becoming more deep and intense by the second. My eyes shot open as he gained the sudden strength to shift completely over me. His hand slid up my bent leg, past my shirt, and onto my bare back. I arched it at his cold touch, but inside, I was begging myself to somehow get closer. Now, my chest was thumping, and soft sounds tried to escape me as we continued. He barely let me let them out.

My hand fell from his chin to his shoulder. I wrapped my leg over him, and he leaned harder into me. All I could hear was my pulse and his heavy breathing. His teeth dragged down my lips and fell to my neck. I wrapped my arms around his hair as he kissed it, over and over again. When he began to slow down, my breathing followed. He laid his head against my chest, and I knew he could feel how fast my heart was beating.

We were panting out of sync. I finally laughed, breathless, and he did the same. He propped his chin on his hands and looked directly into my eyes. He smiled, and for the first time in a while, it was soft and genuine.

"Maliyah... I'm going to say something crazy."

"Say it."

"Marry me."

His request hit me with shock, but my expression was nothing but raw happiness.

"When all of this is over, on the docks, like they used to. I... I want you to be my queen."

"Alaric..."

"Don't! Don't answer yet. I want to ask you again. Properly. Just... later."

I put my hands back in his hair, letting him rest on me. He smiled, and his eyes slowly closed. "Thank you for staying with me."

My voice shrunk to a whisper. "Alaric... I'll never leave your side."

EIGHTEEN

As MY EYES OPENED, the soreness in my limbs overtook my senses. I groaned as I shifted in the bed, but I paused once I felt Alaric's weight. His arm and leg were thrown over me, and his hand was twisted in my top. It was pulled up around me, just barely covering my chest. Alaric's skin felt warm against mine.

I pulled my top back down before I moved toward him. Without opening his eyes, he smiled and held me tighter. I tried to turn to my other side, but he was quick to pull me even closer. His very legs claimed me as their hostage.

"How're you feeling?" My throat hurt as I spoke, despite how I kept its volume low.

"Tired," he groaned back.

I smiled, and I closed my eyes again.

This time, I saw faces in my sleep. I saw Smithy get pulled by his hair, and I saw the blade swing in slow motion. I looked away, but when I looked back, it was Alaric in his place. I was screaming—begging for them to stop—but the blade made contact. My eyes flew open.

"Maliyah! *Maliyah!*" Alaric was hovering over me, his hands tight around my shoulders. My hyperventilations didn't stop when I saw him. He pulled me into a tight hug, but my eyes stayed wide. "It was just a dream. I-I'm here, okay? I'm alright. I'm... I'm here."

As my breathing slowed, he lay back beside me, folded his hands over his face, and exhaled. After just a moment of quiet, I ran my hand down my face. A sudden thought rushed to mind.

"Wait... *do* I talk in my sleep?"

Alaric began to laugh, but he didn't answer until he leaned over to kiss my collarbone. "Only sometimes."

"*What?* Alaric, *why* didn't you tell me—"

"Because then I get to know if your dreams are good."

I covered my face with both of my hands, but Alaric scooped me up in the blankets. I let out a playful yell, and he rolled me over top of him. I could feel the skin of my stomach touching his. My pulse didn't hesitate to quicken.

"I know you've had some pretty good dreams about *me,* right?"

"Maybe that's what you *want* to think."

I was barely finished with my rebuttal when Alaric pulled my face to his. I quickly slid to the side of him as our bodies fought again to get closer. I tried to reach his upper lip, but he pinned me down and kissed me harder. I began to laugh, and he smiled. He smiled against me until he was laughing too. I held my hands around his head as he rose and fell with my chest. Already, my shirt was stretching out. He kissed the skin that was exposed because of it. When there was a knock on the door, he sat straight up, only slowing to clutch his stomach.

"News for the king!"

"Speak!"

"The cruisers have been prepared, sire!"

"What? What's— Do you have the time?"

"Noon, sire."

Alaric theatrically dropped his jaw, then mouthed a slow curse in my direction. I was trying my hardest not to laugh.

"We'll be ready in a moment," he replied. "Prepare my bag."

"Already done, sire."

"Oh... perfect. Um... Inform Clarissa?"

"She's already had breakfast, sire. She requested for us not to disturb you until it was time. Insisted that you needed your rest."

Alaric waved his hands around frantically, and my giggles escaped me.

"Awesome. That is *great.* How are the people?"

"The servants are gathered in the dining room. They joined together in celebration last night."

"And the Royals?"

"They have yet to leave their rooms, sire."

"As expected. Alright, allow me a few minutes, then prepare us a quick meal. And, please, there's no need to address me so formally every time."

"As you wish."

Alaric laughed, but as he spoke, I was too focused on his back to hear. The gashes were already healing, and the nectar was seeping into them, but they still looked so *painful.*

Slowly, I reached my hand out, and I traced one of them.

Alric turned toward me instantly. *"Hey!"*

"Liar. You said you were fine."

"I *am* fine. Just not with your hands all over—"

I rose to my knees and gave him a quick kiss.

213

He smirked at me, then shook his head. *"You* have distracted me *enough* already. Come on, we need to change."

I stood and held out my arms. A few of my buttons had come undone, my shirt was drooping around one shoulder, and I could only imagine what my hair looked like. "What do you mean? I can't go like this?"

"Only if you want me staring the whole trip."

As he made his way to his wardrobe, I felt myself heating up again. I smoothed down my top, regardless of knowing I was about to change out of it. I went to our bathroom, took care of my hair and teeth, and by the time I walked back out, Alaric was already dressed in a fresh pair of black shorts. He found a dark red shirt with short sleeves to throw on with it as I began to look through my own clothes.

"I'm gonna let everyone know the plan, and I'll grab your food to eat on the way, if that's alright with you. We should be there by nightfall, if all goes well. Meet me by the main entrance?"

I nodded, and I saw him look me up and down. I held my arms over myself, but he only smiled.

"Hey, I warned you. I'll see you in five."

I shook my head as he left. My heart was still beating fast, and my head was *screaming* at me:

Maliyah, you are in a load *of trouble.*

After looking through some drawers, I found a short, leathery black skirt with a slit along one side and an orange top that wrapped around one shoulder. It had patterns and accents on it, but either way, the material was the same as my undergarments, and I knew it would resist the water more than some of the other options. I entered the hallway, and a Harpoon saluted at me.

"Where to, m'lady?"

"The main entrance, please."

He nodded, and we were off. This time, I was calm enough to be able to admire the Harpoon's gear. All of them were protected by a thick layer of white, lined with blue and gold. I couldn't imagine how heavy it must have been. Still, each of them walked with immense purpose. It made me realize how long these people were truly the slaves of the Royals.

As we approached the crowd, Alaric was speaking to them. Clarissa stood beside him, listening with her hands folded in front of her. She wore an outfit similar to the day before, but this one was a more salmon-tinted pink. I wondered if it was her favorite color. A part of me hated that I didn't already know.

It wasn't long after that we boarded the cruisers. They were much larger than the motorboat we had first arrived on, even fit with large white sails, and only four were needed to fit us all. By Clarissa's insistent request, they worked together to pull hers onboard, in order for it to arrive home with us by the end.

As the servants passed, I recognized many faces from the crowd. Of the Royals, only a few of the younger ones had actually decided to join us.

On our cruiser, the Harpoons stood tall. Alaric begged them to sit and breathe. While some did, even removing their helmets, most continued to stand guard, their spears and guns remaining at the ready. Alaric held up his finger, then walked away from my view.

"How'd you sleep?" Clarissa asked as soon as he stood.

When I failed to fight a smile, her eyes widened. "Wait. You didn't—"

"No," but I could feel my smile twisting. "It was just... it was a good night."

She raised her eyebrows at me, and I swatted at her hands. "That's all! Nothing else happened!"

Then, Alaric reappeared, a silver tray in his hands. He bowed before me as he uncovered my breakfast. "As promised, m'lady."

"Yeah, *okay,* Maliyah," Clarissa scoffed. "Whatever you say."

I rolled my eyes at them both, but my face was still hot. I was just starting to eat as Alaric sat beside me.

"Alaric, what did she *do* to you? You are *broken!*"

His eyes flicked from her to me. "I suppose it's a... a welcome change." His hand settled comfortably on my leg, just near the end of my skirt. I fought hard not to make another face.

"Clarissa," I tried, "did I mention that dress is really cute on you?"

"Way to change the subject! *I* still think—"

"No, I mean it! Is... is pink your favorite color?"

Her smile softened at my words. "No, but it's my mom's favorite to see me in."

"That's... actually really sweet."

"What's yours?"

"My favorite color?"

Clarissa laughed at my shock. "Yes! I feel like I know everything about you, then I realize I never even asked for your birthday, or your favorite color, or—"

"It's orange." Alaric didn't bother turning to us as he answered, but I could see him fighting his proud smile.

Clarissa scrunched her nose at me, and I nodded slowly. "It's orange."

For most of the ride, we stayed quiet. After about an hour, nausea began to take over, and a Harpoon escorted me to a lower level of the cruiser. With every step, a new thought ran through my head.

What if they poisoned the food? What if there's side effects to the nectar? What if somebody's blade was laced?

As the Harpoon opened the second door, he insisted that my feelings were normal for fast-water travel.

Despite my nerves, it was quiet there, and I didn't hesitate to lie down on one of the many cots that were lined up. It didn't take long for Alaric to come in and check on me.

"I must have left an impression," I teased, barely opening my eyes.

"Must have. How are you feeling?"

"Like I never want to ride a boat again."

We shared a weak laugh, and he sat on the cot beside me. His hand rested on my leg. "Is... Is there anything I can do for you?"

I smiled, but I shook my head. "I think I'm just going to rest for a bit. But let me know if there's anything you need me for, alright?"

He nodded, but I could feel how reluctant he was to move his hand. He sighed and patted my shin awkwardly. "Skirts look... they look good on you."

"Or maybe you just like the way my legs look?"

He swatted at the leg I pointed in front of his face, but he was still smiling when I opened my eyes.

"I'll let you rest."

"Not denying it, though," I sang.

He laughed and patted me again, then I listened to his footsteps retreat. For a moment, he waited at the door, but eventually, it closed behind him, and I let my eyes relax.

"Maliyah?"

"Hmm?"

"It's... We're almost there."

"What?" I felt like I had only just closed my eyes. After I rubbed them, I noticed Alaric standing in front of me. "How?"

He laughed and offered his hand. "How, what? Can you sleep that much? That I can't answer, but... there's less than half an hour left. I thought you might want to join us for the end."

I nodded, and he pulled me to my feet. I looked up at him as he met my eyes. I felt lost in his gaze. He let out a soft laugh, and I quickly turned away.

I hope we never lose this.

Back upstairs, my hand covered my mouth. In the distance, the Lavender Crystalline broke through the haze. The jagged edges of its manufactured gems glistened, all while its soft purple leaves swallowed the dark bark beneath it. Something pulled in my chest looking at it from this far away. I'd always seen it from directly underneath, watching how the bark connected to the giant mass atop it. This way, it seemed much less daunting. Somehow, it felt beautiful. *Magical.*

Things can change.

"Prepare the speaker!" one Harpoon called to another.

"Speaker?"

"We're going to lower it into the water," Alaric explained, "so the sound can travel through. If it works, the Lavenderians should be able to hear me from the air pockets in the Roots."

"That's... pretty handy."

"It's crazy, what some of the people in Cherry came up with. Once we apply it to the *other* Trees..." His voice trailed, but his expression was that of excitement. Just looking at him made me smile.

The closer we got, the more Lavender seemed to loom. The crystals in its top appeared more abundant, and they caught the setting sunlight more than I ever thought they did. I was absolutely awestruck. Maybe there *was* a good reason for the people's prayers.

"I wonder what they're thinking down there," Clarissa mused under her breath. "Just these boats approaching, no explanation in sight... I wonder if they know they're going to be saved."

"No," I quickly corrected. "They think this is the end."

NINETEEN

ON THE CRUISER, ALARIC'S voice was strong, but his volume was low. I could only hope that Cherry's contraption actually worked.

"People of Lavender, this is your king speaking! While it may come as a shock to you, yesterday, what you knew to be the Royal family fell. Favian, Avon, Natasha, and Aaron are all now dead. My name is Alaric, and I was their youngest prince. Despite this, I did not *once* partake in what those Royals stood for. Now that I am king, I am putting into place many changes. No longer will you have to cower in the water, pleading for your lives. With me, I have a team of passionate servants, all of whom had been *stolen* from you. Today, I return them to you, and I call upon you to rejoice! Find your loved ones, feast together, and rekindle what was once lost!

"There is only one thing I must ask of you in return. After you have had your time of reunion, I beg of you to do as they instruct, for I've shared with them great plans for your home. In a few days time, joining you will be the people of Oak. You were told that they were living in pain, but I tell you today that those rumors were just so—rumors—for they have for *years* been living as a prospering community, hidden away from the tyranny. With you, they will share how to construct safer homes, drain the water from your buildings, and flourish once more. Time is not lost among you, and your prayers were not said in vain!"

Throughout Alaric's speech, dozens of heads began to poke from the water, and by the time he was done, dozens more flooded onto the docks. From the boats, the servants cheered and jumped into the water. They joined together with the Lavenderians as fast as they could, hugging, kissing, and crying, while others began to weep just from the anticipation.

While I knew it couldn't be true, a part of me was wishing that everyone would have someone returned to them.

"When are you going to tell them about the Old World...?" Clarissa whispered.

Alaric turned to her, fighting to keep the smile on his face. "One thing at a time."

He turned back to the dock and lifted his device from the water. Now, he yelled into the distance. "Soon, roads will be built, and the three Trees will be connected! People of Lavender, you are not alone!"

Many cheered, but most of the noise was still coming from the cruisers. I could feel the raw emotion evaporating into the air, just to rain on everyone around. More and more of them emerged from the water, and I was sure that, after some time, the entire Branch was there.

You were one of them. You deserve this, too. You can feel what they feel. But I couldn't. Something inside of me felt empty. I found myself slowly backing away from the commotion until I was once again in the isolated interior of our cruiser.

It only took a matter of minutes for Alaric to find me. My breath was uneasy, and tears were rolling down my cheeks. His hands took my arms without hesitation, but I could barely hear his voice through my noise.

"Maliyah, what happened? What's wrong?"

I leaned into him, and he held me. Tight enough to support my weight, but gentle enough to rub my back, over and over, until I was breathing again. I felt like I forgot how to speak.

"You know... this was where I first saw you," he quietly began. "It took me *ages* to swim here. I had to keep stopping at the old Harpoon bases. Once I got to Lavender, though? I watched that dock for *days* on end, just waiting to find *something*. I didn't even know what I was looking for. Then... I saw you."

But you left so fast, I thought.

"I bought the materials to make a small raft before I went back. Two days later, right before I left, there you were again, back on that same dock, praying at that same spot. I shook it off, but you were on my mind for *weeks* after that. You were... you were interrupting my training, and I didn't even know you. That's when I went back. I told myself, if she's still there, you take her home with you. You take her and you train her and you make her a part of your plan. So I got back on my raft, and I paddled. I paddled the entire day, slept a few hours, and I paddled again. And... there you were."

"I miss them," I finally said.

Alaric sighed. "I thought that might be it."

"I-I don't know *why* I thought they might've still been there. But I just... *Watching* everyone here, I... I want to *be* one of them. But I'm just... *not.*"

"You're right. You're not, because you're *more* than that. *You* overthrew the Royals. *You* ended the tyranny. Maliyah... you're amazing."

"I don't want to be anymore." My volume was low. "I... I want to go *home*... I want my mom, and my dad, and my sister, and... and I want *you*. I want to go back to Oak with you, a-and I want to—"

Alaric pulled me into a weak hug.

I exhaled, but I couldn't stop my soft cries. "I'm sorry..."

You're being horrible, Maliyah. Think about the people. Think about the lives *you saved. How are you asking for* more?

"It's not your fault." His voice cut through my hissing brain. "You're right. And... and I do, too. You *changed* me, Maliyah. You made me question if I even wanted to *do* this anymore. But... here we are, and we *won*. This *is* because of you, and if you think I'm going to let you be unhappy after all of it, you're wrong. I-I know there's still a lot of work to do, and I can't just let that go, but none of this is on you. You can have *anything* you desire, alright? You can have your own room—hell, you can have your own *house*—four meals a day, any clothes you want, a—"

"Alaric... I want *you.*"

He stopped and stared at me. His face was blank. "Maliyah..."

"You're the *best* thing that's ever *happened* to me, Alaric. A-and you're the best thing I *have*. I... I don't want to lose you in this..."

His reaction was something I had only ever seen from my sister. Something I hadn't experienced since I was a child. Something so innocent, that made me feel so whole: He took a step back, and he held out his smallest finger.

"You won't. You never, ever will. I'm yours, Maliyah, and I always will be. I promise."

I clasped my pinky around his, and from it, he pulled me into a kiss. His other hand grasped my waist and yanked my body to his. It was like a fight between us, back and forth, stealing the other's air.

But right as we began, the door opened, and Clarissa let out a hard laugh.

"You!" Alaric shouted. His arm was still around me, but I pulled away and turned to her.

"I just wanted to see if Maliyah was okay. But it looks like she's doing *fine,* thank you very much."

"Thanks, Riss. I'm alright now."

"No *kidding!* What the hell are you even *doing?* Is this, like, just until we get home, or is it...?"

As she trailed, I turned to Alaric and smiled. My little finger was still locked in his.

"Why don't you wait and find out?" Alaric challenged. "It's not like we have anyone waiting for us."

"Right... Alright! Yeah, sure. Whatever. *Bye,* you two." She shut the door, and Alaric and I shared a laugh.

"Thank you. I—"

"It's you and me. Always. Alright?"

I nodded, and Alaric gestured with his head toward the door. The sunset had already hit its peak.

"We dock here for the night!" Alaric shouted. "Is there anyone able to supply us with food?"

"Hope you like fish," I muttered, "'cuz that's about all we've got."

"Remind me this place needs some *serious* help."

I chuckled, but soon after, many people were lining up to invite us into their homes. We ducked from Root to Root, answering questions and receiving praise. Whenever someone asked about how we managed to succeed, Alaric held off on the details.

Before long, we were back on the boats, settling down in the cots. Many stayed in Lavender's Roots after dinner, rejoicing with their long-lost families and friends. While they did, the Harpoons spread themselves amongst the cruisers, taking up the spaces that were now left empty.

Plans were made in the morning. Complete plans to redo the entirety of Lavender. We took breaks only to eat, then went right back to work, creating teams to instruct, supply, and construct.

Everyone had a purpose. While some would be working hard for days to come, others would be constantly supporting them with food and drinks. Soon, the Lavenderians were volunteering their homes as entry points. It seemed that everything would be started in only a matter of days. They shared with us a few more baskets of fish, and we began toward Oak, leaving with the promise that we would return in just a few days with dozens of more hands to help.

I continued to sleep through much of the trip. When I was awake, I was either chatting with Clarissa, who was eager to return to her family, or helping Alaric create more plans for Lavender. He wanted to turn it similar in structure to Oak, but still honor the design choices its inhabitants came up with. He was shocked by how many people went along with him without any hesitation. A part of me was, too. I knew everyone was eager for change, but after living in isolation for so long, I didn't expect them to listen to a king's command so quickly.

I wondered what rumors were spreading about us. The thought of it plagued my dreams. Reason told me that no one assumed anything in my regard. *Alaric* was the king, after all. *He* must have been the one to overthrow the crown. Inside, I couldn't decide if I wanted that credit or not.

After another day of travel, Oak was falling into view. I was excited just to touch my bare feet to the bark again. I thought about my room with longing. Meanwhile, Clarissa was talking to some of the Harpoons, her excitement only growing as we got closer.

Cheers and screams erupted before we could even dock. It seemed that everyone was lined up by Oak, as if they'd never moved from when we originally left. I struggled to believe it had only been a few days.

Clarissa's family pushed ahead of everyone else. Clarissa practically jumped from the boat to get to them. They shared a tight hug, all weeping as they sung her praise. A small smile tugged at my lips. As soon as a Harpoon helped me step onto the dock, Oakview was all around me, asking how we did it or how many Royals were left, and I felt swallowed by the sea they were leaving me in.

"Attention!" Alaric finally shouted. Only some of the commotion died down. "Attention, please!" Then, he smiled. It widened as he stood on the edge of the cruiser, throwing his arms into the air. "This is your king speaking!"

The entire crowd screamed, even more violently than before. I felt hands grabbing at me until I was hoisted into the air. Clarissa's father held her on his shoulders. Harpoons in the way were the only reason Alaric was left alone on the boat.

He let them all cheer before interrupting again, but after a short while, he gestured for silence.

"While we are back, the battle is not yet over. Yesterday, we spoke with our brothers and sisters at Lavender. They are suffering there, but I have promised them peace. Peace, as we have had here for years. I beg of you, please, to anyone willing... Gather your belongings, and tomorrow, return with us to Lavender! Those of you that built up Oakview from nothing, help us to save the rest of our people!"

Cheers rang out again, and already, the water was disturbed by divers. As I was set down, my cheeks were hurting from how hard I was smiling.

Despite the hands reaching out to him, Alaric pushed through the crowd and made his way to me. Then, in front of everyone, he pulled me in for a tight kiss. The cheering continued, but my ears were on fire. I began to smile again, and he pulled away. He held up my arm, even when I found myself looking at the floor.

At some point, Alaric dragged me into Oak. The Harpoons waited on the cruisers only after he insisted they didn't have to stand guard at the door. Clarissa and her family made their way to us, still wet-faced and intertwined in each other's embraces.

While they all smiled, Clarissa spoke out. "I want to spend the night with my family before we set back out. I-I'll be back in the morning, though. I won't—"

"Clarissa... why don't you just stay here?"

"What?"

Her family turned to look at her. Who I assumed to be her younger brother took her hand.

Alaric met her eyes as he continued. "I mean... we have a driver now, and we're going to be coming and going a *lot*. Why don't you stay here and help the people who stay behind? You've already assisted us more than I could ever thank you for, and... I don't want to keep you while you have people waiting."

"I mean... are you *sure* you won't need me?"

"If we do, I know we can always come and get you. Besides, the Harpoons have their own means of communicating. Trust me."

I could see her hesitation taking over.

"Please?" a young girl finally asked. "We missed you..."

"Yeah, please?" the little boy copied.

This made her smile. "Alright, I'll stay. But you all have to behave extra good for Momma then, alright?"

Both of them cheered and tackled her in a hug.

"Clarissa... you risked a *lot* by coming with us," Alaric continued, "but... I want to be the first to thank you for doing it. We wouldn't have been *near* successful without you."

She smiled and tipped an imaginary hat. "Now come on, little ones. You have to get to sleep."

"But Momma made cake!"

"Aidyn! You spoiled it!"

"Spoiled what? I didn't hear anything! What'd I miss?" Clarissa flashed us a smile, then waved.

Before she could walk away, I ran over to tackle her in one more hug. "Thank you, Clarissa. For everything. I'll be visiting as soon as I can."

"Me too, babe. Take care of yourself, alright?"

I nodded, and off they went, shuffling together, until they were completely submerged in the water.

"You know," Alaric's voice was tired, yet playful. "The last time we were here, there was something in particular I was *dying* to do."

"Oh, yeah? And why didn't you?"

"I don't know. Maybe I was waiting for a better time."

I tried to hide the smile growing on my face. "I guess... No time like the present?"

"That's what I was thinking." His arm slid around me, and he pulled me to his side. He held me in a deep kiss, and my hands gravitated to his face. I smiled wide, and he dropped his head on my shoulder, swaying with me in our tight hug.

"You saved me," he whispered. "You know that?"

"Alaric..."

"And every time I see you, you do it again." He looked down, pressing one last kiss to my forehead. "I never want to lose you. You mean *everything* to me."

I stayed quiet and took in the peaceful silence. Alaric and I kept swaying, and I drew in a long, deep breath through my nose. Something in the air felt different. Fresher. As if it was just a little easier to breathe.

After I showered, I unpacked everything I was able to retrieve from before we left Cherry. It felt good just to be in my own clothes again.

Tomorrow, I ruled, *I'm packing things for me.*

I decided to sleep in my own bed, but I smiled when Alaric knocked on the frame of my door. Without a word, I moved over, and he slid in beside me. His arms around me made me feel whole. I fell asleep in no time, and I slept more soundly than I had in days.

By the time morning came, I didn't want to move. I curled closer into Alaric, my only thoughts yearning for him to keep holding me.

As I moved, he sighed. He squeezed me just a little tighter before he tried to get up. I weakly reached for his arm, but he winced in his movement.

"I need more nectar. I left some in my bag, but—"

"Let me grab it for you. Is it in your room?"

"I-It's okay, I can—"

"How do you feel?"

"Better. A lot better. Probably just one more day of the stuff. And..." He laughed. "It felt nice to sleep here again."

I sighed and slid out of my bed. As I made my way to Alaric's room, I could feel my grogginess creeping up on me. *Can't we just stay here...?*

I stopped as I grabbed his bag. On the dresser beside his bed sat his sister's shell. I took a few strips of nectar in one hand and the necklace in the other. The chain was cold against my skin.

"Hey, you... you forgot this." It felt weird to say, especially as I held the seemingly sacred item out in front of me.

"Oh... Thanks." He ran his finger along the surface of the pink shell, tracing over the two darker divots in the middle. I could tell thoughts were speeding through his mind. I set it on the bed and began to pull apart the nectar strips. Once the sticky substance clung to my fingers, I began to rub it into his wounds.

They were much thinner now, but I wondered how much lighter each line would get. He arched his back as I got lower and lower, finally resting on where the first spearhead had entered. It amazed me that he was able to keep fighting through something like that.

"Keep it."

"What?"

Alaric turned around, still holding the shell in his hand. "I want you to keep it."

"Alaric, no. That's—"

"A reminder. It's... it's a reminder of my goals. And right now, my biggest goal is to keep you safe and with me."

My mouth hung open, but before any more words could escape, Alaric was behind me, moving my hair to the side.

A sudden thought rushed to mind. "Maybe... Do you think Clarissa would want it...?"

He paused. Just before he could clip it around my neck. He stayed frozen long enough for me to continue.

"I just... I never knew her, and it seems like she meant a lot to her. Plus, she never really got to—"

"Yes." In a single motion, he retreated and slid it into his pocket. We sat in silence for just another moment.

Soon after, without sharing a word, he stood up and left the room. I sighed and began to pack my things back up. This time, just as I had promised myself, I brought a bag packed in perfect accordance to my own desires. I filled it with comfortable clothes, my shampoo and conditioner, my favorite snacks, and the like.

I took my time preparing myself and my personal items, but right before I left my room, something caught my eye—Celia was still sitting on my dresser. I reached for her, but I hesitated. My hand hovered over her surface, as if it was teasing me. After staring for a second too long, I sighed, sheathed it, and threw it into my bag.

On the dock, families were back to hugging and cheering. Already, Alaric had found Clarissa. I rapidly approached them, just in time to see her wrap him in a hug. Tears were pouring from her eyes, and she squeezed him tight.

"This means *everything* to me," she sobbed. "Thank you—*thank* you!"

"You should thank Maliyah," he calmly replied. "It was her idea first."

She turned to me and tried to wipe her face, but it was impossible for her to stop her tears. She ran to me, and I braced myself for the lofty impact. As I squeezed her, it felt like the noise around me stopped. I smiled, and she drew back to look at me. She nodded a few times, clutching the shell tight in her hand. I watched as she held it to her lips, whispering something small, before finally letting it fall near her chest.

"It suits you," Alaric was quick to say.

She smiled big and ran back to him for one last hug. "Safe travels, you two. Come back soon, alright?"

We nodded, and I turned around. As I took another step toward the water, I heard her final call: "And don't do anything too crazy without me!"

Ahead of us, Oakview was loading materials onto one of the cruisers. All in a line, the whole town seemed to be working together to carry items from below the surface. They dove in and out of the water, barely stopping to take a breath. The sight alone left me in awe.

"Maliyah?" Alaric's voice cut through it all. I whipped around, and he was holding two small boxes in his hands.

"What's—"

"I had this planned for... before we left, but..." He sighed before he continued. "It's something to remember our time together. I already told Clarissa about it, I just—"

I reached over and impatiently opened the boxes. Inside each, a new shell and chain rested comfortably. One was a dusty red, and the other a faint orange.

"*Oh* my— Alaric... When did— *How*—?"

"I planned to keep Alana's, but... you're right. I think Clarissa deserves it. And... and—"

"Alaric..." I grabbed the orange one before my thoughts could fully filter. It was thinner and pointier than the others, curving around itself as if something could have once lived inside. "It's perfect."

He set down the boxes and picked up his own. It was curved, going from a round shape to a pointed one, and dotted in tiny white speckles. As he slid it on, a sad smile crossed his face. I almost missed his final remark.

"I asked Smithy to make the chains."

Before I could comment further, a Harpoon made his way to the side of us. "The first cruiser is ready, sire. Shall we begin to board the passengers?"

Alaric turned to me, and I nodded. The Harpoon copied my movement, then turned to the nearest group of people.

We found Clarissa for one last hug before we left. We laughed as her siblings, and eventually, even her parents, joined in. After we finally backed up, she pointed at us and gasped. "Those look *perfect* on you!"

I smiled, but my eyes were set above her chest. Regardless of what she said, her hands seldom left her new, pink shell.

It was strange to see it away from Alaric, but I was proud to see her wear it. After everything, the visualization seemed perfect.

TWENTY

It took half an hour for everyone who was joining us to board the cruisers. Space was more cramped, as nearly all of the Harpoons had to fit in the same one as us, but as soon as I retreated to the lower levels, I could breathe with ease. Alaric sat with me for most of the trip, and my hand rested comfortably over the one he set on my thigh. I thought about what Lavender could become. As hard as I tried, it was always difficult to visualize.

I leaned against Alaric and tried to tune out the rest. When the Harpoons came in and out, I closed my eyes. Inside, I was still at Oak. Going back filled me with an insatiable longing, clawing at my heart and begging for me to cave. I stayed quiet, even when Alaric tried to chat with me. The only replies I could manage were short nods. Already, I was beginning to miss Clarissa.

After the first hour, I stood up and stretched. I was tempted to try to sleep, but it felt like the only thing I'd done over the past few days. Here and there, I took bites of food and went back to the upper deck. Eventually, I pushed past some Harpoons and forced my way to the end of the cruiser. There, I looked back at the three that were following us. The people were still singing and dancing, holding each other, and proudly reminiscing about Oakview. They were far enough away for their words to be lost, but their every movement was clear—whoever came with us was *proud* of what they were doing.

A hand wrapped itself around my waist, and I turned around. Alaric squeezed me against him as soon as I did. "How're you feeling?"

"Like I never want to ride a boat again," I muttered.

He chuckled, then sighed. "I know. Hopefully, soon, you won't have to."

"How're you planning to do this, though? We can't *walk* the whole way, and—"

"We'll figure something out. The people from Oakview have already started running ideas by me. We're going to try *everything*. All we need first are the roads. Once those are there, whoever wants to can start building their houses along them. Spread themselves out, you know? Then there won't be such a journey between each place, anyways, if there's—"

"Do you think there are still people outside Watertowne?" I wasn't sure where my question came from, but it made Alaric freeze.

"I... I don't know, but... after construction has taken off, I want to tell everyone what we saw. I want to send a search party out."

"Wait... *Send* a party, or go *with* them?" I took a step back as soon as I felt him tense. "Alaric—"

"I *have* to. I know how to travel best, and Smithy taught me how to keep direction. I know we can—"

"No. No, you can't! We *just* took over Cherry. The people still need you here, Alaric! *I* still need you here! How is construction supposed to—"

"Oakview is capable of handling it. I've seen them do it before, and I *know* they can do it again. Maliyah—"

"I can't *believe* you're not considering— Do you even know what's *out* there?!"

"Maliy—"

"No! *None* of us do! The only *one* of us with any sensible clue was *Smithy,* and now he's *dead!*"

Alaric's mouth opened and closed. He bobbed his fist at his side, then, without another word, turned and walked through the Harpoons. All of them were staring at me.

For a while, I clutched the side of the cruiser and stared into the water. Eventually, I lost my stomach to it. I stood, and I waited, but Alaric never came back.

I was mad. I was so mad that I didn't want to find him. I knew the reasons for why he had made such a plan, but everything was moving *way* too fast. After Cherry, I thought we could rest again. One way or another. And now, here was Alaric, planning to venture into the *complete* unknown. Thoughts were spiraling through my head.

What if the war *was* still going on, and we were just in a forgotten area? Wasn't that the plan for the flood in the first place? We *saw* what was left! Who *knows* what kind of weapons they had, with the ability to decimate an entire visual range? What if there *were* no people left?

Suddenly, the sky was changing, and the clouds were moving faster. Before I knew it, the Harpoons were escorting me onto the dock.

I couldn't hear a thing as I helped the people of Oakview move materials off of the cruiser. The Lavenderians gladly took them off my hands, but their gracious words were muffled by my hot, ringing ears. All around me, Oakview was gawking at the barren wasteland that was Lavender. I saw their struggle to keep positive as they introduced themselves.

Where's Alaric?

I found myself craving his touch, but bitterness burned inside my chest. Without him, I felt like a lost little girl, trapped within the sweltering sea of people. I was sure someone would trample me.

We finished unloading the materials from the cruiser, and Watertowne began handing out resources to one another. As soon as I wasn't needed, I turned back to the boats. Only a few Harpoons were left on one of them. Already, they'd spread themselves out, and they were offering their services in any ways they could. Slowly, my legs carried me back to our cruiser. I opened the door and went down the stairs. Silence followed me.

"Alaric...?"

There was no sound in return. I poked my head around the corner. I was completely alone.

I could feel my chest tighten instantly. The air itself felt as if it was closing in on me. I ran back to the upper deck and pushed past any Harpoons, even when they tried to call out to me. I looked around, and without thinking, I stripped off my top layer and jumped into the water.

Many people passed me as I swam. Some clutched planks of wood under their arms, and others held their meals tightly encased in glass containers. A few even waved at me as I passed, but my vision was narrow. I kicked my feet until I was entangled in the

Roots of Lavender. In one of the many nooks, I found what was once my home.

As soon as I yanked on the door, I was ushered forward by the rapid water. The front room was always encased by it. I trudged through, shivering, until I stepped over a stray root and reached my sad excuse for a hallway. There, the Roots opened up to each other, leading to the kitchen, what was once my parents' room, and my room.

Everything was damp, and I felt oddly claustrophobic. It seemed that every inhalation was filled with moist air. I found the few cushions that I had left behind, and I pushed them back together with my feet. I threw myself down and pulled my knees to my chest. Already, it felt like my lungs were coated in water droplets.

I grabbed my pillow and clasped it to my chest. My eyes squeezed shut as I tried to listen, but the only thing to hear was the water leaking into the front room.

I'm alone, I'm alone, I'm alone. I sucked in a long, troubled breath. I could practically feel Alaric's hand on my back, and I wanted to jump back into his arms. Alas, I sat back up. I knew he wasn't coming. *How could he?*

I sighed and began to walk around.

I thought about when my sister and I shared this room. It was so cramped that, sometimes, we would push our cushions together to make a padded surface over the whole floor, then fall asleep in the same space. In the morning, my hair would be a scraggly, damp mess. I don't think I brushed it a single time. If I was ever going to, Leilani did it for me. I remembered wincing and yelling, and sometimes even turning back to hit her a few times. She would always laugh at me, then pull just a little harder.

"Mom, she's hurting me!" I yelled.

"Honey, she's just trying to help. Why don't you girls go out as-is?"

I stuck my tongue out at her, as if I'd won something. She rolled her eyes and pulled me out the door.

I would always go with her, even if it was for something as simple as picking up groceries. By carrying one item, I thought I was helping just as much as she was. At that age, I had no concept of money, time, or anything like it. All I knew was that life was normal.

In my parents' room, there were times I would sneak into their bed. Unlike us, they actually owned a small mattress. After being sent to sleep, I would climb into it and giggle under the blankets. I know now that it must have been obvious, but my parents humored me either way.

My dad climbed in and reached his arm across me to get to my mom. "Hon, it's awfully roomy in here... Why don't you scoot a little closer?"

I laughed as she moved in. "You're squishing me!"

"What? Did you hear something?"

"Daddy, it's me!" I popped out of the sheets, and he grabbed me to tickle my stomach and legs.

"Maliyah? What are *you* doing in here? I thought you went to bed!"

"Can I sleep with you tonight? Pretty please?"

He would laugh before looking to my mother, who always had a smile on her face as she shook her head. "But what about Leilani, honey? Won't she be lonely?"

"She can come, too! Leilei, come here!"

I smiled sadly as I stood back up. Everything seemed so vivid—I couldn't believe it had been so long.

I traced the dust-coated furniture back to the hallway, and I entered the kitchen. Anything left was already beyond rotten. I was afraid to open the broken refrigerator.

I used to complain about food a lot. My parents always told me to be grateful for what we had, that we could have lived in Oak. I scoffed at the thought. *If only we had gone to Oak, we would all still be together.*

I paused. *I did go to Oak.* I looked to the side as my thoughts began to shift. *This was where I first saw you.*

When I first saw Alaric, I was *sure* I was going to die. I thought I would finally get to know if my mother was right about what came next. Instead, it led to my first conversation. My first walk in a park. *My first kiss.*

My hand went to my lips. It was a strange realization, when I thought about it as an isolated event. At the time, it had felt so desperate. Insisting on being a goodbye, while refusing the idea altogether. I started to rewind. I thought of all the moments that led up to it. I thought about how far away Clarissa was. I thought about trying to fix Alaric's broken hands. I thought about fighting with him while he was trying to save my life.

I was shot by a Harpoon. The thought had never fully settled with me. I don't think I even *understood* it at the time. It seemed so distant—so foreign—so *impossible.* I couldn't fully picture Alaric's panic. I knew now that it must have been exactly what he was doing. The entire time, rowing back to Oak, a bleeding stranger in his arms.

And he never let me go. He never let me drown. He never let me die.

He tried to act so collected as soon as I was awake, but he broke so fast. I wondered if he ever wanted me to see that side of him. I wondered if I was meant to.

That was the first time we truly spoke. Barely clothed, away from home, and exposed to raw wounds. And still, I trusted him. I trusted him when there was nothing else to trust. And now, I was back where I started: barely clothed, away from home, and exposed to raw wounds. But this time, I didn't have Alaric to teach me how to walk.

I bent down into the pool of water at my feet, and I splashed myself in the face. I took a deep breath, then dunked it completely in. I shook my head, and I splashed it again and again.

"Wake *up*, Maliyah!" I screamed at myself. "What the *hell* are you doing?"

I slammed my fist against the counter, and I ran for the front door. I threw it open, somehow managing to forget how the water attacked. I stumbled back, but I didn't let it stop me. I jumped through, slammed the door shut behind me, and swam. I only looked back once. Once, as everyone else passed me. I closed my eyes, and a single thought ran through my mind: *Goodbye, Leilani.*

Just swimming by everyone, it was easy to see their glowing dedication. As they tampered with the Roots, the first thing they did was create more air pockets for themselves. Ducking in and out of them, they worked with ease. Something inside me clicked as I looked from person to person, for I realized it was easier for me to recognize those from Oak. It was funny to see them underwater.

As I climbed back onto the dock, Harpoons grabbed my arms. I whipped around, embalmed in sudden terror. "What? What's happening?"

A million thoughts sped through my head at once. *Alaric betrayed me. He sent them to come get me. He wants to reconcile. They killed him. They came to kill me. They're killing us. Something's wrong.*

"Lady Maliyah, we've been searching for you. King Alaric is on a cruiser heading back to Cherry. We've gotten word that the Royals are planning a mutiny."

"*What?* Who went with him?!"

"Only a handful of Harpoons, m'lady. He requested that many of us stay at Oak, and now here. Above all else, he demanded for your safety."

"Get another boat ready! We need to catch up!" I stepped forward, but another Harpoon stopped me.

"Please be aware that only some can accompany you, if we are to follow the king's orders correctly."

"I don't care! I— We need to go, *now!*"

They shared a look with each other, but I was already running for an empty cruiser. I picked the smallest of the three, and soon after, a few Harpoons joined me.

"Did he tell anyone where he was going? Do the Lavenderians—"

"He said he would be returning shortly with more help."

"*Holy—* Drive, *drive!*"

The motors revved, and the sails were dropped. I held myself tight. I wanted to say so many things, but at the same time, none at all. I muttered under my breath, but I didn't even know what was coming out.

Everything around me seemed to stop. Harpoons tried again and again to kneel by my side and offer me comfort or assistance, but again and again all I could hear were my deafening thoughts.

He left without you because you weren't there for him. The only one who was *there for him was Smithy, and now he's gone. He's gone, and you brought it up just when Alaric was looking for a friend. He's gone. He's gone. Smithy is gone.*

"Lady Maliyah."

The voice cut through me. I was sobbing, holding myself, rocking gently to and fro. My throat and lips were dry. I was muttering, and everyone could see it.

"He's gone. He's gone—"

"Lady Maliyah, please. Is there anything we can do to—"

"Just *leave me alone!*" I felt like a child as I sprinted to the lower deck. I pressed my hands tightly over my face, and I threw myself onto the nearest cot. I knew that no one was coming to get me after that.

TWENTY-ONE

I WASN'T SURE HOW much time passed before I moved. My face was numb and wet, and my body was shaking from how hard I was holding it. It could have been hours just as likely as it could have been minutes. Either way, I was completely alone for the entirety of the time.

Eventually, my mind started to work again. I began to see pictures, none of them having crossed my eyes before. A part of me preferred the silence.

I saw Alaric trying to talk sense into the Royals. He was giving one of his big speeches again, but this time, no one was listening. They just jutted their spears into the air, yelling and shouting at him to leave. Then, someone fired one of the Harpoon's guns. It hit him right in the chest, and he fell to the ground. People cheered and swarmed his lifeless body. I felt my heart slam against my chest. I wanted to scream. I squeezed my eyes as hard as I could before I even tried to open them again, but now, I could barely keep them that way. Images were continually flashing before me, taking over my very existence. I fought to focus on something else.

What was the last thing you said to him? I thought about my old place in the Roots, and I had to remind myself that he wasn't there.

I want to show him one day. I want him to know where I used to live. How my life was before him. I want him to know what he took me from.

I continued to travel back. Then, I froze. A shiver spread through my entire body.

The only one of us with any sensible clue was Smithy, and now he's dead!

How could I have *said* something like that? I let out a disgusted noise as I replayed the scene in my brain. What made it worse was that he didn't say a word in return. He just turned and walked away.

I made him leave. Over something that *I* brought up. Something that hadn't even happened yet. And now, something that might not happen at all.

I closed my eyes and tried to piece together the information that I had. Smithy was a Harpoon, and he ended up assigned to Oak, where Alaric was meant to rule. Alana went with him in secrecy, and at some point, she befriended Clarissa. Alaric worked from the inside. Then, they made the plan. Alana started the takeover, but left before it was finished. She was going *straight* to Cherry while the Harpoons were distracted by the situation at Oak, carried out by Alaric. Smithy joined him, taking out his colleagues from an unexpected angle.

I was starting to see the scene in my mind. The more the Harpoons fell, the more the citizens of Watertowne joined in. I've seen how they could rally together with my own eyes. Of *course* they were able to win the fight.

Then, there was the aftermath. About the Harpoon's families. Clearly, the takeover was never relayed back to Cherry. If that was the case, they would have been invaded. They must have simply assumed that the conditions there were so bad that the people weren't worth watching, or something like that. But that was the same time Alana arrived at Cherry.

I couldn't understand why she went alone. Maybe there wasn't as much security before she arrived. Either way, did they really not suspect she came from Oak? Based on what Alaric said, they must have. Why else would they punish the families from there, specifically? That raises the question, why wouldn't they have come back for Alaric? Was he really not perceived as a threat?

His father's words seeped through my memories. *"Not you. Not my precious boy."*

My head was spinning. Maybe they thought he went to Lavender, seeing as his brother never tried to occupy the space. After all, he *was* able to freely cross the waters between Trees without getting shot at.

I was shot at. The thought kept creeping back. I, a complete nothing, was shot by the pulse of a Harpoon's gun. And I'm still here.

I bit my lip. I started remembering Alaric's topless form as I woke up in what would become my bedroom. I wondered if he used his shirt to suppress my bleeding while he paddled back. I wondered if he tried to push the water from my lungs. I wondered if he ever pressed his lips to mine, breathed his air into me, in a desperate attempt to keep me from leaving him.

Me, one of countless girls from the broken Roots of Lavender. Me, the smallest glimpse of hope for the prince. The prince that ruined his family tree. The prince that lived alone for years.

He wasn't alone. He had Smithy. Again, I went back to Smithy. Trying—*searching*—to find what was left of him. I wondered if Alaric kept his eyes open. I wondered if he watched his body drop to the floor.

My heart stopped. There *was* something I hadn't thought of. *I wonder if he blames himself.*

Disgust settled on me like the emptiness of the room. Smithy was the only one there for him for *years*. He was one of the only people who felt what he felt, and he was the only one who Alaric could *go* to about it. They had each other, and that *was* all they had.

Smithy wanted to train us, but only to ensure our safety. Before me, he didn't want any part of this. He wanted to be done with all of it nearly as much as he wanted all of it to be done. And yet, in his final breath, he *still* tried to encourage Alaric.

Why didn't he fight? The anger bubbled inside of me, but not for the question. It was because I already knew the answer.

They would have killed us if he did. He did it for *us*. He did it so we could make it out of there. I realized then that it was the only real reason he went at all. If he didn't, we would have ended up just like Alana.

And again, there was me. Me, who could throw his name right back in Alaric's face. And now, Alaric was going back there *alone*. Alone, to the place his family was slaughtered. Alone, to the place his world fell apart. Without his friends, without guidance, without *me. Just* like Alana. And it was my own damned fault.

"Lady Maliyah...?" There was hesitance in the Harpoon's voice. He sounded younger than the rest of them. When I didn't answer, he stammered through a continuation. "I-I just thought... did you perhaps want something to eat? It may help with your seasickness. It's just— It's nothing big, just some leftover scraps of—"

"Are you new?"

He froze in his tracks. I could barely believe I was questioning him so directly.

"I beg your—"

"How long have you been a Harpoon? Can you— I'm sorry, can you take off your helmet?"

He seemed to hesitate, but soon after, he removed his head-gear. He had a short, neat layer of dark brown hair to match his dark eyes. The tone of his face was somewhere between mine and Clarissa's. My heart fell—he couldn't have been too many years older than me.

"Forgive me, m'lady. I— King Alaric hired me just before we left Cherry. I-I was a servant of Prince Aaron, and I begged to be of service once more. My training is slim, but I know your cause is greater than any of the Royals before you."

"What's your name?"

"Naseem, m'lady."

"When... Were you born in Lavender?"

"No, but my mother lived there. They took her twenty-two years ago—one of the first to ever be taken—and I was born only two years after."

"Are there... are there many people your age still here...?"

"I'm afraid not. A few, yes, but... not many made it past their adolescent years."

"Why?"

"Because the Royals are *sick,* and everyone but them knows it." He sighed and tossed his helmet to the side. "I'm sorry for the informalities, I just—"

"Please, don't worry about it. I... I could use someone to talk to right about now, anyways."

He allowed a smile and took a seat on the cot across from me. I tried my hardest to smile back, but I couldn't bring myself to fully form one.

"Many of us servants saw you and Alaric break into the upper floors. We tried for as long as we could to keep the Royals from noticing. A few of us... a few of us paid with our lives."

I thought about the speech Alaric gave to the Royals before we left. About the servant that was killed as he spoke. He didn't even flinch. I was finally starting to understand how it was possible.

"Did you always work for the Royals?"

"My mother kept me hidden at first. She... wasn't sure which of them I belonged to. That was how it always was with any children. They just... *were,* and then they weren't. When I was old enough to understand basic instructions, then yes, I was old enough to work. If we could walk, we could blend in. If we could blend in... maybe we could survive."

"Your mother, is she—"

"Killed." A sad smile crossed his face. "Three years ago. I... I don't even remember why."

I dropped my head, but already, a new thought sprung to my mind. "There were a lot of people on the upper floors, with food and music. Was something going on? Is that why Alaric—?"

"Every day is like that for them. They sing, they eat, and they *breed.* They just— They *take* whatever they want, *whenever* they want it, and they dispose of any remnants from the day, just to repeat it the next. It's... hideous."

I couldn't reply. My head was already somewhere else. I was begging myself to let it go, to move on from the idea, but I couldn't help myself. I needed to know the answer.

"You said you worked for... for *Aaron*. He— Did he ever mention anyone named Leilani...?"

Naseem dropped his head. His fingers folded together as he let out a long, deep sigh. "I... I was wondering if..." He looked up with another sad smile. One that seemed even sadder than the one he held for his mother. "You *are* that Maliyah."

"Was it Aaron? Who talked about me, who—"

"Leilani did."

I felt my heart slam against my chest. At this point, all I wanted to do was forget her, but she was haunting me like some unobtainable ghost.

"Leilani... She wasn't like the other servants. She ate with the Royals, dressed like them... Aaron kept her pampered, as if she *was* one of them. No servant could speak to her, but often did we listen. She... was one of the rare ones. The ones who tricked the rest into thinking they had a chance for something better. Only those of us that worked directly for Aaron knew that it was... it was actually something much, much worse."

"And... she talked about me...?"

"Whenever she could. Aaron's hands would find her shoulders, and he would whisper for her to tell him a story. So she closed her eyes and rattled off every detail she could think of, remembering you and your parents. I think... I think there were times it was the only thing keeping her with us."

A bitter taste rose to my lips. I couldn't make out the expression on his face.

"Tell me about her."

"She was kind, and she was helpful. Even when she was stuck. She tried to make it easier for us, and everyone *prayed* it would be her they were assigned to serve. Alas... there was seldom a moment she wasn't with Aaron. They bathed together, slept together, dressed together... We all knew it was only a matter of time before she broke."

With every new word he spoke, I wanted to retreat into my skin. A shiver ran down my back, and it spread across me like an iced hand, gripping me to my very core. I imagined Aaron's face, heard his conniving voice. He was so *confident* in himself, in his ability, in his *life.* I wanted to watch Desiderium run through him all over again.

"I'm very sorry... Please, if there is any other information I could provide you—"

"Were you there?" I straightened through the shivers and dug my eyes into Naseem's every secret. "When he died, were you there?"

"I was in charge of tending to his wounds, along with two others."

"Did you?"

He tried to take his eyes away from me, but I knew I had him.

"There was so much chaos, and with the Harpoons stationed at the outer rooms, we really couldn't—"

"Did you *let* him die?" My words were sharp. It gave me a satisfaction I didn't know I needed.

"Yes." He took a deep breath before he finally looked away. "I... One of the eldest servants took the blame. She said she faked the nectar applications, that his life was in fate's hands now. She... she was smiling as they shot her down."

I leaned against my small pillow. It felt like something had been lifted off of my soul. My next words spilled from my mouth like a drink that couldn't be caught.

"Alaric didn't kill the Royals. *I* did."

"But Aaron—"

"Alaric killed Aaron, but I... *I* killed the rest."

"Natasha...?"

"Avon."

Naseem changed the way he was sitting. I could tell the idea didn't rest right with him. The silence lingered for only a moment.

"Does the name John Feeney mean anything to you?"

"It... it sounds familiar, but—"

"He was killed protecting us against Favian, but he was a Harpoon before he trained us. Alaric, Alana, and I. Alana... She was the reason Alaric started all this."

"Alana... I haven't heard that name in *years.*"

"Well, get used to it, 'cuz she was a *huge* part of this."

"Isn't she... Isn't she dead?"

"What do you know about the Royal family?"

"As in...?"

"Their lineage."

"Oh." He stopped and looked at me, then returned to fiddling with his fingers. "I know it's not... *right,* but... I don't know the details."

"What are your thoughts on Alaric?"

"The king?"

"Yes, the king."

"He... he's my king, and I am proud to call him such."

"Why?"

"Why? I don't quite—"

"Because... he's a *Royal?*"

Naseem paused again. He threw a confused look in my direction.

I continued my thought. "Do you take pride in calling him king for your own reasons, or do you take pride in calling him king because it's all you know?"

"What I know is that Favian was *not* a king. He was an evil man with a lot of power. Alaric... *Alaric* is a *king.*"

I began to nod, and Naseem squinted at me. I could visibly see him thinking something over.

"And King Alaric... What is he to *you?*"

"You know what, Naseem? I would *love* something to eat."

By the time Naseem returned, another Harpoon had entered the lower deck. He was sifting through a bag that was left on one of the cots, but he kept looking in my direction. I tried to ignore it, but I kept my guard high until Naseem was back. He offered me a small plate of cheese and crackers. I crossed my legs and set it down on top of them. Naseem stared at the other Harpoon until he finally nodded once and left.

"They scare me," he said without missing a beat.

"The Harpoons?"

"Yes. I-I can't trust them. Not after all they've done." He turned his head and reached for the plate, but he drew back almost instantly. "Forgive me. I... I wasn't thinking."

"No, please. Help yourself."

"Are you certain?"

"Of course."

Slowly, he reached for a broken cracker. He didn't take his eyes off of me as he lifted it to his lips. "It's just... I feel like I'm speaking less to a Royal and more to another servant. A-and I mean that in the *best* way possible."

"It would make sense, considering I'm *not* a Royal."

"I heard King Alaric's speech. Is it true that you're from Lavender...?"

I nodded, and he widened his eyes. "What's it like, living there? Knowing that every day could be your last?"

"You stop caring after a while. You just... start waiting for the day to come, instead. No one knows where you go after you disappear. No one knows it's *Cherry.*"

"It's not anymore, thanks to you. And... the Lavenderians seem very welcome to the change. I was certainly expecting some questioning and reluctance."

"I was, too. It... It's almost too good to be true, but I guess *anything* is better than what they had. I don't know... I didn't consider that the reluctance would be coming from the *Royals.*"

"We servants did. It was... We tried to adapt to the new lifestyle immediately. Many of us... The night after Alaric's speech, we... The Royals didn't take it very well, and we were eager to help Alaric. We just... didn't share that it was for our own, selfish reasons."

"Wanting to live isn't selfish. I wish one of you had *told* us! We might've been able to—"

"With all due respect, this is all *very* new to us, Lady Maliyah. Many of us barely trust *Alaric,* especially after he was *gone* for so long. Most of us doubted he was even still *alive.* It's... it's strange."

"What do you think they're doing there? At Cherry?"

"I know that any servants who stayed behind are already gone. I know that... I know that they're going to try to forcefully over-throw Alaric. But I don't know how it will start or end."

"How many of them are there?"

"It's *all* of them. *Nobody* wants—"

"Naseem," I said again. "How many?"

"Maybe... maybe four hundred."

My eyes shot open. I was shocked by the amount of people in *Oak,* and I was sure there were less than *two* hundred there.

"But—"

"On the upper floors, there are halls and halls of bedrooms. A wing is set aside for each family, and the families... Despite when they intertwine, there are many of them, most of them grown at this point. It was the original Royals, like Favian, who set up this entire system, and... and they *spread.*"

"How was Favian in control for so long if there were so many who could have challenged him? There *had* to have been—"

"Nobody *cared,* Lady Maliyah. They were all happy, all living the ideal life... Why would they want the extra work of *organizing* the events, when they could simply reap their benefits?"

"You're telling me there's *four* hundred Royals living in Cher-ry?"

"It's... it's an estimate. In certain occasions, like Leilani's, it's hard to distinguish the Royals from the servants. But, yes. Laven-der... They needed Lavender for a reason."

I leaned back against my pillow. Lavender always seemed so small to me. Everyone knew each other, but nobody dared *know* each other. After seeing so many of them return home, even after knowing how many of them were lost to the Royals, it never felt like they were so *big.*

"But during Alaric's speech—"

"Many were in the rooms next to yours. Even in Cherry, they still separate the great from the good."

"And... and *all* of them want to overthrow Alaric."

"I'm afraid so."

"Why did you let him go back, then?! *Why* did you—"

"It was by his own wishes, m'lady. The Harpoons insisted, but they can't go against their king. It's... it's not in their nature."

"How many Harpoons were left at Cherry?"

"A few dozen, I'm sure. But... I'm *not* so sure if *all* of them will support him."

"But I thought they had to! You *just said*—"

"All they knew was Favian. For all they're concerned, he *killed* Favian."

"But in his room, before he died— They *let* him die, they *let* us kill him!"

"Confusion rises in a dire moment, m'lady. And... it's usually those who know you best who will betray you in the end."

"No, that's... that's not true! It *can't*—"

"It is with the Royals. It always has been. All of Aaron's servants *despised* him. I know that at least *some* of Favian's Harpoons had their minds left. From the very beginning, they were trained to do only one thing, and they were *broken* when they didn't obey. It's what made some of them stronger in other ways, like their hatred and their will. And... those were the ones who helped you."

"Like... like Smithy..."

"I-I apologize, but—"

"John. John Feeney. The— Geez..." I let out a loose breath. "So you think... you think the lower-level Harpoons will go against us?"

"The ones who fought against your entrance but failed to kill you at the door. The ones who lived beside their fallen companions. The ones who are assigned to protect the smaller Royal families... who will *demand* they fight against you."

"But... but we have more Harpoons, right? We—"

"I won't lie to you, Lady Maliyah... I don't know how many will be left by the time we get there."

"What? Why?"

"As soon as Alaric left, they had time to build outrage and time to plan. *And* they had their own Harpoons. If you don't think a Harpoon is capable of killing another... I suppose you missed the message from your fallen friend."

Not long after, I asked Naseem for some more time to think. I felt my panic resurging, but I managed to thank him for the food and information. He returned to the upper level, and I finally felt okay enough to rise to my feet. I stretched, but fear was coating my body in numbness.

What if Alaric is already dead?

The boat ride felt agonizingly long. A part of me wished I had just chosen to sleep again.

What if they set a trap? What if they ambushed him? What if the Harpoons turned on him before he even got there? I shook my head and made myself pace. I decided to climb the stairs, and as I did, a Harpoon moved to the side. I felt distrust settle deep in my bones.

They're not gonna hurt you, I tried to convince myself. *If they were, you'd already be dead.*

I doubled back and ran for my bag. I ripped through it until I found my sheath. I slid the leather back up to my thigh, strapped the pouch onto it, and slid Celia in. I felt heavier, as if my right leg was being held down. I tried to shake the feeling by stretching some more.

"Lady Maliyah," I finally heard. My hand flew to my leg instinctively. "We're nearly there."

As I approached the upper floor, I heard a Harpoon talking desperately into a small device. My eyebrows tightened as soon as I made out what he was saying.

"...an update! Can anyone hear me? Hello?"

"What's going on?"

"Lady Maliyah, forgive him, he just—"

"Is *anybody* still there?"

"What's—"

As Naseem burst through the door, my jaw dropped. My legs were carrying me faster than I was able to register what was happening. In the distance, the Great Cherry stood tall, but even through the haze of what we still needed to travel, I could see the introduction of a desperate new color.

Above the delicate, pink blossoms, a giant cloud of smoke was rising steadily above the Tree.

TWENTY-TWO

EVERY NEW WORD THAT came to me tasted bitter. My knuckles were stained white from how hard I was clutching the railing of the cruiser. Naseem was at my side, his mouth stuck open. Behind us, the Harpoon was still screaming into his device, but the only noise being sent back was one of static and popping.

"We have to go faster," I tried under my breath. "There *has* to be a way to—"

"We're already going at maximum speed. Any faster, and we'll be unable to stop once we arrive."

"How long will this take?! We *have* to—"

"Oak has been informed, and Lavender is getting the word now. Still no response from Cherry."

"Cherry! Cherry, do you *copy?"*

"How did this *happen?"* Naseem yelled. *"How* did this—"

"I *can't* get word from *Cherry!"*

"Can we call for backup?"

"Backup won't arrive in time! There's no *way* we can—"

"Get a team on collecting the blossoms. We *need* to preserve—"

"We don't *have* a team!"

The sudden silence slammed into us. My eyes hurt from how wide I was keeping them.

"Is... is this it, then?" Naseem's small voice was lost to the sound of our motor.

"This *can't* be it. There— There *is* no *it*. This is the *Great Cherry*, it's stood beyond the war, it's—"

"We can use the water. W-we can bring it to the top, we can—"

"With *what?* We have no *contact* with the *others!*"

"Oh, my soul..." The pain in Naseem's words was enough to grab back our attention. He was looking out into the water, leaning far over the edge. He pointed weakly into the distance, but his hand was shaking violently. "Look..."

But we already were. The closer we got, the more definition was brought to the scene. Petals fell in heaps into the water, which was fully coloring itself pink and red. Bodies were packed together, all made up of hands that were reaching into the air, trying desperately to clutch onto as many of the falling leaves as they could. Beside them, others floated limply, face down in the mess. Blood spread all around them, rippling with the crowd's motions.

I was still too far away to make out any faces, but I scanned and scanned for Alaric. I ignored Naseem as he emptied his stomach over the side of the cruiser. A Harpoon had to escort him back to the interior.

Again, I didn't notice my muttering. My entire body felt pulled to the scene, and I was urging myself to somehow get closer.

The motor turned off, and we drifted through the bodies. They thumped against us, lifelessly, until we finally came to a stop. The Harpoons jumped out, tied the boat to the dock, and immediately spread out. I watched in horror as they turned over countless bloodied and burned bodies, casting aside person after person. It seemed like more and more were bobbing to the surface, emerging from the dense Roots. They tried again and again to shake answers out of the Royals, but everyone seemed to be stuck in a trance, weeping as they reached for the falling petals. Their cries only grew as the delicate pinks shriveled before they could reach their hands.

Royals were still pouring out of the Tree. Naseem tried to run in, but he was quickly pushed aside. I jumped out of the cruiser and onto the dock, but I felt weak on my knees. Screams filled the sea, and I whipped back around. I turned just in time to see someone falling from the sky.

Not Alaric, not Alaric, not Alaric. My mind was wailing as they smacked into the surface of the water. The blonde mop of hair was slowly sinking as I turned back around.

"Get me in there!" I shouted to Naseem.

He nodded and pulled on his helmet.

It seemed like we were pushing through people every step we took. As soon as we got inside, I saw more bodies lining the floor. The only difference was that these were coated in white armor, and a clean line of blood was left across all of their middles.

"Alaric!" I screamed, but I was quickly winded. Someone launched themselves at me, pinning me hard against the wall.

"You were with him! *You* let this happen!"

Naseem was quick to grab their arms, but I slid to the floor. They escaped his grip just long enough to slam their forearm into my neck. I was left coughing and sputtering.

"You did this! *You* did this!"

I heard a thud, and when I looked back over, Naseem was wrestling them to the floor. I shook myself off, but Naseem yelled out as another woman joined their pile. I grabbed Celia from her sheath. After one hit to the back of the head, the woman crumbled beside them.

"What is *happening?"* Naseem yelled as I yanked him back to his feet. My answer was to turn around and sprint for the first staircase.

The higher we got, the hotter I felt. Naseem was shedding layers faster than the Royals could run through every window and door.

When we got to the fourth floor, screams filled the area. Everything began to shake, and Naseem and I fell to the ground. We clawed our way to the staircase, but just as we reached it, the floor above us began to crack with a skull-splitting noise. In the middle of the room, wood, furniture, and Royals began spilling onto our level. Many of them didn't get back up, but those who did were dazed and bloodied. I stared at them, noticing the gashes across their bodies.

"Maliyah!" Naseem's finger thrust at the still-crumbling ceiling. Above us, the fire was raging, and a hoard of people were swinging their daggers and swords.

I ran up the stairs faster than I knew my legs could carry me. Naseem, on the other hand, struggled to keep up in his remaining gear. As I reached the top, he took the time to leave his solid boots behind.

"Alaric!" I screamed again, but the swords kept swinging, and I couldn't see through the people. *"Alaric!"*

We all stumbled back as the floor continued to shake, then jumped to the side as the floors above us completely caved in. The screams were almost as deafening as the crashing and splitting wood.

I heard him yell just as I got back to my feet. I whipped around in perfect time to see his bare arm block the blade of a sword.

"You are no *king!"* The Royal before him hissed.

Alaric dropped to his knees as he ripped the blade out of his skin.

"You are a *traitor!*"

"Alaric didn't kill the king!"

The man turned his head as soon as the words left my mouth. As more people jumped back to their feet, Alaric stumbled to regain his own footing. His head was searching the tattered remains of the floor for his weapon. He held his arm tight to his stomach. Blood was smeared all over his clothes.

"Lies!"

"Alaric didn't kill the king!" I screeched again. *"I did!"*

Naseem was barely able to block the woman who dove at me. Both of them ended up on the floor as the rumbling picked back up.

"I killed Favian! I killed Avon! *I* killed the king! *I* destroyed the Cherry Tree!"

Someone swung at Alaric's back, but he picked up his sword and turned just in time to block it. He fell to his knee, but the sheer sound brought us all to drop down with him as the cracking began again.

Then, we fell.

Everything was happening faster than I could think. The next thing I knew, I was gasping and choking, clawing my way through charred pieces of wood. I felt like every breath was more ash than air.

Naseem was next to me, helping me to dig, but again, we were thrown by impact. The screaming was unbearable, but with every new movement, it grew quieter and quieter.

Eventually, Naseem stopped digging. I was screaming, but I couldn't hear myself. As I broke through the surface, I could feel the heat slam into my body. My mouth could only form a single word, over and over again.

"Alaric!" I squeezed my eyes and took a step forward. Above me, piercing blue shot through the flames. My heart dropped as I realized what was happening—the entire left side of the Tree was falling.

I sprinted to the side, watching as the bark tore away from itself. I was still above the water level, but before I could see more, I had to drop down and cover my ears again. Wood flew in every direction. It felt like the whole world slowed down as the Tree began to fall, and as it slammed into the water, everything around me continued to shake.

This time, I was sliding. I screamed and kicked my feet, but there was nothing for me to hold on to. As the Tree lost its balance, wooden piles flew to the opposite edge, and embers rained from the sky. Every time one hit my skin, I had to suck in a sharp breath through my teeth.

A hand reached out and grabbed me. From under the rubble, Naseem was barely visible. He was coughing and gasping, but he still held firmly onto my top. I clawed at his arm, dragging myself back toward the planks he was stuck under.

Everything was falling now. Couches and beds hit the floor hard enough to open more holes on our level. Kitchen utensils flew aimlessly around the room. The sun was bleeding in on all sides of us. More limp bodies rained from the sky.

Then, the cracking began again. I looked up, and a thick branch was falling. I pulled on Naseem as hard as I could, but I couldn't break him free.

"Run, Maliyah!" he shouted at me.

"I can't leave you!"

"Run!"

With one, final pull, we flew away from the wooden pile. Only moments later, it erupted into flames.

The heat was enough to throw us to the side. We rolled and slid until we slammed into what was remaining of the other wall. I was winded, but I fought to get back to my feet. Beside me, Naseem was lying on the floor, his arm bent at a jagged angle, and half his face coated in burns. My scream was shrill. I covered my face before I even tried to shake him.

"Naseem! *Naseem!*" Tears were pouring down my numb face. I knew it was his body that had saved me from the flames.

Then, I was tackled to the side. Someone was pinning me down, wrestling me to the floor.

"Murderer!" His voice pierced through my sorrow. I fought to get him off of me, but his hands were tight around my neck. I wanted to cough, but I couldn't. The panic set in faster than I could move.

As soon as the crackling started again, the man was fast to retreat. I scuttled to the side as the wood chips and embers flew. They shot across the room, and I dug my face into the floor, holding my arms tight around my head. I didn't move until I heard the thunderous crash in the water below.

When I looked up, I was completely exposed to the sky. Only the out-most walls still stood, and even then, the bark was jagged and no higher than my floor. The blossoms were falling into the water in a burning heap, but I knew it wasn't just the water that they would hit. My body was aching, but I made myself sprint for the staircase.

As soon as I ducked in and slid down it, the fiery blossoms came flooding in after me. I was screaming for only a moment. Areas across my back felt agonizing, then like nothing at all. I continued down the stairs on my stomach and arms, then forced myself up, only to keep running.

As I reached the second floor, the third was quickly turning to black. Bodies crumbled through any holes they could find. Some were so burned that I could barely make them out as people.

The cracking began again, but this time, I wanted to collapse. I clutched the wall—leaned against it with my side—but I could only feel the pain in my chest as I coughed. The sounds were deep and unnatural. I stayed where I was as more holes in the floor opened up. As the middle began to split, I thought my heart would beat for the last time. There, Alaric was still fighting, severely bloodied and burned. I wanted to call out to him, but I was gasping for air. I watched as a sword swung. As he was thrown over the edge. As he was falling... falling... falling...

He smacked into the ground, and I couldn't see him move. Screams filled the air above me. Then, I couldn't see anything past the blinding orange and yellow.

I felt a pair of arms wrap around each of mine. Without hesitation, a familiar, sticky substance was being slathered onto my back. It felt like that alone breathed air into my lungs. It was cold, and it clung to every burn. They spread it to my arms, neck, and legs as they dragged me out of the room. Before everything went dark, I spat out one more word:

"Alaric."

TWENTY-THREE

IT COULDN'T HAVE BEEN long before I woke up again. I was gasping, clutching at my chest, and every breath hurt.

"Where's Alaric? Where's Alaric?!"

"Easy, my lady. You've only just—"

I was already prepared to jump back onto my feet. It took two Harpoons just to keep me in my cot.

"*Where* am I?"

"You're back on the cruiser, my lady. We've driven it away and begun tending to the wounded."

"Where's Alaric?!"

"We're doing what we can, miss. We just—"

I shoved past them with as much force as I could muster. They chased after me, but I was running, the only thing I could hear being the pulsing heartbeat in my ears.

Lub dub, lub dub. My back was throbbing in time with my every step. Hands sprawled out around me.

Lub dub, lub dub. I hit them away. I couldn't listen as they screamed my name.

Lub dub, lub dub, lub dub. My feet left the dock, and I was ripping my way through the water.

I pictured how Alaric used to move his arms. One in front of the other, throwing my head to the side for air. Nectar peeled off of me with every stroke. The closer I got to the Tree, the more the red water took its place. Just kicking my feet seemed to want to drown me.

I shoved bodies aside, disregarding their state of life. Charred petals began to fill my view. I thought of Alaric as they brushed across my lips.

Lub dub, lub dub. On either side of the Tree, giant masses of wood protruded from the water. It seemed as if it had split right down the middle, all the way down to the second floor, where sharp stokes were still flaking away. I wondered if the Roots were still as intact as they were before, or if the pressure from the fall had torn them from their resting place deep under the surface of the water.

Lub dub, lub dub. As I yanked myself back onto the dock, I stuffed handfuls of petals into my clothes. While I scooped them up, people tried to grab me from the water. I kicked them away as hard as I possibly could.

The bark above me was still burning. The sky was no longer any hue of blue, and the grays had turned dark.

There was no one left in the doorway of Cherry. Only bodies were lying sparsely on the floor.

My vision was tunneling before I could even reach the stairs. But I knew it wasn't myself that was carrying me.

It can't end like this. It can't *end like this.* As I got to the second floor, my hand flew to my pocket, and I clutched a handful of the petals there. If I couldn't find him, I knew what I would have to do.

I shoved my way past rubble and wood, and I was able to find my footing. Many areas were still intact, and the patches of fire were small compared to what the other floors experienced. I threw my eyes around the room.

Lub— I spotted Alaric. He was lying limp underneath the man who had previously launched a blade into his arm. The wound left over looked minuscule compared to the burns on his entire left side. I screamed as I pushed the man off of him. I realized that he had taken many of Alaric's burns as soon as I turned him around. My mind whispered something vengeful, but I was too busy shaking him for the thought to linger.

"Hey!" I shouted. "Alaric, listen to me! Can you hear me?!" I did a double take at the familiar scene. It instantly brought me to tears. "Alaric! Alaric, *please!*"

Only soft moans came from his lips, but it was enough for me to throw myself onto him and weep. Behind me, Harpoons rushed up the stairs. They gathered the bodies of only those who showed signs of life. I knew they wouldn't need many trips back.

They began to approach, but before they could, I realized I was running my hands all over Alaric. Through my tears, I had squeezed handfuls of blossoms, and I was clutching them to his wounds. He continued to mutter, but the more he did, the less I was convinced there was still life left in him. As they carried him away, they forced a cup into my hands. Every gulp brought new terror and realization with it.

Somehow, I was back on the boat. In a moment of panic, I wondered if I had dreamt going back to the Tree. As I turned to the side, I saw a sheer curtain pulled around my cot. Past it, silhouettes of Harpoons were standing with guns and spears.

One movement made me realize I was nude. Only a thin blanket and layers of bandages covered my body. Nectar was smeared all over me, from my face to my legs. I turned to my side, and there was Alaric, lying on the cot beside mine. A thin strip of a sheet was the only fabric covering him. Nectar and bandages were tied all around him, covering parts of his face, coating his side, and wrapping around his legs.

"Alaric..." It hurt just to whisper. I gathered my strength to drape the blanket around my shoulders. My front side was cold as I fell to my feet.

With every step, I noticed a new imperfection in his body. Barely visible strips of nectar were cut and carefully placed on his every surface, where small embers and flying pieces of wood must have connected. Slowly, I brought my hands to his arms. I closed my eyes and slid them up, leading me to his chest, his neck, and his face. Tears laced my vision as I opened them again. I traced the edge of his hair. It was uneven now, one side having been singed much farther back. I brushed it away regardless, staring into his sharp features. His lips were dry and chapped. His nose had a thick strip of nectar on one side. I dropped myself on top of him, and I began to cry.

It was weak, as if I had no voice left. My chest bobbed up and down, and my face and arms buried themselves in his chest. I kept grabbing him, but every time he failed to grab me back, new sorrow filled my heart.

"I'm sorry." It came out as a choked whisper. I repeated it a little louder each time. "I'm sorry. I'm so sorry."

I slid into the cot and pressed myself beside him. I curled myself in my blanket, but not before resting my head on his unmoving shoulder. I couldn't stop the tears from falling. I shifted myself even closer to him, wrapping my arm and leg around his. My eyes closed as desperate whispers continued to escape from my lips.

"Please wake up... Talk to me. *Talk* to me..." I knew there would be no response, but I couldn't stop myself from trying.

When a Harpoon pulled the curtain back, all I could do was look at him. With only a small nod, he shut it again and called over another to stand guard. I couldn't imagine there were many of them left.

I began to think about Cherry. Its image loomed in my memory like a haunting gravestone. I thought about how it protruded from the ground, light wood turned black, only jagged edges still sticking up from the water. I knew now that none of it remained untouched.

Favian is dead, my mind was suddenly saying. *Avon is dead. Natasha is dead. Aaron is dead. Alana is dead.* I paused and squeezed my eyes shut. I was begging myself not to will it into existence.

Alaric is dead.

I woke up to a Harpoon on the side of my cot. He was changing some of Alaric's bandages and adding new strips of nectar to the collection on his skin.

"Excuse me, m'lady."

"What..." My throat was raw. "What time is it?"

"It's noon, m'lady. We've let you rest since yesterday evening."

"Has Alaric...?"

"No, m'lady."

I turned to him, but as I moved, I felt the cold air hit my raw back. I pulled the blanket back to my chest, but I could barely care. I dropped my hand over Alaric's chest, and I waited.

"How are you feeling?"

I held my breath. Finally, his chest rose. *He's alive.*

"I'm... alright." Physically, I was. My back was sore if I laid on it, but the nectar seemed to be working without falter. I prayed it did the same for Alaric.

"Would you mind...?" He gestured to Alaric, and I nodded slowly. I nearly tripped as I stood, and pain shot up my spine, but I stumbled back over to my cot within a few seconds. As he continued to patch up Alaric, I stared. I stared at every bandage he moved, every burn he quenched.

"I'm afraid to report that we experienced many casualties last night."

"How many...?"

"We... haven't finished collecting the bodies, but... nearly a third of the Royals are already gone."

"And the Harpoons?"

"We know that six survived, including two of the four that arrived with us."

I felt a sudden pang in my chest. "Naseem...?"

"Gone, m'lady."

I let out a deep breath before we could continue. In my plea for comfort, one of my hands shifted to the area above my chest. As soon as I felt my bare skin under the blanket, my eyes shot open.

"My necklace."

"I beg—"

"My *necklace!* It had an orange shell on it, it—"

"It was removed with the rest of your clothes, m'lady. Any contacts with your burns—"

"Give it *back!*" My shrill voice seemed to resonate within the room. As the Harpoon stared at me, I tried as hard as I could to control myself.

Think, Maliyah. Breathe. I turned to Alaric, and I focused on the blank spot that was left around his own neck. Slowly, I let out a long, troubled breath.

"Leave your post here. One of you may stay, if you see it fit, but focus on healing those who are still fighting for life."

"There... aren't many." His every word hit me with increasing force. I closed my eyes as he continued. "And... one of our men is struggling to collect more blossoms. I believe... For the first time in our history, we're running on a finite amount."

"Do you know how this happened...?"

The Harpoon's gaze shifted to Alaric. My muscles tensed.

"All I know... was that it wasn't fire that killed our men."

I felt the sudden urge to grab Celia, but I had no clue where she—or *any* of my things—was. The beat of my heart was suddenly deafening in my ears. I tightened my grip on the blanket over my chest.

"Maliyah... is it true that... that *you* killed Favian?"

"I could use a new patch of nectar for my back, if it doesn't trouble you."

From under his helmet, I could fully imagine his glare.

"Right away, miss." He moved back through the curtain, and I saw him talking to the other Harpoon there. He left shortly after, and the original returned with a large slip of nectar.

"Actually..." I realized, "how much of this do we have left?"

"It usually takes a handful of blossoms to make the nectar, and it's a process that takes up to a few days, in order to extract it and press it together. In our current stock—" He froze. I even saw his armored hands twitch. "Pardon my correction. We have... We have what came with us on the cruiser."

"Save it for Alaric." There was no hesitation in my words.

"M'lady—"

"Save it for Alaric."

"His last request to us—"

"Can be corrected once he wakes up."

"The process slows immensely once the nectar dries. You may begin to feel the pain again. You may—"

"Save it for Alaric."

The Harpoon dropped his hands, hung his head, and turned to the curtain. "I will return to check on Alaric by nightfall. May I fetch you anything to eat?"

"No, thank you."

"Simply call for me if you are in need of anything."

I nodded, and he left. As soon as he did, I dropped my face into my pillow. I was frustrated, more than anything else. I felt like I needed to *do* something.

Slowly, I stood back up. I tried to stretch out every muscle. Even when I winced, it felt good to expand my body. As I turned my neck, I saw the Harpoon glancing through the thin curtain. I quickly reached for my blanket. His head turned back, but discomfort was already resting on me.

"Fetch me something loose," I called out. "Like a gown or large shirt. Please."

"M'lady," he replied within the second, "it would be better for your burns if you—"

"*Please,* and thank you."

The Harpoon shook his head as he began to walk away, but stopped again as I finished, "Oh, and I expect you bring my necklace with it."

Past the curtain, he resumed his journey to the other end of the cruiser, and I shuddered. I turned to Alaric and approached his bedside. His eyebrows were turned in, as if he was in pain even while he rested. I dropped my hands to his collarbones, where my fingers explored the barren area. Even without the chain, his skin was cold.

I found myself staring at his chest, counting the seconds between each rise and fall. My heartbeat quickened just thinking about it.

"There's none, m'lady." The Harpoon's voice nearly made me jump.

"*Excuse* me?"

"No such articles exist on the cruiser. Perhaps there was something in your personal items that I could retrieve for you?"

I had to fight myself not to alter my expression. "No, that's... that's quite alright. Could you simply retrieve the clothes I came here in?"

"They're being cleaned and repaired. There were blood stains on everything, m'lady, and most was burned through. For both you and the king."

"Who's cleaning them? I thought we were low on staff?"

"A volunteer, m'lady. I believe she was struck with guilt."

"A *Royal?*"

"Yes, m'lady."

"I'd like to speak with her."

"I don't believe that would be appropriate in your... current attire."

I rolled my eyes. Impatience was bubbling within me, and I wanted him to know it. "What would *you* suggest I do, then?"

"Rest, m'lady. Heal your wounds."

"I'm feeling just fine."

"You may not within just a few hours. As the nectar dries—"

"I'll continue to be fine. I need to clear my head a moment. You're sure there's *nothing* I can wear."

"Nothing, m'lady."

"Then stand guard here. I'll be back."

As I began to walk, my blanket clutched tight around me, the Harpoon reached out and grabbed my arm. Panic shot up within me, but I whipped my head around and shot him a dangerous glare. He was fast to drop his hand.

"I simply wanted to warn you, m'lady. Some of the Royals can be very... say, *demanding*. Should you need an escort, I'll be—"

"Watch Alaric. Call me if anything goes wrong." I pushed the curtain aside with great force, but as soon as I did, my jaw dropped. Before me were rows and rows of barely conscious Royals. Spare blankets and pillows were laid out on the floor to accommodate for the sudden increase in occupancy. A Harpoon walked up and down the makeshift aisle, checking pulses regularly. He stopped a few times, only to try the motion again, before roughly grabbing unmoving Royals by their arms and legs. He lugged them up the stairs, despite whether blood trailed behind them or not.

Walking past them felt surreal. Some had gashes on various parts of their bodies, while others were burned to the point of their skin appearing charred. Soft groaning followed every small movement. I questioned how many of them would actually live.

When are we going to run out of nectar? The thought felt dangerous.

As I approached the stairs, someone jutted out their leg. I gasped at the sudden movement and watched as the limb twitched. It kicked for just a moment before falling silent and unmoving. Hesitantly, I gathered my blanket and stepped over. I was more eager to get to the upper deck than I ever had been.

The longer I stood still, the more the smell of burnt flesh settled on me. I realized I had been smelling it the whole time, but as soon as I opened the door to the upper deck, I nearly retched. It was potent enough to make me pull my blanket over my nose. As I looked around, I saw the other Harpoon from below. He had a small pile of bodies near him, and he was tossing them into the water. I flinched as he picked up his most recent one.

"W-wait!" Though choked, it was easy to make out the man's cry. I stared as he tried to scream. His body was charred and bloodied. I followed it with my eyes as he went soaring into the abyss below.

Peering over the edge was my worst mistake. Bodies seemed to fill all layers of the red and black water. Following them led all the way back to what was once the Great Cherry. No longer was it a great blaze, but now a dimming light in the distance. I wondered how long it would take for it to stop burning entirely.

Above, the sky was a gray and black plume. I couldn't have guessed how many bodies were still burning inside.

In the water, there was still a collection of bobbing heads and desperate hands near the dock. It appeared as if they had never given up in their attempts to collect the blossoms, despite how they no longer fell from the sky. They wrestled each other for them, as if their very lives depended on it. Some even held others away from the air.

On the dock, those still able to move were crouched over others, desperately rubbing petals against them. I knew that it was all in vain.

"Lady Maliyah." I recognized the strong voice as the other Harpoon who had been on the boat with us. "I've retrieved your bag of personal items for you. I thought it may be of service."

"Yes, I was looking for this. Thank you."

"Looking for it? Did the Harpoon on the lower deck not retrieve it for you?"

"I beg your pardon?"

"He was holding it for you, to give to you when you woke up. He assumed it was what the king would have wanted. At least... that was what he told us."

I straightened in an attempt to hide the shiver that spread across my skin. The Harpoon must have noticed, because he quickly thrust the bag into my hand.

"I'll have a... a *chat* with my associate. I beg for your forgiveness, my lady."

I didn't reply. As he walked away, a question bubbled on my tongue. "Wait. Is there... There wouldn't be anyone currently working to repair my clothes, would there be?"

"My sincerest apologies, miss, but we don't really have the hands for it at the moment. Should I try to find someone—"

"Could you ask him about that too, then? And... see if he can't find a certain *necklace* of mine, while you're at it."

He froze, but his hands were already balled into fists. "Right away, m'lady."

I sighed as he walked back down the stairs. I set my bag down on one of the leathery seats and clicked it open, but as soon as I saw what was inside, I physically doubled back. All of my clothes had been tampered with, none of them folded as I had left them. Even my undergarments were turned inside-out. I had a growing urge to throw it off the boat altogether.

My attention was stolen as soon as the door burst back open. I whipped around, and the two Harpoons were locked in a fight. The one in back had a tight grasp on the frontmost's neck. As he was thrown to the floor, I saw the faint glint of silver escape the protection of the underside of his armor. The winning Harpoon ripped it from around his neck and tossed it in my direction before retrieving his sword and pressing it just below the other's helmet.

"Explain yourself!"

"There's nothing to explain! I—"

"*Where* are her clothes?"

"They're— I washed them! They're drying over the—" His pleading turned to choking as the sword crept closer to his neck. "Okay, okay! They're... they're under my cot."

After a hard kick to the chin, the Harpoon's helmet came flying off. By the time his head dropped to the floor, his lip was already erupting in blood.

"Do *anything* like this to the lady *again,* and it's *over* for you. *Is* that understood?"

His head slowly turned toward me. A smile stretched across his slightly wrinkled face. I took a step back, clutching my necklace in my hand. I gasped as my back bumped into my bag, then harder as it teetered over the edge. I tried to grab it, but my blanket nearly fell. Just as it slipped below my lower back, I managed to clutch it tight to my chest. Then, I was forced to watch, helplessly, as my personal items splashed into the bloody pool below. The Harpoon behind me screamed, and as I turned back toward him, I saw that his chin was now bleeding, too. He turned to the side to spit more of it out, but the Harpoon over him pressed his boot against his chest.

"You can't kill *me!*" he fought with a single laugh.

"And why is that?" the other challenged.

"You *need* me! We're already too low on numbers. The lady needs my care. *Alaric* needs my care!"

"That's *King* Alaric to you." The Harpoon lifted his sword, and I turned away. Before he could finish his scream, his companion's blade made a clean slice across his neck. I didn't open my eyes again until I heard heavy footsteps approaching me. There were two loud splashes in the water below.

"There," he said as he dusted off his hands. "He won't be bothering you anymore. Please, notify me immediately if anyone else gives you trouble. I know there may be certain... conflicting interests after yesterday's events."

"Yesterday's..." I didn't mean to say it out loud. The thought of him watching me as I slept—the thought of him *undressing* me—made me hug myself even tighter.

"We do have a place to bathe on board. You may have seen the tub in the restroom. It's very small, but if you'd like to—"

"Please."

"Very well, then. I will try to find a way to warm the water. Help yourself to any clothes that may fit. I give my sincerest apologies for all of this, m'lady."

"Just... call me Maliyah. What was your name again?"

He froze, then pulled off his helmet. He was dark-skinned and very muscular for his apparent age. "Forty-Seven, at your service."

"Is that... What is that? You don't have a name?"

"Numbers are assigned to us at birth. If we had names before... Regardless, I believe I was the fourth Forty-Seven."

"Well... How do you like the name Jeremy?" A sad smile grew on my face. I couldn't believe how fast it popped into my head.

"I don't—"

"It was my father's name. He... he was a good man."

"In that case, I will carry it with great honor. I am proud to hold the legacy of your family. May I never let you down." He dropped to his knee, but as he lifted his helmet back to his head, I threw out one of my arms.

"Wait! Keep it off. I don't think there's much of a threat anymore, and... I'd like to be able to recognize you."

He nodded, then headed back toward the door. I let out a breath, but I couldn't bring myself to look back over the edge.

I tried to shift my focus, and I found that my hands had occupied themselves by repeatedly rubbing the blood and grime away from my shell and chain. The realization made me frown. In one hand, I gathered the fabric of my blanket, and in the other, I brought the faint orange coloring to my line of sight. At some point, I must have cracked it, because there was a chip on the front of the delicate shape. I turned it around and let it hang against my skin, regardless. With a soft sigh, I sat down, and I waited for Jeremy to return.

Twenty-Four

"Your bath has been drawn." His words snapped me out of my deep thoughts. It felt as if only seconds had passed. "I could only get the water so warm, but I hope it is enjoyable to you nonetheless. I did notice, however, that someone already placed some hair cleaning products in the room. Feel welcome to use them. Were you able to find any garments to change into?"

"Oh, no, I wasn't—"

"No worries, then. Allow me to find you something as you bathe. The room is yours for as long as you desire."

I nodded and slowly stood back up.

The bathroom was small and cramped, and the wooden tub was uncomfortably close to the toilet. Still, I looked around, then dropped my blanket. I glanced at my skin, and I found myself staring at all of the slowly drying nectar. I peeled it off of every large surface—despite how it made me flinch—and picked it from every smaller crack. It crumbed all around me, but the bigger slabs stuck to the wooden floor. I looked over my arms and legs. There were still some small patches of discolored skin left over, but nothing that hurt too much. The only thing left touching me was that same, broken orange shell. I reached for it, but as soon as I tried to remove it, my eyes closed. The image of Alaric's hands passing over mine stole my thoughts. I drew in a long breath as I pictured him being the one to drop it around my neck. I wanted to reach for him. Instead, I looked at the tub and sighed.

I was chilled at first, but I was grateful to sink into the clean water. I submerged my entire body and stayed under for as long as I could hold my breath. Slowly, I opened my eyes, and I watched my shell fight to float away. It seemed graceful and strong, but still so full of longing, like it was begging to escape with my bubbles. I let out a long breath when I broke back through the surface.

I turned to the side of me, where a familiar bottle sat. The orange label brought me many emotions at once. I tried not to think of how it got there, but instead, the first time I had used it. I remembered Alaric's shy, excited expression when he handed me his bag of gifts. I wondered if it was the same way I looked at him with that purple flower so long ago.

Fear rested on my chest as I lathered my hair. I badly wanted to hear his voice again. I wanted to feel his touch, look into his eyes. A part of me wished he was there with me then.

I sank under the water and returned my hands to my hair. I moved to my arms, my stomach, my legs, as I continued to scrub, only growing in the aggressiveness of the motion. I thought about anywhere the Harpoon might have touched, and if one arose, it gave me just another reason to keep going.

The door popped open. I covered myself fast enough for the water to fly to every side of me. "Occupied!"

"I apologize, m'lady. Another Harpoon instructed me to bring you this." He dropped a towel and a dress onto the blanket I had left on the floor.

I didn't reply. He was quick to shut the door again, but I no longer felt the relief I once had. I didn't bother conditioning my hair before I got back out of the tub.

The dress the Harpoon brought me was much larger than I was, but I didn't care to ask where he found it, or even who it belonged to before me. All I knew was that it was better than a blanket.

I left the towel and blanket on the floor, but I grabbed my shampoo and conditioner before I left. As I walked back to my cot, I kept my arms crossed, and I passed the groaning people without giving them a second look. When I finally got back to my curtain, I was pleased to see that it was Jeremy who was left to guard it.

"Feeling any better?" he asked.

"Do you want my honest answer?"

He smiled. It was nice to see his smile.

"Lady Maliyah... May I confess to you something that has been weighing heavy on my heart?"

I felt myself tense again, but he pushed aside the curtain so I could sit. Alaric stole my vision. I didn't speak until I saw his chest move. "I suppose so."

"The young boy you were talking to, the one who used his freedom to join the Harpoons—"

"Naseem?"

"So you did know him. Did he... did he speak to you of himself? Of his family, perhaps?"

"A small amount, yeah. He... he said he was born as a servant. He never knew his father, but he knew he was some smug Royal. His mother was killed a few years back."

"My deepest fears were correct, then."

"Fears?"

"That the boy would die without knowing the truth."

"And... what was the truth?"

A sad smile found him. "His mother's name was Naiomi. She was a *wonderful* woman. Tender-hearted, wise... but she fell bitter, as most did. She was beautiful, and it was her curse. The Royals... they are rather grim people, you know that. They took turns bedding her, and she never fought them. Not after the first time. There was one Royal in particular that always seemed to have a special interest in her. When Naseem was born... We were grateful that he shared more in appearance with her than any other."

"You speak... like you were her friend."

"We were more than friends. Naiomi was my lover. *My* lover, as I was hers. It was supposed to be forbidden, that the servants were reserved for the Royals, but many of us Harpoons still met with them. During meals, in the morning hours..."

"Was Naseem—"

"I am not sure, but... we always said he was. For Naiomi. For me."

"Why didn't you tell him?"

"I thought... When this was over... I thought we would have more time."

We sat in silence, and I felt a new added sorrow to our loss. A part of me wished these people would stop talking to me. I didn't *know* them, and I shouldn't have had to. But not once did I have the heart to stop them. If this had been just a few months before, I wondered if I would have.

"Naseem was a good man. His heart was in the right place. Even after everything."

Jeremy nodded. Slowly, but surely. "Thank you. Forgive me for putting my burden onto you, but—"

"I'm just glad there's at least one person on this boat I can trust."

"Two." Jeremy turned to Alaric, and I began to nod. I stood back up, and I walked over to his side.

"I'll give you some time. Thank you for listening." As Jeremy closed the curtain, I turned my attention back to Alaric. My breath was staggered just by looking at him. I propped my knee near his side, then decided to sit. I slid in beside him, but as I leaned, I felt sudden pain spread throughout my back. I sucked in air before I flipped onto my stomach. I lay again with my arm over his chest, begging myself to somehow get closer. In that moment, I couldn't care about anything else.

TWENTY-FIVE

I DIDN'T KNOW WHAT time it was. I barely knew what day it was. I just pressed my face into Alaric's butchered chest. It was difficult to find a spot without nectar. I decided to close my eyes, and I didn't plan on opening them until someone gave me an immaculate reason to do so.

When that reason came, I wasn't sure if I had slept or not. It could have been minutes just as well as it could have been hours. But my eyes shot open the second I heard Alaric mumble.

I turned to him and pressed my hand firmly on his chest. "Alaric?"

His eyebrows tightly knit as he continued to whine.

"Alaric!"

He moved his head to the side just enough for it to be noticeable. Under my hand, I could feel the beat of his heart stronger than I had before. Its speed grew and grew, until I feared it would jump straight into my hand.

I moved my grip to his shoulders, where I grasped him and shook. "Alaric! Alaric, come on, wake *up!*"

"Smithy..."

The name hit me harder than any punch could. That, at least, I would have been able to brace for. I instantly loosened my grip and sat up straighter. My hands went back to his chest, where his heart was still pounding. "Alaric... *please*—"

"Smith—!" As Alaric tried to sit up, he let out an agonizing sound of pain. My hands were quick to find him, fighting to get him back into a relaxed position, but he continued to thrash against me. "The blossoms, the *fucking* blossoms—"

"Hey." My voice stayed soft. It was easy to do while on the brink of tears. "Hey, it's alright. Just breathe for me, okay? You're... you're alright."

He stopped. His eyes flicked me up and down. He took in a breath. "Maliyah...?"

"Hi..."

"You're... you're here?"

I nodded slowly, and now, a tear did roll down my cheek.

His eyes widened as soon as he must have processed the thought. "Are you *hurt?* Tell me you didn't go in there, tell me—"

"I was *with* you in there, you dummy. You were—"

"You told them you did it. Maliyah, you— They'll *kill* you for that! Y-you can't—"

"It's okay." I forced a sad smile, and my hand found his cheek. "It's over now."

"The Cherry—"

"It's gone."

A look of horror crossed his face. I could tell words were biting at him from the inside.

"It's... They're gone..."

"We *did* it, Alaric. Remember?"

"No, I... Maliyah... They're *gone.*"

Sudden anticipation was resting on me. I feared he was about to say something much worse than I could conceive.

"M-my mom, my brother... *Smithy*—"

"We did what we had to do. We *saved*—"

"No. No, not... I killed them. I *killed* them!"

I grabbed his shoulders as he tried to sit back up. Tears were welling in my eyes. "Alaric, you're scaring me! What are you *talking* about?!"

"*I* did it! I-I ate the blossoms again, Maliyah! I-I-I... *I* killed the Harpoons, *I* killed the Royals, and *I* burnt the Cherry Tree!"

I froze. For a moment, all I could do was blink. "You... *you* did it?"

Alaric released a choppy breath, then threw his head back on his pillow. As his eyes began to gloss over, I wanted to tear myself up from the inside out.

"Maliyah, I can't... I can't *feel* anything..."

I squeezed my eyes shut and turned off my thoughts.

It's Alaric. Alaric is back. He's okay. I dropped my hand onto his, and I gave it a tight squeeze. "Can you feel this?"

He let out another choppy exhalation, but very briefly, he nodded. I slid my hand to his wrist, and after moving forward, I brought it to my face. I saw him tense, and a quick smile tugged at my mouth. I know he saw it, because it didn't take long for his own to flick back. It persisted for only a moment, but his breath changed altogether as I slowly slid his hand from my face to my shoulder.

"Can you... Can you still feel this?"

He nodded again, this time more sure. I continued leaning forward, sliding his hand across me, until I was dropping myself on top of him. He closed his eyes and sucked in air, but I took his other hand and moved it to my waist. I flinched toward him when I felt him grasp it tighter.

Another smile tugged at his mouth, but it was much more sinister than the last. I continued sliding his hand down until it sat on my breast. I stared at him. *Challenged* him. His eyes flicked down just once. When they returned to mine, he broke free of my moderating grip. His hands jumped to the backs of my thighs, and he pulled me forward fast enough for me to let out a surprised gasp. I begged that no one came in to check on us.

I didn't know what to say, but it didn't matter. In just one motion, my breath was stolen away. He pulled on me again until I was fully leaning against him. I saw the pain laced in his expression, but I knew he was choosing to ignore it. *Fighting* it. *For me.*

"Never make me leave you again." It sounded more like a demand than a request.

My expression warped into a twisted smile. I bent down and let my nose pass his. I whispered right against his lips. "Can you feel this?"

"Why don't you find out?"

I stopped trying to hold myself up. I let his arms wrap around me, consuming me in his tattered embrace. I bit down as I kissed him, and he threw his head back to suck in air through his teeth. He pulled me to the side of him, and my dress was hoisted up to my thighs. He rested one of his hands there, and my heart began to pulse. I didn't know if it was my chills or breath that gave me away, but he stopped. He stopped his movement, stopped his staggered breath, stopped *everything,* and he stared. Right up at me, only inches away. And he smiled again.

"Bastard," I hissed.

"You know it."

My leg was bent over his. His grip on the back of my thigh loosened, and he slowly slid his hand over my hip, to the clear area where a waistband should have been. He raised an eyebrow at me. I knew what he was thinking. I didn't say a word.

And still, he didn't touch me. Instead, he looped his arm around my waist and used it to pull me closer to him. He exhaled, but I couldn't help but whisper, "What're you waiting for?"

His eyes shot up to me. They were almost filled with disbelief. I saw something tug at his mouth, begging him to let it free. And I watched as he swallowed it back down. "More of my senses."

I rolled my eyes and shook my head. I lowered myself again, lying by his side, and without looking, he pulled on my dress to better cover my lower half. I turned my head, watching his hand in my own disbelief, and he laughed softly from beside me.

"What?"

"Did you just take a shower?"

Now, I couldn't hold back. I let myself laugh until tears were streaming down my cheeks. "It's been a long day."

"Do you... want to tell me about it?"

"Not... Not now. Just know... One of your Harpoons was relieved of his duty."

"*Shit.* I was hoping you wouldn't— I'm so sorry, Maliyah. When we first came into this, I really should have thought more about—"

"Alaric, *no.* Don't you *dare* apologize right now. You just fought a swarm of Royals in a *burning* Tree. I think I'd much rather hear about *that.*"

Alaric laughed weakly at my words, but I prodded him on with my expression. When he finally sighed, I propped my chin on the back of my hands.

"Is it just me, or does this seem oddly familiar?" he teased.

"You have *no* idea."

I continued to smile, so he gave another laugh, then tried to straighten himself against the wall. He grunted with every movement, and I helped him to steady himself. I leaned over top of him, but I found myself staring into his eyes. There was something different about them from when we first met.

His hand found my face. I leaned into him with incredible longing. He brushed my hair to the side, and as he did, I noticed his eyes shift to my neck. He fished my pendant from under my dress, and he examined it in his fingers.

"Hey... It's broken."

"It's perfect."

"I'll get you a new one as soon as we get home. I can—"

"Alaric," I repeated, "it's perfect."

He smiled softly as he tucked it back under my shirt, but I held his hand against me before he could retract it. Despite everything, he looked into my eyes and smiled.

"Did you still want that story, or did you just want to tease me some more? Because, I won't lie, I'm starting to fancy the second option."

My bottom lip slipped through my teeth. I saw him watching it. His mouth lingered dangerously close to mine.

"Maliyah..."

"Yes?"

"You're going to make me say something crazy again."

I inched my way closer to him. I felt his breath mixing with mine. Life felt like one big whisper, and somehow, I was caught in the middle.

"Say it."

"I love you."

I drew back and stared at him.

He laughed just once, as if it was at himself. He nodded and tried it again. This time, it was softer, but it was even more certain. "I love you..."

I bit back a smile and replied with the first thing that came to mind. "You *would* say it first, wouldn't you?"

He chuckled under his breath, but I could tell that he was relaxed. And I could tell that he really, really meant it. Finally, a smile stretched across my lips. A genuine, happy smile. My mind whispered one, simple phrase: *I love you, too.*

TWENTY-SIX

"Close your eyes." Alaric's instructions were simple, and it didn't take any insisting for me to follow them. I folded my hands against his chest, leaned my chin atop them, and closed my eyes.

"I'm... going to tell you a story now, alright? All I want you to do is listen. And just... Remember that it's here in the end. Remember that it's us."

My expression tightened, but I let out a soft hum, so he continued.

"Okay... Okay. When I was out, I was... It was like my mind was just *running*, and I saw... Okay. Let me just—"

"Alaric," I tried. I could feel him tense underneath me. "You can tell me."

He took a deep breath, and he began.

"Twenty-five years ago, a man loved a woman. He loved her a *lot*. By the time they were married, everything had been encased in water, but they didn't *care* what their world looked like. They were happy together, and that was all that mattered to them. That same year, they had their first baby. He was a happy baby, and his father... His father loved him. It wasn't long after that he decided he wanted another. They tried, and they tried, but... his wife wasn't getting pregnant. Anger took the forefront in his life, because, on the inside, he knew it must have been his fault.

"When a miracle happened, all of his rage was turned to joy. After three, heavy years, his wife was finally able to carry their daughter, and only a year and a half after that, they even had another son. They were raised as a family. *Together.* Their love... their love was unmatched by any other.

"Then everything went to hell, because that man found out it *was* his fault his wife couldn't get pregnant. Side effects from hanging around his father's lab so much as a kid must have caught up to him, because he went completely sterile. The last two babies... They were his father's. What was said to be a gracious gift was really that of selfishness, lust, and power. Absolute *hatred* consumed the man's heart. Hatred for his kids, hatred for his father, and hatred for his wife.

"So, the youngest two left, and their mother was heartbroken. Her first son was corrupted more each day by his father's teachings, but she continued to love him. Away from them, anger was growing in her daughter's heart. She wanted *vengeance.* Vengeance for the man who should have been her father, and vengeance for the woman who should have been a happy mother. Not a day passed where she let it slip her mind. Even when her friends tried to be there for her. Even... even when her brother just wanted to see her happy again.

"She went back to their home against everyone's wishes. They *begged* her to stay, but her heart was set on one thing—ending the life of the man who took her family's happiness.

"Her friends helped her. Trained her. Gave her supplies. They backed her up even after she left. But... she never came back. She never came back, and all that was left of her was a *damned* family heirloom." Alaric slammed his fist against the cot but immediately yelled out from his sudden movement. I rose and fell with his chest, but I didn't say a word.

"The boy—her brother—took on her burden. Hatred grew in his heart. He adopted her vow as his own, along with her friends, her lifestyle, all of it. All he was missing was a way to follow through.

"He set out, days and days on end, until he found someone who would join him. Someone who he knew would have the determination he needed to bring with him. What he found... what he found was the most beautiful girl he'd seen in his life."

"Alairc..."

"That's when things began to change. His priorities were shifting, and the more time he spent with this *girl,* the worse it got. He felt *happy.* Like it wasn't *worth* holding onto the hate anymore. But he couldn't let go of his sister. Even after his friends begged him. Even after they warned him.

"When he set off... they had his back. Just like they had hers. But this time, he brought them along for the journey, all of them intent on making it back alive.

"And... they did it. They ended the man who ruined the lives of so many. But in the meantime... that boy lost his mother. He lost his brother. He lost the man who should have been his father. He lost the man who loved him like one. And he lost... he lost *himself.*

"Inside... Inside, he didn't... He knew it was over for him. He became *exactly* what he hated, and now, he had *no one.* Not if they knew the truth. So he looked for a way out. He got away from everyone who would stop him from what was coming next, and he made up his mind—if the evil was going to stop, it needed to end with him. It was in his *blood.* He knew there would be a revolt after what he did. People would come after him. And... it was exactly what he wanted to happen."

"Alaric—"

"At the very first sign of it, he jumped. He got rid of everyone, got back on a boat, and he returned to his opposition. But this time... This time it was going to be his *last* journey there.

"As soon as he arrived, swords were drawn. Guns were fired. But he wasn't done just yet. He took a handful of blossoms, knowing it would keep him going until the end. Then, it would take him.

"The blossoms... They had a greater effect on him than he originally thought they would. He started to think, and as soon as he did, they powered his anger. He broke through the defenses and ran for the bedrooms. The bedrooms where his... his *parents* used to stay. The bedroom where he was so *grossly* made. The bedroom where his... where his *father* was murdered.

"In that room, they all came spilling in. They knew what he had done, and they were outraged. But he still had his sister's sword, and as long as he held it, he refused to be brought down.

"What they *didn't* know was that he had laced the blade before he climbed the stairs, and in that bedroom was a fireplace. It was tightly concealed from the wood of the home, but it was made to bring endless warmth to the room. As they pinned him to the corner, screaming, chanting, and swinging, he tore apart the metal cage and thrust his blade inside.

"Embers flew, and everyone was screaming, but that boy's blade was flaming, and he had another handful of blossoms in his pocket. At least... he *thought* he did.

"His back and hands were burned from the cage, but he still wasn't ready to give up. He fought his way to the window, despite the people still spilling in. He leaned out, desperately reaching for the blossoms, but he was pushed. And before he could even take in a breath... the leaves went up in flames.

"Everyone flew back, *sprinting* for the stairs, but... He stood in their way. The boy and his sister's *unforgiving* blade. Not *one* person left that room. Not one person... but him.

"Now he was ready to let the fire take him. Consume him like the hellish beast he was. But the people kept running up the stairs, screams *filled* his ears, and the floor began to crumble.

"Everyone started to fall. Some began to jump. The smell alone gave away what was happening. *Everyone* was swinging now, and for some reason, he couldn't stop. The floor broke, the walls toppled, and still, all they could do was fight. A blade went into his arm. He knew it was over, and he was ready for it to *finally* take him. At least he would go down fighting. At least he would go down in a blaze of glory.

"Then... he saw *her.* His reason for living. His reason for letting it all go. She was standing there, *screaming* that it was *her* fault, *not* his, and to leave him alone. Despite *everything...* She came back. It hit him all at once. He knew he *needed* to keep her alive. She didn't deserve this. *Any* of this. It was *him* who brought her into it, strung her along, and... and even made her care for him.

"But it was too late for him. He... he did it. Every-thing—every*one*—was already gone. She... she didn't need to live knowing what she'd trusted. And when he closed his eyes, *swearing* to himself that it would be the last time... He opened them again to see hers staring back."

Alaric didn't look at me. Tears were streaming down my cheeks. I knew my voice would break, but I tried to use it anyway.

"Alaric—"

"Don't. I... I can't—"

"I'm going to tell *you* a story now, alright?" My insides were clawing at me, but through my sniffling, I smiled. I smiled just in time for him to turn back and see it. He tried to peel his eyes away again, but before he could, I laid my head back down on his chest. I could feel him trying to leave his own skin, but I closed my eyes, and I spoke what I saw.

"Over two decades ago, a little girl grew up in green. She ran her toes through the grass, saw flowers bloom, and she met a boy. That boy... he loved her. He loved her a *lot.* And eventually... they had a baby of their own. A happy little girl. But... their lives changed just a handful of years later. Without warning, they were cast into a world of water. Through their confusion, they taught their little girl. They taught her not only letters and numbers, but what was right and wrong. They taught her how to smile. Tried to keep her safe, fed, and *breathing.* Then... they got pregnant. Some would say they didn't even *want* to. And when they had that baby, they pulled her from the water of their own flooded living room.

"Despite everything, they tried to keep that baby happy. And she *was,* for a really long time. The water was all she knew. Her *family* was all she knew. And then... they were gone.

"That little girl spent *years* wondering if they were coming back, but eventually... she had to learn how to feed herself. How to swim. And, after a long time, how to pray again. Finally, that girl was ready for it to end. She made what she was sure to be her last swim ever, and she kicked up to the docks above her."

"Maliyah, don't—"

"When she got there, she prayed. Without even knowing *what* she was praying to. But... she prayed that it would end. She prayed to see her family again, after years of being alone. Only, it *wasn't* her family she was blessed with. It was a boy. A boy with the blackest hair she had ever seen. A boy a lot paler than she thought someone from Watertowne could be. And she had never seen him before in her life.

"She bet he was the Grim Reaper, ready to bring her to the home her mother had promised to her, but... he spoke. And then, he swam. Then, that girl's life had *purpose* again. So she prayed, and she prayed, and she *prayed,* and it took him a while, but eventually, that boy came back. Then, her life changed. Because that pathetic little girl was *shot,* and the boy was determined enough to keep her alive. He took her in. Taught her not only how to swim, but how to walk. Not only how to fight, but how to *smile* again. And, oh my *gosh*, did he make that girl smile.

"Then... nothing else mattered. Not if she lived. Not if she survived. So long as she... she got to feel his skin before she fell asleep. So long as she had his shoulder to lean into. His hand, to fit into hers. His lips... to say dumb stuff that she never would've thought of, like when he was wanting so badly to let go, but breathing into her words like 'I love you,' and making *her* hold on even tighter."

"Maliyah—"

"Alaric." I clutched his hand against mine. "I will never—*ever*—let you leave me." A smile crossed my lips. "Besides... what's a queen without her king?"

He pressed his lips tight to mine, and all of my air seemed to escape. I wrapped my arms around him, as if he was my only life source left. He pulled me toward him, even when I could feel him squeezing everything tighter to mask the pain. Everything, including me.

He spun me to the side, and I knew his body was exposed. My own top was falling around one of my shoulders. He didn't hesitate to find the skin, and I threw my head back as he kissed it. He moved to my neck, and my breath turned shaky. I continued to hold him, but my grip loosened. He brushed my hair aside, but his hand didn't go with it. It moved down the back of my dress, and I heard the fabric rip. He looked at me once, and we shared a deep laugh. I fell silent again as soon as he continued to rip. My arm escaped through the hole he made, and it clutched his hair to keep pushing him closer and closer to me. He continued to slide his hand down until he was back to my waist, clinging my skin tight to his. His mouth moved to my ear. In one exhale, I knew his every thought.

"Maliyah Celestia Adley... You *ruined* me."

TWENTY-SEVEN

THE SOUND OF THE curtain tearing open could have been equivalent to that of glass breaking. Alaric flew back, yelling as he did. I threw the bottom of my dress over him, simultaneously holding it over my chest to keep it from falling. My mouth hung open as I saw who stood in front of us.

"I have *never* driven *faster* in my *life*. When I heard what happened... Alaric, you're going to *kill* me with the panic you give me! Then, I get here. I haven't slept in *days*—I passed rotting *corpses*—just to see you two *macking* all over each other! Why the hell do I even *bother?!*"

"To be fair, I am dying over here."

"Oh, *shut* up, Alaric! If *that's* dying, shoot me now!"

"Clarissa... how did you *get* here?" Disbelief clouded my every emotion. My heart was still slamming against my chest from the moments prior.

"Weren't you *listening?!* I *drove! Alone*, for *two days straight!* They said the Cherry was in flames, and I *knew* you were gonna be in it! You leave for *just* a—"

"Clarissa, *breathe!*" I couldn't help but smile at Alaric's tone. It felt good to hear him like that again. "We're okay!"

"*Clearly!*" She slapped her hand to her head and drew in a long breath. Alaric straightened himself against the wall, still grunting as he did. I looked him up and down. I was amazed he was even able to move at all.

"Alaric..." she tried again. "What *happened* here?"

"It's over now," he said with certainty. "For good this time."

"I heard there was a... a *revolt.* Are you...?"

"I'm alive, and that's... more than I was asking for in the first place. So... we'll take this one as a victory."

"Have you... Have you *seen* Cherry?"

I turned to him. I knew he hadn't yet. Not like I did. "He'll see it soon."

"Is it..." He couldn't finish his thought. He looked up, but I knew he was looking right past us. "Let's go see it, then."

"Alaric, wait—" I held my hand over his chest, and Clarissa even winced as more of his skin fell exposed. "Can you *walk?*"

"Of course I can *walk.* I-I just need to—"

"Get dressed?" I asked with a soft laugh.

Alaric looked down, then had to bite back his smile. "Oh, yeah. *That.*"

"Speaking of which," I lowered my voice to a whisper, "I think you ripped my only dress."

"*What?* Didn't you pack a bag?"

"Yeah, then it got hit overboard."

"I think I missed a lot more than I... How long was I out for?"

"He was *out?*" New panic seeped into Clarissa's voice. "Tell me he didn't eat the blossoms again."

"Why did *you* think she was all over me? Clearly she missed me."

"Oh, yeah. Because you haven't done anything like that *before.*"

"Clarissa, you have a *long* story ahead of you," I mused. "Jeremy! Are you there?"

"Who's Jeremy?"

Alaric's question was answered as soon as the Harpoon appeared, bowing, only seconds later.

"Were you able to prepare our clothes?" I asked him.

"I salvaged what I was able."

"Great. Could you bring them over please?"

"Of course. My king, it is excellent to see you communicating again. May you need anything at all, know that I am forever at your service. Shall I fetch more nectar before you rise?"

"Uh... Yeah." Alaric's expression was that of bewilderment. "That would be great."

"Right away then, sire." He closed the curtain again, and both of my friends stared at me dumbly.

I laughed as I looked back at them. "A *very* long story."

Clarissa sat in my cot, her head turned, as I helped Alaric to sit up. Jeremy was quick to hand me the nectar and clothes we had asked for. I was gentle with Alaric as I applied the strips and slabs, but nearly every touch brought him to flinch.

"Is this it?" I asked as I smoothed one onto his back.

"What?"

I smiled before I clarified. "Is this the last time I have to do this for you?"

"Depends... Can you keep me out of trouble?"

"You're kidding, right?" Clarissa choked out. "Do you just make *everything* like that now?"

I laughed, then continued to peel apart the nectar. I moved around his arm to get a better look at him. His left side was much worse off than his right, especially when it came to burns. I slid my hand across his chest, then looked up at him. He started to smile, but quickly looked away.

You're still ashamed. As I ran my hand down his arm, he pulled back with force. His forearm was tightly bandaged where he had blocked the hit from the sword. I stared at it, then looked up at him again. Still he evaded my gaze. I brought my hand to his cheek, and he couldn't help but fall into it.

"Are you two done yet?"

"Clarissa, *give* us a minute!" Alaric yelled back.

"You've had *plenty!*"

"Jealousy doesn't look good on you, babe."

"Jealousy?! Now you're just being airheaded."

After he turned to send her a smile, I tossed Alaric his clothes. I pulled my undergarments on under my dress, then let it fall around me. I was pulling on what remained of my tight black top when Alaric audibly winced.

"You alright over there?" Clarissa was quicker than even I was.

"Yeah, yeah. I... I'm fine."

"I'm betting on this. If you can't walk, you owe me."

"Wow, what *happened* to you? You lose your heart on the way here?"

I rolled my eyes as I tugged on my tattered brown pants. I was grateful they still held themselves up properly, especially with all of the holes and missing pieces that were now in them.

After getting dressed, the first thing I did was climb over the cot and tackle Clarissa in a hug. She smiled as I peeked my head over her shoulder.

"It's good to see you again, Riss."

"Maliyah, I was *so* scared. I-I didn't think—"

"I know." I smiled down at her necklace, then met her eyes again. "By the way... pink still looks good on you."

Genuineness grew in her smile.

A loud thud made us both turn around. Cussing was soon to follow it. I ran to Alaric's side, hoisting him off of the floor. He leaned against me, and I looked him up and down. He had barely managed to finish tightening his loose black shorts before he lost his balance. I steadied him, but I couldn't peel my eyes off of the giant bandages that wrapped around his stomach.

"I'm okay." But I knew he wasn't talking about his stumble.

"Alright, pay up." Clarissa teased as she walked over.

"Pay? The view isn't good enough a reward for you?"

"The *view* got burned down, presumably with you in it."

"I meant *me,* genius."

"Then *you* clearly have to work on your flirting skills. And yet—*somehow*—you pulled *her.* " She looked me up and down, then clicked her tongue. "What a waste."

We all shared a laugh, and I opened my arms to invite her into a hug. She turned to me, but before we could connect, her attention was stolen by the bandages on Alaric's arm.

"Woah, what happened *there?*"

"Sword fight."

"Many sword fights," I corrected. *"Alone. "*

"You weren't *with* him? I thought—"

"Not right now, Claire. Can I at *least* get some fresh air before you start chastising me?"

"Oh, hon, you *really* haven't been outside yet, have you?"

"Is it... is it that bad?"

"I think..." I interrupted, "you should maybe see for yourself."

As soon as Jeremy pulled the curtain back, I saw Alaric's eyes dart to the floor. Clarissa and I helped him hobble through the aisle, and as we did, mostly dragging him, the groaning in the room multiplied. Alaric squeezed his eyes shut and turned his head to the side.

"Man... how did this *happen?*" Clarissa asked under her breath. Both of us stayed quiet.

The rotten stench seemed even worse than it did before. It brought Clarissa to the point of covering her nose with her free hand. Alaric stopped altogether as soon as we opened the door. Clarissa stepped aside, and I loosened my grip as he stumbled to the edge of the boat. His mouth was open and his eyes were wide. The water was stained red, and even more bodies had managed to float to the surface. The persistent pops and crackles of the Tree were overbearing as pieces large and small flaked off, sending ripples through the water. It didn't take Clarissa long to puke over the edge. I wondered how many times she had to do that on the way here.

"I did this..." Alaric's words almost slipped by me.

"No. The Royals did."

"Maliyah, I *am*—"

"*No.*"

"I... I wanted to build him a memorial. In the king's room. I-I wanted to—"

"A memorial for—"

"*Smithy.*"

I froze. My answer came fast and simple. "Build it at Oak."

He dropped his head, and his hair fell over his face.

"He... He would have wanted it that way."

"Maliyah... I wanted to marry you on this dock..."

"Marry me at Oak." My words were barely a whisper, but they made him whip his head back around. His eyes, still wide, were glossed over. Even when his lips parted, he didn't speak. I sent him a small smile.

"This is *vile.*" Clarissa wiped her mouth with her baggy sleeve as she approached us.

Alaric looked down.

"It was—" I flinched. "It's over now.

"I can't believe they could just *do* something like this. I—"

I shot her a nervous glance. She looked to me, then to Alaric. When her eyes came back to mine, they were wider than I'd ever seen them.

"You didn't."

Alaric slammed his fist onto the rail, and we both turned to him. I didn't know what to say. The look on his face pained me more than any of my wounds.

"Alaric... What *happened?*" Clarissa's voice, while demanding, was laced with terror.

Alaric turned, and his expression wavered. I couldn't tell how many words were fighting to make the first escape. He tried to take a step forward, and I rushed to his side when he began to collapse. His next words made me look away altogether.

"Please don't hate me."

"Alaric, what did you *do?!*"

"I burned the Tree!" He started to yell, but his voice broke almost instantly. Sucking in a desperate breath, he threw his gaze to the floor. "I— I burned the Tree..."

"Why?"

"I just— I don't know, okay?! I was just— I-I—"

"He didn't have a choice."

"*Choice?* I don't see how *choice* has a play in *any* of this! I-I-I've never seen so many *corpses* in a room before, and now you're telling me it's because of *him?*"

Alaric fought to get away from my grip. I had to pull him back as he spoke.

"*Yes,* Clarissa! It *was* because of me! And I didn't just burn them, I slit their *throats! I gutted* them! It was *my* blade that did it, is *that* what you wanted to hear?!"

"Alaric..."

"*No!* No, I'll tell it how it is! I'm a *monster,* okay? *Their* blood is the *same* kind that runs through *my* veins! The kind that ran through *Alana's* veins! Are you *happy* now?!"

Then, we all jumped back. As if a miracle itself was sent straight from the heavens, thunder cracked across the sky.

The rain started pouring almost immediately. I turned back to them with excitement, but Clarissa only stared at Alaric. Stared at *me.* Her fist clenched, but before she could speak, a Harpoon ran toward us.

"Rain, Your Highness!"

He didn't answer. He was staring back at Clarissa, tightness locked on his face. With a disgusted noise, she turned and made her way back to the door.

I turned my head toward the Great Cherry. All around it, smoke thickened, and already, the light inside was beginning to dim.

"I'll prepare a crew to investigate the wreckage as soon as the flames die down," the Harpoon continued. "Is there anything we should prioritize in the retrieval?"

"People." Alaric's tone was cold. It hurt me to look at his hardened expression. "Heal as many as you can."

"My king, we are running low on our supplies. We can only serve so many—"

"Do what you can. Use the rest, if you must. I... I don't care." His last words were low and staggered.

I placed my hand on his chest, but he tried to shake me off. As the Harpoon turned away again, I pinned him against the railing. I *made* him meet my eyes. "You are *not* a monster."

"Oh, yeah? Look *around*, Maliyah. What else could do this kind of damage?"

"What do you think Smithy would say about that?"

He grit his teeth at me as he tried to push past me again. *"Don't* bring him into this."

"Smithy was a *fighter*. A fighter for *good*. A fighter for *justice*. And *so* are *you*. And if he were here right now, he would say—"

"The only reason he *isn't* here is because of me!" Now, he did push me back. The sky flashed, and thunder cracked soon after.

Alaric tried to take a step forward, but I pinned him back again. This time, he grabbed my arms and spun me around, until I was the one with my back against the railing. He pressed his forehead to mine. His breath was heavy and hot.

"Maybe it *was* a mistake bringing you here. Maybe I *should* have come alone."

"Why? So you could *die?*" I let the aggravation in my voice show, even when he turned away from it. "Then what, huh? What then?"

He took a step back, but I watched as he tripped over himself. He braced his fall with his bandaged arm. I turned away as he yelled, fighting to get back to his feet. "I don't *know*, Maliyah! *You* tell me! Do the people get to live? Does *Smithy* get to live? Does Clarissa get to be happy?"

"This isn't about me, Alaric." Her voice made me let out a sigh of relief. It was hard to turn back to Alaric.

As soon as he stood, he turned toward the sound of her voice, but he avoided meeting her eyes.

"I *saw* what Alana became. I... I knew her better than *anyone*. You *know* that. I just... I *can't* see that happen to you."

"It already *did.*"

"No," she countered. "You have us."

"So did she!"

"Alaric... Why are you fighting this? You *know* that we—"

"Look *around!* I *know* you see what I do! I *did* this, Clarissa! That doesn't *bother* you?!"

"The difference between you and Alana"—she lowered her voice as she continued—"is that Alana never felt bad."

Alaric shook his fists at his sides, then let out a distressed breath. Now beside him, I tried to rest my hand against his cheek, but he pushed it away. Again, he tried to take a step, but this time, before he could fall, Clarissa pulled him back to his feet. Almost instantly, he pushed away and leaned against the railing, staring back into the distance.

"Alaric... What do you want us to do here?"

"Go home. Be with your family. Geez, I just... Why couldn't you just stay *home?*"

"Because we care about you." I took a step closer to him as I spoke.

"And we need you," Clarissa finished.

He turned toward her, and the moment he did, I knew he regretted it.

Behind her, someone screamed. She didn't even turn her head as he was thrown overboard by a Harpoon. Instead, she offered

Alaric her hand. "I *did* look around, and I saw a *mess.* But there's only *one* person that I know who's actually going to *want* to clean it up. And... he already started."

As he let out a long breath, I found a smile tugging at the corners of my lips.

Clarissa sent a nod in my direction. "Alaric... Oak is *empty* right now. Do you know why?"

"Claire..."

"It's because they're all *together,* with the people of *Lavender.* Do you know the last time that happened? *Never. You* did that, Alaric. They *need* you to be their king."

"Maybe you'd make a better king than I would."

"Maybe." Her mouth twisted into a smile. "But I heard a rumor that you already picked a queen. And, frankly... she's taken." She offered her hand again, and this time, he did take it. As she pulled him forward, he groaned and reached for his stomach, but it didn't take him long to steady himself.

"Damn... When are you finally going to give up on me?"

"Few hundred more years, my friend."

He smiled and let out one long breath of air. He gave her a firm nod, then returned his gaze to the distance. Her final words were what brought him back to us fully.

"And may I just say... I'm proud of you."

"Oh, yeah? What *for?*"

"Your upgrade."

"In?"

"Title."

"My *upgrade* in—"

"In becoming His *Highness,* the Royal Pain in my Ass."

He lent her a small smile, so she nudged his arm with her shoulder. "Now, how about we make a plan? I think the Harpoons are simply *dying* to talk to you... Your *Majesty.*"

"Yeah, that's not happening," he scoffed. "But I will, in fact, speak to the Harpoon. Do you mind?"

"Not at all, my—"

"Stop it!"

We shared a laugh, then she gestured to me with her head. As we moved to the other side of the cruiser, I mouthed a 'thank you' in her direction.

"Please, I had to deal with him after Alana left. *Nothing* was worse than that."

"I... really thought you were mad at us there."

"I was. I *am.* I-I don't— This is *horrible.* But... what's done is done. Speaking of which... What *happened?*"

I sighed, then glanced back to look at Alaric. He seemed to be in deep conversation with the Harpoon, and another had already shown up.

"We were at Lavender, and some... complications came up. I wasn't there, and he took the boat back here with some Harpoons. I grabbed a few more and followed shortly after, but... They ambushed him the second he got here. They *really* wanted to kill him, Riss. It was... It was *bad.*"

"And... he still won."

"Yeah, 'cuz he took the *blossoms* again."

"He did... Of *course* he did." She moved her hand to her forehead as I nodded. "So that *does* explain the sleeping, then... This boy is gonna get himself *killed.*"

"He..." I dropped my voice. "That was his plan."

Her expression sank with my words. She looked over her shoulder. "He didn't... Did he...?"

"He was gonna go down with the Tree."

"He *did* set it on fire, then."

"Not intentionally. Well, he... He laced Alana's sword, and he used it to open the fireplace. It was half-planned, but..." My voice dropped to a whisper. "I don't know..."

"And he woke up...?"

"Just before you got here."

"So... you know what I do."

"I think you're mostly caught up."

She froze and bit her lip. She even closed her eyes before she continued. "I heard... I heard him talking with Smithy about something, and I just... I want to know if it's true."

"Try me."

"It's about... It's about his family."

My facial expression alone must have given me away.

"You *do* know something, then."

"I think... I think that's a conversation for you to have with him."

"Is that why Alana hated them so much...?" I watched as she began to fiddle with her necklace.

I let a sigh be my response. "Clarissa... I'm just glad you're safe."

"Excuse me, ladies, but the king requests your presence."

Clarissa rolled her eyes at me, but a small smile stayed on her face. As we turned, Alaric was waving at us, still leaning heavily against the railing. As soon as we approached him, the door to the lower deck burst open. Harpoons were carrying up cots, dropping them off, and heading back down instantly.

"What's going on?" Clarissa asked.

"Do you still have your boat?"

"I don't like where this is going..."

"We have around a dozen Harpoons left here, and more are on their way with another cruiser. We're going to bring anyone conscious back to Oak to get them better access to medical supplies and staff. A few Harpoons are getting ready to go back into Cherry and gather anything they can find of use. As for us... Do you think you can bring us back to Lavender?"

"To...?"

"Check up on their progress. Try to—"

"Alaric, I hate to break it to you, but I don't think you're going to be much help like this."

"I-I'm fine. I can—"

In one, swift motion, Clarissa kicked out his feet, and he dropped to his knee. It took him immense strain and noise just to pull himself back up.

"Well what do *you* suggest I do?"

"Go *home*, Alaric, and take Maliyah with you! Just... just *rest* for a few days. Is that so hard?"

I turned to him, a silent plea in my eyes. As soon as he saw me, he sighed. "Jeremy!"

"At your service."

"Tell the others there's been a change of plans. As soon as they arrive, we load their cruiser with anything of use. Go with them to monitor work at Lavender. Keep the bodies here, but pack on as many more as you can. Follow behind us. My crew will escort the others back to Oak. Oh, and get me a driver, please."

"Right away, sire."

"What?" Clarissa fought. "I'm perfectly fine to—"

"If I recall correctly, you mentioned that you haven't slept in days. And with that, I assume you haven't eaten?"

"You *sly* little—"

"Jeremy!"

"Yes, sire!"

"Get these girls some food, immediately. Please."

"And for him," I tacked on. He turned to me, but I only raised my eyebrows. *"You,* my good king, have been *unconscious.* And that is *also* not eating."

He gave me a shallow laugh, but I could tell something else was in his eyes as he looked at me. It was enough to make my skin burn.

As soon as the thunder cracked again, I turned back to the Great Cherry. "I'm going with the retrieval team."

"Maliyah, *what?* You *can't.* What if—"

"Queen's orders." I sent him a smile, but fear clouded his expression.

"Of course," the nearest Harpoon answered as he helped to lower a cot. "Join them by the dock. They're preparing to go inside now."

I took a step forward, but Alaric caught my arm. "What are you *doing?"*

"Talk to Clarissa. It would be good for you both."

"Maliyah—"

I pressed a quick kiss against his mouth, but already I knew it was a mistake. I felt the very pull of gravity begging me to stay with him, asking me for just one more taste. I gave him only that before I turned away and dove into the grime below.

TWENTY-EIGHT

I SWAM UNDER THE water as much as I could. Every time I emerged, I had to push aside another floating corpse, and I was completely coated in sticky, red liquid. It was one of the most disturbing experiences I'd ever had the displeasure of going through, and in the end, it wasn't even worth it.

As soon as we reached the dock, the few Harpoons remaining explained that they were going to search the lower levels, to see if the fire had been as effective under the water as above. We dove back into the murk and swam down to the Roots. Just doing that made my stomach churn.

As we broke through the water's tension, shouting filled the area. Even in the sub-water floors, the fire was still persisting, charring everything in its path. As soon as the first door was opened, the Harpoon in front flew back, and everyone began to yell new plans. I looked around rapidly, even as everyone was diving back into the water.

"Lady Maliyah, bail!" but I was determined to find something of use. *Anything* that was spared. I tried to think fast, reasoning if there was any other way to reach the upper levels.

Maybe if I can get past the dock— My thoughts were cut short when all I could feel was heat. My ears began to ring, and just like the first Harpoon, I was tossed back by new, sudden flames.

When I opened my eyes, I felt cold. I had no clue what time it was, what day it was, or even *where* I was. All I knew was that Alaric was hovering over me, and he was fast to press his lips against mine, over and over again, until I was pleading for air.

"Maliyah, *never* again. Never, *ever* again—"

"What...?" I could barely finish my thought. I tried to focus on my senses to stop my head from spinning. I closed my eyes again, and I listened. The familiar sound of Clarissa's humming motor brought me to a place of understanding.

From there, I drew in a breath. A long, fresh breath through my nose. I smelled the *air*. Clean, untainted air.

"Maliyah, *why* did you go in there? They said you were *looking* for something, *why*—"

"There's nothing left." My voice was hoarse. Without hesitation, Clarissa was over me with a glass of water.

They helped me to sit up as I drank, and both of them sat beside me. I was tired, and as I leaned against Alaric's chest, it was all I wanted to continue doing.

Still, he whispered, "what were you *looking* for...?"

"Desiderium..."

"What?"

"There... there was a painting. In your old room. I just... I wanted to see if—"

"Maliyah, you're not making any—"

"*Desiderium!*" Tears were forming in my eyes. I barely even knew what I was saying. "You said it means longing, right? Well, I-I just... I wanted to see what was *left* in there!"

"But—"

"It's *rubble!* It's rubble and flame. I... I don't even know how much longer the dock has. Even *with* the rain."

Alaric didn't question me any further. He just rubbed my arms, letting me lean into him with all of my strength. My entire body felt weak. As I looked down, I realized that I, too, was covered in nectar.

Alaric continued to rub me as he stared into the distance. "I think... I know."

"Wh-what...?"

"When you thought I... *Maliyah*... That was *the worst* thing I have *ever* felt. *No* more..." He didn't finish his thought. He only held me closer, pressing me tight against his bare chest. It was at that moment that I realized I was wearing his shirt. I had so many questions, yet the strength to ask none of them. All I wanted to do was sleep.

"We're almost there."

Clarissa stood and walked to the railing. I followed her with my eyes. In the distance, the Great Oak was falling into view. Behind us, one of the larger boats was following. I closed my eyes again, but when they flickered back open, I was in Alaric's arms as he was speaking to a Harpoon.

"Can you walk?"

"What?"

"Maliyah, can you *walk?*"

I squinted at him, then rubbed my eyes. It seemed like a silly question to me, but even as I raised my arms, they were exploding with soreness. When I looked down, I noticed that there was more nectar visible on my legs than skin.

"Come here." Clarissa held out her arms as soon as Alaric helped me to my feet. I collapsed into her, my weight begging to send me to the floor. She fought to keep me upright, and Alaric yanked himself up with his arms. I was dizzy as we crossed over onto the dock. I could barely believe we were there.

"How...?"

"We're home," Clarissa whispered as we hobbled closer to the Great Oak. "Maliyah... we made it."

Twenty-Nine

Everything seemed fuzzy and strange to me, as if I was walking through a distorted memory. Clarissa held me tight, and I realized that she might have been the only reason I was focusing at all. I had no clue how much time had passed from the last time words left my mouth.

"What *happened...?*"

"It doesn't matter now. We're home, and you need to rest."

As we walked, the blurry haze worsened. My eyes weren't fully opened until cold water was being poured over my head. I gasped for air and looked around. I was sitting in a tub of water, surrounded by familiar walls. I almost laughed as I covered my chest. There was Clarissa, smiling wide, an empty bucket in her hands.

"Girl, I already seen all there is to see. Trust me, it ain't much."

"That's coming from *you*. A-K-A, *not* a fair claim." I smiled and leaned back as Clarissa laughed at me. "Damn... What *happened?*"

"I think you've asked me that about five times in the past hour. A-K-A... It's good to have you back."

"I-I don't—"

"You were *out*. You got burned again, but I think... The Harpoons said something about nectar wearing off?"

"Ah, yes. *That.*"

"Tell me you pulled an Alaric or some crazy shit like that."

"He needed it more than I did. Trust me, it wasn't any noble feat."

"Maliyah... Why did you go back *in* there...?"

"I just..." I blinked as I leaned back. Clarissa offered me my shampoo, and I scrubbed it into my hair, despite the persistent soreness in my arms. "I wanted to know what was *left.*"

"You said... Back on the boat, you said something about a painting. And... and Desiderium...?"

I froze, my lips stuck slightly parted. Clarissa was quick to pour more water over my head.

"Hey!" I giggled when she raised an eyebrow at me. "Okay, okay, relax. I think... I was probably dreaming, or something. I don't—"

"I'm not stupid. I *know* what Desiderium is. It was—"

"It was what started the fire."

Clarissa paused, then leaned back in her chair. I tried to stand, but my legs were still weak.

"Where are you trying to get?"

"The *shower.*"

"I don't think that's happening right now, hon. What can I help you with?"

"Do you... Do you know where Alaric is?"

She laughed lightly before she replied. "What, I'm not good enough? I can flirt, if that's what you're missing."

"No, it's not that, I just—"

"Is he your shower buddy now? Is *that* what y'all are?"

"No! I was—"

"I know, I know. I'm *teasing*. Last I saw, he was talking with some Harpoons. He... he *really* cares about you, you know that? More than he has for anyone else."

I looked down. As she handed me my conditioner, I stared at the orange label.

"Maliyah... I think he's *lost* without you."

"He... He's fine. He just—"

"He was in *shambles* on that boat. I told him you were tough, that as long as you were breathing you'd make it out, but... He couldn't set you down. Even when the Harpoons asked to address his wounds, even as I *slept*... His eyes were *fixed* on *you.*"

"Did you... Did you two ever get to talk?"

"We did. I... I didn't know things were so bad in his head. I've never heard something so... *wrong.*"

"So you know about—"

"I know who you killed was really his dad." She laughed, but it was short and cold. "Both of them."

"I-I don't—"

"It's good. I mean... I'm glad it wasn't him who did it."

Slowly, I nodded. She dumped the bucket over me again, and I couldn't help but laugh. When she reached behind her for a towel, I did my best to climb out of the tub. I fell against her as soon as I was wrapped in it. I didn't know if it was the cold or the weight that was making me shiver.

"Has he seen you like this yet?"

"What, weak?"

"No, Maliyah. Naked."

"Oh." We shared a laugh, and I pursed my lips. "No. No, he—" Then, I paused.

She raised her eyebrow at me, so I continued. "I'm... not sure, actually."

"So not, like..."

"If you're asking what I think you're asking, then the answer is *no.*"

"*How,* though?!"

"What do you *mean,* how? You just don't—"

"I get *that* part! I just... Do you think... Do you think you're the type to... *Geez,* Maliyah, I *still* don't know what the hell you two are!"

I smiled as I looked down at my necklace.

Clarissa gave a short laugh. "You know, you almost slapped me for trying to take that thing off of you."

"I did *not.*"

"You did. I'm gonna have to keep an eye on you from now on—you're getting worse than *him.*"

I sighed and rolled my eyes, but my smile persisted as Clarissa prepared herself to help me walk.

As soon as we stepped out of my bathroom, Alaric was there to greet us, his arms crossed as he leaned against the wall. "Is it wrong of me to be here?"

"*Yes!*"

"*No,*" Clarissa countered just as fast. She tossed me toward him, and I found myself clinging to my towel. "You can *have* her. She's too crazy for me."

"Just my type."

"Oh, what the hell? You're *both* insane."

We shared a laugh, and Alaric turned me to face him. He looked me up and down, and his smile morphed into something much sadder. "How're you feeling?"

"Alive, that's for sure. I—"

My mouth fell open as he pulled me into a desperate hug. "I sent someone out to get you more clothes. They should be back at any moment. If there's anything I can do for you, *please* just—"

"Alaric, slow down! I'm okay! How are *you?*"

"Me?" He questioned. I turned my head so I could see him again. He looked confused, even after I nodded. "I-I'm doing fine, I just—"

"Alaric..."

"I missed you..."

A sad smile spread across my face. When I turned back around, Clarissa was rolling her eyes, standing to one hip, her arms already crossed.

"Delivery!"

"Mom?" Clarissa's eyes went wide before she even turned around. She rushed into the hall, and excited sounds followed.

"I hope you don't mind, but I saw the man outside as I was about to come in. I believe this is for your friend?"

Clarissa came back in with two handfuls of bags. My face was full of shock as I turned back to Alaric.

"I-I didn't know how much you packed, so... Help yourself? It should all be your size, I just—"

"Hold up," Clarissa interrupted. "Before you two go back to doing... *whatever* it is you do, do you mind if I head out?"

We turned to her, but she was already laughing. "Oh, who am I kidding? I'll see you tomorrow. Don't be stupid, alright?"

"No promises," Alaric shot back with a smile.

"Thank you for *everything,*" I added.

"Oh, please." As she made her way down the hall, I could hear her shout, "I know you need me!"

I chuckled, but when I turned back around, Alaric was already staring at me. I tried to ignore the heat rising to my face.

"You know what that reminds me of?" I asked.

"What's that?"

"We still need *doors.*" I gave a soft laugh at my joke, but Alaric just kept staring. I could feel my pulse growing faster. "What?!"

"It's nothing, just..."

"Just *what?*"

"You're beautiful."

I bit my lips together—I thought I was going to burst. I looked at the bags, trying to take my attention away from him, but he took notice and held them out in front of me.

"Is there... is there anything I can help you with? I know I'm not Clarissa, but—" He started to trail as soon as I dropped my towel to the floor. His mouth hung open, and he blinked a few times, but he cleared his throat loudly in a weak attempt to recover.

My bashful laughter escaped at once. "Do you think... Can you help me reapply some nectar?"

"*Hell* yeah," he yelled.

I laughed again, hoping that my face wasn't burning too red.

He pulled me closer to him, but his eyes stayed locked in mine. "But only if you'll help me next."

He tried to take a step forward, but both of us immediately stumbled. Luckily, my bed was close enough to break our fall. He twisted himself, so as not to land on me, but already, I was pressed against his top half. His expression twisted again, and I could feel his heart thumping fast against mine.

"*Damn...*"

"Damn at me, or damn at what just happened? Because, either way—"

Before I could finish, Alaric pulled me into a tight kiss. I curled into him, smiling uncontrollably as I did. I rested my head in the crook of his shoulder, and he wrapped his arms around my waist.

He pulled me back, sitting my bare form atop his lap, just to take another glance up and down. "Damn, because you're *gorgeous.*"

"Maybe you just haven't seen enough women before."

"Maybe I don't *have* to." He ran his hands down my hips, staring at my small, subtle curves. When he looked back up at me, a smile was trapped on his face. "I mean, *damn!* This is all *mine?*"

I shook my head at his gawking. He continued to look me up and down, and although I smiled, I squeezed my eyes shut. Soon, I crossed my arms over my chest again, but he pried them away from me and kissed the now-exposed skin.

"You're beautiful. You're really, *really* beautiful."

I looked down at him for just another moment before I laid my head on his shoulder. His hands rested on my lower back, and as they slid across my skin, I felt a chill run down my spine.

"Are you cold?" he quickly asked.

"Something like that."

He looked confused for a moment, then sent me an expression both shocked and proud. I laughed again, then leaned in to kiss the tip of his nose. I was happy there. I let him hold me, and for the moment, nothing else mattered. It was just his hands on my back and my skin against his. I closed my eyes, wrapped my arms around him, and I smiled.

"Sire!"

"Just a moment!"

My eyes shot open, and Alaric practically threw me onto the bed. I laughed as I pulled over the covers, and he tossed the bags of clothes in my direction. He stumbled as he walked, but before he left the room, he turned to me and shook his head.

"I'm sold. We need doors *yesterday.*"

I laughed again, and he brushed out his uneven hair with his fingers. Then, he stepped into the hall to continue his conversation with the Harpoon.

I leaned over, but the drying nectar was already starting to catch up to me. I began to think, and suddenly, I was wondering how long Alaric had let me lie there with him. I was completely vulnerable, completely open, and still, he just let me sleep. As I poked through the bag, I tried to find the loosest article of clothing there was. Luckily, I had a selection to choose from.

I decided to slip on the simplest top I could find. It was large, and it reminded me of the one I had worn during our night at Cherry. A part of me wondered if that was why Alaric had requested it in the first place. Regardless, I slid on my lower undergarments, then got under the covers. I curled against my pillow, but already, my body was longing for his. I wanted to feel him against me, holding me, watching me. A smile crept across my lips.

King Alaric... Maliyah Adley, what the hell do you think you're doing?

It didn't take him long to re-enter the room. "Maliyah...?"

"I'm awake."

"Do you... Should I let you rest now?"

"Yes." My voice sounded more tired than I thought it would. "Now come join me so I can."

I could practically feel his smile from across the room.

"Here... I won't— It's just the nectar, I'm not—"

"Alaric?"

"Yes?"

"I trust you."

He fell silent, so I turned back around. I met his eyes, and I repeated my words. "I trust you."

In his hands was nothing other than a few strips of nectar.

"We... We're starting to run low. They have more of a supply at Lavender, so if you end up needing it—"

"Is there enough for you?"

"What?"

I found myself laughing again as I turned back to my stomach. "Why do you always sound so surprised? I care about you, doofus. Get used to it."

"There's... I'm not sure."

"Then split it. Do mine wherever it looks the worst, and save the rest for you."

"I-I don't think—"

"Alaric, I mean it. I'll be fine."

"Fine. Where does it hurt the worst?"

"Why don't you find out?"

He laughed under his breath, then slowly began to lift my shirt. As his hands trailed down my back, I couldn't focus on the pain. When I shivered again, I imagined his sly smile. His hands wandered, and whenever I winced, I felt him smooth the cold strip onto my skin.

I closed my eyes as he continued. It took me too long to realize that he had run out of nectar quite some time ago. It was only his hands against my back, rubbing me gently, allowing me to finally relax. Freely. *Safe.*

"How's your arm doing?" I groggily asked.

He only shushed me as a response.

"Do you... do you need help reapplying?" I tried anyway.

"In the morning." His hands continued sliding farther up my shirt, until they were on my shoulders, and I could feel his bandages next to me. As his cold chain grazed my skin, I reached back and tugged upwards at it until he took it off. I heard him drop it on the table beside us. Right after, he reached for my necklace.

"No," I weakly whined.

"If *I* can take it off, so can you."

I only hummed in response.

"Come on, you'll sleep better without it." He pulled at it again, and this time, I let him take it. He moved my hair to the side, pressing a soft kiss on my now-exposed shoulder. Then, he leaned against my back. I smiled at the feeling of his warm pressure against me. Despite all of its cuts, divots, and scabs, it still made me feel at home. It didn't take much longer for me to drift into a deep, sound sleep.

When I woke up, a smile was still resting on my face. As Alaric curled closer to me, I made a soft sound. His hands were under my shirt, which hung loosely around my ribs. I put my hands over his, guiding him to hold onto me tighter, and I felt his lower half inch closer to mine. As he leaned his chest against my back, I fell into him, and he craned his neck to kiss my collar bone. One of my hands cupped his jaw. He kissed me again, and my eyebrows curled in. As he hugged me harder, squeezing my skin, my mouth fell the smallest bit open. His lips took the opportunity to lean in and graze over my bottom of the pair. I smiled as he moved my chin toward him.

"Glad to be home." He laughed softly as I hummed in agreement. Then, he leaned away and sighed. "So, what's the plan for today?"

"Why are you always in such a rush?" My words turned into a scream as he returned his grip around me and yanked me over top of him.

"Me, rushing? Love, I could stay here all day."

"Wanna bet on that?" I turned around with a confident smile, but as soon as he slid his hands back under my top, my expression changed altogether.

"That's what I thought."

"What's—"

Before I could finish, he pulled me to the side again, trapping me in another kiss. I laughed against his lips, but he dug his fingers into my back until I was arching closer and closer to him. My chest was moving up and down, quicker and quicker, until he was kissing my neck again. I felt like I could barely breathe.

"Payback," he whispered between kisses, "for all the times you tortured me."

"I would never."

My breath left in a flash. With just one hand, he grabbed my wrists and pinned them above my head. His mouth twisted into a devious smile. I knew he had me now. I was at his very will. And I didn't even try to fight him.

"Tell me, Maliyah. Where do I go from here?"

"You—"

"Sire!"

"*Damn* it!"

Still breathless, I began to laugh at his anger. He sat up again and let go of my wrists. I rubbed them as soon as he did, watching as he turned to the door, then back to me. He scoffed and shook his head. As he stood up, he pointed fiercely in my direction. "We are *not* done here."

"Whatever you say... Your *Highness.*"

He threw his head back and groaned as he struggled to kick a blanket off of his foot. "Why do I *like* when you say it?"

I bit my lip, but my smile broke through. I continued to watch as he threw the blankets aside, but before he could get a few steps forward, he had to lean against the wall, doubled over, to catch his breath. My smile faded as I stared at his back. While they looked much better than they once did, his burns and cuts were still very visible.

"Alaric, the nectar. Should I—"

"I'm fine. I just... need a second."

Regardless of his words, I kicked the messy blankets aside. On the bedside table, above our entangled necklaces, still sat some unused strips of nectar. I grabbed them and rushed to his side.

"Save them. I'm—" He quieted as soon as I ran my hands around each side of his lower back.

I reached around him, dragging my hands with me, to show him my own suggestive smile. "That's what I thought."

"*Witch,*" he hissed.

"You know it."

He shook his head and let out a sigh as I continued to smear the nectar over the worst of his burns. "What would I do without you?"

"Seeing as you insist you'd be dead? Probably not much." I said, only half-joking. He gave a soft chuckle, and I nudged him with my arm. "Go do your kingly things. I'll be right here when you get back."

"You better be." He looked reluctant, but he made his way to my bathroom. When he returned, he was sliding his shirt over his head. I rubbed my arms as I watched him leave. Inside, I wished he would never have to again.

I let out a slow breath—my heartbeat was only just beginning to calm itself. The way it made me think of him brought a smile to my face.

King Alaric... With one last nod, I made my way back to the bed, and I waited.

THIRTY

WHEN ALARIC RETURNED, HE was carrying a few containers on a silver tray.

I opened my mouth dramatically as soon as I saw him. "What's all *this?*"

"Only the best for you, m'lady."

I began to laugh as he sat in front of me on the bed. As I lifted one of the lids, I tried my best to mock his accent. "Only the best... like eggs and toast."

"That's for me, actually."

We shared a laugh, and he handed me a silver fork. I smiled at him, then looked down as he laughed.

"Told you she'd like it."

Alaric instantly threw his head back. "*You* said you wouldn't tell."

"Hey, Riss." I patted the bed next to me as she walked into the room, my smile staying wide.

"Heard you two had a fun night."

"Oh, did you now?" I turned to Alaric with raised eyebrows.

"No, she did not. Not from me, at least."

I looked back to her, and she slid in beside me. "What? A girl can try!"

I took my turn laughing with her, then lifted a piece of toast to raise against hers. Alaric didn't stop me from taking my first bite from off of his tray.

After we ate, Alaric was in and out of the room. Clarissa and I held a light conversation, and for the majority of the day, I stayed in my bed. The next day went very similarly to our first back home. Throughout the third, Alaric helped me to stretch and stand for the first time without using any nectar. Both of us were worse for wear, but we were recovering. Slowly. Together.

By the second week, I finally convinced him to tell me some of the plans he and the Harpoons had been working on. Reports from Lavender said that progress was going much faster than expected. Construction had already started on the foundations, and the people were working non-stop to create stable homes and places of work for each other. Alaric also informed me that more motorboats—similar to Clarissa's—were being built to make travel easier before the roads were finished.

I asked him if I could see Lavender. He replied that he was only waiting for me to ask.

As our cruiser pulled into the dock, my mouth hung open. *"Wow..."*

Already, the outlines of new structures were starting to show through the water, and the dock was lengthening and expanding, even when exact materials didn't match.

"Here, look at this." Alaric took my hand, and I looked down. We met each other's eyes at the same time. All over again, I felt like I had just arrived at Oak. But this time, it was *my* home.

We dove into the water, and Alaric held tight onto my waist as we guided each other's movements. I couldn't close my eyes.

Everyone who wasn't in deep focus toward their work took the time to wave at us. All of them seemed happy to be making so much progress.

All around us, people swam, delivered items, and continued construction on the buildings. I could already see where a Tube was starting to form. We stopped in an air pocket, and Alaric held me while I caught my breath. I paused in the anticipation of my sudden thought.

"Alaric... Can I show you something?"

"Of course you can."

I slipped his fingers into mine, and a sad smile crossed my face. I sucked in a deep breath, and I dove back into the water.

The closer we got to the original Roots, the more I could feel my heart against my chest. As we approached the small, still untouched door, it felt like my two worlds were colliding. I gave it a tug, pulled Alaric inside, and slammed it shut again before too much water could spill in. The house smelled even worse than I remembered.

"Is this...?"

"Welcome to *my* home." I turned back to him, but I could already see his curiosity taking over. His hand ran over the dusty surfaces, and his legs tread awkwardly through the low level of water.

"You... really lived here?"

"Born and raised."

"This..." His laugh was full of air. "I-I didn't think—"

"I know. I was born right here, at the front of this room. And... my sister and I stayed right down there."

Alaric turned back to me, then began to walk down the hall. His movement was slow, even after he stepped out of the water. He looked as if he'd seen a ghost.

As my bedroom door creaked open, a smile cracked on my face. "At least I had one thing you never did."

"A family?" he shot.

I let out a loud laugh. *"Doors,* Alaric. Geez, not even *I* try to cut *that* deep!"

"If I recall correctly, you *are* the girl who brought up Smithy's death to prove a point."

"Okay, *that's...* " I flinched. "I shouldn't have— You still think about that...?"

"Don't worry about it. If I didn't forgive you, you wouldn't still be living with me."

"Hey, *you're* the one sleeping in *my* room."

"And I never got a 'thank you' for that, either."

After I rolled my eyes, Alaric looped his hand around my waist, but it only lasted a moment. As he looked ahead, something new caught his attention. He crouched down, brushing his fingers over faded lines, long since etched into the wood. "Is this from you?"

I couldn't help but smile. "I was keeping the time."

"What were you waiting for?"

"You."

He whipped his head back at me, and I held my smile. As he reapproached, he was again distracted. This time, it was by tripping over a pillow on the floor.

"Is this where you slept?"

"That's Leilani's spot, actually. I just moved in the cushions from the living room when it got dark. I... I couldn't take her place, even *years* after she was gone. It just... It didn't feel right."

"I knew it was *bad,* but..." He couldn't bring himself to finish. I slid my hand onto his back, and he turned to face me. I blinked a few times, then found myself stuck in a weak hug.

"Thank you..." My voice was barely a whisper.

"No. Thank *you.* "

"Alaric..."

"It's okay. I'm here."

I looked up at him, and he brushed a tear away just as it broke through my thin eyelashes. He sighed before resting his head against my shoulder. We stayed there for a while, and everything was quiet.

Just before I closed the door on my old home, I let out a long sigh. "Goodbye..."

As soon as we got back to the dock, I told the Harpoons to add it to the list of houses ready for demolition. That way, it could be used as an entrance for when they began to hollow out parts of the Lavender Crystalline. It was hard to imagine what would become of my old Branch, but after only a few months of work, it was becoming clearer and clearer.

Alaric and I stopped by to help whenever we could. On my off days, I ate dinner with Clarissa and her family. Sometimes, Alaric would even join us.

In Oakview, people began to return home. Kids ran in The Tube again, families conversed of their progress, and soon after, Alaric was guiding me down a familiar path, holding his hands over my eyes.

As we entered the Greenland Preserve, I found myself gasping. There, in the center of the park, was a large, bubbling fountain. In the middle, a stone statue of a familiar, lost friend stood proud. All around the memorial, people cried and tossed small stones into the pond. As Alaric walked me over, I read the inscription on the sign at the front:

Memorial of John "Smithy" Feeney
Husband, Soldier, Friend
Inscribe a name, toss in a stone
Lost, but never forgotten

Tears welled in my eyes as Alaric handed me a stone and one of the small chisels that had been laid on the side of the fountain. I began to chip away, and I realized that Alaric was doing the same.

When I finished, I saw that he was still going. I pursed my lips before grabbing another two stones.

When he turned to me, I showed him mine. In one, I inscribed *Jeremy+Kalea*. In another, I wrote *Naseem*. In my final one, finished with a dark heart beside it, I wrote *LEILANI*.

Without a word, Alaric turned his around. In the first stone sat the name *Alana*. In the second, *Natasha, my Mom*. It was after this that I began to tear up, for in his third, he had even inscribed the name *Avon*, and in his fourth, *Aaron*. Then, in his final stone, he wrote the words *Smithy—Dad*.

I was sniffling as I took his hand. Together, we set down the stones, and we pushed them into the pool. With his arm now around me, Alaric pulled me close. We didn't move until they had fully finished sinking to the bottom.

EPILOGUE

ONLY A FEW MONTHS ago, I felt like just a drop in an endless pool of water. Now, when I walk by, people call me queen.

Many would say that I changed the tides of our ever-still lives. I still say that it was Alaric. Alaric, the lonely prince of Oakview. Alaric, the boy who chose to fight. Alaric, the one who burned the Great Cherry Tree.

Sometimes, it's hard for me to remember that life wasn't always how it is now. But that's when I think back to all of our adventures together. I think back to the first time I learned how to swim, and to the first time I held a blade. I think of Smithy's training and Clarissa's tiny shop. I think of what it felt like to be so close to losing it all.

Lavender began to flourish after Cherry was destroyed. After Alaric became king. *Everything* changed then.

We began to build boats and roads so everyone could visit each other without restraints. We stretched ourselves above the water, proving that life could find a way. That we were still here. That we survived.

But that wasn't all that changed. We built places to honor our lost—to remember their names. We made lives for those who were subjected to hopelessness for so many years. Everything that once seemed small, we changed to prove it was big.

After everyone returned to Oak, Clarissa's Boutique found booming business. Shortly after, her biggest competitor, Julie, was forced to relocate. Although, no one was entirely sure as to where. Clarissa, on the other hand, was hailed as a hero, and people stopped in just to ask about her part in their rescue. At the end of every week, she taught her siblings how to drive, and many more of Oakview's kids were left begging for their own turns.

I was visiting her one day when we decided to pay a visit to Smithy's old forge. It was left completely untouched since before we left, other than a few flowers dropped by the door. As we got closer, we noticed an envelope slid underneath. I turned to Clarissa, and even though she shook her head, I opened it up. A pile of coins sat inside, along with a small note:

We made it back. Both of us. Thank you for everything.

With a sad smile and tears in my eyes, I turned back to Clarissa. After giving her a single nod, I slid it farther under the door.

The remainder of the Harpoons spread themselves out, helping as they saw fit, but also learning how to exist as normal people in a healing world. I smiled every time I saw Jeremy. He always looked like a weight had been lifted off his shoulders. I found him nearly every time I went to the Greenland Preserve.

Many freshwater animals began to roam Watertowne and beyond. They multiplied quicker than we could even release all of them. It became a priority to help create more places like the

Preserve, in the hopes that, one day, *all* of Oak's creatures could again roam free.

Alaric and I stayed at Oak until progress at Lavender was certain. I'll never forget the day that I thought we were going to check on it. It was then that he brought me out to the dock at sunrise, dropped to his knee, and asked me properly to become his queen. I wished he wasn't as surprised when I gave him an enthusiastic "yes!"

It wasn't long after that progress began to slow. As the Lavenderians were becoming more comfortable, and more intricate jobs were in need of fulfilling, Alaric gathered Watertowne to deliver an announcement.

Many nights I lay awake, trapped in the thoughts of what was lost on our journey. But it was always the same question that bothered me most: At the end of it all, as the Great Cherry burned, *why* did I run back to the fire?

When Alaric told everyone about the world beyond our small Watertowne, uncertainty spread throughout us all. Just as fast, citizens approached him, volunteering to join the expedition that he was setting up. He warned that there was a chance for no return, that he needed only those who were overly capable, then only the fewest of them.

A variety of people lined up at Oak's door. Old and young, male and female, lost and found. But one common theme united nearly all of them: their families were never returned to them after what became known as the Liberation of Cherry.

A list of names was formed within days, and dates were set to begin the journey to the edge of what was known.

As Alaric was reviewing the list with a few of his Harpoons, I approached him with a pen. His eyes were wide as I signed my own name at the bottom.

Maybe I wouldn't know for certain why I ran into that fire. What I did know was that a part of it burned inside of me ever since. An undying, never ending flame. One that yearned for adventure. One that was spurred on by uncertainty. And one that raged for Alaric.

Just before we thought the list was done, Clarissa showed up at our newly installed front door. She bowed dramatically before unrolling Alaric's scroll, stealing a pen from our table, and signing her name just a few below mine.

Alaric shot her a nervous glance. "But what about—"

"You never know when you'll need a driver."

A smile crept onto Alaric's face. He rolled up the list again, tied it with a red string, and handed it to the nearest Harpoon.

The night before we set out, it seemed that everyone was gathered at the dock. It was hard to distinguish between those who hailed from Oak and the Lavenderians who had joined us. As we dined, they played music, chattered merrily with one another, and toasted to the brave souls who offered to set out with us.

When Alaric walked by, he slid his arm across my shoulder. Before he was fully past, he tugged on my hand. I followed him into the hall, and it was easy to slip away with all of the commotion.

I smiled as he pulled me into his room, but that smile only grew when he locked the door behind us.

"What? Does the poor king need a breather?"

"Only if it's your breath I'm taking."

"Ah," I teased. *"That* kind of breather."

"Are you *sure* you want to do this?"

"There's a few things you *know* I want to be doing, but just to make sure we're on the same page—"

"Tomorrow, Maliyah. Are you... You're *sure* you want to come?"

The closer I got to Alaric, the more he had to look down. His head turned until I was right below him, running my hands up his chest. "Wherever you go, I follow. Even if it's to the ends of this earth and back."

"And... if we don't make it back?"

"Then I'll be waiting for you in the World Beyond." I rose to my toes and sealed my words with a kiss. Then, I held out my smallest finger. "Promise."

He smiled as he interlocked it with his own.

Just as he pulled me into another kiss, I saw our door handle twist, and we froze. A knock was quick to follow. I held my hand over Alaric's mouth, and soon after, footsteps hurried away. I began to laugh, but I was silenced by Alaric running his finger under my chin, guiding me back to his lips. As we kissed, I ran my hands through his freshly cut hair. I smiled, and slowly, I opened my eyes.

"Alaric?"

"M'lady?"

"Can I say something crazy?"

I saw the smile tug at his mouth. He nodded once with his chin. "Anything to me, love."

I looked deep into his eyes, and I kissed him again. I slid my arms around his shoulders before I whispered directly into his ear.

"I love you, too."

ACKNOWLEDGEMENTS

I honestly can't believe I'm here right now, writing the acknowledgements of my first *real* novel. This has been my dream since before I can remember, and actually sitting here with a completed book feels so unreal, *especially* after what I went through to get here.

That being said, my first thank-you has to go to the Creator Himself. I was on a *severe* three-year writer's block when I published my first book, *Roses and Thorns: 100 Poems for Life*. It was only then that I decided to take a long-needed vacation, during which I woke up from a sudden, vivid dream—a dream that contained the setting and plot for *Trees of Fate*. I knew that I had to start writing—that the idea itself was a gift—and in only an hour, a prologue and two pages of chapter one had been written.

I rushed down to the beach, leaping into the ocean to tell my loving parents about my idea. As always, they were super supportive, but this time, something was different. This time, I was radiating with total pride in my concept, and they could absolutely feel its potential. Mom, Dad… thank you *so* much for always letting me follow my dreams, even when they came out of nowhere.

A thank-you is also reserved for my younger siblings. You both guide me in knowing what will work and make sense, and you constantly keep me inspired and motivated. Not to mention how my sister took the time to edit the back of my book, even when she was supposed to be doing schoolwork. I was stuck on that last step for months, and without her, I don't think I *ever* would have finished.

And the excitement that came from my little brother for this one! I wasn't surprised when he seemed to be interested in my idea, but I was blown away by the amount. Before I knew it, we were sitting down together for hours at a time, discussing storylines and character deaths, listening to music that would fit the story's theme, and suddenly, I had thought up the biggest plot twist I had ever written.

As soon as my first copy was done, my best friend Izzy was there to help me read, re-read, and edit. She sat by my side countless days as I acted out dialogue and picked apart paragraphs, and of course, she kept me fed along the way. Izzy, you're an invaluable member of my team and life, and I'm so happy to have had you along for this journey. Plus, your love for Smithy is unmatched!

Then began the time of beta reading. It is here I introduce my friend Kate, who spent her late nights online, reading and offering insightful feedback on my beginning chapters. Kate, thank you for your excitement for my characters and storytelling, and for keeping me on track with editing, even when it was by mistake. I truly hope you enjoy the final copy.

Now for the girl who not only helped me beta read, but re-read the *entire* book, helped me structure, edit, and format, debated scenes with me both at home and in public, and sang my praises to others before the book was even out. Here's to Taylor Krol, who single-handedly left the most comments on my documents, screamed with me when I needed the motivation, and kept me excitedly moving along the whole way through. Taylor, I am SO thankful for your help, and I can whole-heartedly say that this book wouldn't be the same without you.

And, of course, thank you to all of the friends and family—near and far—who supported and encouraged me throughout this wonderful and trying journey. At first, I had no clue that it would get this far, but somehow, you did. Thank you for keeping me smiling, excited, and most importantly, believing in myself. I truly hope you know who you are.

To anyone out there reading this... Thank you. Thank you for being a part of my first published novel. I hope you enjoyed every page, and I hope you'll stick around for what's to come. See you in the next book!

Angelina Scriptor

Also By Angelina Scriptor

Roses and Thorns: 100 Poems for Life

About the Author

Angelina Scriptor

 After graduating high school with highest honors and the state-certified Seal of Biliteracy in Latin and English, Angelina Scriptor instantly began work on publishing her first book, *Roses and Thorns: 100 Poems for Life.* It was shortly after when the ideas for *Trees of Fate,* her first completed novel, came to mind. She currently lives with her loving parents, inspiring younger sister, boisterous little brother, and lazy dog, where she not-so-secretly hopes to soon meet the love of her life. Her next planned project is to finish writing a medieval fantasy novel series, the drafts of which she began working on at the age of 13... or whatever idea interrupts her train of thought next.

She can also be found on Instagram (@Angelina.Scriptor)